The

Vampire

of Venice

Beach

Also by Jennifer Colt:

The Mangler of Malibu Canyon

The Butcher of Beverly Hills

Jennifer Colt

Broadway Books
New York

The Vampire of Venice Beach

a novel

PUBLISHED BY BROADWAY BOOKS

Copyright © 2006 by Tessera Productions, Inc.

All Rights Reserved

Published in the United States by Broadway Books, an imprint of The
Doubleday Broadway Publishing Group, a division of Random House,
Inc., New York.
www.broadwaybooks.com

BROADWAY BOOKS and its logo, a letter B bisected on the diagonal, are
trademarks of Random House, Inc.

"On the Good Ship Lollipop" Lyrics/Music S. Clare & R. Whiting

"I'm the Greatest Star" from the musical *Funny Girl*
Lyrics by Bob Merrill, music by Jule Styne

Book design by Caroline Cunningham

Library of Congress Cataloging-in-Publication Data
Colt, Jennifer.
    The Vampire of Venice Beach : a novel / Jennifer Colt. — 1st ed.
        p.   cm.
    1. Women private investigators—California—Los Angeles—Fiction.
2. Los Angeles (Calif.)—Fiction. 3. Sisters—Fiction. 4. Twins—Fiction.
I. Title.

PS3603.O467V36   2007
813'.6—dc22

                                                    2006043869

ISBN-13: 978-0-7679-2013-1
ISBN-10: 0-7679-2013-9

PRINTED IN THE UNITED STATES OF AMERICA

10 9 8 7 6 5 4 3 2 1

First Edition

For Lisa, Mary Linda,
and Ginger—collectively,
the Smith Tarts

acknowledgments

The research for this book was done by crewing on a documentary film produced by W. K. Border exploring the phenomenon of social vampires. We spent a riotous four days at the Dracula '97 convention in Los Angeles—a celebration of the hundredth anniversary of Bram Stoker's classic novel. There I met and talked with bloodsuckers, dominants and submissives, hearse collectors, body artists, poets, black humorists, Edwardian costumers, fang purveyors, goth musicians, horror writers, Transylvanian vintners, vampire historians . . . (I could go on.) It was a fun and enlightening experience, for which I'm indebted to my great friend Keith.

And while we're on the subject of friends, I would strongly advise aspiring writers to find one like Claudia Hoover, who will dismiss your fears with "Well of course you can write and publish a book. Get busy!" This followed by a steady drumbeat of *yes you can, yes you can* when courage falters. This series began with her.

Thanks also to Lynn Fager, who pointed out that "V" stands for Vampire.

The
Vampire
of Venice
Beach

prologue

*O*nce upon a time there were two sisters.

One sister was good and pure of heart. Gentle as the raindrops, delicate as a butterfly, bright as a star in the nighttime sky. The other sister was a dangerous psychotic—

Strike that.

I'm Kerry McAfee. My twin sister, Terry, and I are private investigators in Los Angeles, not characters in a fairy tale, so I'll ditch the flowery language and tell it like it is. Anyway, why strain for metaphor when *Star Trek* says it best?

Remember that episode where James T. Kirk comes swaggering out of his captain's quarters all sweaty and gimlet-eyed, ogling the women crew members, roughing up his fellow officers, and cackling insanely as he barrels through the USS *Enterprise* wreaking all kinds of havoc? This can't be the real Jim, you say, the one we love and admire. No, somehow they have intersected a parallel universe and this guy is none other than . . . (drum roll) . . .

Evil Jim.

Jimmy Darko. Kirk the Knife.

That's what it's like having Terry for a sister.

She runs around with my red hair, my green eyes—*my very DNA*—cutting an antisocial swath through this topsy-turvy reality where good is bad, black is white, cats are dogs—and I'm trapped in that other universe, waving my arms and yelling, "Over here! It's me, Good Jim!"

She's Huck to my Tom, Hyde to my Jekyll, yang to my wimpy yin.

If this were some artsy movie, it would be revealed in the end that I am not actually a twin but an individual nutcase who has projected her destructive and rage-filled impulses onto an imaginary sister.

I wish.

If that were the case, I could pop some Thorazine and get on with life.

I'm afraid she's real. There's no cure for Terry but death. And even then I expect she'll be poking me in my astral ribs, saying, "Hey, heaven's no fun. Let's go check out the *other* place."

We had a normal suburban childhood. Our mom stayed at home and our teamster dad worked as a gaffer in the movies. Terry always made things interesting; while I was in study hall working on extra credit, she was sneaking cigarettes in the girls' bathroom. While I was lusting after the quarterback of the football team, Terry was pining after the head cheerleader, Missy Mancuso. But our parents died young and then Terry fell apart. She started doing coke. Let me rephrase that—she set a world record by inhaling her body weight in cocaine in one evening and then set a land speed record trying to outrun the cops on a residential street in Brentwood.

So she went to prison. I went to work.

For three years I was apprenticed to an investigator in the offices of her criminal attorney—Eli Weintraub, Esq. Eventually I qualified for a PI license and set myself up in business. When Terry got out of prison I hired her. We call our agency Double Indemnity Investigations.

In the past year we've tracked down deadbeat dads, retrieved teenage runaways, busted a worker's comp faker doing cannonballs into his pool at a backyard barbecue. We've taped romantic getaways at the Motel 6, delivered dating histories of grooms to their prospective brides, even conducted urine tests on Wal-Mart employees suspected of getting high on the job. (I know. Why would anyone need mood-altering drugs to get through a shift at Wal-Mart?)

And—oh, yes—we uncovered an illegal painkiller ring in Beverly Hills and infiltrated an extraterrestrial cult in Malibu.

You might say we'd done it all, but that would be sadly underestimating my sister. She'd been complaining that I didn't give her enough responsibility in our two-person firm. Said she was tired of being second banana. (Her felony conviction technically prevents her from being top banana, but try explaining that to her.) She insisted that I let her bring in some business on her own.

That's how we ended up working for vampires.

I wasn't a big believer in the paranormal. My worldview didn't encompass Bigfoot or ET, and the Men in Black were just the Blues Brothers in outer space. Vampires were the stuff of blockbuster movies and best-selling books, as far as I was concerned, and I never even dreamed they'd enter my working life.

Kerry McAfee, Night Stalker?

I guess there's a first time for everything. Especially when you have Terry for a business partner.

one

*I*s this payback?" I said as I jogged alongside a powder blue hearse, wearing a zippered black jumpsuit and Reeboks and panting in the eighty degree heat. "This is payback, right?"

Terry tossed me a pitying look. "Save your breath," she said. "We'll talk about it after we pick up our check."

She was jogging on the passenger side of the hearse and seemed to be having an easier time of it—she looked cool and comfortable and quite the bad-ass in her black wraparound Christian Dior sunglasses.

"Is it because I forced you to wear mascara and laughed at you in a dress?" I said, wiping at the sweaty white makeup on my forehead. "That's it, isn't it?"

She pulled down her glasses so I could see her eyes rolling. "Zip it, okay? We'll talk about it *later*."

The two of us were doing our impression of Secret Service agents guarding the presidential limousine. We were there for crowd control, but I suspected we were actually more like window dressing for the motorcade making its way down Main Street in Venice, California. We aren't trained fighters, we don't carry weapons, and we aren't all that imposing physically. An unruly mob could flatten us like bunnies under a bulldozer. But we'd gotten an inflated reputation for toughness after thwarting a hijacking a while back (long story), and Terry was all for exploiting it.

The occasion was the Coming Out of the Coffin Parade, a celebration of the vampire in contemporary society. But it was also a publicity stunt for the new Dark Arts Gallery, a collection of businesses that planned to sell clothing, artwork, and furniture to the gothic demographic. Venice has long been a quirky beachside city that is home to artists, bodybuilders, chain-saw jugglers, tarot card readers, gangbangers, street basketballers, punks, hippies, scads of homeless persons, and a few yuppies. Now, with the influx of Anne Rice devotees, you could officially add vampires to the list of subcultures thriving here.

"Coming out of the coffin?" I'd said when Terry first told me about the job. "Are these gay vampires?"

"Why am I the world's expert on gay people?"

I just stared at her. "Um, because you're a flaming lesbo?"

"Why do you straight people always insist on knowing if someone's gay?"

"Well, the name kind of implies—"

"It's none of your business what they do in the privacy of their own coffins!"

"Okay . . . you're right. I don't care if they perform same-sex sucks. It's really unimportant in the scheme of things."

She gave me a *You're so unenlightened* look. "They're just regular people with a slightly different fashion sense and different preferences in recreational activities."

"Recreational activities? Oh, of course," I said, putting a finger to my cheek. "Let's see, shall we go boating on Lake Arrowhead today, or go chomp on someone's jugular? It's so lovely out, let's go jugular-chomping!"

Terry explained to me in a tone usually reserved for very small, retarded children that the occasion was for throwing off the yoke of oppression, an opportunity for vampires to come out into the light and assert themselves as an unappreciated and misunderstood minority.

"And what *about* the light?" I said. "Don't they disintegrate if they go out in the sun?"

"They're not real vampires, moron. They're *social* vampires."

"Oh. So what you're telling me is that vampirism is a 'life-style choice' now."

"Right."

"And we need to be more tolerant of people who make this lifestyle choice."

"Right."

"Just like gay people."

She let out an exasperated sigh. "See, this is exactly why I took the job! You're so judgmental. You need to be exposed to more diversity, broaden your horizons a little."

And there you had it. The reason we were working for vampires was that I needed horizon-broadening. I let her bully me into it rather than appear bigoted against an oppressed minority. Now, as I slogged forward in a black microfiber outfit that stuck to me like tar on asphalt, lips and nails painted in matching obsidian, carrying a silver-tipped walking stick to ward off dogs and vampire hunters, I was feeling the tiniest bit silly for getting sucked in (sorry).

The sidewalks were full of summer crowds milling in front of vintage clothing stores, massage parlors, cafés, and neighborhood bars. People dressed for the season, I noted with envy. Sandals and shorts and tank tops, their arms and legs free to breathe.

They turned to watch us pass. Even in jaded, seen-it-all Venice this merited a glance: a motorcade of multicolored hearses trailing black and red bunting with two redheads dressed like refugees from *The Matrix* jogging next to the lead car. Three giant bodybuilders, also clad in black, ran alongside the next hearses in line.

"Anyhow, I couldn't turn down an old friend," Terry said over the hood of the hearse.

An old friend?

I was still reeling from the news that we'd been hired for this gig by Darby Applewhite, the onetime homecoming queen of Burbank High, now reigning as Ephemera, Queen of the Undead. Our former schoolmate was a real fixture on the goth scene, according to Terry—she was lead singer in a band called the Flatlining Femmes. For some reason, Terry had kept this little tidbit from me until this morning when we'd gone to Darby's house to pick her up in her coffin. I could only guess why.

Did my sister have a secret life? Maybe when I'd been out on dates she'd been transforming herself into Batgirl and flying off in pursuit of forbidden thrills. No one who knew her would put it past her.

"I'm not buying the for-old-times'-sake BS," I said. "Since when do you care about Darby Applewhite? You hated her in school."

"Shhh! She'll hear you."

"Oh, she's gonna hear me through the walls of a hearse and the ebony coffin? Does she have supersonic vampire ears? She didn't in high school. How do you go from being the Princess of Perkiness to the Queen of Darkness, anyway?"

Terry shook her head. "People change, you know. It's not as if we're poured into a mold at birth that defines us our entire lives."

There was no talking to her when she was in righteous mode. And I had to concentrate on oxygenating myself before I collapsed and was carted away by one of the hearses on parade. The two of us would have it out good when we got home, I promised myself. Yes sir, the red fur would fly tonight.

Anyway, I had my own problems right now. In fact, I was perched on the horns of a real dilemma.

I was interested in two different men. A nice change from my usual state of dateless celibacy—except now I was not only celibate, I was frustrated. I had been *that close* to ending my dry spell a few weeks ago with a homicide detective named John Boatwright when he'd been called away on business. Only moments later, however, a cute FBI agent named Dwight Franzen happened upon me in my underwear inside a tent on the beach at Malibu (another long story).

I'd sent Franzen back out of the tent in order to get myself dressed. I hardly knew the guy, but I'd had a secret thing for him ever since he'd interviewed us after the hijacking incident. He waited outside the tent until I was decent, then he and I sat on the beach, talking and laughing into the wee hours. He had a nice sense of humor and was totally edible—short blond hair, broken nose, killer body. But he was the straightest of arrows—said no thank you to the champagne and didn't so much as remove his shoes as we sat on the sand.

Kind of an Eagle Scout. But a dead sexy one.

I could only imagine what Mr. Straight Arrow thought when he'd found me in my bra and panties, guzzling champagne in a tent at midnight. *Wild woman out of control. Runs with the wolves. Howls at the moon. Leaves the mattress in shreds.*

The truth was somewhat different.

I was a dyed-in-the-wool good girl. Terry had co-opted all the wicked traits before we were out of diapers, and I sometimes think that I became the good twin in order to compensate. I suspected there was a wild woman out of control lurking somewhere deep inside me, but I was too scared to rattle her cage—not sure I wanted to reap the whirlwind.

But Franzen had struck me as so normal and nonthreatening—such a good egg—that I started to get ideas. This was someone I could trust, I thought. Someone who was most likely not a sexual deviant. Someone who might be perfect for taking WWOC out for a test drive.

As we watched the surf crashing in the moonlight I entertained a slow fantasy of peeling off those perfectly pressed pants, slowly unbuttoning the starched shirt, slipping off the spit-shined shoes. Just when I reached the point where I had his FBI badge propped up on the sand and his hands bound at the wrist in agency-issue cuffs, trailing my tongue up the length of his muscled stomach, he suddenly shot to his feet, freaking me out.

Had he read my mind? Was he going to arrest me for having impure thoughts about a government employee?

He looked at his watch and uttered an unprofane curse like *Drat!* and apologized for having to leave. He had a big surveillance planned the next day, he said—a suspected terrorist cell operating out of an apartment in Van Nuys. I think he only divulged this information as a way of apologizing for bugging out on our moonlit moment.

He swore me to secrecy and promised to call, sealing the promise with a kiss.

I couldn't detain him; my country was at stake. Couldn't exhaust him with sexual acrobatics when he needed to be alert, couldn't send him off with sand in his ears when he needed to listen for massive plots being hatched over his headphones. It would be unpatriotic.

Not to mention slutty. As I indicated earlier, the reason I was in my underwear in the first place was that I had been rolling around in the tent with Detective John Boatwright of the Beverly Hills homicide division, just minutes before Franzen arrived.

Franzen fell off the face of the earth after that. I waited for him to call. And I waited. If an Eagle Scout says he'll call, he'll crawl over broken glass to do so, right? I told myself that he was prevented by his work. The man was hunting domestic terrorists, for crying out loud! I resolved to be patient.

Boatwright was equally gorgeous, but ten years older and a lot more worldly. Battle scarred, his soul a shade darker. I wouldn't want to try out WWOC with him. Might be inviting more trouble than I could handle. We'd mauled each other in a couple of frenzied make-out sessions but never got past go. One way or another we were always interrupted.

His phone, my sister.

I'd said I thought we should take it slower, and he'd accepted it like a gentleman. But I could tell he was getting frustrated, and I was slowly losing the battle against my libido. Make no mistake, Boatwright was fine. I just wanted one more date with Franzen so I could make an informed choice.

Now, suddenly, the thought came: *Why do I have to choose at all?*

There's no law against sleeping with two men at once, not in this great country. And if Boatwright and I happened to be involved when Franzen came back from the Van Nuys front, then maybe I'd assert my feminine prerogative to do a little comparison shopping.

Maybe you'd be a slut, said a voice in my head.

"I am not a slut!" I yelled.

Terry turned and stared at me, openmouthed. "I wish you'd stop torturing yourself and do the deed with Boatwright," she said, shaking her head. "You're coming unglued."

"When I want your sexual advice I'll ask for it!" I snapped back.

"Sorry." She raised her hands in the air. "Just thought it'd be healthier than running around yelling '*Slut*' at yourself like some spaz with Tourette's—but hey, you do what you want."

I hadn't told Terry about my evening with Franzen. Hadn't shared the dilemma with her. The less she knew about my horns the better. She'd only find some way to complicate matters.

I glanced in the window of the blue hearse and got a thumbs-up from the driver, who was grinning at me like mad.

Must have heard my outburst through the glass. *Story of my life,* I thought. *Born without the filter that keeps every stray thought from popping out of my mouth.*

The driver was one of Darby's two male roommates, a wraith-like blond of five feet five with heavily lined blue eyes, who went by the name of Lucian. Her other roommate, Morgoth, was driving the tiger-striped hearse. He was a chubby little thing with thick black hair in a widow's peak that he enhanced with shoe polish so that it reached halfway down to his eyes. With Darby they formed the odd trio, sharing a dilapidated wooden house festooned with human skulls, iron torture implements, and body parts floating in formaldehyde. The place had made my blood curdle even in the bright light of a July morning.

The motorcade slowed to round the corner at Main and Rose. Three blocks to go. No thoughts of sex now. I was only thinking about getting this stupid job over with.

We traveled past run-down craftsman houses, weed-clogged yards, low-cost housing, and the occasional luxury condo that looked like it had gotten lost on its way to Santa Monica. Then our destination came into view, a warehouse that resembled a blue airplane hangar looming over the mixed neighborhood. There was a gaggle of local news types on the curb eager to get a sound bite (sorry) for the nightly broadcast.

I could hear it now: "Would you buy a used hearse from these people? Venice vampires open the Dark Arts Gallery on Jim Morrison's old stomping grounds."

The procession came to a stop by the curb. A black satin bow was stretched across the front door of the warehouse for the ribbon-cutting ceremony. Goth groupies began pressing toward the motorcade. Time for crowd control.

"Move back, everybody! Stay clear of the hearse, thank you!" I pointed at a man in a long black cape who was trying to peer inside the car. "You sir, could you move away from the hearse, please?"

I checked in with the crew. "This is Red One to Bruce One," I said into my walkie-talkie. "Do you copy, Bruce One?"

The black box crackled. "Copy."

"We're about to unload the first hearse. Keep the crowd back from the vehicles but don't let them block the cameras. Publicity is the whole point here. Bruce Two, you in place?"

"Roger that."

"Bruce Three?"

"These people have fangs!" said a panicked falsetto.

"Easy, Bruce," I said in a calming tone. "They're here to shop, not to feed."

We had commandeered a group of actors to help out for the day—cohorts of our friend Lance Manley, who was now a rookie in the Malibu sheriff's department. These guys weren't the brightest bulbs in the bug zapper, I'd discovered, and though they were billed as martial arts experts, they turned out to be clueless about bodyguarding. Terry had suggested they imitate an action hero as a Method acting technique, and they all wanted to be Bruce Willis. Not an Arnold Schwarzenegger or Jackie Chan or Vin Diesel in the bunch. When fists were about to fly over the issue, Terry settled the matter by making them all Bruce for a Day.

"Bruce Three, was that a copy?" I asked.

Crackle. "Back! Back, bloodsuckers!" I heard Bruce Three shouting.

I signaled to Terry that I'd be back and jogged down the line of hearses past the mob that was cheering and howling, demanding an appearance by the vampire queen. Bruce Three was stationed next to a royal purple hearse with a matching coffin inside. My first thought on seeing it was that Elizabeth Taylor had given up the ghost, but I was told that the hearse belonged to a famous artist named Viscera Vicious, who was also partial to purple.

On the curb, black-clad arms were flying. A vamp with a

bicycle chain looped through one side of his nose, shoulder-length maroon hair, and Freddy Krueger torso rippers attached to his fingers was slashing at Bruce Three. Bruce dodged the spikes, brandishing a large wooden crucifix.

"Back! Back, thou fiend of the dark!" Bruce yelled at the vampire.

I guess Bruce had had some classical theater training.

"Hey!" I ran up to the brawlers and jammed my walking stick between them. Steel spikes clanged on the stick and the crucifix slammed into the shaft hard enough to crack wood.

"Way to go, Bruce," I said. "Crack the crucifix."

"He was trying to bite me!" Bruce Three was six feet, four inches of bulging muscle, blond hair, and tanning-parlor skin. You wouldn't think he'd be threatened by the anemic-looking goth who barely came up to his shoulder, but I guess you could say the same thing about me and spiders.

"Both of you . . . chill!" I said, then turned to the vampire. "Sir, did you attempt to bite my bodyguard?"

"Shyah. Like I want a mouthful of steroids," the vamp grumbled, then added, "He was waving a cross at us!"

"Bruce, what are you doing with a crucifix?" I scolded him. "That's so not PC at a vampire gathering. You provoked them!"

Bruce Three looked down at his shoes. "I brought it just in case," he said petulantly. "You never know with vampires. They can transfix you with their eyes and turn you into their sex slave."

The vampires protested, screeching and brandishing their long nails. With visions of a riot breaking out, I clicked on my walkie-talkie. "Bruce Two, do you copy?"

"Copy."

"Come replace Bruce Three at the purple hearse."

"Rrrrroger."

I grabbed Bruce Three by the arm and dragged him away. His muscled replacement, Bruce Two, jogged by with a snappy little salute. I didn't think the vamps would give *him* any trouble. He looked like a slightly shorter version of Shaquille O'Neal.

"These people give me the creeps," Bruce Three said with a shudder.

"They're not real vampires, Bruce. You don't fight them off with crucifixes. That's a Hollywood myth."

"What do you fight them with?"

"Nothing!" I said, spouting the party line. "They're harmless slackers dressed up like Dracula. They're no different from you or me."

He gave me a skeptical frown.

"Okay, they're different," I conceded. "But they're not necessarily monsters."

We arrived at the first hearse just as Lucian and Morgoth were unloading Ephemera's coffin. After that, they would move to the tiger-striped hearse and unload Vlad the Retailer. His name was a pun on Vlad the Impaler, the fifteenth-century Romanian prince who had been the inspiration for the fictional Count Dracula, famous for skewering Ottoman invaders like cocktail shrimps and staking their squirming bodies across the countryside before consuming their blood.

Hence Dracula's bad rap.

I hadn't actually met Vlad or Viscera, and neither had I seen the so-called vampire queen when we picked up her coffin this morning. They'd be revealed to me in all their glory at the same time as they were to the audience. After a few words for the camera, Ephemera would move to the front of the gallery and cut the black ribbon, after which the whole crowd would move inside to drink blood red cocktails, which I hoped got their color from grenadine, and to consume finger foods, which I hoped were not actual digits.

The drivers stood Ephemera's casket on end and began to unlatch it.

A cutie-pie reporter chirped into a video camera, "We're here at the culmination of the Coming Out of the Coffin Parade in Venice, where the well-known vampire personality Ephemera will be emerging from her coffin for the grand opening of the new Dark Arts Gallery, catering to those whose tastes run to the macabre . . ."

The coffin lid swung open on a nightmare vision of Snow White in a poison-apple coma. The big blond hair I remembered from high school was now raven black and hung in raggy shanks down the front of her crimson gown. Her lips were purple; her sun-starved skin like boiled potato. She had a black widow spider tattoo high on her right cheek, eyebrows that were inverted black *v*'s, and fang caps on her canines that dug into her bottom lip.

It looked like she'd had a makeover in hell.

One of her acolytes blared on a bullhorn, "Ephemera, Queen of the Undead! Awaken to the world of the living! Grace us with your unearthly presence!"

The crowd went insane.

I guessed Darby hadn't caused this much of a sensation since the regional playoffs, when instead of the regulation underpants she'd worn a red thong under her cheerleading outfit. Although she claimed it was an honest wardrobe malfunction (years before Janet Jackson thought she'd coined that phrase), it got Darby's butt kicked right off the squad. But nothing could keep the Applewhite juggernaut from the homecoming court. She was too popular, too pretty, and too obliging to the football team to be deprived of the honor, and her coronation took place the very same week of her thong disgrace.

Now she had reinvented herself as a vampire goddess. I looked at her standing there in the coffin surrounded by white satin, hands clutching a gleaming set of shears, and thought about how strange life could be. As the noise from the crowd reached a deafening roar, she slowly inclined forward, head nodding as if she were awakening from a deep, blood-drugged sleep.

Then her whole body pitched out of the coffin and she hit the asphalt face-first, the shears skittering away on the street.

Someone screamed. A girl in a ripped-up wedding gown fell over in a faint. I charged through the crowd, shoving my way through the vampires to get to Ephemera, who was sprawled flat on her face, arms akimbo, red velvet skirt hiked up over her black fishnet stockings.

"Call 911!" I yelled, kneeling at her side.

Terry whipped out her cell phone, stabbing in the number. "We need an ambulance! The corner of Rose and Fourth!" she yelled at the dispatcher. "Vampire down! I repeat: vampire down!"

The Bruces tried to contain the crowd, pushing the noisy peasant throng back from its fallen queen. I ignored the mayhem breaking out around me and turned Ephemera over onto her back, feeling for a pulse.

Her arm was as cold as lunch meat.

I brushed the hair away from her face and winced when I saw that her nose had been smashed on the street. The makeup lay thick and waxy on her blanched face. I lifted her wrist and the delicate hand flopped like a bag of bird bones.

"What happened?" Terry crouched next to me. "Did she suffocate?"

"I don't think so. Look at this."

I pointed to two gaping puncture wounds on her neck. They were several millimeters in diameter, with black edges, surrounded by a painful-looking purple hickey.

Terry took in a sharp breath. "Omigod. She was bitten?"

"She was more than bitten," I said. "She was sucked dry."

This queen wasn't undead.

She was dead dead.

two

A patrol car screeched to the scene, the EMS truck right behind them. At the sound of sirens the vampires dispersed like a colony of bats after a gunshot. They had an aversion to the boys in blue, apparently, not trusting them to look too kindly on citizen bloodsuckers.

The EMTs jumped off their truck with a defibrillator. We stood next to the cops on the sidewalk, waiting for the paramedics to give Darby a blast, but after taking her pulse and feeling her skin they pronounced her dead at the scene. There'd be no jolting this girl back to life.

Sergeant Alvarez was one of the responding officers. "What killed her?" he asked a paramedic.

"Blood loss, I guess. Looks like she's down a couple of quarts. But I can't say for sure."

They stored the machine and loaded Darby's gurney into the

back of the truck to await onsite inspection by the medical examiner.

A breathless blond reporter charged at Terry, microphone at the ready. "Aren't you those twins who foiled the hijacking of the Hawaii flight?" She didn't wait for an answer. "What did you think when Ephemera fell out of the coffin *dead*?"

"I thought, 'I sure hope some bimbo reporter gets in my face and asks me how I feel about this,'" Terry said, turning to smile into the camera. "You may quote me."

The reporter gave her an *Eat shit* look, cut off the cameraman, and went in search of a better sound bite.

Soon the newspeople had their footage of the dead body, their B-roll of the crowds, coffins, cops, and ambulance, and a couple of *Gee, she was a real up-and-comer* quotes from the few remaining vampires, a couple of *There'll be an investigation* quotes from the cops, and hurried back to their stations to edit the pieces. The story was hot, probably the lead for most of the local broadcasts and a pickup for the twenty-four-hour cable news services.

As for me, I was feeling like a total jerk. Sadness for my former schoolmate was compounded with guilt. I'd been trashing Darby pretty heavily ever since we got this gig, and there she'd been, dead in her traveling coffin, while I'd made snarky remarks and gloated over the thong episode in my mind.

I saw Terry's eyes confirming my guilt and became defensive. "I didn't know she was dead. I wouldn't have said those things if I'd known."

"Oh, that makes it okay then." She shook her head, muttering under her breath, "So judgmental."

"I didn't even want this job!"

"What?" Alvarez said, angling our way. "What exactly are you ladies doing here?"

I grabbed my wallet and flipped it open to the investigator's license. "I'm a licensed private investigator. My sister and I were hired to do crowd control."

He motioned for his African-American partner to join us. Patrolman Dawson took the wallet and perused the license.

"What crowd?" Alvarez said.

"Gone," Terry said, "as soon as they heard your siren. There were at least a couple hundred."

"How did this go down?" Dawson asked. "The victim was in a coffin in that vehicle there . . . ?" He pointed to the powder blue hearse.

I nodded. "Yeah, she was in that one and the others were in . . . *Holy schneikes!*"

Dawson and Alvarez jerked back.

"The other guys!" I yelled at them. "We left them in their coffins!"

I raced to the tiger-striped hearse, followed by Terry and the policemen, hoping against hope that it didn't contain another corpse. I threw open the back door and the four of us reached in to grab the silver coffin by the handles, lowering it down to the street. Terry snapped the locks on the lid and a tall bald man with a tattoo of a bat on the back of his head sat up, fangs bared. Vlad the Retailer. A giant tarantula was inching its way down the front of his red silk shirt.

The officers pulled their guns in panic.

Vlad's eyes bugged out of his head. "Don't shoot! She's not poisonous!" he said, grabbing the tarantula and perching her on his shoulder where she sat like Blackbeard's parrot. "Her name's Tallulah."

Dawson looked like he was ready to take the dealer down at the slightest quiver of his fangs. "Sir, put your hands in the air and step away from the coffin."

Vlad's pale hands went up and he looked around in confusion. "What the hell's going on here? Where is everybody?"

"There's another one back here!" I shouted, ignoring Vlad's complaints.

Terry and I ran to the purple hearse with Alvarez right behind us. We started to unload the color-coordinated coffin but had vastly underestimated its weight. As it cleared the back of the hearse, it slipped through our fingers and crashed to the ground with latches popping. The lid slammed open and a heavily made up three-hundred-pounder sat up in the lavender silk padding.

"Okay, who dropped the coffin?" he demanded. "This is a five-thousand-dollar, top-of-the-line Eternal Slumber! Somebody's gonna pay for the damage!"

His royal purple gown was covered with black netting and accented with a black feather boa. He wore a lavender wig with blunt bangs and Cleopatra cornrows, and gold bangles hung from his ears and encircled his thick wrists.

Alvarez stared at him in confusion. "Ma'am . . . sir . . . whatever . . . step away from the coffin, please," he said.

"What*ever*? *Fine* way to talk to a taxpayer."

"Your name, please?"

"Viscera Vicious, Queen of the Queer Undead. But you can call me Vishy. Rhymes with dishy." Vishy struggled to hoist himself up by means of the coffin sides. "Could I get a little help here?" he said snippily.

Alvarez holstered his gun and reached out to help the transvestite vamp to his feet. Vishy took the officer's hands and grunted, straining to pull himself up. But gravity had other ideas. Alvarez's feet slipped out from under him and he was yanked into the coffin headfirst, landing facedown in Vishy's purple lap.

Vishy looked down at him and grinned. "Well, that's what I call protecting and servicing!" he quipped.

We gathered in the large gallery portion of the warehouse, redheaded twins and other assorted freaks being interrogated as a group, like Agatha Christie characters dumped into a John Waters movie. Two caterers had been questioned and released, leaving their champagne and canapés behind. The Bruces answered a few perfunctory questions, then left to wait for us down the street at the Firehouse restaurant.

Vlad, Vishy, and the hearse drivers were seated in folding chairs around the edges of the room. Above them the walls were hung with paintings depicting blood and death and sex mixed up together in a gruesome kind of erotica. Buxom maidens with their throats slashed, a man and a woman coupling in a shower of blood, orgy scenes featuring simultaneous copulation and exsanguination. Hieronymus Bosch by way of Transylvania.

I jerked my eyes away from the lurid artwork and focused on the scene in front of me.

The uniformed cops had been replaced by two LAPD homicide detectives. The older one, Bagdasarian, had the unhealthy look of a donut hound. Big fleshy face under a gunmetal gray military cut, exploded blood vessels on his cheeks from chasing the donuts with bourbon. His partner, Kenneally, had the unhealthy look of a health nut. Tall and rangy and starved of dietary fat, with a sharp nose pointing down to an even sharper chin and long brown hair combed straight back and held in place with mousse or wallpaper paste—hard to say which.

Terry crept up beside me. "Should we call Eli?" she whispered.

"No. They're not treating us like suspects yet."

Eli Weintraub was our surrogate dad—Terry's lawyer during the drug fiasco and my employer during the time she was in prison. Recently our relationship with him had been complicated by a torrid affair he'd had with our great-aunt Reba. There had been instant attraction, followed by cohabitation, engagement, then breakup—and, lately, Mexican standoff. I was finding the current state of estrangement kind of restful, but Aunt Reba was an emotional wreck.

She'd responded to her heartbreak by having a full-blown midlife crisis (assuming she was going to live to a hundred and forty). Her son, our cousin Robert, had rented a studio here in Venice to show his paintings during the annual Art Walk. When Reba saw the neighborhood she pronounced it *so bohemian, dears!* and purchased a high-end condo in a very iffy area. Venice was slowly losing the fight against gentrification, but there was still a lot of gang activity in the parts of the city you didn't see on the tourist Web sites. Crips and the V-8, mostly—dealing, tagging, and sponsoring the occasional neighborhood shoot-a-thon.

Not the ideal place for an elderly Beverly Hills widow, but I didn't think it would last long. At the merest hint of automatic gunfire, Reba'd be hightailing it out of there, broken heart and all. Right now I had other worries—namely, dead vampire royalty and a suspicion that we were in this mess up to our jugulars, thanks to Terry.

Vlad leapt from his chair and began loping around the warehouse space, the bat tattoo on his head seeming to flap in agitation.

"I hold these two responsible!" He pointed at Terry and me. "They were hired for protection!"

I started to sputter a protest, but Terry's comeback was calm and matter-of-fact.

"We can't protect someone who's sealed inside a coffin," she said. "Anyway, the girl had to be dead, or getting there, when we went to pick her up." She pointed at the drivers. "These guys were in the house when we went to get her."

Lucian flushed pink under his white pancake makeup. "We live there!" he said. "We wouldn't kill her. We need her to pay the rent!"

Bagdasarian reacted coolly to the little blond's outburst. "What time did you see her last?" he asked him.

Lucian gulped air to relax. "Last night around midnight."

"And you?" This question was aimed at the Eddie Munster look-alike.

"Same thing," Morgoth said, chewing his bottom lip with his fangs. "She told me she was going to be in the coffin in the morning, getting in the mood, and we should just load her onto the hearse when the twins got there."

Bagdasarian looked at the third driver, Dagon. "And what about you?"

With his spiked orange hair and red lips, Dagon looked more circus clown than coffin-dweller. "Man, I just drove a hearse, okay?" he said like a surly teenager being busted for a joyride. "I never saw her. I don't even know these people."

"Which hearse were you driving?"

Dagon nodded at Vishy. "The purple one, for Slim Jim here."

Vishy shot Dagon a look that left no doubt where he got the name Vicious. "Obviously I couldn't drive it *and* pop out of the coffin," he told the cops, "so I hired this person. He was referred by a mutual friend."

I looked around and saw Kenneally gazing at the statue of a bat on a pedestal. It stood four feet tall, webbed wings fanning out, fangs open, with a slick pink tongue rearing up in its mouth. Very realistic and pretty terrifying.

He ran his hand down the bat's gnarled brown surface, which was covered in a thick layer of varnish. "What's this one going for?" he asked Vlad.

Vlad perked up at the whiff of a possible sale. "A thousand dollars. And we'll finance."

"What's it made of, driftwood?"

"Certified authentic bat guano, from a cave in Panama."

Kenneally made a little *gck* noise in his throat and jerked back, wiping his hand on his pants.

POW!

An explosion echoed off the cavernous walls and wooden floor. The cops whipped around in a crouch, going for their guns.

Vishy stood next to the bar, a green bottle frothing in his hand. "Champagne, anyone?" he said, smiling.

The cops relaxed their gun hands and shook their heads. Bagdasarian gave Vishy a jaundiced look. "You feel like celebrating something?"

"I need a little something to calm my nerves." Vishy's plump hand fluttered to his brow. "You'll have to excuse me. What with the murder and everything, I'm not my usual self."

I didn't know what his usual self was, but right now he struck me as a cross between Bette Midler and Barney the purple dinosaur.

Bagdasarian shook his head and turned back to the drivers. "All right, let me get this straight." He pointed to the orange-haired Dagon. "You picked up Mr. Vicious here at his house at nine o'clock. Was he in his coffin?"

"No. The coffin was in the back of the hearse. He opened it and climbed in."

"So you didn't load it with him already inside?"

Dagon gave him an incredulous look. "Me and what army?"

Vishy gave an indignant snort. Bagdasarian directed his next question to Vlad. "And you met these two guys"—he pointed to Lucian and Morgoth—"at their house?"

"Yeah," Vlad answered. "I drove myself there, then I got into my coffin and Morgoth drove me to the parade."

"And you two"—he pointed to Terry and me—"did you ever see Ms. Applewhite alive?"

I shook my head. "She was already in the coffin when we got to her house. We helped the boys carry her down and load her into the blue hearse."

"Wouldn't it make more sense to do it like the others? Carry the empty coffin to the car then let her get in?" he asked.

I made an exasperated gesture. "Detective, these people wear fangs and sleep in caskets. You want it to make sense?" I looked around at the assembled vampires. "No offense."

"None taken," Vishy said, toasting me with his glass.

"So nobody'd seen the victim since last night?" Bagdasarian said.

We all shook our heads. He scribbled something in his spiral notebook.

Kenneally stepped up to face Vlad nose to nose, trying to intimidate. "Tell us about your little group here. You were all renting this space together, equal partners?"

"I'm on the lease," Vlad said. "Everyone else rents space from me."

"If it's your place, why was Ms. Applewhite in the lead hearse?"

"Glamour. Crowd appeal. She was a big draw, always the center of attention. Leave it to Femmy to steal our thunder with her last hurrah."

Bagdasarian looked up from his notes. "Are you suggesting she might have drained her own blood to get one up on you?"

Vlad hiked the shoulder with Tallulah on it, bouncing her up and down. "You never know."

"Oh, Mary, give it a rest." Vishy plopped down on a black vinyl beanbag chair, champagne in hand. I had no idea how he planned to get back out of the beans. Maybe there was a fork-lift nearby. "Look, detectives, this was our big day. Our grand opening. We needed her celebrity to make the gallery a success. We spent a fortune on this promotion. Look at all the chilled champagne no one's drinking, all the advance publicity—wasted!"

Bagdasarian gave him a cynical smile. "Oh, you couldn't have asked for better publicity. You'll be the lead story on every local newscast, probably go all the way to CNN."

The mention of CNN seemed to spark a memory. He turned

to Terry and me. "Say, haven't I seen you two somewhere before?" he said, studying our faces.

I started to say no, but Terry couldn't resist the opportunity to grandstand.

"You may have," she said. "Um, did you hear about the Hawaii flight that was hijacked?"

Kenneally's mouth fell open. "Oh, you're *those* twins," he said.

"Good work with the terrorists," Bagdasarian added, with renewed respect. "Wish we had more like you."

"Thanks," Terry said, pretending to blush. "It was nothing."

I changed the subject before she could start signing autographs.

"That's why Darby hired us," I told them. "She heard about the hijacking incident and brought us on to make sure there were no disturbances at the opening."

"Disturbances?" Bagdasarian said. "What kind of disturbances?"

Terry shrugged. "She said there'd been threats from rival vampires. And she was worried about reaction in the neighborhood. You never know how Joe Citizen is going to react to a bunch of fanged shopkeepers moving in."

"If you can find Joe Citizen in this town, let us know," Kenneally said. "We'll have him stuffed. Who are these rivals she was talking about?" He looked around at the vampires for an answer but got only shrugs.

Vishy waved a hand, bracelets jangling. "Girlfriend always was rather dramatic," he said. "She imagined everyone was jealous of her, out to knock her off her pedestal."

"She got knocked off pretty good," Bagdasarian replied evenly. "Who wanted her out of circulation?"

Vlad looked at Vishy. Vishy looked at Vlad. They turned back to the cops with the feigned innocence of five-year-old bubblegum thieves caught in the act.

"No idea," they said in unison.

Bagdasarian wasn't buying. "Think about it real hard, and get back to me." He handed them each a business card.

"We need you to take us to the house," Kenneally said to Darby's two roommates. "And we're impounding the blue hearse."

Lucian made a face but relented, handing over the keys. Kenneally did a double take at the plastic severed hand hanging from the ring.

"Not to be insensitive or anything," Vishy said, "but when can we open the gallery? We've sunk a ton of money into this thing. It's not like it's a crime scene."

"I'm sure the public is clamoring for bat guano art," Bagdasarian said, "but I'd think you'd want to close it. You know, out of respect."

"All due *respect*, Officer"—Vishy gave a theatrical sigh—"a girl's gotta pay the rent."

Bagdasarian snapped his notebook shut. "Yeah, go ahead." He looked at Terry and me. "I suppose you know it's illegal for private detectives to investigate a homicide in California."

Terry stiffened. "Who says we were going to investigate?"

He held her eyes for a second. "Don't, is all I'm saying. It could cost you your license." So much for our antiterrorist goodwill.

He signaled to Kenneally and the two of them led Lucian and Morgoth out of the warehouse, Dagon dragging his baggy-pants ass behind.

After they'd gone, I heard *ugh, ugh* and saw Vishy attempting to launch himself out of the beanbag chair. Terry and I went over to give him a hand. I grabbed an upper arm, which was like gripping a rump roast two-handed, and Terry tugged on the other. After much grunting and heaving, the big purple thing was on his feet.

"Remind me never to do that again," Vishy said, straightening his gown. "It's like lounging in quicksand. Feels like your butt's being sucked to the center of the earth."

I rubbed my shoulder. "Consider yourself reminded."

Terry got in Vishy's face, arms crossed over her chest. "Okay, the cops are gone," she said. "I don't know why you were holding out on them, but I want an answer. You must have some idea who did this."

Vishy adjusted his lavender wig. "Yeah, I've got an idea."

"Who?"

"He doesn't," Vlad said, shooting Vishy a warning look. "He's just being provocative."

Terry stared at them for a second, waiting. When it became obvious that the two of them were not going to come clean, she gave it up. "O-*kay* then, I guess there's nothing for us to do but take our check and vamoose." She held out her hand for the payment.

"Oh, uh. There's a wee problem with that . . ." Vishy said.

"*Yeah?*" Terry said, eyes narrowing. "What problem?"

"We were going to pay you from the proceeds of today's sales." He spun in a little circle, palms out. "No customers, no sales!"

I glowered at him, fists on my black-spandexed hips. "Look, we jogged through half of Venice in these stupid outfits in the middle of the summer and nearly got sunstroke. We did our job keeping the crowds in line. And we have to pay the Bruces."

"How much?" Vlad said.

"We contracted with Darby for a thousand dollars."

He pulled out the empty pockets of his black velvet pants, shrugging.

Terry sighed and looked around the room. "Okay, we'll take it out in trade. What do you have here that's worth a thousand?"

"That iron maiden ought to be worth a grand." Vishy pointed to a medieval torture device shaped like a woman, metal spikes jutting from her insides.

Vlad scowled at Vishy. "Why don't they take your scatological bat?"

"Welcome to it."

"We'll take the maiden," Terry said, touching a spike with the pad of her finger. "It's really cool."

Vlad sprang to her side. "That's one of our showpieces! If we're going to get you your money, we need to have this to sell! Anyway, it's priced at two thousand."

I grabbed Terry by the sleeve. "Come on, Ter. We're not taking anything on the motorcycle. We'll work this out later." She let me lead her to the door.

"I swear I'll get you the money," Vlad said. "Come back Monday."

What choice did we have? "Look, somebody's got to speak to Darby's family," I said to them. "Are you going to do it?"

"Us?" Vishy stopped with his champagne in midair. "Why us?"

"Oh, I don't know," Terry said sarcastically. "Maybe because you were her *friends?*"

"She never talked about her family," Vlad said. "I think she was estranged. Anyway, won't the police do that?"

"Don't you think it would be the decent thing to help break the news?"

"No one's ever accused me of being decent," Vishy said, vamping like Mae West. "Look, if you knew her better, you'd know that girlfriend had a definite death wish. Most of them do."

"Most of who?"

"The goths."

"Aren't you one of them?"

He flipped the cornrows behind his shoulder. "Honey, if

there wasn't a dedicated market, you could *keep* all this dark side stuff. But as long as it lasts, I'm there."

"You think it's on the way out?" Terry asked.

"Nothing lasts forever, doll. The little vampires will tire of this fad and move on to another. I've been through several incarnations myself—punk, glam rocker, the whole *Paris Is Burning* transvestite scene. I've seen them come and go. You always have to be ready to leap into the new."

Vlad gave him a snide look. "Trend whore," he muttered.

Suddenly, Vishy whipped around and sloshed his champagne into the bald vampire's face. Vlad sputtered in shock, wiping his eyes and smearing his makeup. "What was that for!" he yelled.

"Ephemera isn't the only one who needs to be brought down a peg," Vishy said, brimming with contempt. "Frankly, this pretentious vampire crap is starting to bore the hell out of me."

"Well take your bored fat ass somewhere else!" Vlad said, reaching up to grab Tallulah, who was climbing on top of his head to avoid the next onslaught of champagne.

"Come on," Terry said to me. "Let's get out of here before they start bitch-slapping each other."

"I guess *we'll* go by and talk to Darby's parents," I said to Terry. "Think they're still living in that little house off Victory?"

Vishy gave a shudder. "Valley white trash," he said, wrinkling his nose snobbishly. "And you wonder why she had a death wish?"

three

I wanted that iron maiden," Terry said. "It would have looked awesome in the living room."

"Sure it would," I said. "And I guess when the county assessor comes by, we could lure him into it and show him what we think of his stinking taxes."

We were headed to the Firehouse at the corner of Main Street and Rose Avenue, a bright red remnant from 1920s Venice. The city had been completely different back then. There had been a pier crammed with carnival attractions, a huge indoor saltwater swimming pool, and gondolas gliding down the manmade canals.

Unfortunately, the fine citizens of Los Angeles decided they didn't like the gambling and drinking and loose morals of the fleshpot next door, so they annexed the town and shut down all the vendors and hawkers by levying taxes on them, making sure the banks wouldn't loan them the money to pay up.

Eventually the unique character of the place was eroded. There were still some great houses on the canals, but the waterways themselves resembled undredged swamps. And now the miniature trains, the swimming pool, the pier, were all history. The boardwalk next to the beach remained an ongoing human carnival, a gathering place for the weird and funky— but given time and Starbucks, that could change too.

We spotted Bruce One's gleaming head in the crowded bar. He was completely hairless—no eyebrows, facial hair, not even arm hairs—sporting two golden hoops in his ears. He looked like Mr. Clean's brother, Mr. Even Cleaner. He and the other two guys sat at a table eating peanuts and nursing beers. A waitress stopped by, but I waved her on.

"So," Bruce Three said when we sat down, "pretty weird day."

"Say that again," I said.

"Pretty weird day."

Bruce Two bopped him on the head. "You don't actually say it again. It's a figure of speech."

"Oh," Three said.

"I'm sorry, guys," I said, "but they stiffed us."

"They didn't pay?" Bruce One asked.

"They said they would, but we'll make good in any case. Can you come by our house Monday night?"

"We didn't really expect the whole payment," Two said. "I mean, we were supposed to be on watch until closing time."

"Not your fault there was an unanticipated murder," I said.

Bruce Three made the sign of the cross on his chest. "I knew this was bad news. These people are twisted. They suck blood and worship the devil. I just hope we haven't been tainted. I'm going to church tomorrow to be on the safe side."

Terry made a dismissive gesture. "Oh, most of them are harmless—romantic misfits, is all. A variation on beatniks or hippies."

Bruce Two shook his head. "But a girl is dead."

"Yeah," Terry said, "and it's terrible, but you can't lay it at the feet of every vampire out there. Crimes happen in every segment of society."

"I don't know," One said, his voice low and almost fearful. "I'm with Bruce. You're better off not messing with the dark side."

"What*ever*." Terry was anxious to drop the subject, never very good with death and dying. "You guys did a great job. If we need crowd control again we'll call you, okay?"

The Bruces downed their beers, handed us their head shots—eight-and-a-half-by-eleven black-and-white photos, the actor's version of a business card—and took off, biceps rippling as they waved goodbye.

"Ciao . . . See ya . . . Bye!"

Terry spread the photos out on the table in front of her. Each Bruce was side-lit and posed to masculine perfection. One black, one white, one blond. "Hey, nine more of these and we can make a Bruce calendar," she said.

"Or we could tack 'em on the wall and play pin the brain on the airhead."

She made a face. "You're so mean. They're sweet guys."

"I know. I'd take them home and try to teach them amusing tricks, but we already have two lapdogs. Are they really martial arts experts?"

She turned over the head shots, looking at the résumés on the back. "That's what it says here—kung fu, tae kwon do, karate."

"They seem kind of light in the loafers for kung fu fighters."

"Shows what you know," she said, sneering. "The martial arts are spiritual disciplines, not just fighting methods."

"Okay, so they're spiritual sissies."

She sat back in her chair. "My, aren't we the crabby one?"

"Murder has that effect on me," I said, standing. "C'mon, let's get out of here."

We paid the Bruces' bill and headed out to the back lot where we'd parked our Harley-Davidson. After Dad died, Terry had taken her share of his life insurance and bought the Softail Deuce as consolation. I was furious with her for blowing all that cash, but even I had been awed by the precision-engineered machine crouched in the driveway like a lethal black jungle cat.

Then she got tooted up one day and painted it shocking pink.

That's right, a shocking pink Harley. Engine cover, wheel wells, gas tank—all fuchsia. She recovered the seat in pink leather and somehow got matching handlebar grips. Now, instead of a Hells Angel's wet dream, it looks like Barbie's getaway vehicle after a toy bank heist.

It didn't get Terry far on that fateful night in Brentwood, though, and while she was in prison it sat in the garage like a blushing bride waiting for her groom to be sprung from the joint. I, traffic law–abiding, cautious, responsible Kerry, was forbidden to take it out, on the grounds that I wasn't a good enough driver.

My '82 Toyota Celica gave out around the time that Terry was released, and the bike had been our ride ever since. Terry'd already had one fight defending its honor—against a biker who thought she'd blasphemed by painting a Harley pink—but I'd given up on asking her to change it. It was her *grrrl power* statement, and besides, it set off her fringed pink leather jacket and matching helmet with a purple "flower power" daisy on the side.

Just as we rounded the corner of the back of the restaurant on our way to our bike, I saw a piece of black cloth flapping in the wind. A cloaked and hooded figure darted around the side of the building. I'd had only a fleeting glimpse of him, but I felt a chill go up between my shoulder blades—an intuitive sense of evil.

"Oh, no!" Terry yelled, running to the bike.

It was covered in a glistening red substance that drenched

the seat and dripped down the chassis, forming a puddle of co-agulating goo on the asphalt.

I dashed around the corner of the building to get another look at the creep who'd poured blood over our motorcycle. An engine roared to life and tires squealed. A black VW Beetle winged a right out of the parking lot. I caught the letters DE on the car's rear license plate. Then it was gone.

I stood there for a minute, willing my heart to slow down before walking back to the bike.

Terry pointed to the mirrors. "He left a message."

Black lipstick was scrawled on the reflective glass. On the left: *Die*. And on the right: *redhead bitches*.

"Remind me never to let you book us jobs again," I said to Terry.

But she didn't seem to hear. She stared at the bike, shaking her head and muttering, "What kind of *animal* would desecrate a Harley?"

Bagdasarian was there in fifteen minutes, along with a crime scene tech he called Wayne. Wayne took a sample of the blood with a Q-tip and photographed the mirrors. He dusted the bike for prints, scoring a few—probably ours. Then he packed up and quickly disappeared.

I told Bagdasarian about the man in the hooded cloak who drove off in a black Beetle. He told us to be sure to get the whole license number if we saw it again.

"So . . . you girls knew the vic in high school?" he asked, returning to our earlier topic of conversation.

I nodded. "Yes, she was perky and popular. Voted least likely to die standing up in a coffin dressed like Lily Munster."

"Any old grudges from those days that you know of? A jilted boyfriend who was crazy for her?"

"I don't think this has anything to do with the old days," Terry said. "I asked around when we first got the job, and not too many people knew what had happened to her after graduation."

"What do you know about her family?"

I flashed on an image of a little girl—gawky and homely, living in her big sister's shadow. "She had a sister, Pammy. Remember Pammy Applewhite, Ter?"

Terry nodded. "I think she was two years behind us. Whatever happened to her?"

"Who knows?" I turned to Bagdasarian. "She was different from Darby. Kinda shy, not as cute or popular. I remember seeing her in the background at Girl Scout meetings."

"What about her parents? What are they like?"

"Your average Valley types, Herb and Sandra. They were older than our parents, I think. He's a furniture wholesaler. They live in Burbank."

"We were going to go pay them a condolence call," Terry said. "Have they been told yet?"

"Yeah, I sent an officer by an hour ago," Bagdasarian said. "I'll go see them myself after I have a look at the victim's house." He nodded to the bike. "I want you to take that threat seriously."

I swallowed hard. "You don't think it's random vandalism?"

"Die redhead bitches?" he said. "Sounds pretty targeted to me. If we get a match between this blood and the vic's, there's a definite connection between the two crimes. If you're harassed any further, I want you to let me know."

"Sure," Terry said. "Your number still 911?"

Bagdasarian gave a short laugh, then waved and got into his unmarked car, parked illegally next to a red curb.

Terry and I went back inside the restaurant and described our plight to the waitress. She and one of the guys from the kitchen followed us out to the bike with towels and a bucket of industrial-strength cleanser. Terry snapped on the latex gloves we usually carried and scoured the bike as they watched.

"Is it real blood?" the kitchen guy said.

"Afraid so." Terry scrubbed the chassis with a sponge. "We just don't know if it's human."

"Dios mio."

I looked up at the waitress. "You don't happen to know someone in the neighborhood who wears a long black hooded cloak, do you?"

She shook her head. "Most people around here are beach-combers or Gold's Gym types. No matter what the weather, they're always in muscle shirts."

"That's what we thought." I handed each of them a business card. "If you do see anyone wearing one, or if you spot a black Beetle that has a license plate with the letters DE in it, give us a call, okay?"

They promised to call if they saw anything. When Terry was done cleaning the bike, I steeled myself to sit where the blood had been.

"It's clean," Terry said, swinging a leg over the seat.

"But it's never completely gone, is it?"

"Get on, wimp."

I closed my eyes and got on behind her with an involuntary shudder. "Memory Lane to the Applewhites'?"

She pulled on her helmet. "They're owed that much, aren't they?"

I nodded and we took off for the 10 freeway headed east.

four

*F*our o'clock on a Saturday. Normally the Applewhites would be outside doing yard work or having cocktails while firing up the barbecue. We'd grown up in Burbank and we knew the weekend drill: mall, mower, burgers on the grill.

But this was no ordinary day. Their elder daughter had been murdered, and they had heard the news only a couple of hours ago. They were probably inside crying their hearts out, asking themselves the question asked by all victims of senseless violence—

Why us?

They lived a couple of miles from our childhood home, in a white A-frame house with green trim. The trees in the cul-de-sac had grown so huge over the years that the houses were dwarfed, like gremlin toys tossed at the foot of the enormous oaks.

Terry slowed the bike at the curb, and I felt a little frog shimmying into my throat. The Applewhites' house was virtually interchangeable with the one we grew up in. Same floor plan, same yard planted with yucca and impatiens. I half expected to see our mom throw open the front door in leggings and an oversize sweater, a plate of fudge brownies in her hand.

We hadn't been here since our Girl Scout days. We'd gone to all the same schools as Darby, but our paths diverged in junior high. She got boobs and we didn't. Biology being destiny, I wasn't destined to be part of the popular crowd. I went the nerd route: class president, valedictorian, chess club. Terry wasn't a nerd, but she definitely wasn't into the social scene, either. She went the smoking-on-the-blacktop, setting-fire-to-the-principal's-desk, hacking-into-the-school's-computer-to-post-the-guidance-counselor's-head-on-Pamela-Anderson's-body route.

And Darby? It appeared Darby Applewhite had been hiding a darker side from all of us under her tiara.

"What are we gonna say, we're sorry?" Terry whispered as we went up the walk.

"Among other things."

Sandra Applewhite came to the door dressed in high-heeled sandals and stretch pants that stopped at midcalf. But there the similarity to our mother ended. Instead of a plate of brownies, she held a highball glass. Instead of a brilliant smile, she blasted us with gin vapors and cigarette smoke. Her eyes were red and wet, her skin pasty white. In her grief, she looked deader than her daughter.

Terry averted her gaze from the pathetic woman, preferring to focus on the toes of her motorcycle boots.

"Mrs. Applewhite?" I said. "We're the McAfees. Remember us?"

Sandra's swollen eyelids narrowed, then opened wide in recognition. "Omigod. The *twins*! You're all grown up, and so *pretty*."

She threw her arms around us, tossing gin into the flower bed, ice cubes bouncing off the mailbox.

"My baby's dead!" she wailed.

We declined Sandra's ("Please, call me Sandra") offer of gin and tonics and sat on the southwestern-print couch—Santa Fe pastels dotted with ketchup and coffee stains. She faced us in a wooden rocking chair, pitching back and forth in a hypnotic rhythm. Herb Applewhite sat in a cloud blue recliner angled toward the TV. All we saw were his spindly legs in black socks and sandals on the footrest. Every now and then his voice floated up over the top of the Barcalounger.

"Bad crowd," Herb muttered. "Started running with a bad crowd."

"Tell me how this happened," Sandra begged us. "Tell me where we went wrong."

I had no idea what to say to the poor woman, and Terry was no help at all. She sat speechless in the face of Sandra's tipsy misery, staring at the fake paneling on the family room wall.

"People change," I said. "I'm sure it's not your fault."

"But why all this satanic stuff?" Sandra rose to freshen her drink. "We took her to church, didn't we, Herb?"

"Every Christmas, every Easter," said the Barcalounger.

"Let me do that." Terry jumped up to take the glass out of Sandra's hand. Sandra relinquished the tumbler and fell back in her seat, rocking backwards at an alarming angle, her feet in the air.

"There's a jigger next to the bottle in the kitchen," she called to Terry. "Two parts gin, one part tonic."

I'd hate to be a microorganism on this woman's liver, I thought.

"It's not satanic," I said as Terry slipped away into the kitchen. "With goths, their guy isn't Satan, it's Dracula."

Sandra rolled her eyes. "Satan, Dracula. What's the difference?"

"I don't really know," I said truthfully. Both were mythical bogeymen to me.

"So she hired you for this . . . opening thing?" Sandra asked, struggling to understand the circumstances of her daughter's death.

"Yes, it was a publicity stunt. She was supposed to come out of a coffin dressed like a vampire and cut the ribbon on the door."

"But if it was just a stunt—if it was all costumes and playacting—why did someone kill her?" A sob caught in Sandra's throat. "The police told us . . . they said somebody drained her blood!"

"Jesus," said the Barcalounger.

Terry returned from the kitchen and handed Sandra her glass, then sat back down next to me on the couch.

"She mentioned a rival group of vampires when she hired us," Terry said. "She thought they might do something to disrupt the opening."

"Rival vampires," said the Barcalounger. "Christ."

Sandra whipped around in Herb's direction. "Stop taking the Lord's name in vain, Herb!"

"Not taking it in vain. Got a goddamn good reason."

Sandra made a face at the chair, then turned to us with tears in her eyes. "Here's what I want," she said, leaning forward in the rocker, high-heeled sandals planted on the faux Navajo rug. My eyes were irresistibly drawn to her feet. Somehow I didn't expect gold glitter polish on the toenails of a bereaved mother. "You're investigators? You find out who did this to our baby. You find the bastard—"

"—or bastards," Herb said.

"You find them and make sure they pay for what they did." Sandra picked up a Virginia Slims menthol and clamped it between her teeth. She torched it with a silver and turquoise lighter, sucking smoke into her lungs with a dragon's vengeance.

I looked at her tortured face through the smoky haze. Now was not the time to discuss the limitations imposed on practitioners of the PI trade, I thought. Bagdasarian was right—strictly speaking, we weren't supposed to insert ourselves into a homicide investigation.

But we wouldn't be inserting, I rationalized. We'd be skirting the edges. We'd be in the background, picking up what we could while attempting to remain inconspicuous. If we happened to uncover something of interest, we'd turn it over to Bagdasarian and Kenneally for them to pursue.

If our own mother had lived to Sandra's age, and if one of us had been senselessly murdered, I would have wanted our old friends to rise to the occasion and help her out. I'd also like to think Mom wouldn't have been blunting her sorrow with Virginia Slims and gin, but who knows? Fortunately, our image of her would never be corrupted. Pretty and caring, she'd forever be bearing us brownies in our minds.

"Okay," I said, standing. "We'll find out what we can."

"Thank you." Sandra grabbed my hand to pull herself out of the rocker. "You always were sweet little girls," she said, smiling fondly. "Funny-looking, but sweet."

I forced myself to smile back at her, then led the way past the Barcalounger to the front door. Herb muttered a goodbye without ever taking his eyes off the ceiling. Maybe it was his intense focus on the water spot there that was keeping him from going to pieces.

I turned in the doorway, remembering the little sister. "What about Pammy?" I asked Sandra. "Does she know yet?"

Sandra took a drink and ended up with an ice cube in each cheek, looking like a chipmunk on a barstool. "No, she doesn't know. And she won't—at least not for a while."

"Why not?"

"She married an abuser. Damien Turnbo. Ever heard of him?"

Terry nodded. "Oh yeah. Pro football player, right? Local boy who made good."

"Worthless scum," Herb said to the water spot.

"He beat Pammy," Sandra said, crunching the ice as if wishing it were Damien's head. "She tried to get away from him, but he stalked her. Threatened to kill her. A few years ago she took little Jimmy and ran."

"She went underground?" I'd heard of women doing that. Taking on a new identity and living a different kind of life. The trouble with those arrangements was that the women had to leave their loved ones behind for good. Or at least until the abuser got locked up or killed in a barroom brawl.

Sandra dabbed at her eyes. "Jimmy's six now. How old was he last time we saw him, Herb?"

"Three," Herb said in a small voice.

"We get letters now and then, but we can't get in touch with her," Sandra said. "She and Darby never got along very well. Too different, I guess. But they loved each other as sisters. Pammy's gonna be devastated when she finally hears."

Sandra opened the door to let us out. Her shoulders slumped and her gin belly sloped outward. She seemed to be melting, her skeletal system liquefying with sorrow. I thought she wouldn't be on her feet much longer.

"Take care, Mrs. Applewhite," Terry said. "We'll be in touch."

I handed Sandra our card. " 'Double Indemnity . . . discreet inquiries,' " she read to herself as she shut the door.

Yeah, I thought. *Discreetly inquiring after bloodsucking fiends.*

Terry zipped left through Beverly Glen traffic and onto the gravel driveway of our house. Willed to us by our grandparents, it's a tiny cabin that looks like a summer home for Santa's elves: one and a half stories tall, with barely enough square footage to equal the master bathroom of one of the McMansions that have sprung up around us. Wooden shingles cover the outside, the oak floors are scarred and warped and missing the occasional wood knot, and the Santa Ana winds whistle up from the floor and groan through the eaves in winter like spirits going noisily into that good night.

I slept in a loft with a skylight. Terry had made a bedroom out of the bay window alcove at the front of the house, rigging up an accordion door for privacy. I had no real door, but there was a wall that blocked off most of the rest of the house.

Now the cabin was also home to our two dogs, Muffy the pug and Paquito, a Pomeranian-Chihuahua mix. We'd acquired them on a case we had a few months ago, and they'd quickly become the loves of our lives, giving up the Beverly Hills high life for us. Coming home to them was a daily pleasure, not to mention a source of unending comfort.

A day full of false leads? *Lick, lick.*

Whole world treating you like scum? *Nuzzle, nuzzle.*

Person who hired you dead in her coffin? *Toss me the ball!*

Terry threw open the door and the teeny welcoming committee lunged at our feet. I scooped Paquito up in one hand and lifted him to my face for a kiss. Terry picked up Muffy with two hands and did the same.

"She's getting heavy," Terry said, hoisting Muffy up in the air. "Has our little girl been pigging out?"

Muffy snorted and smiled, a long tongue happily jutting from her harlequin mouth.

I weighed tiny Paquito in my hand. "Now that you mention it, I think he's losing weight. He feels a couple of ounces lighter."

"She's probably been eating his food," Terry said, pointing an accusing finger at Muffy's smashed-in snout. "Snarfs down her kibble then sits there with a *You gonna eat that?* look on her face until he backs off."

I laughed and rubbed my cheek against Paquito's wet nose. "We'll have to change their names to Jack and Jackie Sprat," I said.

Terry set Muffy on her lap and picked up the phone to check messages. She listened a few moments, and I watched as her face acquired a strange, almost confused expression. Then she punched the Repeat button and held the receiver out to me.

"You'll want to hear this."

I put the phone to my ear.

"Hello, Terry? It's me, Darby . . ." Her breathing was irregular—like she'd been caught in the midst of some strenuous physical activity. "I'm sorry, I don't have your cell number with me . . . Uh listen, I've decided to pull out of the Dark Arts deal. I'm sort of in the process of leaving the scene, and it's . . . well, it's too complicated to get into on the phone. I'm sorry for the short notice . . . I'll pay you something, a cancellation fee, whatever. Talk to you soon, okay? Thanks."

Beep.

I punched the button to save the message. Hearing Darby's voice from beyond the grave left me weak-kneed. I fell down on the couch next to Terry, setting Paquito on the floor. "What time did that come in?"

"Eight o'clock," she said, frowning. "If we hadn't left early for coffee, we would've gotten it."

"Any other messages from her?"

Terry shook her head.

"So," I said, doing the math, "she died sometime between eight o'clock and nine-thirty, when we went to her house."

"Well, obviously somebody didn't want her pulling out of the deal," Terry said. "Not alive, anyway."

I thought about it for a second. "You know, this puts the spotlight directly on Vlad and Vishy."

"You think?"

"Yeah. They're the ones who had something to lose if the

promotion didn't go through. She was billed as the main attraction. If she didn't show, those fans of hers might have caused some real trouble. They were close to rioting as it was."

"So you think she told them she wanted out, and the other guys killed her rather than cancel their big opening?"

I shrugged. "They got her there, one way or the other. And the cops are right—this is going to get them even more publicity."

Terry made a skeptical face. "I didn't get a killer vibe off those guys. Anyway, how could they snuff her between eight and nine-thirty, drain her blood, dump it, then get back in their hearses for the parade?"

"The only way would be if everyone was in on it. Morgoth and Lucian . . . that other guy Dagon, possibly."

"If they did it, it would explain why they were being coy about those rival vampires," she said. "The rival vampires don't exist."

She hit *69 on the phone.

"You're calling the dead girl?" I said. "Why? She's not going to answer."

"Let's see who does." I saw from her face that someone had picked up. "Who's this?" Terry listened for another few seconds before disconnecting. She turned and stared at me, her eyes wide.

"Who was it?" I said.

"A woman," Terry said, her mouth twisting cynically. "And I would have sworn it was dear departed Darby."

five

*T*erry instantly became convinced that Darby had pulled a switcheroo on us. "I'll kick her ass!" she said, jumping up from the couch.

"Now there's a good idea," I said, crossing my arms over my chest. "Go down to the morgue and kick a corpse."

She glared at me. "She's not *at* the morgue, Ker."

I knew the reason she was running with this: something similar had happened on our last case, and it still pissed her off that we'd been duped. But pointing this out would only have the effect of cementing Terry's convictions. When she got stuck on an idea, it took heaven and earth to shake her loose.

"Ter, it *had* to be Darby in the coffin!"

She paced the room, twisting her braided pigtail over one finger. "Why did it *have* to be? We haven't seen her since high school, remember, and she had a ton of makeup on. Under those conditions—the shock of it and everything—we'd see whoever we expected to see. It's an old magician's trick."

"But they're vampires, not magicians."

"I'm telling you, I know this in my gut."

Often referred to as "the golden gut," Terry's amazing intuition was usually right on. But this time I was sure she was just plain wrong.

"If it wasn't her, then who was it?" I said. "And are you saying Darby killed whoever it was?"

"Not necessarily. It could have been one of their crowd. Maybe someone who OD'd or something. Then all they had to do was dress her up in Ephemera's outfit, put Ephemera's makeup on her—"

"And Ephemera's spider tattoo . . . a postmortem tattoo?"

"We don't even know for sure that Darby had a tattoo, do we?"

"There's one way to find out," I said, rising. "Let's go online and find a picture of her in her Ephemera getup."

Terry followed me to the computer, where I did a quick online search. Darby had amassed quite a few fan sites associated with the Flatlining Femmes. There were dozens of photos of the band performing at goth clubs—four girls in Morticia Addams drag, framed against red or purple backdrops, all of them looking vaguely alike in their makeup. But high on the lead singer's right cheek was a black spider with a blood red spot on its abdomen.

"There you go." I pointed to the tattoo. "Same spider as the dead girl's. It was definitely Darby in the coffin."

Terry mulled it over, eyebrows knitted. "I don't know. A tattoo isn't definitive. We were fooled by a tattoo once before," she reminded me, referring to that earlier case.

"You're saying no one in the whole crowd recognized her as a fake?"

"Who got the chance? All the vampires scattered."

"And what about Vlad and Vishy? Are they in on your switcheroo scenario?"

She paced around the computer nook, Paquito at her heels. "Yeah, maybe . . ."

"But what would be the point of all this?"

"Who knows? All I know is, there's more here than meets the eye."

"Fine. Somehow Darby dressed up some other girl like herself, drained her blood, and put her in her coffin to fall out at the opening. Great conspiracy theory. Let's call Bagdasarian and Kenneally and share it with them."

"As if!"

"Terry, you're running with this idea because you *think* you heard Darby's voice on the phone just now?"

"I'd know it anywhere," she insisted. "It's exactly the same as it was in school." She broke into a singsongy voice: *"Hi! Cute shoes!"*

Mimicry was one of Terry's special talents. I could see the high school Darby standing before me, bubbly and full of class spirit.

"But this would be beyond the pale," I said. "It would be just plain sick. Not to mention that even if she didn't kill the girl, using a body like that is abusing a corpse. That's *way* illegal."

Terry shook her head. "I'm gonna love saying 'I told you so.' "

Could she be right? Suddenly I wasn't so sure. Terry could be very persuasive, especially when she was confabulating or hallucinating. She had the paranoid schizophrenic's faith in the veracity of her own voices. But was I entering into her insanity?

"Try calling her back," I said at last.

She hit the Redial button and waited. "No answer. No voice mail. The number's probably being disconnected as we speak. Let's get over to the house and see what we see."

"No!"

"Why not?"

"Because *a*, she's not going to go running home if she's supposed to be dead . . ."

Terry shrugged. "So we'll talk to her roommates, get a line on her."

"And *b*, the police are probably still there and they already warned us off . . ."

She drummed her fingers on her arm. "Okay, we'll go after the police have left. Do we have a *c*? Or would you like to buy a vowel?"

"I don't need a *c*—I'm the boss! We're not going and that's that."

She stalked past me into the kitchen. "Not gonna be very good for our reputation if we walk away from a murder . . ."

I followed her into the kitchen and watched her pour kibble into the dogs' bowls. Nails clickety-clacked on the floor as the pups ran into the room and dove into the bowls snout-first.

Muffy's food was gone in two gulps. She sat back on her haunches and looked longingly at Paquito's bowl.

"Don't steal his food!" I said.

She looked up with hurt in her round black eyes. *Me, steal?*

"Yeah, you. And it's gonna be low-fat kibble from now on."

She plopped to the ground and put her head down, looking like an unhappy little propane tank with paws. I felt bad for being so harsh, but I figured we needed to nip this eating addiction in the bud. It was time for some tough puppy love.

"Don't take out your frustration on her," Terry said, pushing past me into the living room. She snatched up her jacket and helmet. "I'm outta here."

"Where are you going?"

"Somewhere they don't mistreat dogs."

"Terry . . . where?"

She threw open front door. "I'm going riding!"

"You're *not* going over to that house," I said.

She turned and shot me a fake smile. "Course not. I would never disobey a direct order from Her High Holiness the Boss of the Universe." She pulled on her helmet and was halfway through the door when I grabbed the hem of her jacket.

"Okay," I said. "We'll go by first thing in the morning." She let me stop her. "But if the police are still there, we bail. All right?"

A moment passed before she turned back to me, grinning in triumph. "In that case, I'll go pick up some DVDs and Chinese food." She jumped off the porch, running for the bike. "Don't kick any four-legged creatures while I'm gone!"

six

The next morning we parked down the street from the large wooden house Darby had shared with Morgoth and Lucian, approaching it on foot. The place was horror heaven, the yard filled to bursting with vampire paraphernalia. Rubber bats hung from tree limbs, plaster gnomes that were painted to look like vampires stood sentry in the garden, and wind chimes made of finger bones clacked in the breeze. A taxidermy crow unfurled his wings above the door. Red paint dripped like blood down the front windowpanes in a mockery of snow-flocked Christmas windows.

There were no police cars out front. Nobody milling around, in uniform or out. I saw a remnant of yellow crime scene tape flapping on a corner of the house.

"They've released the scene," I said. "Must not have found much."

We went up the stairs to the front porch. A new decoration

had been added since we'd been there the day before. A wreath of garlic hung from a hunting knife jammed into the wood of the front door. The buds on the bottom of the wreath were soaked with still wet blood, dripping to the porch below like some kind of diabolical fondue.

Terry stared at the wreath, then started to back down the stairs, shaking her head. *What is this?* I thought. *Terry's afraid?* Couldn't be. She was born without the fear gene (or the common sense gene, for that matter).

"What?" I said, as I watched her retreat.

"I'm not going in there."

My hands went to my hips. "This was totally your idea! What's the big deal? We were just here yesterday!"

She shook her head again. "Yeah, but that was before the Angel of Death popped by to leave blood on the door." Her eyes went from the wreath to mine, naked in their entreaty. She wanted out of there, bad.

I peered at the wreath more closely. "I don't think it's real blood."

"It was real blood on the bike."

"Stay here, then." I punched the doorbell and heard the first bar of The Funeral March ringing through the house. Hollow, deep tones like those of an ancient pipe organ.

Dum dum da DUM, dum da dum, da dum, da DUM.

"That does it." Terry turned and ran down the walk toward the street. "See ya, Sis. Happy hunting!"

"Terry, if you don't get back here right now, you're gonna hear about this the rest of your life!" I yelled at her. "You can never call *me* a wimp again!"

She stopped dead on the sidewalk.

"Ha!" I grinned and turned back to the house, thinking, *Who's the ballsy sister now? The worm turns, baby.* I tried the knob and found that the door was unlocked. I pushed it open.

"See, Terry?" I said, full of bravado. "There's absolutely nothing to be afr—"

A dead body swung into my line of vision, hanging from a noose. It wore leather pants and a gauzy blouse with bell sleeves that hung down to its black fingernails. Its head was cocked at an impossible angle, an obscenely long tongue wagging from its gaping mouth, and its bugged blue eyes stared at me in sightless reproach.

I screamed and my mind blanked out before I hit the porch.

I came to with Terry slapping my face. Slapping it harder than was strictly necessary in order to revive me. My hand lashed out and slapped her back.

"Owww!" She rubbed at her cheek. "Easy!"

"What happened?" I said, trying to sit up. "Did someone hit me?"

"No, you were hit by the scaredy stick." She laughed as she reached out to help me up. "I called the cops. They're on their way."

I let her pull me to my feet, feeling the back of my head with my other hand. A bump had formed there, and my cheeks were still stinging from Terry's overzealous resuscitation efforts. I smoothed down my hiked-up jean skirt.

"Don't try to be brave, okay? It's not your style," she said.

"Are you going to tell me what happened?" I looked over and saw that the door was now closed, the garlic wreath lying on the porch where it had landed. The knife blade was still jammed in the wood.

"You screamed and keeled over," Terry said. "The body hit the door, I guess, and it slammed shut again."

It all came back to me in a rush. "You saw . . . ?" I asked her, my knees starting to shake.

She nodded. "I saw."

"Who was it?"

"Hard to tell with the contorted face," Terry said. "But I'm guessing it was Lucian."

It *was* Lucian, I realized, as I mentally superimposed the image of the skinny driver with wispy blond hair and tons of eyeliner over that of the corpse. Even before he was suspended from the rafters, he'd looked as if he were in need of a blood transfusion.

We heard a siren in the distance. "Buck up," Terry said, straightening my yellow baby tee. "Don't want to look chicken in front of the cops, do we? After all, we *are* professional investigators."

"Save the sales pitch for *them*," I said. "I'm scared out of my mind."

The cruiser screeched to a stop at the curb, siren going off with a final *wheep*. Two male officers got out of the car. One Latino, one black—our pals Alvarez and Dawson.

"You two again?" Dawson said, his brown eyes wide in surprise. "Did you call in a dead body?"

Terry nodded. "We came by to talk to a couple of the people who live here," she said, "but one of them isn't living anymore."

I pointed toward the house. "He's hanging from a noose inside the door."

The veil of serious cop business dropped down over their faces. Their eyes flicked to the knife stuck in the door, then to the blood-drenched garlic on the porch floor.

Alvarez put out an arm and shoved us aside, unholstering his gun. "Stay out of the way," he commanded us.

Dawson positioned himself on the other side of the entrance, his own gun at the ready. Their eyes met, communicating something without words. Alvarez gave Dawson a nod, then Dawson reached out and threw open the door.

I squinched my eyes shut. I didn't want to see the horrific hanging dead thing again.

Turns out I needn't have bothered.

"It was right there!" I heard Terry yell.

I opened my eyes and saw the officers giving us a look of rank skepticism. *The body was gone.*

"I passed out when I saw it," I said. "You think I'd faint for no reason? Feel this knot on my head! I hit my head when I fell to the porch!"

No one made a move to verify my bump.

"It's true," Terry said. "I just got her conscious again." She banged on the doorjamb. "I'm telling you guys, there was a hideous corpse hanging right by this door!"

Alvarez looked over at Dawson. Dawson shrugged back. "Was it the person you came to talk to?" Alvarez asked Terry.

"Yeah, one of them. His name is Lucian."

"What did you want to talk to him about?" he asked.

"We went to see the parents of the vampire queen—we'd known her at school—and they asked us to look into her death."

"Not officially, like an investigation or anything," I hastened to add. "But they'd been out of touch with her. They just wanted to know what her life had been like. She was a stranger to them and now she's gone. They wanted to know what went wrong with their daughter."

Alvarez smirked at Dawson. "Uh-huh, and how were you going to do that?"

I shrugged. "Talk to her roommates and get a line on her life."

"Interfering with an ongoing investigation, sounds like," Dawson said.

"No!" I looked over at Terry, who was shaking her head madly. "No, sir, that's the job of the police. We know that. We'd never do anything to interfere."

Dawson jerked his head toward the inside of the house. "Security sweep?" he said to his partner.

Alvarez nodded. Evidently he thought a report of a dead body qualified as probable cause for entering the premises. The cops stepped over the threshold, guns drawn.

"Stay here," Alvarez said to us.

"Police!" Dawson called as they moved cautiously into the foyer. "Anybody here?"

"Go on," Terry whispered to me, pointing inside.

I slapped her hand away. "He said to stay here!"

She shoved me and I went stumbling inside the door. Terry rushed in behind me. The cops turned and gave us a warning look.

"We're in," Terry said, shrugging. "Might as well hang out awhile."

"Now stay *there*," Alvarez said.

He and Dawson walked to the end of the foyer and looked into the living room, eyes traveling across the gruesome paraphernalia that covered every available surface. Skulls, severed limbs in plastic, even a fanged baby doll with blood staining its bib.

"They move Halloween to July?" Dawson said queasily.

"Vampire decor," Terry explained.

Alvarez crossed himself and turned to face the front door. There was a thick noose caught on a hook next to the frame, the rope slung over a pole that ran the length of the ceiling. The noose was empty.

"*Desaparecido,*" he said of the missing body.

"Looks like someone played a prank on you." Dawson pointed to a footstool ladder next to the door. "It was probably some kind of dummy."

"Look, I'm a bit of a fraidy cat, I admit"—I ignored the snort that came from Terry—"but I don't think I'd black out from seeing a mannequin swinging by a rope. It was definitely a person. And let's not forget the blood on the garlic out front."

Dawson walked through the living room and over to a window that faced the backyard. On the windowsill was a row of jars containing a yellowish substance, with various biological specimens floating inside. He leaned in and took a long look before jerking back.

"Jesus! It's an eyeball!" He turned around with a horrified look. "There's gotta be an ordinance against keeping eyeballs in your house, isn't there?"

"Don't look at us," Terry said, shrugging. "You're the law."

Dawson turned back to the jars. "And this is a frickin' finger!" he yelled.

"I'm sure you can buy those on the open market," I said. "There's probably a whole eBay section devoted to preserved body parts. Don't they use them in medical schools for teaching?"

"Teach me to lose my lunch," Dawson said on the exhale.

Alvarez pointed upstairs. "You've been here before?" he said. "What's up there?"

I got the feeling he didn't want to go. "Bedrooms, sort of."

"No beds," Terry added. "Just coffins."

Dawson rolled his eyes and took the baton off his belt. He pointed up the stairs with it. Alvarez led the way up the dark staircase, moving slowly. Halfway up, his arms started flailing.

"Ackkk . . . *Yickkk!*" he yelled.

Dawson bounded up the stairs to him. "What?"

Alvarez brushed at his uniform frantically. "Cobwebs."

"They probably raise spiders like my grandfather raised bees," Dawson said, shaking his head.

After Alvarez got a grip on himself, we continued upstairs, wooden treads creaking underfoot. Three rooms opened onto the second-floor landing—two near the staircase and one at the far end. We approached the first open bedroom. It was dark, the morning sun blocked by maroon velvet drapes. Two crossed swords hung over a mahogany coffin on the far side of the room.

The foot of the coffin was pointed toward the door. The upper half of the lid was open on its hinges. And in the middle of the opening was a luminescent white face that seemed to float in the darkness.

"The body?" Alvarez whispered to Dawson.

Dawson nodded, serious again, and the two of them moved into the room, with Terry and me following right behind them. We stopped next to the side of the coffin and peered in.

But it wasn't Lucian lying there. It was Morgoth.

He lay peacefully, his face pale and still. The widow's peak looked like a dead blackbird perched on his forehead. The four of us held our breath.

"Omigod," Terry said at last. "They killed him, too?"

Morgoth's eyes popped open. *"What?"* he said.

We shrieked and jumped back.

"Can't a guy take a nap?" Morgoth blinked sleepily at the cops. "I thought you guys were gone!"

"What are you talking about?" Dawson said.

"The investigators, they left an hour ago. They just let us back in. I thought I could get some shut-eye."

"We had a report of a dead body," Alvarez told him.

"A body . . . ?" Morgoth said. *"Where?"*

"Ms. McAfee saw it hanging over the front door by the neck," he said, indicating me with his head. "It caused her to faint."

"Oh-h-h." Morgoth chuckled and flipped open the bottom section of the lid, climbing out in his Batman pajamas. "That was no body, that was Lucian. He does that to freak out solicitors and Jehovah's Witnesses. He hooks the noose onto a harness and goes flying in their faces. They don't usually come back."

"Who is this guy Lucian?" Alvarez said, clearly not amused by his high jinks.

"My roommate," Morgoth said.

"Where is he now?"

"He probably took off when he saw you passed out," he said, giving me an apologetic look. "People usually just scream and run away. Sometimes they wet their little black business suits. I don't think he's ever made anyone faint before."

"I'm happy to have that distinction," I said, turning to Alvarez. "I'm very sorry, Officer. But I'm sure you can understand our jumpiness after what happened at the gallery yesterday."

Alvarez gave me a nod of acknowledgment. "You rent this place?" he asked Morgoth.

"Yeah, a few of us. Well, two of us now."

"What do you do for a living, if anything?"

Morgoth looked affronted. "I work in a photo lab darkroom."

"Okay, let me make this perfectly clear," Dawson said, crossing his arms and causing his muscles to bulge. "If I ever get another call back to this house on account of a body hanging from a rope"—he stepped up and pointed a blunt finger at Morgoth's pug nose—"you *and* your roommate are gonna be booked on nuisance charges. Understand?"

Morgoth twisted the corner of his PJs, exposing his round little belly. "Yes, sir, Officer," he said meekly.

Dawson and Alvarez turned to leave.

"We're really sorry," I said as they exited the room. "We weren't *trying* to file a false report."

"Forget it," Alvarez said, waving a hand in the air. "It's L.A."

They took the stairs, grumbling and swatting at cobwebs as they went.

As soon as they were out the front door and out of earshot, I let loose on Morgoth. "Why would Lucian pull a stunt like that just hours after your friend was killed? How totally inappropriate!"

He shrugged. "Stress reaction?"

"It was gruesome!"

"Gruesome is what we do well," he said with an impish grin.

"We need to ask you some questions," Terry said. "Now that you're awake, can you give us ten minutes?"

"Sure, I guess. Ask away."

"First, though, we want to take a look at Darby's room."

He glanced out into the hall. "Oh, I don't know about that. They might need to do some more investigating or—"

"They're finished with it," I said. "Anyway, our fingerprints are already on record."

"What are you looking for?" he asked apprehensively.

"Well, for one thing," Terry said, "we're looking for a cell phone."

"Okay, but if there was anything interesting in there, I'm sure the police took it."

He led us down the landing and Terry pushed open the door. We entered a black-walled room with black velvet curtains. Morgoth flipped the wall switch and rose-colored light glowed from art deco sconces. There was a platform in the middle of the room where the coffin had been. Chest-high iron candelabra sat at the corners, congealed black wax forming two-foot stalagmites on the surface underneath. The room was crammed with dusty bric-a-brac, but here it was more fanciful than ghoulish: a pewter unicorn, crystals in all colors and shapes hanging from the ceiling, glittery pentagrams spinning in the draft from the open window. One particular item gave me a shiver—a crucifix in hand-tooled silver, hanging upside down on the wall facing the platform.

Maybe Darby *had* been a devil-worshipper.

Terry and I scoured the place looking for a phone or anything else of interest, but nothing presented itself. I went to the closet and slid open the door. It was empty except for a few dust bunnies.

"Hey," I said, turning to Morgoth, "where're all her clothes?"

He walked up and peered into the closet, shrugging. "Maybe she took 'em all to the gallery to sell 'em."

"Or maybe she's on the run," Terry whispered to me.

"Did the police determine that there was a break-in?" I asked him.

"No, but her window was wide open, like it is now. She slept with it that way."

"Always?"

"Uh-huh. She said she didn't want to miss it if a real vampire came by."

"A real vampire?" I said, shooting Terry a look. "You mean *you're* not a real vampire?"

"I'm a real vampire spiritually, but I haven't been turned out yet. We all hope to be chosen by one of the immortals someday. You know, transformed into the undead."

"I see." I bit my tongue and walked to the window. Fingerprint dust was smudged on the sill. "Do vampires have fingerprints?"

Morgoth scoffed. "Of *course*."

"Well, how am I supposed to know? They don't have reflections, right?"

He wrinkled his nose. "Hollywood bunk."

So hard to know the difference. "Do the cops think her killer came in through here?" I gestured to the window.

"*If* she was killed," Morgoth said pointedly.

"You're thinking she might have been 'chosen'?" Terry said. "That she's not really dead, but one of the undead?"

"Like I said, it's everyone's goal."

We leaned over the sill and looked down into the yard. The grass appeared to be flattened in the shape of four rectangles, as from the base of a heavy ladder.

"Looks like someone put a ladder against the house and climbed right in," I said. "I thought vampires changed into bats and flew in the window."

Morgoth joined us and looked down into the yard. "They didn't find a ladder."

"How about blood?" Terry asked him. "Did they find any blood?"

"Not that I'm aware of."

"So whoever drained her was very careful," Terry said, looking around the room.

"Vampires tend to be fastidious," Morgoth said. "Besides, they wouldn't let blood go to waste on the floor."

"Did you share your 'real vampire' theory with the police?" I asked him.

"Yeah, but I could see they were skeptical." He gave a philosophical shrug. "That's okay, we're used to skepticism."

"They don't consider you a suspect?"

"I'm sure they do, but they don't have enough evidence to arrest me. I didn't do it, you know. I'm a lover, not a killer." He rubbed his tummy. "Hey, I'm starved. Could anyone go for some Count Chocula?"

This is pretty good," I said, spooning in another delicious and nutritious mouthful of sugary chocolate cereal. The three of us were seated around the Formica table in the kitchen, nice and cozy. If it weren't for the black cereal bowls and the spoons made of skulls, it would have been just like home.

I looked at the cartoon character on the box. Count Chocula had a single fang hanging from the top of his mouth. "Dude, Chocula's only got one tooth. What's up with that? He looks like Bugs Bunny."

"He used to have two," Morgoth said, "but they extracted one in the eighties."

"Why?"

"Fear of the occult, I guess."

"Kind of defeats the purpose, doesn't it?"

"What're you gonna do? They're always out to defang us, one way or the other."

Terry pointed to the prongs jutting from Morgoth's mouth. "Are those permanent?"

"Yeah. They're caps."

"Okay, here's the real question," she said, leaning into him. "Do you eat Count Chocula because you're a vampire? Or are you a vampire because you ate Count Chocula as a kid?"

He seemed baffled by the question. "Didn't you eat it?" he asked her.

"Nope. Froot Loops."

He smirked. "That explains a lot."

"So which is it?" Terry insisted, laughing. "Which came first?"

"I was always obsessed with vampires, even as a kid. I used to pitch a fit if I couldn't have the cereal every morning. And it was all my mother could do to keep me from wearing my Halloween costume to school every day. Eventually we compromised on just the black cloak. I got beaten up a lot, but hey—can't deny who you are."

"So you're saying you always knew you were a vampire," Terry said. "Like people who know they're gay from the age of three?"

"Yeah. I've been in vampire support groups where other people have said the same thing."

Terry and I exchanged a look. "Vampire *support* groups?" we said.

"You think it's easy being a night creature in a daylight world?"

"Maybe your mother weaned you too soon," I suggested. "And that's why you want to suck blood."

"No, I think it's the romance of it all." His eyes went off into the distance. "You're *other*—apart, isolated. Your victim swoons at the bite of her neck, her life essence going into your mouth . . ."

Ugh. "Is her life essence screened for dangerous organisms?" I said. "Or don't vampires have to worry about stuff like that?"

He turned back to me. "Right—well, these days the blood thing's not so simple. You have to practice safe sucks. Most of us have donors we're sure are clean, and we don't usually go for the jugular. We make a cut with a sterile surgical knife and suck on that."

I pushed my bowl away with a moan. I thought I might chuck my Chocula.

"Oh, come on," Morgoth said. "Haven't you ever cut your finger and put it in your mouth to stop the bleeding?"

"Yes," I admitted.

"Did it taste bad?"

I made a face, but Terry answered truthfully. "No, not really."

"Some people think we have a medical condition called iron deficiency porphyria, meaning we're lacking an enzyme that we can only get from the blood of someone else."

"Have you checked online for this enzyme?" Terry said. "I mean, if you can click your way to a larger penis . . ."

"Blood drinking is done in lots of cultures," he said, ignoring her. "Have you heard of the Masai tribesmen of Kenya? Maybe you've seen them in that Audi commercial?"

We shook our heads.

"They're cattle herders. They wear red robes and carry spears. Anyway, they drink raw cow's blood for its nutritional value. They milk the cow into a cup, then they slice the cow's flank, drain some blood into the milk, and have themselves a little snack. A blood smoothie."

"Omigod," I said, squirming. "Doesn't the cow get woozy?"

"They've been doing it forever. They know just how much to take so the cow doesn't pass out."

"Do those fangs bother you when you eat?" Terry asked him.

He dragged his bottom lip across the tips. "Not anymore. When I first got them I went around with a bloody mouth all the time. But you learn how to manage."

"But what about your workplace? They don't mind that you have fangs?"

"Nah. They're just happy to have someone who'll work the night shift."

I thought about his roommate, the swinging corpse. "What does Lucian do? Does he have a job?"

"He works at the L.A. County morgue, but his teeth are a bridge. I doubt he could get away with wearing them to work for the government."

"A vampire who works at the morgue?" Terry said. "What does he do, drain body fluids or something?"

"He's a cashier in the gift shop."

"The *what?*" she said.

"It's called Skeletons in the Closet. They sell beach towels with chalk body outlines on them, baseball caps with the coroner's logo, toe-tag key chains, piggy banks made to look like meat wagons—tons of cool stuff."

I looked over at Terry. "It's L.A.," she said, echoing the cops.

"This is all very interesting," I said, "but we're no closer to knowing what happened to Ephemera. Assuming she was murdered and wasn't taken as the bride of Chocula, who do you think might have wanted to do this?"

Morgoth sucked at his dripping fangs. "There were people who didn't like her, or were jealous. Thought she wasn't sincere, just milking the vampire scene on her way to becoming a media star."

I remembered the phone call from Darby saying she was planning to get out of the scene. If she was killed by someone who was jealous, it was just too bad she hadn't done it sooner.

"Vishy was about to say who the rival vampires were," I said, "but Vlad shut him up. You know who he was talking about, don't you?"

Morgoth gave me a long look. "He was talking about Shatán," he said finally.

"Shatán? What kind of name is that?"

"Supposedly it's Sanskrit for Satan. He's the big vamp on campus. He and Ephemera had a rivalry going. He thinks the Dark Arts types are exploiting the true faith for the sake of commerce."

"The true faith?" Terry said. "What is he, a fundamentalist vampire?"

"You could call him that. He claims to have been turned out for real."

"And if he was," I said in an *Oh, right* tone, "he could fly in windows and suck the blood of someone in their sleep?"

Morgoth pushed his lips out through the fangs as he considered it. "Anything's possible, I guess."

"How would we get in touch with this Shatán?" Terry asked him.

"Oh, uh"—Morgoth pointed to our bowls—"are you done?"

We nodded and he took the bowls to the sink, then rinsed them out and stuck them in the dishwasher. It was an incongruous sight, to say the least. Somehow I couldn't picture Bela Lugosi using a labor-saving device from Maytag.

He turned around with a worried look. "I wouldn't recommend trying to find him. He's kind of . . . extreme."

This from a guy with permanent fang caps who admitted to sucking donor blood.

"Extreme?" I said.

"A real sadist. Likes to inflict pain. Doesn't always get permission before he rips into someone's neck with his canines. That's probably why Vlad backed off from accusing him. You wouldn't want to get on his bad side. Even the gangs won't mess with Shatán. He's pure evil."

"You let us worry about that," Terry said, unfazed. "Now, how do we get in touch with him?" Her tone implied it was the last time she was going to ask nicely.

"He's at the Inferno Club most nights, holding court. He owns it. Spends a lot of time in the private room upstairs. It's on Pico around La Brea."

"Okay, we'll check him out tonight," Terry said. "Is there a dress code at this place?"

"Think black."

"I mostly think pink."

"Not if you're going goth, you don't. Got any cat's-eye contacts?"

"Um, no."

"Well, put on a lot of pale face makeup and black lipstick, and whatever you do, don't smile."

"Okay," I said, rising from the chair, "thanks for the insights."

"You're welcome." He poured some Liquid Sunlight into the soap compartment and started the wash cycle.

"Anything else we should know about Shatán?" I said, turning in the doorway.

Morgoth looked down at his long black fingernails. "Yeah," he said. "Rumor is, he's killed three people."

"You mean 'turned' three people?"

He gave me an enigmatic smile. "No, I mean murdered."

Fabulous, I thought, then said, "Cheery bye!"

seven

*W*hen we got back to the bike the cell phone vibrated in my pocket. I flipped it open and took it a few yards away, plugging my ear against the noise of Terry starting the engine.

"Hello, dear." It was Great-Aunt Reba.

"Hi, Reba. How's it going?"

"Well, I'm a little shorthanded. Could you two come help me out for an hour?"

"Sure. Where are you?"

"I'm at the Compassion House, on Broadway Court."

"The *what* house?" It didn't sound like one of Reba's normal hangouts. "Compassion" wasn't exactly her strong suit. "What is this place?" I asked as Terry looked back at me impatiently.

"It's a soup kitchen. I'd no idea there were so many homeless people in my new neighborhood. I couldn't stand myself if I didn't do something to help these poor unfortunates."

So the pampered Beverly Hills widow was taking notice of

the needy people around her—would wonders ever cease? A little alarm bell went off in my head, but I ignored it. *Everybody's entitled to change*, I told myself.

"Sure, we'd love to help."

"When can you get here?"

"In a few minutes. We're in Venice now."

"Oh, good," Reba said. "We're two blocks up from Abbott Kinney. The white house with all the loaded-up shopping carts parked out front."

"Okay, we'll be there soon."

"Thank you so much, dear."

I shut the phone and went back to the bike.

"Who was it?" Terry asked.

"Reba. She needs some help serving lunch at a soup kitchen."

She laughed. "Ha. Good one. So who was it?"

"It was Reba. She needs some help serving lunch at a soup kitchen."

"Here's what you need to know about comedy, Ker—you can't get a laugh twice with the exact same joke. You have to either expand on it or go in another direction altogether with the next line."

"I'm not trying to be funny," I said, though by now I was laughing, too. "I'm trying to tell you that Reba is volunteering at a soup kitchen because she's shocked—*shocked*—to find there are homeless people in the world. She can't bear their suffering, so she's slopping food at a place called the Compassion House."

Terry's mouth dropped open. "Omigod. Reba's got a social conscience now?"

I shrugged and grinned. "Looks that way."

"The end is near, people," she said, shaking her head. "The end is *near*."

The Compassion House was the best-maintained building on the street, a wooden two-story in a seedy section of Venice just blocks from trendy Main Street. There were no upscale shops here, no coffee bars, no canals. This part of town was down and dirty, where gangbangers and crackheads ruled the roost. A few retirees lived among them, staying out of sight in their houses and trying to keep their heads clear of drive-by shootings.

And Reba Price-Slatherton was inside, doing her impersonation of Mother Teresa.

Reba had had five husbands in her life, each richer than the last, and each on his last legs by the time she got hitched to him. All my childhood memories of Reba were of attending her husbands' funerals. They were elaborate affairs, with Reba draped in black couture, stoic in her grief.

She was a combination black widow spider and Queen Midas, except that everything she touched turned to platinum instead of mere gold. Was it possible that marriage and money were no longer doing it for her? Maybe the end of her affair with Eli had been the last straw and she'd finally made the decision to live for someone other than herself.

It's a good thing, a good thing, I chanted mentally in an attempt to drown out the little voice that was screaming, *Danger, Will Robinson!*

Terry switched off the engine. "Think the bike's gonna be okay here?"

"We'll find out, I guess."

Terry gazed toward the house. "It's temporary insanity, it has to be. She'll do it for one day and then realize she's better off sending a check."

"I don't know—maybe she's seen the light. Maybe Robert's conversion was contagious."

Our cousin Robert had been a confirmed drunk until he went hurtling down the stairs in Aunt Reba's mansion, hit his head and knocked himself out, and subsequently decided to put his life in order. He got off the sauce, started meditating, and dedicated himself to profound philosophical pursuits.

I gave it six months.

"Maybe," Terry said. "Well, let's go in."

There was a line snaking out of the house and across the yard, made up of individuals who'd clearly been living outdoors—weathered skin like riding chaps, hair scraggly and bug-ridden. Most of them had multiple layers of clothing on despite the balmy weather; everything they owned was on their backs. Some looked at us as we passed, but many kept their eyes on the ground or stared into space.

Inside, the place was stark and clean. We found hardwood floors, plastic tables and benches, and rows of men and women slumped over metal plates with peanut butter and jelly sandwiches and bowls of soup. I'd expected the atmosphere to be a little ripe, since no one here got much of a chance to shower, but instead of the smell of unwashed bodies we were hit by the overpowering scent of Chanel No. 5.

Terry sniffed the air, frowning. "Smells like a French cathouse in here."

"Wanna bet who the French cat is?"

We made our way to a service window that had been cut into the wall, exposing the kitchen beyond. Inside there was an assembly line of volunteer chefs huddled around an industrial stove and a huge sink, all of them in jeans and aprons.

All except one.

"There you are!" Reba chirped through the window, her face steamed up from the soup boiling on the stove. She wore a sleek little Dolce & Gabbana pantsuit under her apron. Her hennaed hair was caught up in a hairnet, and she wore a flesh-colored nose plug, like a swimmer's. With the pinched nostrils, her voice sounded like it was leaking out of her ears. "Just in time," she said. "Here, have a hairnet."

She handed us two little balled-up pieces of net. I unfolded mine and stretched it out, then snapped it on over my head. Terry burst out laughing.

Reba gave her a look. "Hygiene is no laughing matter, Terry."

"Sorry."

Terry stuffed my loose red tresses under my net, then bunched her braided pigtails up next to her head in little coils, pulling her hairnet on over them.

"You look like Princess Leia, just rolled out of bed," I told her.

"I feel ridiculous in this thing," Terry said.

"Would Jesus feel ridiculous?" Reba retorted.

Excuse me?

What were we looking at here, a full-blown religious conversion? Born-again Reba? Saul struck blind on Rodeo Drive?

Reba shook a finger at us. "Did Jesus say, 'I won't touch those nasty scabs, Mr. Leper'?" She gave us a self-righteous flick of her chin. "No, he simply ministered to the sick and the lame."

"Okay, Reba, we got it," Terry said. "We'll be Jesus. Now, what are we supposed to do?"

Reba handed her a tray of sandwiches through the window. "Every patron gets one of these sandwiches—two halves—and one ladle of soup. If they ask for more, tell them to go to the end of the line for anything that's left over. They're supposed to bus their own trays, but obviously the ones who think we're the CIA beaming messages into their heads run out directly after eating."

Terry and I snapped on latex gloves, and I carried the sandwich tray to a table at the head of the room. The soup kettles were already in place. I positioned myself behind the sandwich tray and Terry picked up the ladle to serve the soup. Reba came to the end of the table to supervise.

"Now, let's see you serve." She signaled to the next person in line, a toothless man of about seventy. He stepped up with a tray.

"Hi," I said to him. "Peanut butter sandwich?"

"Unless you got lobster Newberg."

"Right." I plunked a sandwich down on his plate. "Peanut butter it is."

He shuffled over to Terry. "Would you like some soup?" she said.

"What kind is it?"

Terry peered into the pot. "Potato, is my guess."

"I'd rather eat pig swill."

"Okey-dokey." Terry slopped some soup into his bowl. "Enjoy."

He nodded his thanks and shuffled off.

Terry leaned in and whispered to me, "That was easy enough."

As the man walked past Reba, her hand snaked out and I heard the *pssst* of an atomizer. The scent of Chanel No. 5 floated over the yeasty smell of the soup. Reba whipped her hand behind her back as the old man spun around, nostrils flared.

"What the hell was that?" he said.

Reba gave him a wide-eyed look of innocence. "What?"

"Did you just spray me with perfume?"

Her mouth made an *O* of indignation. "Certainly not. Now move along, we have other patrons."

"How come you have your nose plugged?" the man asked.

"I'm allergic to pollen. It's pollen season."

"No it ain't. That's in the spring."

"If you're so smart, why are you homeless?" she barked at him. "Now *move along*!"

The man glowered at her, then looked back at Terry and me with watery, accusing eyes. "She ain't right in the head," he said.

It's a good thing, a good thing, I chanted mentally.

The man shuffled away, and a lady of indeterminate age in a green knit cap, wearing several sweaters over her flowered shift, stepped up for a sandwich. She was tiny, standing barely five feet high.

"Pile it high and deep," she said to me.

"Here you go." I put a sandwich on her plate, and she moved over to the soup.

"Don't be stingy, honey," she said to Terry. "Slop it to the top."

Terry smiled and scooped up some soup. "Here you go."

"Come on, Red, you can do better than that for old Lola, can'tcha? Know who I am? I was Shirley Temple's stand-in. Maybe you caught some of my pictures. I was in *Bright Eyes* and *The Little Princess*, buncha others, too. Think you were always looking at Shirley's feet? No, siree. Who do you think took over when Miss Priss was too pooped to do another take? I was the better dancer, I'll tell you that. But she was jealous. She did everything she could to keep me down. That's why I'm here, instead of the United Nations, like Miss Fancy Feet."

"Well, how about that?" Terry said. "We'll watch the movies tonight. I'll pick 'em up at the video store."

"Video . . . *pah!*" Lola said. "That stuff ruined the movies. That and the damn TV. C'mon, gimme some more soup. Tap dancing takes calories."

Terry started to ladle up some more soup, but Reba was there in a flash, slapping Terry's wrist.

"Ow!" Terry yelled.

"You know better, Lola," Reba said, shooing her away. "End of the line, end of the line."

Lola scowled with her toothless mouth. "Mean old bitch," she said to Terry, then picked up her tray and headed for the tables.

I saw Reba's hand dart out again and spritz Lola's back. Lola froze in place. She leaned over and sniffed her food.

"This food is poisoned! It's Shirley Temple! She's still trying to kill me!"

Terry turned to me in horror. "Is she gonna spray every single one of them with perfume?"

"What can we do?" I asked helplessly. "It's her gig."

By the time we'd replenished the sandwiches and refilled the soup kettle and served everyone in line, our eyes were burning from the perfume-polluted air. The homeless people were coughing as they tried to eat, choking down the food in a noxious fog of Parisian fragrance.

"She's like one of those crazed women at the department stores who spray you while you're shopping," Terry said.

"Yeah, but at least *they* do it to your face."

"This is so wrong."

I sighed. "I'll go talk to her."

I caught up to Reba in the kitchen. She was buzzing around the room, stacking dishes and cleaning up, humming "Lara's Theme" from *Dr. Zhivago*.

"Reba?"

"Yes, dear?"

She looked so pleased with herself, I hated to rain on her humanitarian parade. But something had to be said.

"Reba, you can't keep spritzing these people with perfume," I told her. "They're human beings, you know. They have a right to their dignity."

Her beatific smile turned down. "And *I* have a right not to smell BO."

"You're going to asphyxiate everybody! There's hardly any air left to breathe in that room."

"I simply cannot *bear* the odor."

I threw her words back at her. "Would Jesus wear a nose plug? Would Jesus spritz the unfortunate with Chanel No. 5?"

Her eyes went sideways. "Well, I don't suppose they *had* Chanel No. 5 in ancient Judea . . ."

"Reba," I said, shaking my head, "if you want to be compassionate, you have to go all the way. You have to treat these people with respect. Anyway, you're going to cause an uproar if you don't stop attacking them with perfume."

"Oh, I suppose you're right." She yanked off the nose plug with a sigh. "I'll just have to think of some other way around it."

After lunch we helped with the washing up, threw away our hairnets, and turned in our aprons. The homeless people left to retrieve their shopping carts and get back to business.

"You girls haven't seen my new place yet," Reba said. "Want to come by for a cuppa joe?"

Cuppa joe? Reba was evidently learning some hip beach lingo here in Venice. Terry looked over at me, and I shrugged back at her. "Sure, let's go have a look," I said.

We found the Harley unharmed, and followed Reba's mint green Mercedes SL to her new digs, a condo on Vernon Avenue. Some brave soul had built the sleek modern structure in the spirit of inner-city revitalization, but the gang graffiti told us who the real civic leaders were around here.

"Think Reba knows she's moved into a war zone?" Terry said.

"I doubt it."

Reba zapped open her automatic garage door, and we followed her into the spotless empty space. No tools, no oil cans, no sign of automotive life other than the car itself.

"Smashing, isn't it?" she said, as she closed the door to the Mercedes. "I feel so unencumbered. I never knew how weighted down I was by those large properties! Got it for a song, too. There are three other condos in the building that are still unoccupied. The seller was very motivated."

"Oh, really?" Terry said. "How long had it been on the market?"

"Two years, can you imagine? I don't know what the problem could be."

I almost said *location, location, location* but decided to keep it to myself. "Is Robert home?"

"No, he's at the beach getting in shape for his gallery opening. He leaves every morning half dressed for some kind of *workout*." She gave us a little smirk, whispering, "I think it's a midlife crisis, but don't tell him I said so."

Oh, you're *one to talk,* I thought to myself.

The garage opened directly into the kitchen, a large open affair with marble counters and light wood cabinets. There were copper pots hanging from a wrought-iron overhang, sunflowers in a vase of blue glass, and one heavyset Irish woman in a white uniform, scrubbing the counter—Reba's maid, Griselda.

"Hey, Grizzie," Terry and I said.

She waved a sponge in the air without turning around. "Humph."

Grizzie had been with Reba and Robert for thirty years. She was grumpy at the best of times, and you could see that she didn't consider these the best of times. She was a super housekeeper and a rock of a human being, but Reba's late-life adventures in moving were obviously taking their toll on her. First they had gone to Malibu, where they'd stayed only a few weeks due to a dead body found in the spare bedroom (long story), and then they had moved from Malibu to Venice.

"She doesn't like the neighborhood," Reba whispered, making a face at Grizzie's back. "I think she considers it too low-rent. I'd no idea the woman was such a snob."

We had recently learned that Grizzie was wealthy in her own right due to careful investment of her paychecks, but she remained with Reba's household as if on some kind of housekeeping autopilot. She had a daughter in Belfast, married to a "blighter," and no grandchildren, no compelling reason to go home. So she stayed, keeping Reba's various domiciles spotless with her bloated red hands, grumbling unintelligibly all the while. I guess it worked for her.

I looked around the kitchen. "It's a great place," I said to Reba. "Very hip, very now."

This got me a pleased smile. "Well, I like to think so. Say, you girls haven't heard from Eli, have you?"

The question caught us unawares. Reba was still pretty raw after her breakup, and we didn't want to say the wrong thing here.

"Um, no," Terry said casually.

"Uh-uh," I said. "Why do you ask?"

Reba gave a one-shouldered shrug. "Just curious, is all. Wondered how he's getting along."

Terry cut her eyes to me. "Well, we haven't heard a peep."

"Probably licking his wounds like a grouchy old bear," Reba said with a wink.

"Yeah, probably," I lied.

"Well, if you do see him, feel free to mention that I'm completely over him. I've got my work with the homeless, now . . . I'm 'giving back,' as they say, and it's even more satisfying than great sex."

Terry gagged and turned away, a hand covering her mouth.

"Glad to hear it," I said, forcing my mind to go blank before it could supply me with a geriatric porno film starring Reba and Eli.

Reba took no notice of our reactions. "Grizzie," she said in her lady-of-the-manor voice, "we'll have coffee on the roof."

Grizzie grunted in reply, which translated to *As you wish, madam.*

Reba led us up a stairway and out onto the second-story deck. We sat at a whitewashed table with deck chairs and a red striped umbrella. I took a deep breath of the fresh beach air, humid and salty with the promise of umbrella drinks and sandy towels.

"Look at that view!" Reba said, waving an arm.

It was indeed a great view. You could see the ocean shimmering beyond the palm trees in the distance. And if you didn't look down, you wouldn't see the crack dealers trolling the streets in their brand-new SUVs.

"Aren't you a little concerned about the tagging?" Terry asked.

Reba looked at her curiously. "Tagging?"

"Gang graffiti."

"Oh, posh. It's just an alternative form of artistic expression. It's part of what makes this neighborhood so fascinating."

"But it might be dangerous—" I started to say.

No sooner were the words out of my mouth than a series of hot popping sounds cut the air.

I looked at Terry in panic. "Were those gunshots?"

She spun around in her chair, eyes wide. "Sure sounded like it."

Reba pooh-poohed us, waving a hand in the air. "Firecrackers. Don't be so nervous. Look, that's Dennis Hopper's house right over there, see?" She pointed to a starkly modern house surrounded by a high wall and barbed wire. Looked like Dennis was expecting a recurrence of the L.A. riots or a resurgence of the Viet Cong.

"Well," Terry said, "I guess you could always duck over to Dennis's bunker if a war breaks out."

Grizzie huffed and puffed out of the stairwell door, holding a tray with the coffee service, silver urn, and china cups. Just then a bunch of police cars screamed into the area with their earsplitting clarions.

Wheeeeeeeeeeee-eeee-eee!

Then we heard the rotor of a helicopter on approach—*whop-whop-whop-whop-whop!*

Grizzie froze in place, looking up.

The helicopter raced across the sky, pursuing a speeding

vehicle on the street below. A black luxury SUV burned rubber through the intersection next to the building, tires squealing like pigs being slaughtered.

WHOP-WHOP-WHOP-WHOP-WHOP-WHOP-WHOP!

The helicopter swooped down, buzzing the roof. The wind whipped up around us, swirling our hair up into the air, our eardrums imploding from the pressure and the noise. The umbrella rose up from the table and spun off into the atmosphere, carried tornado-style to someone's yard two blocks away.

The passenger of the SUV stuck the barrel of an AK-47 out the window, sending up a volley of gunfire at the helicopter.

POW-POW-POW-POW-POW!

Terry and I dove under the table.

Grizzie chucked the serving tray and hit the deck, rolling behind a chimney with her hands over her head. The china cups exploded into a million fragments, and the silver coffee urn went clanging across the rooftop.

We held our breath, waiting for death to take us.

Then, as quickly as it came, the maelstrom passed. The helicopter engine and the sirens faded into the distance. Terry and I looked at each other, shell-shocked. We crawled out from beneath the table. Grizzie pulled herself up from the rooftop by means of the chimney, groaning and rubbing her backside.

"What the hell was that?" Terry yelled.

Reba grinned, clasping her hands together at her breast. "It's positively invigorating, isn't it? Life on the edge!"

Terry and I helped Grizzie sweep up the china shards, mopping up the coffee and cream with paper towels. She buffed the dent in the silver coffee urn with her apron, shaking her head.

"I tell ye, girls, I don't know how much more o' this I can take. It's like livin' in downtown bloody Baghdad."

"Oh, you know Reba," I said. "She just needs a change of pace every now and then."

"Time we quit trampin' about like a bunch o' gypsies and moved back to Beverly Hills."

"Did she sell the house on Palm Drive?" Terry asked her.

"Not yet, but it's on the market."

"Well, don't worry. We'll think of something before it's too late."

"It'll be back to Belfast with this lass if ye don't," Grizzie said, polishing the urn. "I'll take me chances with the IRA."

We declined her offer of replacement coffee and headed back home. Between the swinging corpse and the perfumed soup kitchen and the sudden outbreak of gang warfare, we'd had enough of this charming seaside hamlet for one day.

eight

*T*erry was eager to pursue Shatán that night at the Inferno Club. Problem was, I had accepted a dinner date with Boatwright, in spite of knowing this would probably be it: the proverbial fork in the road. The intersection of To Do It and Not to Do It streets.

Like I said, I wanted him bad. I just didn't want the ghost of an FBI agent in bed with us. So I was actually relieved that I had the excuse of the vampire club to forestall the inevitable.

"That's okay, you go on your date," Terry said. "I'll check out Shatán."

"Like I'm gonna let you infiltrate a bunch of vampires by yourself!" I said, shaking my head. "I'll go with Boatwright for an early dinner, then have him drop me off. I'm sure things don't get hopping at the club until ten or eleven."

"But I figured this was gonna be the big night," she said with a smirk. "Moonbeams and condoms?"

I still didn't want to tell Terry about my dilemma.

"Nah, I don't think it's right just yet."

She frowned in disgust. "If you put him off anymore, he'll lose interest. Or he'll think you're diseased."

The phone rang and I snatched it up before Terry could get to it, hoping it was Boatwright calling to cancel. *Homicide detectives do tend to have erratic schedules*, I reminded myself.

"Ms. McAfee?"

I couldn't place the gravelly voice. "Yes, it's Kerry. Who's this, please?"

"Detective Bagdasarian, LAPD."

"Oh, hi, Detective."

"I'm calling about that incident with your motorcycle. I got the lab to do a rush job for me."

"Was it pig's blood or something?" Even as I said it, I knew it wasn't going to be good news—as if pig's blood in your carburetor could ever be construed as good news.

"No, it's human. After the autopsy we'll be able to determine if it belonged to your Ms. Applewhite."

I felt an electric charge go down to my toes. "And what if it is hers?" I asked.

"It would mean that the murderer had a specific message for you, and it ain't friendly. I want to talk to you again, see if there's something I missed. Can you and your sister come by the Pacific station first thing tomorrow? Say, nine o'clock?"

"We'll be there."

"On second thought, make it eight-forty-five. And Kerry . . ."

"Yes?"

"I want your solemn word that you're not going to do any more investigating."

"My solemn word that we won't investigate?" This got Terry's attention. She pulled a finger across her throat, telling me to cut the conversation. "My word wouldn't be very solemn if I threw it around willy-nilly, Detective."

There was silence on the line.

"Okay, then. I just don't want it on my head if you end up a couple of gallons short of a tank. See you tomorrow."

"See ya."

I hung up the phone and turned to Terry. "Bagdasarian says the blood on the bike was human. He says it's possible we've been targeted by the murderer for some reason, and he doesn't want it on his head if we get offed."

"Nice of him to be concerned."

"Yeah." I waited for a few seconds. "Maybe he's right, Ter. Maybe we'd better call it quits."

"You want to leave Sandra and Herb on their own in that little house, swilling highballs, wondering what happened to *both* their daughters? I don't know about you, but that would keep me awake nights."

I sighed, shaking my head. "I hate it when you're right."

"And you *know* I am."

"I just said so, didn't I?" I started for the bathroom. "I'm gonna go get ready for my date."

"And I'm gonna stand by the front door, pretending I'm you so I can get a big wet kiss from the hot detective."

"If you do, it'll be the last tongue kiss you ever get, 'cause I'll rip yours out with pincers!"

She laughed. "Down, girl. Your dude's safe with me."

"You know what your problem is?" I asked her. "You're not just gay, you're . . . universally horny. I wouldn't be surprised if you find some vampire to go off into the sunset with."

"Would it freak you out totally if I did?"

"You know it would!"

She grinned. "I'll see what I can do."

"God, you make me crazy!"

"It's mutual, babe."

As I showered, lathering my body with jasmine-scented body wash, I found myself thinking about Agent Franzen again.

Why was I torturing myself over a guy that wasn't here, when there was a very fine specimen on his way over to take me out at this very moment? This wasn't a dilemma—it was just plain stupidity. Self-defeating stupidity, a means of avoidance.

Well, I wouldn't avoid him forever, I thought. Just tonight.

Then why are you knocking yourself out to be attractive? said the damned little voice inside my head.

"Shut up, little voice," I said, turning off the water and getting out of the shower.

You're being inconsistent. Insulting me won't change that.

"Oh, yeah? Well, consistency is the hobgoblin of little minds. Little voices, little minds. Whatever."

"Who are you talking to?" Terry called to me.

"Myself," I yelled back.

There was a pause. "You're scaring me!"

I ignored her, blowing out my hair as Jennifer Aniston straight as I could get it, dabbing on eyeliner, mascara, and a little blush. Then I hurried up to my loft to get dressed. I threw on a Theory v-neck sweater in light green (deliberately chosen to set off my eyes, I'll admit), and tied on some stiletto sandals with Roman slave girl leather straps that laced all the way up my calves—very sexy, reminiscent of orgies. And even though I would be riding the motorcycle home after the Inferno Club, I put on a short white A-line skirt.

I'd done my best to cover up the freckles on my face, but I didn't mind them on my legs. They gave me a little color and kept my legs from looking like leftover Popsicle sticks. I grabbed my vintage leather jacket along with the black lipstick I'd worn for the parade. The lipstick wasn't for kissing Boatwright—I didn't think black lips were one of his turn-ons—but I certainly wasn't dressed properly for a goth club and I thought the lips and black leather might be my entrée.

I hurried down from my loft the second I heard the doorbell. I knew Boatwright was very cautious about grabbing the first twin he saw ever since the time he'd planted a big one on Terry by mistake. But I was taking no chances.

Terry heard me clomping down the stairs and charged out of the kitchen to the front door. She swung it open.

"Hi, John!" She reached for him, turning her face up for a kiss.

He smiled and gave her shoulder a squeeze. "Nice try, but you're not dressed for a date."

Terry pouted. "This is how I dress for dates."

"Yeah, but I'm not one of your truck driver girlfriends. I like my dates a little more feminine."

She slugged him in the gut. "How's that for feminine?"

He bowed in the middle, clutching his stomach. "Good punch," he said, grimacing. "Ready?" he asked me.

"Yeah," I said, sashaying to the door. At least I was trying to sashay. The heels on the sandals were so high that it was more like galumphing.

I pecked him on the lips. "Good to see you."

"You, too."

"Hungry?"

"I was before the internal bleeding."

"The Masai tribesmen consider blood to be a nutritious snack," I said, getting a baffled look in return. "Fun fact to know and tell?"

"Yeah, real fun." He opened the door. "See ya later, Terry. Don't take any wooden nickels."

"I won't. And don't you take any woodys," she said to me. "See you around eleven?"

Boatwright looked at me, frowning.

"Oh, uh—I was going to tell you over drinks," I said, glaring at Terry for blurting it out like that.

"Tell me what?"

"I have to work later tonight."

He put a hand in the small of my back and ushered me outside. "She'll see you tomorrow morning, Terry."

"You're very sure of yourself," I teased as he closed the door.

He wrapped his arms around my waist and jerked me to him. My body slammed against his, the breath going out of me. He sunk his fingers into my hair and pulled my head back, and for a second I thought he was going to bite my exposed neck. *Get a grip, Kerry. You have vampires on the brain.* Instead, he mashed his lips against mine and held me tight in his strong arms.

I was barely aware of traffic whizzing by below us on Beverly Glen as I melted into a blob of desire, helpless to resist him. He pressed hard on my mouth—no sweet little courtship kiss, this, but pure animal lust. I moaned as he filled my mouth with his tongue.

Franzen who? Boatwright was the sexiest man alive, the sexiest man who'd *ever* lived. I wanted him more than I'd ever wanted anything in my entire life. I'd been an idiot to even consider throwing him over for someone else!

We pressed our bodies even closer together. My legs were getting wobbly, my panties steaming up. I reached around and gripped his backside with my hands, pressing his pelvis into me. He was so hard, I almost swooned. My right leg swung up on its own and wrapped itself around his waist. I balanced precariously on my left foot, positioning myself directly on top of the bulge in his jeans—

Then the porch light flashed on. And off again. On-off. On-off. On-off, flickering like strobe lights on boogie night.

I groaned and brought my leg down from Boatwright's waist, my heel slamming the concrete. "I'll kill her!" I said.

"Not if I kill her first." He grabbed my elbow, and we stumbled down the stairs onto the driveway. Next to the detached garage was an old Ford Torino, a mint-condition gas guzzler in factory royal blue.

"What's this?" I said on seeing the car.

"This is my baby. I only take her out on special occasions. Just got new plugs and a brake overhaul."

"Wow. A real muscle ride."

"No, that comes later."

He opened the door and put his hand on my head, protecting it as he would for an arrest in handcuffs.

He grinned adorably. "Sorry, force of habit."

I fastened my seat belt as he got behind the wheel. He looked over at me and his blue eyes shone in the dome light, reflecting the blue interior of the car.

"You got this car to go with your eyes," I said.

"I got this car to go with my lead foot," he said.

"But it really sets off your eyes."

"And your sweater sets off yours. They're beautiful."

I felt myself blush. "Oh."

"Has anyone ever told you—you have the sweetest lips?"

"I don't . . . I don't think so."

"Good. Then I'm the first."

I smiled at him shyly.

"And I want to be the last."

My smile froze in place.

He closed the door, extinguishing the overhead light, and started up the engine, which sounded like a 747 on the tarmac. I sat back against my bucket seat and thought about what he'd just said. True, I wanted him badly. But did I want him to be the *last* man I ever wanted? That was too much to contemplate, even in my desperately desirous condition. If I was completely honest, his statement had actually dampened that desire just a bit.

Maybe it wasn't meant to sound as possessive as it had. I looked over at Boatwright and he looked back. His eyes told me exactly where he stood. There was no lightness in his gaze, no humor. It was pure ownership, all the way. He was laying claim to me.

Well, that settles the issue of Franzen, I thought sadly. Even if I were capable of dating two men simultaneously, it didn't look like alpha male over there would go for it.

I saw the porch lights in the side mirror, flashing on and off again, as we pulled out of the driveway.

"Your sister needs a life," Boatwright said, seeing them, too.

I sighed. "Why, when she can have so much fun messing with mine?"

Dinner was at Anna's in West L.A., an old-fashioned Italian restaurant with checked tablecloths, red bubble-glass candles, and heavy entrées designed to stick to your ribs. No angel hair pasta or pesto or parchment-thin slices of Parmesan, thank you very much. Just spaghetti and meatballs and lasagna and a little jar of dry cheese shavings. Cops loved this place, according to Boatwright.

We ordered spaghetti and Chianti. The waiter came back and presented us with a basket of greasy garlic bread.

"I will if you will," I said to Boatwright, eyeing the bread hungrily.

"You'd better, if you're gonna be hanging around vampires."

"Oh," I said sheepishly. "Been watching the news?"

"Didn't have to. The news came to me."

"Cop grapevine?" He nodded. "That makes me feel really comfortable," I said. "Like having a hidden video camera aimed at my toilet."

He showed me his hands. "Hey, not my fault I'm dating one of the pink avengers. You have a way of getting talked about."

"Terry has the way of getting talked about. I just get dragged along."

Boatwright folded his arms on the table. "Look, I don't mean to interfere, but I have to state my opinion."

My teeth clenched, but I gave him a nod. "Lay it on me."

"You don't want to mess with those people." It sounded like an order.

"What do you mean, 'those people'?" I gave a careless laugh. "As far as I can tell they're just like everyone else, except for their taste in clothes and bling. So what? That doesn't necessarily make them dangerous."

"Oh, yeah? How about the kid in Kentucky who thought he was Transylvania's answer to Charlie Manson? Killed a girl's parents and drove off with her in their SUV?"

"There are twistos in every crowd. Most of the vampires are peace-loving people with an artistic bent. Counterculture types who want to set themselves apart from 'normal' society. Kids have been doing that since forever."

"They're not all kids, either."

I couldn't dispute that.

"You think they'll outgrow their fangs one day?" He shook his head. "They're misfits and malcontents, and they have an unhealthy interest in dark stuff."

"Look," I reassured him, "I'm not hanging out with them. It's a case. When it's over, I'm never going near them again. And it wasn't my idea to take the job, it was Terry's."

"Yeah, that worries me, too." He sat back in his chair, frowning.

"What?"

"She's impressionable. And she's got that contrary kind of personality. She's the type to flirt with it, especially if she thinks it will bug you."

"I won't let her."

"Would you be able to stop her?"

Good question, I thought. I had long ago appointed myself Terry's protector, being one and a half minutes older and, let's face it, the more responsible one by a mile. Looking at us from the outside, you wouldn't think she needed protecting. She was the one who jumped first and asked questions later—if ever—and always came up smelling like a rose.

But Terry had a self-destructive side, and she could be her own worst enemy. Part of me was afraid that if I got too involved with a guy, any guy—she might take it as her cue to start acting out. Get into drugs again and go off the deep end. Aside from our wacky aunt and our cousin, we were all we had left in the world. Sometimes it felt like we were adrift on a little lifeboat, the two of us against the big ocean full of slimy monsters.

"It's too bad you don't have a sister," I said, reaching for the garlic bread.

"For Terry?" He laughed. "Sorry, my sister's married with two kids."

"You're an uncle?"

"Yep. Jared and Amber. He's nine, she's three." He pulled out his wallet and showed me a picture.

They had his intense blue eyes, his strong nose, and thick dark hair, like his. The girl was adorably chubby. The boy was skinnier and snaggletoothed, but I could see his potential for gorgeousness.

"Cute," I said.

"You like kids?"

"Sure, they're fun to play with." *And give back to their parents.* "I didn't know you were an uncle. What else don't I know about you?"

"How do I know what you don't know?"

"You never talk about yourself. Ever been married?"

"I wondered why you never asked me that before." He looked straight into my eyes. "No, I haven't."

"Why not?"

He smiled. "Why haven't I sworn to love, honor, and cherish somebody till I croak? I don't know. I guess I thought if you took an oath like that, you'd better mean it."

The waiter arrived, setting huge steaming plates of spaghetti with meatballs in front of us. We paused a minute to start swirling spaghetti around our forks.

"So how did you get into policing?" I asked him.

"I always wanted to be a cop."

"Did you study law enforcement in school? Did you go to college?"

"Cal State Northridge. And yeah, I studied criminology."

"And you joined the force right out of school?"

He hesitated a second. "No, I took a little detour."

"What kind of detour?"

"I'd rather not say."

"Was it illegal?"

"No!"

"Immoral?"

"Of course not!"

"Well, if it's not immoral or illegal, I don't know why you won't tell me," I said.

He gave me a long look. "If I tell you . . . you promise not to laugh?"

"Why would I laugh?" He gave me the big eye. "Okay, I promise." I held up two fingers. "Girl Scout's honor."

He tortured a meatball for a second. "I was a fashion model," he said finally.

I guffawed, spitting out my spaghetti.

He speared the meatball and shoved it in his mouth. "I can see I'm the only one here who takes an oath seriously."

"I'm sorry, it's just such a . . . what kind of model? What exactly *did* you model?"

"Underwear, mostly."

"*Pfffaaah!*" I grabbed a piece of garlic bread and stuffed it into my mouth as a gag. "*Hmmmmm-hmmm-hmm-hm.*"

His eyes narrowed. "You're starting to piss me off."

Other patrons turned to stare. Boatwright gave them his *I*

bust people for a living scowl and they turned back around quickly.

"That's so great!" I said, chewing the bread. "I'm not laughing at you, I swear, I'm laughing at—"

What was I laughing at? At a world where underwear models became homicide detectives? Why not, if movie actors could be governors and presidents?

"It's how I paid my way through school!" he said defensively.

"Okay," I said, taking a deep breath, "but you have to understand, I just never thought I'd be dating a model. You have no idea what a complete nerd I was. Kerry McAfee dates chess champions, not male models."

"I can play chess!"

"I'm sure you can!" Still giggling, I wiped at my eyes with a cotton napkin. "There's nothing wrong with being a model."

"Then why did you bust a gut laughing?"

"I told you, I can't imagine myself going out with . . . a hunk."

This got me a smile. "Okay, so I'm a *hunky* laughingstock."

"Really, I think it's wonderful. But I'm having trouble picturing you like this—" I jumped up from the booth with my hands on my hips, gazing out across the restaurant with that *Here comes the Robert E. Lee!* face you see on models.

He grabbed my arm and jerked me back down on the banquette. "Teach me to be honest," he grumbled.

"But I've been honest with *you*. I told you I was a nerd. Class president. Secretary of the chess club. Valedictorian."

"Well, you're not a nerd anymore."

"Thanks, but once a geek—"

"You're a gorgeous geek."

I almost choked. "Oh, yeah . . ." I said, rolling my eyes.

"You are. Don't try to deny it."

I sat there for a moment in stunned silence. Had someone stolen into my room in the middle of the night and exchanged my body for someone else's? Was this the Invasion of the Pod Babes?

I had trouble even thinking of myself as attractive, let alone gorgeous. When I got compliments they tended to be the *You're cute in your own way* variety. Even Mom had only been able to summon "pleasing-looking" to describe us. *Hey, maybe I'm coming into my own*, I thought.

Or maybe he's blind, my inner bitch said.

"God, get some self-esteem!" I blurted out.

Boatwright jerked back. "What?" he said, thinking I was talking to him.

"Sorry," I looked down, embarrassed. "I was addressing my shadow self."

He glanced around the restaurant. "Terry's here?"

I laughed, and then he leaned in, putting his hand on my knee under the table. My breathing apparatus shut down. *Knees have sweat glands?* I thought, as I felt mine popping out in hot beads of perspiration under his hand.

"I love your long legs and your long red hair. I love your freckles. I love that bump in your nose—"

"Hey."

"And I'm pretty sure I love you, too."

My jaw plummeted.

Boatwright removed his hand and sat back, swirling some pasta with his fork.

"This . . . cooling-off period we've been through," he continued, "it forced me to think."

"Think?"

He nodded. "And I think I'm ready."

"Ready?"

"You know, for something permanent."

Gulp.

Was "permanent" code for marriage?

My God, I couldn't think about marriage now! Marriage was

the beginning of the end, the first step on the road to middle age, decrepitude, and death. First you got married, then you had kids, then your life spun out in front of you like a movie on fast-forward, and then before you knew it you'd become human lichen growing on the surface of a Barcalounger, like Herb.

Even if I never saw Franzen again, and I was beginning to believe I wouldn't, I wasn't prepared for this.

We ate in silence while my brain did a series of flip-flops. I gulped down wine.

It's not supposed to happen this way! I wanted to yell.

Don't you read books? Don't you watch HBO? For crying out loud, don't you read *Cosmo*?

I'm supposed to spend the next ten years going on horrific dates that provide endless fodder for the witty stories I exchange with my women friends over drinks and lunch, becoming increasingly bitter as I wend my way through the series of jerks and perverts I encounter in the dating world, but along the way I'll discover the true joys of sisterhood, relying on my fellow singletons to prop me up, and ultimately coming to the realization that the only thing you can count on in this world, other than the fact that all men are worthless, is your girlfriends.

And then I'm supposed to get desperate when my biological clock starts ticking out of control and get knocked up by the bag boy at the grocery store and struggle through the next ten years as a single mother—

"Hey," Boatwright said. "Penny for your thoughts."

I shot him a bright smile. "I was thinking these are some darn good meatballs."

"Liar."

"I swear."

Which is known in life as a "little white oath."

nine

I spotted the pink Harley outside the Inferno Club, a two-story brick building surrounded by mattress outlets, discount stores, and a taco stand, all closed for the night. Boatwright stopped the car without looking at me. I leaned over and pecked him on the cheek.

"See you soon?" I said.

"Yeah."

Dinner had gone from awkward to excruciating. I'd hardly eaten a thing after Boatwright's declaration of love, if that's what it was. It was actually more of a blurt of love. Like he hadn't meant to say it, and was maybe sorry he had.

I wasn't sure if I was sorry or not. Just confused, as if I'd been told a joke that everyone else thought was a riot but I didn't get. Rather than confront the issue, I decided to take the low road. I ignored it, tuning myself to Light and Cheerful for the rest of the meal.

"Later, then!"

"You girls have fun."

"We will!"

I jumped out of the car and watched as the Torino sped away. Mixed feelings washed over me like ocean crosscurrents. First hot, then cold—sweeping my feet out from under me and dragging me out to sea, before tossing me back up on the beach, breathless and spitting out sand.

This love stuff is dangerous, I thought. *It could drown a person.*

A figure stepped out of the shadows. I jumped in fright, then recognized my other half.

Terry had done quite a number on herself. Her hair was slicked back in a low ponytail, and she was dressed in black from head to toe, her eyes heavily lined. Black lips, white face, and the barest hint of two fangs poking into her bottom lip.

"What the hell is that in your mouth?" I said.

She smiled around glow-in-the-dark fangs, the plastic kind from a drugstore. "Like 'em? They're real handy for tearing into flesh."

"That's so lame. Why don't you just wear a sign that says 'I'm a fake'?"

"Yeah, you're right." She popped the teeth out of her mouth and stuffed them into her pocket. "I just wanted to see what it felt like to have fangs."

She's the type to flirt with it, especially if she thinks it will bug you. Was this how it started? I wondered. First fangs, then a closet full of black capes and blood cocktails every evening at six?

"You're doing a good job of looking like a total outsider," she said, interrupting my paranoid thoughts.

I pulled out the black lipstick and slicked it on. "I'm not trying to convince them of my vampire credentials. I just want to get in the door." I smacked my black lips and grinned at her.

"Now you look like a yuppie with a bad licorice habit," Terry said. "Never mind, I'll play the evil twin who's trying to lure you to the dark side."

"*Play* the evil twin?" I said, arching an eyebrow.

"Lu-u-uke . . . I am your sis-ter . . ." she said in a low raspy voice.

She expected a laugh, but I sighed and leaned back against the brick wall.

"What's wrong with you?" she asked. "Something happen at dinner?"

"Boatwright said . . . he told me he loved me."

"Shut up! What did you say?"

"I spat out some spaghetti."

She howled with laughter. "Such a class act!"

"Or maybe that was when he told me he was an underwear model."

"*What?*"

I nodded, smiling in spite of myself. "Before he became a cop he was a model. It's how he paid his way through school."

"That is hilarious! It's so L.A. You start out modeling underwear, end up modeling a badge." She got an idea. "Hey, does he have any pictures of him in his tightie-whities? After we do the Bruce calendar we can do one with cops. Well-Hung Homicide Detectives. It would kill. This could be a whole new sideline for us."

I scowled at her. "How do you know he's well hung?"

"I have eyes, don't I?"

"Oh." I paused and then felt myself blushing. "He also said I was gorgeous."

"Course you are. You look just like me." Terry started dragging me to the front door. "Come on. Time to party down with the children of the night."

The doorman was dressed like a bouncer version of Mr. Hyde, in a top hat, black coattails, and red waistcoat. He tipped back his hat with a cane and looked at me disapprovingly. Obviously I wasn't wearing enough black.

"There's a dress code, miss."

"I just got off work," I lied.

"Sorry, can't let you in."

"But I'm here with my sister."

He looked Terry up and down. "She can come in."

"Just for a half hour," Terry begged, tugging me forward. "Please?"

She batted her eyelashes at the doorman, who was apparently impervious to her charms. Maybe I should have let her keep the fangs.

"Uh-uh," he said, crossing his arms over his chest. "Dress code is strictly enforced."

"Look, here's what you have to understand," I said, sidling up to him. "We used to be conjoined twins, connected at the head. But when they did they operation to separate us, instead of giving us each half of the brain, they slipped up and I got most of it. So I'm kind of a Seeing Eye dog, you know, for mental impairment. You have to let me in on account of the Americans with Disabilities Act."

The doorman finally gave in, rolling his eyes. "Five bucks per person."

"Pay him," I said to Terry.

"I'm not too impaired to pay, I notice." She handed the bouncer ten dollars and he parted the black velvet curtains to let us inside.

"Try to get with the program next time," he said to me.

"Yes, sir. I will."

We walked through the curtain and into another world.

Discordant music assaulted our ears, with a high-pitched wailing that reminded me of prisoners languishing in dungeons. *Rocky Horror* types sat with red drinks in front of a mirror reflecting hundreds of flickering candles. On the fringes of the club, spectral faces glowed in the dark, gliding in and out of the shadows, trailing long black hair behind them. The dance floor contained solitary dancers moving through pools of light in diaphanous gowns, brocade vests, and long black coats, turning in dizzying circles and making rings in the air with their hands, oblivious to the others around them.

"Tripping," Terry pronounced, watching the dancers.

"On what?"

"Ecstasy, maybe. Or just on themselves."

I pointed to some stairs on the far side of the dance floor. "Shatán is probably up there."

I drew no stares as I crossed the wooden dance floor, conspicuous in my twenty-first-century dress. The dancers were completely wrapped up in themselves, each the star of his or her own vampiric music video.

At the top of the stairs we passed through more velvet curtains, entering the lounge. There was a bar on the near side of the room made of black wood with brass finishes. Velvet-covered tables and benches sat next to a large window overlooking the dance floor. Vamps reclined on big silk throw pillows on the far side of the room.

Terry walked up to the bartender.

"We're looking for Shatán."

"*Who* is looking for Shatán?" he said with a bogus Romanian accent.

"Morgoth sent us," I said, hoping the name would have some currency.

He looked us over, then pointed across the room.

"He's there."

I turned to see a hulking bald man surrounded by a harem of vampire babes. He smoked a clove cigarette in a long black holder, puffs of smoke curling up around his face, which was covered in tattoos—dark green circles radiating out from the center of his cheeks and circling his eyes. His scalp was smooth and completely white underneath a tattoo of a large red pentagram.

"Wow," Terry whispered. "There's no turning back from those tattoos. He's committed to it."

"Nothing like fixing yourself in a specific place and time," I said. "Twenty years from now people will be able to look at him and say, 'Los Angeles, early millennium.' "

The bartender made some kind of signal at Shatán, who nodded, waving us over with a limp wrist.

"Here we go," I said to Terry.

The women around Shatán glared as we approached, looking like they wanted to sink their fangs into us. Didn't like sharing the big dog, probably. They reminded me of the vampire brides that had haunted Dracula's castle, dark and oversexed, baring lots of cleavage.

Shatán indicated the pillows. "Have a seat."

He spoke like someone with a tongue stud on top of a pre-existing speech impediment—a strange sort of lisp I'd never heard before.

The pillows closest to him were occupied by two of the brides. He poked one of them with his foot and she stood up languorously, giving us a little hiss as she slunk away. Another one followed her, pulling the same attitude.

Terry lowered herself onto a purple satin cushion. This was a trickier proposition for me in my short skirt, but I bent my legs and landed in a kneeling position on one of the other pillows, sitting on my heels.

"What can I do for you?" Shatán's contact lenses were yellow with long vertical slits for pupils. In the green striped face, they gave him a cold-blooded, reptilian look. I felt my own blood temperature go down a few points just looking at him.

"We're Terry and Kerry McAfee," Terry began. "We were hired by Ephemera to do crowd control at the opening for the Dark Arts Gallery."

"So I heard," he lisped in a gravelly voice. Or maybe it was a hiss.

"Then I guess you heard what happened to her," I said.

"Yes. Apparently she was a victim of her success*sss*."

Terry glanced sideways at me. "How so?"

"She attracted the attentions of a genuine vampire. They do exist, you know."

Maybe they did, maybe they didn't, but I was getting tired of hearing about it. You can beat any subject to death, even "undeath."

"We've heard that theory," I told him, "but the police are having a little trouble believing it's a paranormal perpetrator. They think it was a human being that killed her. Someone who had a grudge against her."

He shrugged. "Let them spin their wheels looking for a human killer all they want. They won't find one."

"You seriously believe that she was bitten by a real vampire?" Terry asked. "I mean, we're talking Bram Stoker?"

"She didn't know what she was playing with," he said, blowing smoke in Terry's direction, adding, "Most of them don't."

"And what is that?"

He leaned in to her, his eyes gleaming like two bad moons on the rise. "When you invoke the devil," he said in a low voice, "he comes*sss*."

I felt a shiver under my sweater. I had never been terribly religious. I figured there was probably a God, though not some cranky old man in the sky who doled out pain and pleasure according to whether you'd been good or bad, like Santa Claus. But looking at Shatán, I was starting to believe in the devil. Boatwright's words were ringing in my ears: *You don't want to mess with those people.*

Until now they'd seemed like harmless faddists. But Morgoth was right—Shatán was something else. Dangerously deluded. Maybe even psychotic.

One of the brides came back and handed him a drink—a burgundy concoction that shone like fresh blood in the candlelight. But instead of tipping the wineglass into his mouth, he stuck his tongue directly into the bowl and lapped up the drink.

His tongue was black. And it was forked.

Split down the middle and curling up on the sides.

Terry lost all pretense of cool. "Dude!" she cried. "What did you do to your tongue?"

Shatán laughed and poked his tongue out as far as it would go, wiggling the sides like boneless black arms. "I am an artist. My body is my canvas."

"Oh, man," Terry said, a hand covering her mouth. "Is that permanent?"

"Nothing is permanent, not even death," he said with a menacing smile.

"Listen," she said, cringing, "just tell us what you know about Ephemera's death and we'll go."

He pulled on the cigarette holder, smoke streaming from his nose. "You mean her rebirth."

"Okay, have it your way. Who would want to *rebirth* her and why?"

Shatán dunked a finger into his drink and inserted it into the cleft of his tongue, curling the sides around it.

My stomach flipped over.

Then he retracted his tongue with a smack. "She was a poseur. It was a lark for her, a game. Some of us know the truth about the undead. We respect them. Others have to learn the hard way."

Terry's eyes narrowed. "Did you maybe take it upon yourself to teach her?"

He grinned, displaying incisors that had been filed to sharp little points. "And if I did?"

"If you did, you're going to prison, asshole."

Shatán and the brides burst into mocking laughter. They

threw their heads back and wagged their tongues, snarling and making biting motions at us with their fangs.

I wanted to run like hell, but Terry wasn't through with Shatán yet.

"Have the police interviewed you?" she asked him.

"No."

"Well, I'm sure they'll be in touch."

The green lids dropped to half-mast over his yellow irises. "If the police 'get in touch' with me, I'll hold you personally responsible."

Oh, marvelous.

"They'll get to you anyway," Terry said, calling his bluff. "Everyone knows you were Ephemera's enemy."

"I didn't care for her, it's true," he said, lifting his broad shoulders in nonchalance. "*Enemy* is a bit strong."

"Well, you'll need a better story than 'Count Dracula did it.' The police are kind of closed-minded about these issues. They tend to think that if someone's been killed, it was done by a real person."

Shatán turned the cigarette toward his mouth and doused the ember on his tongue, grinning as it sizzled. "You don't know them very well. Cops are very superstitious. I doubt they'll be looking very far into Ephemera's death at all. They don't like to get too close to the dark side."

"Why don't *you* take a walk on the dark side?" a female voice said behind me. I turned and saw one of the brides settling herself in next to me. "I'd really like to taste your blood . . ."

She aimed her teeth at my thigh. I jumped to my feet before she could rip into my femoral artery with her fangs, stumbling backwards. The other brides erupted into jeers and started making their way toward me like serpents drawn to sun-warmed rocks, their eyes shining with evil, flicking their tongues in and out.

"C'mon. We're outta here," I said to Terry, backing up toward the stairs. "Enough of this freak show."

Terry stood up and moved toward me, her gaze locked on Shatán's glassy lizard eyes.

"You'll hear from us again," she told him.

I turned and bolted down the stairs as fast as I could go in my slave girl sandals. My legs were wobbly from both the four-inch heels and the hideous sight of that tongue. Seconds later, I heard Terry pounding down the stairs after me.

We hurried back through the sylph-like dancers still gliding around the dance floor. They spun in their hermetic circles, arms waving, never even registering our presence.

As we reached the exit, the doorman smiled and tipped his hat. "Come again, ladies." His smile was pure Cheshire cat. He could tell from our faces we'd never brighten his door again.

I was only too happy to go through that black velvet curtain, back into the land of the living. We ran to the bike and stood there for a moment, catching our breath.

"How the hell does he get his tongue black?" I asked Terry, shuddering.

"He probably gargles with tar," she said.

ten

Once we were home again, we took the pups out in the yard for their evening toilette, then back into the kitchen for kibble. When they were happily munching away, I stated my position unequivocally.

"Ter, we're dropping this case."

"No."

"Yes."

"How come?"

" 'Cause I say so and I'm the boss."

"Here we go again." She planted her hands on her hips. "We're equal partners until you want your way, then you pull rank."

"I'm serious. This is some weird shit. These people don't play by the same rules."

"What rules?"

"The keep-your-tongue-in-one-piece rule, for one!"

She shook her head. "It's all about appearances with you."

"Come on—it's not just that, it's their whole shtick. I've had it with this dark side stuff. I don't want to work with vampires anymore. If we have to have supernatural clients, I want to work with . . . *cherubs*."

"Cherubs?" she said, laughing. "I don't think too many cherubs run out on their child support or do drugs on the job." She grabbed a salt shaker from atop the stove and walked out of the kitchen.

Curious, I followed her into the living room, and was followed in turn by the dogs. We watched her pour salt around the front door and along the windowsill in her little bedroom/alcove.

"What the hell are you doing?" I said.

"It's to ward off evil spirits," she said, sprinkling the salt. "I read about it online while you were out with Boatwright."

"Give me a break! I thought you didn't buy into that stuff."

"I don't, but why take chances? You're supposed to put dishes of water in the corners, too."

"That is so stupid," I said, heading back to the kitchen to get some saucers. I filled them with water and went back into the living room to hand them to Terry. She set them down in two corners and the dogs immediately started lapping at them.

"No, honeys. That's not for you. That's for the bogeymen." I shooed them away, then looked at Terry. "Want some garlic for the door?"

"Why not?" she said. "It's decorative *and* functional."

I found half a bulb in the kitchen. Terry grabbed a safety pin and stuck it through one of the cloves, pinning it over the window in the front door.

"I can't believe we're doing this," I said.

"Better safe than sorry."

"Look, I'm sorry I pulled rank," I told her. "Of course we're equal partners. Of course I'll give you a say in the decision—"

"As long as I agree with you."

"No, as long as we can discuss it and come to a mutual decision." I hugged my shoulders. "I want you to consider dumping this case. I'm gonna have serious tongue nightmares tonight. Boatwright thinks we should drop it, too," I added to bolster my argument.

Uh-oh. Big mistake.

"Oh, I get it," Terry said, beginning a slow burn. "We're taking orders from Boatwright now."

"No, I didn't mean—"

"Good, 'cause here I was thinking we were capable of making our own decisions and obviously I was wrong. I'm glad you set me straight."

"Terry, listen—"

"I'm glad somebody with a *penis* came along to tell us gals how to run our lives. Because as we all know, the *penis* is a font of wisdom."

"Would you shut up a second?"

"Equal partners. You, me, and the penis . . . McAfee, McAfee, and Johnson. Has a nice ring to it, don't you think?"

"Oh, for God's sake! Twist everything around, why don't you?"

She plopped down on the couch. "Look, Shatán's trying to scare you with those looks, hooking into your superstitions about evil and whatnot. But it's all for show, like a gangbanger who works up a rep for busting caps in the enemy. Only Shatán works up a rep for popping fangs in 'em."

"But gangbangers *do* bust caps in people."

"Well, he doesn't turn people into the undead, I'm pretty sure of that."

"No, but I think he killed Darby."

"She's not dead."

"Then why are we still involved?"

"Because someone played us for fools. Probably Darby herself. And her poor old parents are sitting up there in Burbank mourning a daughter who's still alive somewhere."

"If you believe that, then why did you practically accuse Shatán of her murder?"

She shrugged. "To provoke him, see what happens."

"Oh, great!" I said, stomping around the room. "Let's provoke the psychotic man who looks like a Gila monster. That's a brilliant strategy. And when he sends the brides of Dracula over to shred us to pieces, we'll toss some salt at them. That oughta slow 'em down. You're just *full* of brilliant strategies!"

"I'm not afraid of those fanged bitches."

"Well, *I do* have a healthy fear of fanged bitches! And if you're not afraid, why are we sprinkling salt everywhere?"

The phone rang and I jumped a foot in the air. "Jesus!"

"Quit yelling!" Terry yelled.

"I can't stop!" I grabbed up the phone. "Hello!"

"Ms. McAfee. It's Detective Bagdasarian."

"Oh, hi."

"You're breathing hard. Catch you at a bad time? You got company or something?"

"No such luck, Detective." I let out a sigh. "What's up? Anything new with the investigation?"

"Yeah, something new, all right."

"Hold on, I'll get my sister." I signaled to Terry to pick up the extension. "We're here. What's going on?"

"Well, it's your friend Darby Applewhite."

"Yes?"

"She's disappeared from the morgue."

I gripped the phone. Terry's eyes went wide on the other side of the room.

"What do you mean, 'disappeared'?" I asked him.

"Just what I said. She's gone."

"Someone took her body?"

"Well I don't think she got up and walked out, do you?"

I thought of Shatán's claim that Darby had been converted into one of the undead, but decided to keep that to myself. "No, I guess not."

"But how could somebody have gotten in there and snatched her?" Terry wanted to know. "Don't they have security guards?"

"Yeah, there's a couple of patrol officers on night duty. But it's not a problem they usually have to contend with, bodies disappearing."

"One of her vampire roommates works at the morgue. He only works in the gift shop, but—"

"Yeah, we know. Lucian."

"Did you speak to him?"

"He was a no-show at work today. He's not at home, either."

So Darby's roommate was missing, along with her body.

But I had another vampire on my mind just then. "Listen, we spoke with a guy tonight who hinted that Darby was the victim of a real vampire . . . and he seems to think *he's* a real vampire."

"Yeah, so?"

"So maybe he killed her and stole the body. When we asked him if he had anything to do with it, he didn't deny it."

"Who's this?"

"His name's Shatán. It's Sanskrit for Satan."

"What does he do?"

"He owns the Inferno Club."

"Does he have a real name?"

"Do any of them?"

"Okay, I'll put him on my list. Look, I know I told you not to investigate—"

"And we certainly aren't," I said. "I mean, wouldn't. I mean, *haven't*—"

"Relax. Let me make my point."

"Yes, sir?"

"You obviously know how to move in these circles, so let me put it this way. Anything you turn up, anything interesting you may run across—"

"While we're not investigating—"

"Right . . . keep me informed. And if you tell anyone I said that, I'll deny it to the death."

"Got it," I said.

"Have you told her parents yet?" Terry asked him. "I mean, about Darby's body going missing?"

"No. And I'm not looking forward to it. They're next on my call sheet. I'm still seeing you two in the morning, right?"

I told him we'd be there, then slammed down the phone. "That's it," I said to Terry. "That's the last friggin' straw."

"Chill, Ker."

"*You* chill! We're being threatened by people with heat-seeking tongues, we got blood poured over our motorcycle in broad daylight, and now they're stealing corpses from the morgue. What does it take to make you realize we're in over our heads?"

She waved away my objections with her hand. "Look, the police are practically *asking* us to investigate now. The case requires our special people skills."

"People skills? You're out of your mind—they aren't people! Deadbeat dads are people! People you wouldn't invite to dinner, maybe, but very few of them actually have fangs."

"Tracking deadbeat dads is boring," she said irritably. "And it's small potatoes."

"Yes, but it *pays* for a few potatoes now and then, unlike these undead deadbeats you've got us mixed up with."

She crossed her legs and folded her arms over her chest, nose in the air. "I have higher ambitions."

I mimicked her, crossing my arms and legs until I was a human pretzel. "Oh you do, do you?"

She ignored my mockery. "I think we've been settling for too little. We should set our sights on bigger fish."

"Bigger fish?" I straightened up again. "What'd you have in mind? Marlin . . . ? Sharks?"

She rolled her eyes. "I meant corporate espionage, stuff like that."

I stood there, completely floored. How had we gone from dogging vampires to corporate espionage? "Terry, where did you come up with this idea? What brought this on?"

She picked at the nap of the couch fabric. "I'm just thinking of the future."

"Okay, fine," I said. "We'll do corporate espionage. We don't know how, we aren't equipped for that, but—"

She sat up, energized. "We *could* be equipped."

"Sure. We could spend all our money on some high-tech investigative equipment that would take us years to pay off—"

"But with better equipment we'd be in a different league," she said, leaning forward. "Corporate clients have deep pockets, you know. We could charge rental on the equipment we bought, and it'd pay for itself in no time!" Her eyes were alight and she had a big grin on her face.

Too big.

I squinted at her. "Uh, Terry . . . ?"

"Yes?"

"Where's the money?"

She gave me her Madonna face, full of radiant innocence. "What money?"

"You know what money," I said slowly. "The money we got from the mob."

In a drawer of the sideboard we had stuffed an emergency stash of money that we'd received from the Mafia on our last case. It wasn't the kind of compensation you could put in the bank or report to the IRS. But it was all the money we had, so I was willing to overlook its origins on the grounds that PIs need to eat, too. I had been meaning to get a safe-deposit box for it.

"Oh, *that* money," Terry said, looking sideways. "Well, I figured it wasn't doing us any good collecting dust—"

I ran to the sideboard and yanked open the money drawer. It was empty. *"What'd you do?"* I yelled.

The dogs ran to my side, agitated.

"You're scaring the pups," Terry said.

I ran over to the couch and grabbed her by her lacy black shirt. "Tell me what you did with the money right now, or I'm going to reach down your throat, grab your stomach, and pull you inside out!"

The dogs were yapping, scampering around at my feet. Maybe they knew more about my capacity for homicide than I did. Terry slapped my hands away and stared at me, defiant.

"I invested it in our future," she said.

I fell down on the couch, my head exploding, and buried my face in my hands. "You didn't," I moaned.

"I so did! I went online and bought this amazingly cool detective equipment at one-third the cost of retail."

"How do you know it was one-third the cost of retail?"

"It said so, right on the Web site."

"What Web site?"

"It's called Total PI. Awesome high-tech stuff. Cold war technology from the former Soviet Union."

"Cold war . . . ?" I sat up and stared at her in disbelief. "Who are you, Ronald Reagan? Are we the proud new owners of a satellite defense system?"

"Okay, okay. Let me get the printout and I'll show you. You're gonna be so happy." She ran to the computer and grabbed a piece of paper. "Now, we got a parabolic pen microphone. 'It can pick a whisper out of a crowded room—and it writes!' " she read.

"Fabulous. How much?"

"Only ninety-nine ninety-five. And an advanced pinhole camera with infrared technology. 'For all those dark surveillance areas, small enough to fit in your pocket.' "

"How much?"

"Only one-ninety-nine ninety-five. Oh, you'll love this one . . . if we'd had it when Darby called . . . 'Ever wonder who your spouse is talking to in the other room? Then this unit is for you. It automatically records both sides of all telephone conversations whenever the phone is in use. Note: Federal law prohibits the interception of oral communication without' . . . *Blah blah blah . . .*"

" 'Without blah blah blah'?" I reached over and ripped the paper out of her hands. " 'Without *permission*,' " I read. " 'Check state and local regulations for further guidelines.' " I looked up at Terry. "I don't suppose you checked state and local regulations?"

She shrugged. "I'm sure it's okay."

"Spoken like Linda Tripp. How much?"

She grabbed the paper back. "Only one-seventy-nine ninety-five."

Call me a masochist, but I had to ask: "Anything else?"

"Computer keystroke recorder. You plug it in the back of the computer and the unit records all keystrokes using a state-of-the-art memory chip. And before you ask, it was only one-forty-nine ninety-five."

And so it went. We got the advanced night-vision monocular (only $274.95!) and the Sneak laser listening device with a range of up to four hundred meters, an FM transmitter kit, a GPS vehicle tracker, and two lime green camera phones with text messaging . . .

At some point I had crawled off the couch and curled into a fetal position on the floor. "Why do we need those?" I said referring to the fancy phone features. "Why wouldn't we just call each other?"

"Well, okay. But what if, like, we're on a stakeout, and we have to be real quiet? And one of us is on one side of a house, and the other's on the other side of the house. We'll send text messages, see?"

"Uh-huh."

"And then if someone's coming around to your side of the building, I can send you a picture of him, like: Here he comes! Haul ass!"

"You know, if there's some slavering bad guy coming at me, I might prefer that you convey that information by screaming your brains out rather than taking the time to frame up a nice photo."

She scoffed at this. "That was just an example. We'll figure it out."

"Uh-huh. Anything else?" I lay on the floorboards, my hands over my head.

"Just the *pièce de résistance*—the phaser pain blaster."

I looked out from under my hands. "Pain blaster? It inflicts pain . . . ?"

"Yeah, baby. 'This miniature electronic device, intended for special military operations, can now be yours. This unit can cause nausea, paranoia, slight brain convulsions, and even pain.' Only one-forty-nine ninety-five."

"I'd pay ten times that much for something that would blast you to Arkansas right now," I said.

"Kerry, Kerry, Kerry. When you get over the sticker shock, you're going to realize that this stuff is going to really put us out front—"

"Cancel it."

"What?"

"Cancel all of it. Except the phaser pain blaster. I have plans for that."

"I can't. I've been tracking the shipment online. We should have it tomorrow."

"Tomorrow! When did you order it?"

"Couple of days ago. They ship via air freight for a few extra bucks."

"Oh, by all means, what's a few extra bucks? Why don't you tip the delivery guy ninety-nine ninety-five while you're at it? It's a nice round number."

"*Literally* a few bucks."

I lifted my hands in surrender. "Okay, Terry. We all make mistakes. No harm done, just send it back."

"I can't."

"Why not? You have thirty days to return anything you buy with a credit—"

"I didn't buy it with a credit card."

It took a second for the full horror of this to sink in. "Are you saying you paid *cash*? You sent money through the mail?"

"Of course not. I converted it into a money order and sent that."

"Why?"

"So there'd be no record of it, ditz-face. I mean, most of this stuff is borderline legal. Besides, I knew you'd take this attitude."

"Let me get this straight," I said. "You knew I'd *take this attitude*, so you sneaked around and did it without consulting me?"

She drew herself up, indignant. "If you ever showed the slightest respect for my opinion—"

"Don't make this about me! You took our entire illegal nest egg and blew it all on a bunch of expensive toys!"

"I knew that if we were ever going to expand, if we were ever going to go about our business with more than one cell phone and our mouths, it'd be completely up to me."

I rolled over on my back and moaned. Muffy took it as her cue to jump on me, landing on my bladder like a bag of cement tossed from the back of a truck.

"Ugh!"

"What's your problem now?"

"Muffy just gave me a splenectomy . . . What have you been feeding her, anyway? Cheesecake? Pizza?"

"That would be terrible for her health. Why would I do that?"

"I don't know! Why would you order a bunch of astronomically expensive equipment without telling me?"

"I don't have to sit here for this."

"Neither do I." I got up with Muffy and headed to the stairs. "I'm going to bed."

"Hey, I don't know about you," Terry said, "but if some caped crusader jumps through my window at night to suck my blood, I'm gonna be damn glad to have that pain blaster thingy."

I stopped halfway up to the loft. She had a point. "Did you get two of them?"

"Actually, yes."

"Okay." I sighed. "What's done is done. I'll take it out of your salary."

"*What?*"

"You heard me. No disposable income for you for the foreseeable future. And we ought to make an appointment with the vet. We need to get this kid on some kind of diet."

"I'll call the animal clinic in the morning."

"Good. Lock the doors," I said. "And the windows."

"They're locked."

"Did you put salt on my windowsill?"

She walked up the stairs and handed me the salt shaker.

"Thanks. See you in the morning."

"Sleep tight, Sis."

"Yeah, right."

I curled up in my bed with Muffy, hugging her to me like a hot water bottle in an igloo. It's cold in the canyon at night, even in summer, and the heat of her little body and the sound of her mouth-breathing was solid comfort.

There was so much ricocheting around inside my head—Terry's online shopping spree for one, Boatwright's declaration of love for another.

Was it sincere, or just the wine? Had I blown it with him? What kind of idiot was I, passing up a hottie like that? Was I using Franzen as cover for my own fear of commitment?

I didn't think so.

My oath might not be as solid as Boatwright's, but I couldn't swear to love, honor, and cherish him till I died if I was always secretly thinking of someone else. Besides, I needed time to figure out who I was, to grow up. I had a potential lifespan of ninety years, give or take. Was I supposed to spend sixty-plus years with one man, albeit a very fine one?

And what about Terry? If I got seriously involved with someone, who knew what kind of trouble she'd get into. Look what happened when I turned my back for a few dinner dates. She blew all our money at Bugs 'R' Us.

Of course, all of this cogitating was just a way of avoiding what I really didn't want to think about—those hissing, slithering creeps who were sure to make a star turn in my dreams. I reached up and turned out the lamp and pretended I was flipping the switch on my brain as well.

Good night, brain. Shut up now and go to sleep. We'll think about it tomorrow.

It worked. I was unconscious almost immediately.

And I would have stayed that way if the vampire hadn't come through my skylight.

eleven

I was in a lifeboat with Muffy, bobbing on the swells. Nothing in sight on the horizon. No land, no ships. No sound except the *swish, swish* of the water on the boat's hull. But the ocean was the wrong color. It was a deep red. Maybe that was the setting sun glinting sideways off the water.

It looks like blood on fire.

"Something tells me we're not in Kansas anymore, Muff."

I looked around for an oar, an engine, anything.

I found a parabolic microphone sitting in the boat behind me. I picked it up and aimed it out into the air, hoping to pick up a radio signal. Or maybe the sound of a helicopter flying to our rescue.

There was a scraping noise coming from underwater. Was it the sound of ocean creatures scraping against each other? Or some kind of fish-speak?

The scraping noise grew louder. Muffy got agitated. She started to bark.

"Don't worry, honey. They'll come and get us. We'll be rescued any minute."

There was a jolt. The cabin rocked. I pulled the oxygen mask down over my face, realizing I was now in an airplane. Then I knew I was dreaming. They don't let dogs sit in the passenger seats.

I tried to come to, to force myself awake.

I opened my eyes to see a figure next to my bed. He was cloaked in black, a hood over his head. He had shimmering white skin and a fanged overbite.

I started giggling.

I don't know why, but it was the funniest thing I'd ever seen. I tried to ask the vampire how he got into my bedroom and why he had that plastic mask over my nose and mouth. But truthfully, the whole thing was so hilarious, I couldn't keep myself from laughing.

I laughed and laughed and laughed.

He pressed the mask down with one hand, trying to grab at Muffy with the other. She bounced around on the bed, snapping at him. Yapping, frantic.

Silly dog, barking at the funny vampire!

I heard footsteps pounding on the stairs. Terry, probably. Got her knickers in a twist about something.

Knickers in a twist! I love that expression—it's hilarious! I cracked myself up all over again, laughing so hard, my stomach hurt.

"Hey!" Terry shouted from the doorway. "What's going on here!"

The figure lunged for her at the same instant she sprang at him, swinging an iron skillet. I heard the *clang!* of metal hitting bone.

The figure grabbed her by the waist, knocking her to the floor. The two of them wrestled, grunting, rolling out the door.

Then I heard a scuffle and the sound of tumbling down the stairs and screaming.

The mask fell off my face. I sat up to tell Terry not to worry, everything was all right . . . it was just a dream.

But I was too light-headed. I felt nauseous, but that was probably dream seasickness.

I wanted to go back to sleep, but there were all those scuffling noises and barking and banging, and now a door slamming.

"Can you keep it down, please?" I called out.

It was quiet again.

"Thank you." I closed my eyes and snuggled back under the quilted coverlet.

After a few seconds, Terry came crashing up the stairs, her feet slapping the wood. She threw herself into the room, flicking on the light.

"What are you doing?" she yelled. "Are you going back to sleep?"

I blinked in the sudden brightness. "Of course I'm going back to sleep." I pointed to her hand. "Why do you have a skillet?"

She gawked at me, then saw the canister and gas mask on the floor next to the bed. She picked it up. "What did he give you, stupid gas?"

I frowned. "Who? He?"

She stared at me openmouthed. "THE VAMPIRE I JUST CLOBBERED AND CHASED OUT OF THE HOUSE!"

"Huh?" I grabbed the canister out of her hand and tried to read the label, squinting as it slowly came into focus. "Nitrous oxide?"

"Oh, no wonder," Terry said. "He pumped you full of laughing gas."

I jerked up in bed. My head was still muddled, but it was beginning to clear. "I thought I was having a dream," I said.

"No dream, babe. He came in through there." She pointed to

the open skylight. "Then he gassed you. If Muffy hadn't woken me up—"

"You fought with him?"

She swung the skillet. "I clunked him on the head. But he got away."

The reality of the situation was starting to sink in. "Omigod! Did you see who it was?"

She shook her head. "Too dark."

"Are you sure it was a he?"

She rubbed her elbow. "If it was a she, she was pretty strong."

I lunged over to the phone, punching in 911. The dispatcher came on the line, sounding bored or tired or both. "Yes, 911 operator," she said. "What's your emergency?"

"We had an intruder, a vampire! He left on foot."

"Ma'am, it's a crime to use this line for pranks."

"This isn't a prank! He broke in through the skylight and was about to attack me. My sister hit him over the head with a frying pan and the two of them fell down the stairs. Come quick, he's getting away!"

A moment while she weighed my credibility. "There's a police unit en route. Stay on the line until they get there, please."

"Yeah, I'll stay on the line, no problem . . . just hurry!"

The cops came within minutes and took our statements. They searched the neighborhood for the intruder, but without luck. It would have been very easy to disappear over the ridge in the back without ever being seen. The brush and trees made for excellent cover.

They dusted the canister for prints, although I told them it was probably a waste of time.

"He was wearing gloves," I said to the tech.

"Latex?"

"No, smooth cloth. Like formal gloves."

"Well, we gotta do it anyway."

The paramedic shone a penlight in my eyes. "Any headache? Nausea?" she asked me.

"Yeah, a little headache."

"You're lucky he was interrupted. Nitrous oxide can cause permanent brain damage or death."

Oh, great. My two favorite things. "Where would someone get nitrous oxide?" I asked.

"Well, it's used as an anesthetic in dentists' offices, and sometimes by doctors resetting bones. But these days there's a lot of it on the black market. It's a big recreational drug."

"It was kinda fun," I had to admit. I'd thought the whole episode was just hilarious until the fog cleared and I realized how close I'd come to being murdered in my own bed.

"They mix it with all kinds of stuff," the paramedic went on. "Pot, alcohol, MDMA. People get very creative when it comes to getting high. Too creative. A lot of them end up dead. You should really go to the hospital, both of you."

They'd already examined Terry for signs of concussion or broken bones. She was bruised but insisted she was okay.

"If I feel any aftereffects, I'll go see someone tomorrow," I said. I wanted nothing more than to pretend it had never happened. As if it were just now bedtime and everything was perfectly normal in our little homestead.

"Anybody you want us to call?" one of the officers said to me.

I thought about Boatwright. Then I thought about the tongue-lashing I'd get for staying involved in this case. He'd find out about it soon enough, and he'd have some choice words for me. Words like *idiot*.

"No, no one. We'll be fine on our own."

"You might want to think about an alarm system," another cop said.

"We might want to think about getting some new clients," I said, giving Terry an accusing look. The cop obviously expected me to elaborate, so I muttered something about moving to a city with a lower crime rate. Fortunately, he didn't pursue it. I didn't want to talk about the case we were not supposed to be working on. We'd be meeting with Bagdasarian in a few hours. We'd tell him everything then.

"Think we should move in with Reba for a while?" I said to Terry after the crowd had gone.

"Forget it. He won't be back."

"Wish I were as sure as you." I yawned and headed for the stairs, but my foot wouldn't take the first step up.

"Ter?"

"Yeah?"

"I think I'll sleep on the couch."

"Okay."

I picked up Muffy and hugged her to me once more. "You saved my life, little girl," I whispered into her silky ear. She licked my face happily. "But you're still going on a diet."

twelve

The next morning, we were at the Pacific police station at eight-forty-five.

Bagdasarian sat at a table in the detectives' room, bushy-browed if not bright-eyed. His milky blue orbs were red around the edges, and his face still bore the imprint of a pillow or the floor. It looked as though he'd had a rough weekend.

"Donut?" Bagdasarian held out the box and I took a glazed one as I sat down across from him. Terry took a coconut. Cops and assistants took turns swooping in to snatch one for themselves and grunt "morning" before going on their crime-fighting ways.

"Thanks, my blood sugar's a little low this morning," I said to Bagdasarian. "Aftereffects of being gassed."

"I heard."

Bagdasarian's hand passed over the top of the box with a slight tremor, dipping down occasionally like it was dowsing for cholesterol. He plucked a donut hole out of the box, popping it into his mouth.

"Where's your partner?" I asked him.

"Probably out jogging," Bagdasarian grumbled, then added, "Guy's a body Nazi, know what I mean? Always on about carbs and trans fats and all that. I gotta get in my breakfast before he shows up throwing trail mix around. That's why I asked you here at eight-forty-five."

Terry and I laughed.

"So, tell me about your break-in," he said, licking the sugar from his lips and eyeing the donuts again. His hand twitched toward the box, but instead of diving in, he reached out and pushed it away.

"There's not much to tell," I said. "Someone came in through the skylight in my loft with a canister of nitrous oxide. If it weren't for the dog, Terry might have slept right through it. He could have done anything he wanted to us."

"Did you get a look at him?"

"Yeah," I said, "he was pale with fangs and bloodshot eyes."

"That describes ninety-nine percent of your little vampire friends."

"We know," I said, discouraged. "Listen, I was wondering— could it have been nitrous oxide that was used on Darby? The paramedic told me it could be fatal in large doses."

"It's possible, but now we can't do the tests to find out."

"Her body hasn't turned up?"

He shook his head.

"Did Lucian come up clean?" Terry asked.

"Not exactly."

"What do you mean?"

"He still hasn't shown. Not at work, not at home."

"I wouldn't have pegged Lucian for a murdering body thief, but I guess he has to be a suspect, huh?" I said.

"Unless he shows up dead. We checked with the roommate,

and he said he hadn't seen him since he did his Hang 'em High act for you two yesterday afternoon."

We sat with this information for a second, then Terry piped up.

"Hey, are you absolutely sure the body *was* Darby's?" she asked him.

His eyebrows went north. "Yeah, the parents identified her. Why?"

"Terry's convinced that the dead girl we saw wasn't Darby," I explained. "We called her cell phone after her alleged death. Someone answered, and it sounded like her. Did you happen to recover a cell phone at the house?"

He reached into a metal tray for an evidence sheet and scanned it quickly. "Nope. No cell phone. Could it have been someone else on the phone? Someone with a similar voice?"

Terry looked at me, her eyes going wide. "I never thought about it. What if it was Pam? Sisters can sound a lot alike. We do."

I turned to Bagdasarian. "Darby's sister is supposedly on the run from an abusive husband. Her parents haven't seen her in a few years, although they hear from her occasionally."

"Hmm. Got that cell phone number on you?"

"I remember it," Terry said, "but it's out of service now."

"Write it down for me. We'll check it out with the phone companies."

Terry wrote the number in his spiral notebook.

"How did Herb and Sandra react to the news that the body was missing?" I asked.

"Bad." He shook his head, eyes closed as he recalled the conversation. "The mother was screaming about how she'd already arranged a funeral and she needed 'closure' by laying her daughter to rest. She's threatening to sue, naturally."

"She's already scheduled a funeral? How can she do that? You're in the middle of a murder investigation."

"We can generally release a body the day after autopsy, when the tissue samples have been taken, cause of death confirmed—all that. Hers was supposed to be last night, so I told them they could have her today."

"But when they went to autopsy her, she was gone."

He nodded, his eyes going to the donut box. Terry held it up to him. "That chocolate one's got your name on it," she said.

He went for it. "I'm too friggin' old to worry about my weight, anyway," he said, biting into the donut. "Gotta die from something, right?"

"Right," I said, thinking, *Heart attack, vampire attack, something.*

"Okay, here's another possibility," I said. "What if it *was* Darby Applewhite in the coffin, but she wasn't really dead?"

He almost choked on his donut. "Not dead?"

"Could she have been in some sort of suspended animation? A coma or something? What if she was given gas like I was, but just enough to make her appear dead when she wasn't. Slowed down her vital signs or something . . ."

I could tell I was losing him, but there was no stopping the brain train.

"The whole thing could have been a stunt," I continued. "People arrive at the opening to find her dead. Big scene. Then there's a hunt for the murderer, but she miraculously comes back to life. It's all over the media: The Queen of the Undead actually comes back from the dead!"

His lips curled up in a smirk. "Did you count your brain cells when you got up this morning? I think you mighta lost a few last night."

"I know it's kind of out there," I said, "but these people are completely nuts. Some of them believe in actual vampires. They're just waiting for the moment when a real one comes along and transforms them into an immortal."

He shook his head. "Sorry. Not buying it. The M.E. can spot

a live one—that's what he does for a living. Somebody stole her corpse for reasons unknown. We'll find it."

I was a little disappointed at having my new pet theory shot down like that, but I tried not to show it.

"Tell me more about the guy you mentioned last night," Bagdasarian prompted.

"Yeah, Shatán," Terry said. "Supposedly he was jealous of Darby, and thought she was a poseur, not a real dark soul or whatever. His theory is that she was drained by an honest-to-God vampire. He might be your killer *and* your body thief."

"Why would he do it?"

"To get rid of a rival, and to pump up interest in the myth at the same time. According to some people, the vampire thing is going out of style. But he's a purist, a true believer. And he's mutilated himself so far, there's no going back for him. He has to keep people interested or he's just another out-of-work schnook with a face full of tattoos and a black tongue split down the middle like a snake's."

Bagdasarian made a face. "A split tongue—you shitting me?"

"Swear to God," she said, holding up her hand.

"That's wacked." He shook his head and readied his pen. "How do you spell 'Shatán'?"

"I'm guessing S-H-A-T-A-N."

"And he owns the Inferno Club?"

"Right, on Pico near La Brea."

"Okay, we'll go have a little chat with the guy. Think it coulda been him that came through your window last night?"

"No," I said. "Even with makeup it'd be impossible to cover his facial tattoos. He looks like the view through a kaleidoscope."

"There's something else you might be interested to know," Terry said.

"What?"

"Darby called us at eight o'clock on the morning she was

killed, saying she wasn't going to go through with the opening 'cause she was leaving the vampire scene. We didn't get the message because we left early, but if we had we wouldn't be here right now."

"So if it was Darby on the phone," I said, "she was killed sometime between eight o'clock and nine-thirty, when we picked up her coffin. Does that square with what the M.E. told you?"

"He didn't have a time of death. What with so much blood gone, he couldn't get the usual information from lividity and such. But he gave us a range of ten to twelve hours."

Terry sat back in her chair again. "Well, that supports my theory."

"Which one is that?" Bagdasarian said, massaging his forehead with stubby fingers. "Can't keep 'em straight."

Terry ignored the sarcasm. "I think Darby called us herself and someone else died in her place. And my theory is supported by the fact that all of her clothes are gone from her closet," she said with a note of victory. "She took a powder."

Bagdasarian grinned. "Well, you don't miss much, I'll give you that." His phone rang. " 'S'cuse me, I gotta get this. Yeah? . . . Okay, I'll take it." He whispered "Applewhite" and punched a button on the phone.

"Bagdasarian, Homicide."

We listened to Sandra's voice leaking out of the speaker for a few seconds, Bagdasarian grimacing at the stridency in her voice. Finally, he got some words in edgewise. "Uh-huh. Well, it's your call, ma'am, she was your daughter. Yes . . . Thank you for letting me know." The call went on for another few seconds, punctuated only by Bagdasarian's frequent *Uh-huh*s.

He hung up and looked at us. "The mother. They're going ahead with the funeral."

"What?" Terry said.

He shrugged. "She said there's nothing holding them here anymore, and they want a fresh start in Arizona."

"She must have been talking about a memorial," I said. "You can't have a funeral without a body."

"Nope, a regular funeral with a burial afterward."

Terry and I frowned at each other.

"What are they going to do," Terry asked him, "bury an empty casket? Can you do that?"

"Sure," Bagdasarian said. "They do it with soldiers whose remains haven't been found, or when they can't locate the body of a known murder victim."

Terry and I contemplated this for a moment.

"All righty, then," I said finally, "when's the funeral?"

"Thursday morning."

"Well." Terry looked over at me and smiled. "I guess we'll go; should be interesting. Are we done here, Detective?"

"Yeah, for now." He held out the donut box to us. "One for the road?"

Normally I would have declined, but a brush with death makes you want to grab all the gusto you can. My gusto of choice was a vanilla sprinkle.

"Seize the donut," I said, shoving it into my mouth.

Our next stop was the Applewhites' house. We wanted Sandra to look us in the eye and tell us she knew for a fact that it had been her daughter on the slab at the morgue. It was a gruesome duty, but someone had to do it.

There was a For Sale sign out in front of the house. The grinning photo of the real estate agent looked totally inappropriate under the circumstances. The phrase *dancing on her grave* popped into my head, along with a vision of the realtor doing the robot on top of newly turned sod.

"They didn't waste any time," Terry said, pointing to the sign.

I glanced at my watch. "Eleven a.m. You think it's cocktail hour yet?"

"Hey, it's midnight in China."

I rang the bell and Sandra appeared wearing a black poly-ester pantsuit. Her light blond hair was sprayed into a bouffant sitting high on her head. Coral-colored lipstick had run into the lines around her lips, looking like solar flares shooting out of her mouth. And sure enough, there was the scent of gin mills on the air.

"Girls!" She threw her arms around us, sloshing the highball onto the impatiens again. Those flowers were gonna end up in AA at this rate. "Thank you for coming."

"We wanted to see how you were getting along," I said.

"Okay, I guess." Sandra put the glass to her mouth and saw it was empty. She stared at it, frowning. "I just freshened this. Guess I'm really putting 'em away, huh, girls?"

Terry nodded sympathetically. "Blunting the grief."

"People say 'good grief' all the time," Sandra said, waving us into the house. "I'd like to know what's good about it." She ges-tured toward the kitchen with her glass. "Care for a cocktail?"

I started to say it was too early for us, but Terry surprised me. "Sure, I'll have one."

Sandra closed the door behind us. "Herb! The McAfee girls are here! Get decent!" She padded toward the kitchen in terry-cloth anklets. "Gin or vodka?"

"Vodka. I'll get it. You take a load off." Terry guided Sandra over to the couch. Sandra teetered a little and fell back onto the threadbare cushion, her glass held aloft. Terry grabbed it from her.

"Thanks, sweetie. I'll have a gin and tonic. Two parts gin, one part tonic."

"I remember."

I glanced inside the kitchen and saw gallon jugs of whiskey, gin, and vodka sitting on the counter. Sandra was all set for Ar-mageddon.

"So," I said, taking a seat in the rocker, "how you holding up?"

Sandra shrugged a bony shoulder. "Holding."

"We heard from the police about . . . Darby's body disappearing."

Sandra rolled her liverish eyes. "Can you believe it? Buncha Keystone Kops is what Herb says . . . *Herb!* Come say hello to the McAfee girls!"

I heard shuffling behind me. Herb stuck his face out into the den. He was wearing a white T-shirt, plaid shorts, and black socks with his sandals.

"Hello, girls."

"Hi, Mr. Applewhite. How are you doing?"

He waved a hand in the air and retreated to the back of the house.

"Herb's no good with grief, either. He won't even wear black. Oh, well—he's got his ways, I've got mine. We've managed to stick together through all our differences."

Terry came back in and handed Sandra her drink, then she winked at me before taking a sip of her own. I got the message. It was all soda water in Terry's glass, no alcohol. Her plan was to get Sandra smashed and hope for loose lips aboard sinking ships.

"We wanted to know if there's anything we can do for you, before the funeral," I said to Sandra.

She looked surprised. "Oh, the funeral. I was just going to call you about that. It's Thursday. You can come, can't you?" She'd said it like she was inviting us to a scrapbooking party rather than the final send-off for her own child.

"Sure," Terry said. "Though I guess it can't be open casket, since there's no body."

Sandra snorted into her glass, then took a drink. "Nope, but at least we didn't have to spring for the coffin. Our daughter was thoughtful enough to have one on hand."

I tried not to react to her sarcasm. "Isn't the coffin in evidence?"

"They said we could have it back." Sandra hiccuped. "Ain't

that grand? We can have the coffin she died in, but we can't have our daughter."

Terry shook her head. "Terrible."

"We heard you're moving to Arizona," I said.

Sandra nodded. "We'd always planned to do it when we retired anyway. It's just a few years early. With Herb's furniture business in receivership, and all this . . . *other* . . . we figured it was time to get away. Sign from God, you know?"

"Where will you be living, Tucson?"

"Scottsdale, outside of Phoenix."

Terry raised her eyebrows. "Scottsdale? That's pretty ritzy. Lots of spas and resorts, right?"

"Good golfing!" came the voice from the back of the house.

Sandra tipped her head in his direction. "Herb lo-o-oves his golf."

"Well, I'm glad you're getting a new start," I said. "I don't suppose you've heard from Pam?"

Sandra shook the bouffant sadly. "No. Her sister's gonna be buried, and she won't even know about it. Well, not really buried, but memorialized."

"What will you do if they recover the body?"

She seemed taken aback by the question. "I guess we'll . . . we'll dig up the casket and put her in."

Had they not even considered this eventuality? The question had evidently started her thinking, and the thinking set her to blubbering. "But I don't think that's gonna happen. I think them Satanists took it to . . . to defile her." She reached for a Kleenex and blew her nose one-handed.

I waited a moment for her to compose herself.

"Sandra, did the police give you Darby's cell phone?"

She took a second to think about it, then took a gulp from her glass. Obviously she thought better with a mouthful of gin. "No. Don't recall that . . . why?"

"Well, I ask because we called her cell phone number on Saturday, after she . . . you know . . . and someone answered."

Sandra stared at me while the words made their way like underwater sound waves to the language centers of her brain.

"Who?" she demanded, sitting up straighter.

"We don't know," Terry said. "But it sure sounded like Darby."

Sandra was stumped for a moment, eyes traveling from our faces to the wall and back again.

"Oh, you girls are just like me," she finally said. "I sit here on this couch and pray she's gonna walk back through that door. That it's all been a bad dream. I'll wake up and she's gonna be here, eating my cheese balls and playing spades with me. Sometimes I even hear her voice calling me—*Mommy! Mommy, I'm home . . .*" Another fit of sobbing ensued.

I felt as if I were watching one of those plays where the audience has to figure out what's going on by following the actors through the rooms of a house, listening in on their conversations like invisible spirits inhabiting the world of the living. Seeing, but not being seen. Looking on without the possibility of interacting with those involved with the drama of life.

"But you know that can't happen," Terry said slowly. "You *know* she can't walk in the door again because you saw her body at the morgue, right? You know for a fact that she's dead."

"Yeah." Sandra sighed. "Herb and I needed that. For closure, you know. We had to see it with our own eyes before we could accept it."

Terry gave a sympathetic nod. "I assume they had cleaned off the makeup and everything so you could get a good look."

"She looked so sweet," Sandra said, sniffling. "Just like she did when she was a little girl."

"Except for the tattoo," Terry said.

Sandra took a swallow, her rheumy eyes peering at Terry over the rim of the tumbler. "Huh?" she said.

"You know." Terry pointed to her own cheek. "The spider tattoo that Darby had right here on her face."

Sandra looked sideways. "Oh, yeah. That."

"Well, obviously she didn't have the tattoo when she was a little girl, is what I'm saying—"

"Of course not!"

I cringed, but Terry pushed ahead. "Well, had you seen it before? Had you seen it on her when she was alive? Can you be absolutely sure it *was* Darby?"

Sandra gripped her glass in both hands. "Why are you going on about a goddamn tattoo! Of course I'm sure. That was my girl lying there on that table!"

Terry set down her glass on a crocheted doily and stood. "I've upset you. I'm sorry."

Sandra dipped her head, a phlegmatic sob racking her narrow chest. "That's all right, sweetie," she said after a few seconds. "You two have been so good to us these past few days. Almost like having our own girls back."

"And we're sorry we haven't been able to turn anything up on her killer," I said.

Sandra looked up at me. "Killer?"

"You asked us to find out who killed her, remember?"

"Oh." Sandra waved a hand past her nose, as if fanning away a bad smell. "We've moved on, emotionally," she said. "Darby's gone, there's no bringing her back. At least we have our memories."

What the hell?

Now she had "moved on"? A minute ago she was weeping over the defilement of her baby's corpse. The next minute she expected Darby to walk through the door. Then it's off to the next, childless phase of her life in Arizona, like nothing ever happened. Maybe this confusion was a manifestation of grief mixed up with wet brain.

Or maybe it was something else.

"We'll see you Thursday, then," Terry said. "Where's the funeral?"

"Oh, uh . . . *Herb!* What's the name of the funeral home?"

"Valhalla Mortuary on Victory!" Herb called from the back.

"Eleven in the a.m.," Sandra said. "And then the burial is at Valhalla Memorial Park. It's right down the street in North Hollywood. We'll come back here afterward for refreshments."

"Cocktails and cheese balls?" Terry said.

Sandra nodded. "And Chex Mix."

"Count us in," I said.

When we got outside to the bike, Terry pulled an advertising brochure out of her pocket. "I found this in the kitchen."

"What is it?"

She smiled. "Wheels of grief."

"What?" I took the brochure from her and opened it. It was from a dealer of recreation vehicles. One of the models had been circled in red ink.

"I thought they were moving to Scottsdale," I said.

"Yeah?"

"So why do they want a mobile home?"

"Maybe they're doing both."

"How can they afford that? Equity in the house? Sandra said the furniture business was kaput."

"That, my girl, is a very interesting question." Terry put her hands on an imaginary steering wheel. "You know, I always thought I'd look good behind the wheel of a big honkin' RV."

"By all means," I said, grinning. "Let's go see how you look."

thirteen

The mobile home dealership was in North Hollywood, same as the funeral home, a downtrodden area north of Los Angeles. The dealership's lot consumed half a block, its banks of RVs standing shoulder-to-shoulder like a motor pool for seniors with wanderlust. Overhead, multicolored flags fluttered in the breeze. They were supposed to put you in a festive buying mood but only served to underscore the drabness of the area. On one side of the lot was a liquor store. On the other a 99 Cent store. Across the street was a cocktail bar called the Twilight Lounge.

Twilight Zone was more like it. Or maybe the Outer Limits.

Terry pulled into the lot and we got off the bike. As we started toward the showroom, a guy with a flattop hairdo, dark green polyester pants, and tan cowboy boots came outside, tugging a large silver belt buckle up against his overhanging paunch.

"Helloooo, little ladies. Welcome to RV Heaven. Name's Tucker, Tucker Jones. What can I do you for today?" He pointed to the bike. "I see you came in on a hog. You girls born to be wild? I can set you up with a beauty that'll fit your motorcycle on the back, dirt bike, whatever you *dee-sire*. Deals for wheels, that's me."

Terry took the brochure out of her pocket. "We're interested in this model."

"Oh, yeah, ain't she a peach?" He whistled. "Top-of-the-line Winnebago Rialta. Note the sleek, aerodynamic design. Lessens wind drag and keeps it nice and quiet inside. She's got rear air springs, fully independent front suspension, four-wheel disc brakes, and four-speed automatic transmission. And she's just as fuel efficient as she is pleasing to the eye."

He motioned us over to a vehicle that had the sleek, aerodynamic look of a giant nurse shoe. "This baby'll sleep six, easy."

"We don't need to sleep six. Just two."

"You girls gonna hit the road together? Thelma and Louise? Or in your case, I guess, Thelma and Thelma?" This really cracked him up, paunch bouncing up and down as he laughed.

"Ha ha," I said. "You sell a lot of these?"

"This baby's top of the line, but not our top seller. Most RVers go for the Class A motor homes. The Rialta here usually sells to your rock bands and your celebrities. They like the sleeker look."

"Oh, yeah? Retirees usually go for the bigger models?"

"Yeah, although I did sell one of these for cash the other day to a gentleman of retirement age."

"Really," Terry said.

"Nice fella, came into some money. He wouldn't say, but I'm guessing he won the lottery."

Terry clasped her hands together. "The lottery?"

"Yeah, he was pretty tight-lipped about it. But when somebody named Herb comes in and plunks down a hundred grand for this year's model, customized, you can bet he's not buying it out of his retirement fund. I been doing this for thirty years and I can call 'em, all right."

"Herb, huh?" I said, glancing at Terry. "Sure sounds like a winner. Did he take delivery yet?"

"Naw, we still got some odds and ends to take care of. Installing the plasma TV, quadraphonic stereo system—that sorta thing. He's taking delivery Thursday."

Thursday, the day of the funeral? Odd.

I looked at Terry and saw she was thinking the same thing.

"Huh," she said. "Well, we certainly can't plunk down a hundred grand for a sleeper. We're just a couple of working stiffs."

"You're not with a rock band or something?"

We shook our heads.

"Well, I guess even Tucker Jones can call it wrong once in a while. I thought you girls were celebrities. The Olsen twins?"

"Nope, not them, either," I said.

"We're just thinking ahead to retirement," Terry said. "Wondered how much we should be socking away if we want to see America."

"Well, let me show you something in our Airstream line. I'm sure our finance company can work with you if you got even a speck of credit—"

"No thanks, Tuck," I said, scooting back toward the bike, dragging Terry along with me. "Some other time."

"Hold on there!" He trotted along behind us, locked on to us like he was caught in a tractor beam. "How 'bout we do you a complimentary paint job in pink? Pink with a silver racing stripe?"

"That's enough food for thought for right now," I said to him as we jumped onto the bike. "We'll be back one of these days!"

"See ya!" Terry said, cranking the motor.

"Ya'll come on back and get yourselves a little slice of heaven, any ole time!" he called to us.

As Terry pulled out of the lot, I looked back over my shoulder. I saw Tucker pull out a pocketknife to clean his nails. He caught me looking at him and gave me a little goodbye salute with the blade.

Terry and I wordlessly decided on where to eat lunch. It's true what they say—twins are often telepathic. Food is an area where our mind-meld is particularly efficient, but it works with anything we're really focused on. Sometimes I think that's how Terry got through school. I did the homework, studied my ass off, and she osmosed the information from my brain and transferred it to her tests.

Now she drove straight to Solley's on Van Nuys Boulevard in Sherman Oaks, an old-style deli that was Eli's favorite place. It had lots of customers in lots of booths, always buzzing with activity, and served delicious fatty food piled in heaps on your plate. The waitresses were the kind that can carry two dinners in one hand while writing up an order with the other, and who always called you "hon." Pastrami at Solley's was just the thing we needed. Comfort food for the recently burglarized.

When the sandwiches arrived ("Enjoy, hon") I pulled out my steno pad and opened it to a blank page. Terry hated my habit of diagramming cases, but I maintained hope that she'd acquire some organizational skills one day. "Okay, it's time we got a grip on this case," I said.

A dill pickle flew across the table and landed—*splat*—on the open page. I looked up and glared at her.

"Oops," Terry said innocently. "Slippery pickles."

I threw the pickle back at her. It bounced off her left arm and onto the floor. She looked over at it lying on the linoleum.

"Nice," she said.

"You started it."

"Grow up."

"You grow up."

"Gimme your pickle."

"No!"

She grabbed for it and I smacked her hand with a spoon. "You don't lob a pickle missile at someone and then decide your victim owes you a replacement pickle! That's just wrong, Terry."

"It's your fault. You brought out the steno pad at lunch. You know how much I hate it. You did it to bug me."

I gave her a smirk. "I've figured out why you don't like it."

"Why?"

"You don't want to write anything down because you don't want to have a record to be judged by."

"You think?"

"Yeah, I think."

"Well, I think that every time you diagram stuff, you lock us into some theory of the case that makes sense when you write it down but always happens to be wrong because there's something you didn't take into account."

"Such as?"

"Such as who the bad guy is."

"That's what I'm trying to get at!"

"And you never do, so give it up and let it come to you. Stop trying to force the case into a nice little box."

"I'm not. I'm just trying to analyze what we already know, all right?"

She sighed. "Okay, go. Figure it out. You've got till the last bite of pastrami."

I gave her a smug look and drew a radial graph. I wrote *Darby—dead on opening day* in the center. On the radiating lines I wrote *Sandra and Herb—parents, Vlad and Vishy—partners, Morgoth and Lucian—roommates, Pam—missing sister.*

Underneath Pam's name I wrote: *Not missing?*

Under Sandra and Herb's name I wrote: *RV = Sudden wealth?*

Terry grabbed the pad and spun it around. "What are you saying here?" she demanded. "That somehow Darby's death led to a windfall for Herb and Sandra?"

I sketched a dollar sign next to their names. "Follow the money," I said.

"Oh, come on. Herb and Sandra, child killers?"

I shrugged. "Look, Vlad and Vishy got stuck with the tab for the opening, so they didn't profit."

"What about Shatán?"

"He was trying too hard to convince us he did it, which he wouldn't do if he was really guilty."

"What if he just doesn't give a shit if we think he's guilty? He's supposed to have killed three people in cold blood," Terry reminded me.

"That's talk. Street cred."

"I wouldn't be so sure."

"Consider the source on that—Morgoth, a guy who eats Count Chocula because he identifies with the cartoon on the box. So when we eliminate those who had no profit motive, we're left with Sandra and Herb. No one else had anything to gain from Darby's death."

She shook her head, chewing. "Doesn't feel right."

"That's why I want to chart things, so we aren't influenced by our emotions. What's the saying? Eliminate the impossible, and whatever's left is your answer, even if it seems improbable."

Terry didn't seem to be listening. She was eyeing my pickle again, waiting for her chance.

"Don't even think about it."

She gave me a pout. "It's not as good without a pickle."

"Should have thought of that before."

"Okay, okay." She took another bite of her sandwich. "Give me an improbable scenario that I can buy into a little."

"Well, okay. Maybe they didn't kill Darby. Maybe she died of natural causes, or killed herself, and they made it look like murder so they could cash in on her insurance. Insurance carriers usually won't pay on self-inflicted death."

Terry burst out laughing. "That's so ridiculous! Herb and Sandra defrauding the insurance company by dressing up their dead daughter as a murder victim?"

It *was* kind of ridiculous, but I wouldn't give her the satisfaction of saying so. "Okay, then you tell me where they got the money for the RV."

"No, you tell me how they got a payout from an insurance company that quickly. And why pay cash if it was a legitimate source of income?"

"I'll figure that part out later. Go with me for a minute."

"Jeez, okay." She picked pastrami pieces out of her sandwich and tossed them into her mouth like Juju beans. "So who called to cancel us on the morning of the opening—sister Pammy, who sounds like Darby?"

"Yes."

"Why?"

"Herb and Sandra didn't want us to see Darby dead. They were afraid we'd screw up the insurance deal somehow—figure out it wasn't murder but suicide, let's say, or a drug overdose. I mean, we *are* investigators."

"Okay, so Darby died of a drug overdose, and the family is covering up in order to get the insurance. But aside from not having any evidence that Darby was a druggie, we've got another problem."

"What?"

"You think Herb dressed up in a vampire outfit, shimmied through the skylight, and gassed you with nitrous oxide?"

I got an image of black socks, sandals, and madras shorts under the vampire cloak and had to laugh.

"Guess not," I said.

Terry punched a finger in the air. "Unless . . ."

"Yeah?"

"Pam could have done the break-in or got someone to do it. And she could have been the one to put blood on the bike."

"Why?"

"To throw us off the scent. To make it look like there's a psycho vampire out there who killed Darby instead of Darby killing herself."

"Yeah, and here's the problem with that. We're just speculating about Pam's involvement. She could be in deepest, darkest Idaho for all we know."

"I thought speculation was the point here."

"It is. But if all of this is true, why would they steal Darby's body from the morgue afterward?"

We sat there, stumped.

Terry tapped the steno pad with a greasy finger. "See what this gets you? Brain pain." She gave a little burp. "And indigestion."

I ripped the page off the pad and crumpled it up. "You're right. We shouldn't draw any conclusions until we have more information."

"I say we give up thinking altogether and go get our money from Vlad."

I put the pad back in my shoulder bag. "Let me finish my sandwich first."

A man's voice boomed at us from across the restaurant.

"Yo, yo, yo, if it isn't my star operator and her baby sister!"

I looked up and saw Eli Weintraub waddling over to our table, a restaurant check and credit card in his hand. Eli was my mentor and just about my favorite human. A mensch, a laugh riot, and a crack criminal attorney. I noticed he looked particularly dapper today. His polyester pant legs reached almost to his scuffed wingtips, his shirt almost didn't clash with the tie, and his sport coat was hardly shiny at all. I would have sworn that he was wearing matching socks, too.

"Eli!" I jumped up and hugged him around his big middle, inhaling his scent. I love the smell of cigar smoke. "How you doing?"

"Good, good," he said, grinning. "You girls staying out of trouble?"

"Oh, yeah, staying way out of trouble."

"My aunt Fanny. How's business?"

"Good," Terry said, accepting a kiss on the cheek. "I've been bringing in some new clients." She was beaming with pride like a kid with a stellar report card.

"Oh, yeah?"

"Vampires," I said sardonically.

"Why not?" He shrugged. "I got a few wolf men on the client rolls."

He seemed to be weathering the breakup with Reba pretty well. His pockmarked skin looked very healthy—I would even say it glowed. The kind of glow that comes from really vigorous exercise or really good sex. He had just broken up with Reba, so I knew it couldn't be sex. And even as my mind rebelled against the idea—Eli, exercise?—I said, "You look great. Did you take up jogging or something?"

He looked down at his credit card. "Oh, uh—"

He turned around and caught the eye of a stunning blonde of around fifty who'd just come out of the ladies' room. She headed over to the booth, looking as if she expected an introduction. Terry kicked me hard in the shin.

"Girls," Eli said, putting his arm around the blonde's shoulders. "I'd like you to meet Helen."

Terry looked at me. I looked at Terry. Fortunately Terry spoke, because my tongue was paralyzed on the floor of my mouth.

"Nice to meet you," Terry said to the woman.

"Pleased to meet you, too," the gorgeous blonde who was twenty years younger than our great-aunt said. Well spoken *and* well dressed.

"These little girls are my protégés," Eli said proudly. "Taught 'em everything they know about investigation."

I forced my mouth to work. "Always happy to meet a friend of Eli's," I said. "What do you do, Helen?" *Former exotic dancer?*

Overage porn star? Some bimbo that Eli will tire of in a couple of months, please, God?

"I'm a Superior Court judge."

"Oh," I said, hope sinking like the *Titanic* in grease. "How nice."

Nice and respectable and big trouble. I hated to think what Reba's reaction would be to this news. Would she take up sky-diving? Move to South America? Open her wrists?

"Which reminds me," Helen said, turning to Eli. "Time to go don the robes. Full docket this afternoon."

Eli threw her an admiring look. "Can you imagine? Me going out with someone on the bench?"

"That's great," Terry said with a wink. "Just don't let her make an honest man out of you."

"Not a chance," Eli said, missing the double entendre. "Well, we gotta run. You girls take care."

"Okay," I said, waving. "We'll give Reba your regards." The devil made me do it because the devil wanted to see his reaction.

Eli hesitated, his smile turning into a grimace. "Yeah. You do that. *Bye.*" Then he grabbed the judge's elbow and ushered her quickly to the front door. I watched them hurry out of the restaurant, then turned back to find Terry eating my pickle.

"Hey!" I shouted.

"It was sitting there, calling to me." She gave it a tiny, fly-on-the-wall voice. *"Eat meeeee, eat meeeee."* The last bit went into her mouth and she gobbled it up, grinning. Then her expression turned to one of concern. "Think Reba knows about Superior Court Blondie?" she asked, nodding toward the exit.

I looked through the window and saw Eli gallantly opening his car door for the judge, looking extremely happy.

"If she doesn't," I said, "I'd hate to be within spitting distance when she finds out."

fourteen

$\mathcal{W}$ e had to park a full four blocks away from the Dark Arts Gallery when we went there to get our money. The surrounding streets were full of hearses in a rainbow of colors—blue, gold, cherry red; one covered in hand-painted skulls and crossbones, screaming faces, and bodies impaled on stakes; another one in a subdued gray with bats stenciled onto the whitewall tires.

Inside the gallery, a crowd of wannabe vampires and goth types milled around sipping cappuccinos and champagne, nibbling at canapés, pale as ghosts in the dark warehouse in the middle of a summer afternoon. Overhead track lights sliced through the darkness like laser beams, trained on the sculptures and paintings depicting torture, mutilation, and other uplifting motifs.

Our pupils were dilating to adjust to the dark interior when Vlad came rushing up to us, Tallulah poised primly on the shoulder of his midnight blue velvet coat.

"Hey, girls! How are you?"

His lips were red to match the vermilion contact lenses. He grinned, revealing stylishly stepped fangs. Instead of two large canines, he had three in descending size on each side of his mouth.

"New fangs?" I asked him.

"You like?" He ran a tongue over the points on the left side. "I had them made a couple of weeks ago. They're clip-ons." He yanked off one of the fangs to demonstrate. "Thought I needed a little tarting up for the opening," he explained, popping the fang back into his mouth.

"Looks like business is good," Terry said.

"Business is excellent." He dug a hand into his pants pocket. "I've got your money. Sold the iron maiden. I hate to say it, but Ephemera's demise was great publicity, just like the cop said. Everyone who comes in here has heard about it, and they all want souvenirs from the place where she made her transition." He counted out ten hundred-dollar bills and handed them to Terry.

"Her transition?" she said, taking the money from him.

"You know, her transition from mortal woman to immortal child of the night."

"Did you know her funeral is on Thursday?" I said.

He looked at me in surprise. "Her funeral?"

"Yeah," Terry said laconically, "that's what it's called when someone dies and you bury them."

His mascara-clogged eyelashes blinked rapidly. "But she's *not* dead. She finally realized her dream of becoming one of the *un*-dead."

"New information," I told him. "She left us a message at eight o'clock on Saturday morning saying she wanted to cancel her appearance at the opening. She said she was leaving the vampire scene, so it appears she wanted to remain a normal human being."

"Impossible," Vlad said, reaching up to pet Tallulah.

"It's the truth," I assured him.

"If she called you to cancel on the morning of the parade, why did you show up?"

"We left the house before the message came in," Terry said.

"So if she called us at eight in the morning, it's doubtful a vampire would be zooming around biting people at that hour," I said. "They're night creatures, right? They don't transform their victims by the light of day. So something else must have happened to her."

Before Vlad could formulate an answer, Vishy came swishing up to his side with the ever-present champagne flute.

"Ladies! How nice to see you." He was wearing a saffron Indian sari with large tracts of flesh hanging out above the silk wrap, gold bangles up to his elbows. His eyes were lined with black kohl, and his wig today was a Cher-length black mane, which he kept flipping behind his shoulder. "To what do we owe the honor?"

Terry fanned out the bills. "*We* were owed, remember?"

"Ah, yes," he said with a wrinkled nose. "Gross commerce. Not my thing."

I grabbed the bills from Terry and stuck them in my shoulder bag. "I'll hold on to this, thank you." Then I turned to Vishy. "We were just talking about Darby's funeral. Will you be attending?"

"Someone's throwing her a funeral?" Vishy said. "Isn't that a tad premature?"

Vlad jabbed him in the fat with his elbow, and Vishy gave him a withering look in return, edging away from him.

"What do you mean, 'premature'?" I said.

"Well, we don't know that she *is* dead, do we?"

"She was pronounced dead by the medical examiner. And that's what he does for a living. He's pretty good at it."

"Yes, but I understand—" He stopped midsentence, glancing over at Vlad. Vlad's eyes narrowed around the red irises, and he gave a warning shake of his head.

"What?" Terry said, watching this little exchange. "Spit it out."

Vishy tossed his butt-length hair. "I heard she disappeared from the morgue," he said. "So how are they going to have a funeral without a body?"

Terry looked at him suspiciously. "How did you know? That information hasn't been released to the public."

When he didn't respond, I stepped up and pointed my finger at Vishy's chest. "Look, she hired us, then the very morning we were supposed to go to work, she tried to unhire us, after which she ended up dead. We had blood poured on our bike, and someone came through the skylight and attacked us in the middle of the night. Now Darby's gone from the morgue and her parents are burying an empty coffin, and I'm getting *pret-ty fucking* annoyed with your vampire games. You give us some straight answers or we're going to go talk to a very close friend of ours at the FBI."

"And you don't want to be in *their* files," Terry said.

"The FBI?" Vlad gave me a worried look. "Why would they get involved?"

"She's been kidnapped," I said. "That makes it a federal crime."

"I thought you said she was dead," he protested. "Can you be charged with kidnapping a dead body?"

"We haven't looked into that fine point of the law," Terry said, "but we will as soon as we leave here. Now what do you know about Darby's disappearance? We want the truth."

Vlad pointed to a portion of the warehouse that was blocked from view by—what else?—black curtains. "Can we discuss this in private?"

We followed him over to the curtains, slipping through them into his private lair. There was a laptop computer on a massive claw-footed desk, a spiked iron punishment collar doing duty as a paperweight, a red velvet loveseat, and two straight-backed chairs covered in black satin. Vishy situated himself on the loveseat. It was meant for two but in his case was sagging under the weight of the one. Terry and I sat on the satin-covered chairs.

"Are you telling us she's really dead?" Vlad said to me.

"As a doornail," I said, adding, "whatever that means." Was there such a thing as a living, breathing doornail? "You seem surprised."

Vishy shook his head in disgust. "I told you it was a stupid idea," he said to his cohort.

Terry leaned forward, arms on her knees. "What was a stupid idea?"

Vlad picked up the punishment collar and tapped himself on the thigh with its lethal spikes. "It wasn't our idea . . . I mean, we knew. But I don't think we have any legal responsibility here—"

"Legal responsibility for what?" Terry said.

"The whole thing was staged," Vlad said.

Terry frowned at him. "What was staged? Ephemera's death?"

Vlad nodded. "It was Femmy's idea. She figured we'd get more press if the Queen of the Undead turned up really dead when we opened the coffin, and hiring you two would get us even more publicity—you know, because of the terrorist thing."

"So how was it supposed to go down?" I said. "Was she drugged or something?"

Vishy twirled a long strand of Cher hair around his finger. "Yes, she was supposed to be drugged. Like Juliet, or was it Romeo?"

"Spare us the literary allusions," Vlad said archly. "We know you went to high school." Then he turned to us. "She was supposed to appear dead to the paramedics and be taken away. Once they got her to the hospital she'd be revived. She was going to stay out of sight for a couple of weeks and then come back again after the rumor mill had gone wild."

Terry said, "Well, what about the bite on her neck? Didn't that tip you off that something was wrong?"

Vlad shrugged. "I merely thought she'd taken the gag a step further, getting a vampire hickey to make it more convincing that she'd been turned out."

"But if she was drugged well enough to fool the paramedics, how could she be sure of being revived?" I asked him.

"I wasn't privy to those details," Vlad said. "But Lucian was her backup at the morgue. If she got sent there, he'd make sure they didn't autopsy her before she woke up."

"Was there anybody supervising this little operation?" Terry wanted to know. "Someone with medical knowledge?"

Vlad nodded. "Gutzeit."

"Did I sneeze?"

"His *name* is Adam Gutzeit, DDS," Vlad said, rolling his red eyes. "He's the major fang supplier in the community. His office is in Beverly Hills. He gave Femmy something to take, I don't know what. It was supposed to last a few hours, tops."

A dentist fang supplier? Well, of course. The fangs had to be fitted by a professional, just like regular caps. And, what do you know? Dentists have access to nitrous oxide.

Boy, is this ever an interesting little tidbit, I beamed to Terry, who nodded back at me.

"Who knew about this plan besides the dentist?" she asked.

"We did, obviously," Vishy said. "Morgoth and Lucian were in on it, too."

"That's why no one was broken up about her death," I said to Terry. "They didn't believe she *was* dead." I looked back at the vamps. "What about the redheaded guy, Dagon?"

Vishy shook his head. "He's innocent. He had no idea what was going on."

The word *innocent* didn't seem to apply to anyone in this scenario, but I let that slide.

"Now Lucian hasn't shown up for his job at the morgue," Terry told them. "And Darby's body's been removed from there by someone."

"So we heard," Vlad said. "We thought it was going brilliantly—a trip to the morgue, then a disappearance from the morgue. Lucian revived her and helped her escape."

"But she was really killed instead," Terry said. "*Somebody* was, anyway."

Vishy waved a hand in the air. "You can't convince me of that," he said. "I won't believe it until I see her cold dead body for myself."

I was realizing that we couldn't be one hundred percent convinced ourselves, in spite of Bagdasarian's assurances from the medical examiner.

"This Dr. Gootsomething—" I started to say.

"Gutzeit."

"He's the one who did your fangs?"

Vlad touched his tongue to one of his canines. "Yes, he's the best in the biz. Expensive, but worth it."

"Did he use nitrous oxide on you?"

"Not when I got the fangs, but he did when I had my wisdom teeth out." He smiled dreamily at the memory. "It's good stuff—almost makes it worth it to get your teeth pulled."

Vishy shook his head. "I'll take my recreational gas in champagne, thank you very much." He drained his glass.

"We'd like to have a chat with your Dr. Fang," Terry said. "You have an address for him?"

"Yes, but I'm sure he'll deny the whole thing," Vlad told her. "It could be pretty bad for his reputation, being involved with a stunt like this. Maybe even cost him his license."

"You let us worry about what he confirms or denies," she said, holding out her hand for the address.

He wrote it down on a piece of red paper, and we got him to promise not to tip off the fang purveyor that we were planning to pay him a visit sometime soon.

fifteen

When Terry and I pulled up at our house, we saw a Chevy van parked in the driveway. The Bruces were sitting on the front porch amid the boxes from the PI company, which had just been delivered.

"Hi, guys," Terry said as we got off the bike. "What's shaking?"

"Not much," Bruce One said. "We signed for your delivery. Then we thought we ought to stick around and make sure nothing got stolen."

"Thanks," Terry said. "Good thinking."

"Got your money right here," I said to them. "Want to come in and have something to drink?"

"Sure," Bruce Two said. "What's in all the boxes?"

"Oh, it's some electronic surveillance equipment Terry bought. She spent everything we had on it."

"Sweet!" Bruce Three said. "Real spy stuff?"

"Well," I said, "Terry claims it's real spy stuff."

"Some of this technology was developed by the KGB," Terry boasted, hoisting a box. "It's primo, top of the line."

"Whoa . . . the K-G-B," Bruce Three said, awed. "What's that?"

"Never mind," Terry said, shooting me a look.

"Here, let us help with that," Bruce One offered.

I unlocked the door and the boys of burden picked up the boxes, their arm muscles bulging in their tight T-shirts. The pups jumped up excitedly at the entrance of all these humans, and we spent a few minutes making introductions and cataloging personal smells.

"This is Bruce One."

Sniff, sniff, lick.

"And this is Bruce Two."

Sniff, sniff, lick.

"And we call this handsome dude Bruce Three."

Sniff, sniff, lick.

The Bruces were an immediate hit with Muffy and Paquito, and the feeling was mutual, judging by all the handling and kissing. Both pups could fit in their massive hands like little doggie dolls with "real tongue action."

I went into the kitchen to put down some kibble and grab some sodas for our guests. Terry and the guys went to work unpacking the equipment. I heard "Way cool!" and "Awesome!" and "I want one!" from the living room as they opened the packages and pored over the operating instructions.

Bruce Two came running into the kitchen.

"Double A batteries?"

I pointed. "In the drawer."

He yanked open the junk drawer, rummaged around, and came up with a bonus pack of batteries.

"Thanks." He dashed back out of the room.

I looked around for a place to hide the money we'd gotten

from Vlad. I took out three hundreds and put the rest in a Baggie, which I stuffed on top of the spice cabinet. Neither Terry nor I really cooked, so it was a perfect place for stash. This time around, I felt I had a fiscal responsibility to hide the money from her. It wasn't just us anymore; we had mouths to feed.

A voracious mouth, in Muffy's case.

I went back into the living room and gave each of the Bruces a hundred. They were happy to get it, but even happier to be playing with the surveillance equipment.

I set four Cokes and a bag of chocolate-covered pretzels on the table. "Dig in," I said. "I'm gonna take a little nap." Last night's sleep deprivation had suddenly hit me hard.

I left them to it and went upstairs to my loft, my steps slowing as I got toward the platform. All at once I was struck by the memory of that horrific white face looming over me.

It had seemed funny at the time. But under the gas, a heart attack would have been funny. In the light of day, the idea of that creep invading my space was much less amusing.

I steeled myself and stepped onto the loft.

Against the left wall was my double bed with Grandma's patchwork quilt. The scene of the crime. My eyes traveled up to the skylight in the middle of the ceiling that had served as a portal for home invasion. The cops had helped us put it back in place, but I was determined to get a couple of padlocks for added security.

I lay on the bed, closed my eyes, and tried to imagine my attacker letting himself in. Had he flown in through the skylight as a bat and transformed himself back into human shape once inside? No, I reasoned, a bat couldn't have toted the gas canister all the way here.

No, Kerry. Humans don't turn into bats in the first place.

Was I going soft in the head?

I tried to clear my mind and let the intruder's image come back to me.

Was he tall? Heavy? He wasn't Vishy's size, that much I knew.

Could I even be sure it was a male? It seemed to me that he was strong, but where had that impression come from? I hadn't actually engaged him; I'd just lain there in the bed, immobilized by laughing gas, while Terry beat the crap out of him.

But he'd have had to climb up to the roof, then lower himself into the room by his arms, so that argued for good upper-body strength. A man, then.

Before I knew it, I'd drifted off.

I awoke to a buzzing sensation. There was a lime green cell phone on my stomach. I picked it up and saw an envelope icon in the middle of the screen. I clicked on it.

A text message appeared: *get yr ass down hre*.

Hey, this text messaging thing was pretty cool. It might actually be more efficient than relying on our twins' mental telepathy. I futzed around with the buttons and typed back a message: *yes master*.

As I walked to the edge of the loft, I heard an electronic whine coming from the living room. "Hey, what's going on down there?" I called to them.

"Whisper something," Terry said from the base of the stairs. "We're doing an experiment."

"What's going on down there?" I repeated in a whisper.

Terry ran to the window and shouted outside, "Did you get it?"

"Got it!" came an excited voice from the yard. Bruce Three ran in through the back door with earphones on. "I heard her loud and clear."

Terry held up a pen with a cable running across the floor to a receiver in Three's hand. "Your parabolic pen microphone in action!"

"Oh," I said as I came down the stairs. "I didn't know it'd be trailing a cable. Isn't that kind of conspicuous?"

Bruce Two piped up. "If you don't want the cable, you can transmit with this little baby to an FM radio." He held up a small round microphone to his mouth. "Do you read me, Bruce One?"

There was a thump on the side of the house, then Bruce One came in carrying a radio the size of a cigarette pack. "You're on the air, Bruce Dude."

Terry grabbed my hand. "C'mere." She dragged me into the coat closet and shut the door. She stuck something on my head, pulling down a lens in front of my right eye.

It was a night-vision monocular. I got a greenish glimpse of Terry waving her fingers in front of my face, producing thermal energy tracers in the blackness.

She giggled. "Isn't that the bomb?"

"Awesome." I was beginning to think these purchases might have been a good idea, in spite of myself. Maybe there *was* corporate espionage in our future. Microsoft, here we come.

The door swung open and Bruce Three slipped in. There was a faint clicking sound.

"Gotcha red-handed!" he said.

He reopened the door and showed us a miniature camera. "Superspeed film lets you photograph in the dark!"

"Over here!" said Bruce One. He pulled me by the arm over to the TV, pushing me down on the couch. "Smile, you're on TV!"

I looked at the screen and saw myself sitting on the couch, looking at myself sitting on the couch.

"It's a hidden camera!" One said.

I looked around the room. "Where'd you put it?"

"Paquito! Here, boy!" Terry called. Paquito jumped off the chair and trotted up to us as my face zoomed larger on the screen. I looked down and saw the tiny camera stowed on his rhinestone collar.

"A Pom cam!" Bruce Two slapped his knee. "Is that great or what?"

The Bruces and Terry started high-fiving each other and jumping around, their combined tonnage shaking the house in double Richter digits. I had visions of it sliding off its foundation and right onto Beverly Glen into the middle of rush-hour traffic.

"Hey, easy on the floorboards!" I yelled.

The jumping stopped. "Sorry," everyone said.

I noticed a contract sitting on the end table. I picked it up and read: " 'In accepting this merchandise, I acknowledge that I am under obligation to determine the legality of using it in my jurisdiction.' " I gave Terry a look. "I'm not signing this."

"Don't worry, I signed it online."

"Oh, great."

"The Bruces are really into this," Terry said. "They're thinking they might like detective work better than acting—"

"We don't even do that much acting," Two said. "Mostly we just go on auditions."

"Cattle calls," Bruce Three said, disgusted. "They treat you like a piece of meat."

A side of beef, in his case.

"We asked if we could help you out on this case," Bruce One said, his bald pate turning pink from excitement. "You know, to see if we have any natural ability."

"Terry said we could," Two said, grinning from ear to ear. "Is that okay with you?"

"Did Terry happen to mention that we're flat broke because of her KGB spending spree, and we couldn't possibly pay you?" I asked.

"We don't need payment," Bruce Two assured me. "We'll consider ourselves apprentices."

"Hey, Lance told us what you did for him," Bruce One said

reverently. "You saved his life, then you got him a job as a sheriff's deputy."

Oh, so now we're in the business of rehabilitating actors?

"I don't know," I demurred, running a hand through my hair. "I didn't even want to keep going with this case. It's getting too risky."

"All the more reason we should add three giant guys to our staff!" Terry said. "Even a vampire's gonna think twice about going up against these mothers, huh?"

The Bruces lined up in front of me like kids on Christmas Eve begging to open their presents early.

"Please . . . ?" they said.

"Oh, okay."

"Sweet!" More jumping and high-fiving. Pictures rattled on the walls and furniture skittered across the room.

"No jumping!"

They stopped abruptly. "Sorry."

"We're going to turn the Bruces' van into a mobile command center," Terry said excitedly. "We're drawing up the plans now. Our first job will be bugging the funeral."

I frowned at her. "Bugging the funeral?"

"Here's what we'll do." She rubbed her hands together as she cooked up her scheme. "There'll be flowers on the casket, right? So the Bruces will dress up like deliverymen and show up at the funeral home with a floral arrangement—"

"What kind of floral arrangement?" Bruce One asked.

"How about calla lilies and purple irises?" Two suggested. "That would be nice."

"It's a girl's funeral," Three put in. "Gotta have pink roses, don't you think?"

"Guys!" Terry yelled, trying to get their attention. "You're missing the point!"

They clammed up and looked at her expectantly.

Terry sighed and started again. "So . . . the guys will dress up in deliverymen jumpsuits—"

"I have a lineman's jumpsuit I wore in my Village People tribute," One said, "but it's neon orange. That might be kind of garish at a funeral—"

"Well, leave the hard hat at home," Two said, shaking his head. "Florists don't *wear* hard hats—"

"What kind of shoes should we wear?" Three wanted to know. "Lace-up work boots?"

"Wear your mother's shoes! It doesn't matter!" Terry slapped her forehead. "Sheesh! Would you guys zip it for a second so I can give you your assignment?"

They did the imaginary mouth-zipping thing with their fingers.

"Okay," Terry said with exaggerated patience, "you'll wear appropriate clothing for deliverymen—*I'll leave the wardrobe and floral details to you*—and when you drop off the arrangement in the parlor, you'll jam that microphone into the flowers on Darby's casket." She pointed to the small round mike in Two's hand. "The microphone will transmit to that FM radio, which I'll carry in a fanny pack. I'll have earphones on, like I've got an iPod."

"Won't it look a little strange, listening to music at a funeral?" I said.

"Nobody'll notice," she said. "They'll be caught up in their grief."

"Okay," I said, "dare I ask why we're going through this exercise? You think the murderer's going to be overcome with guilt and blurt out a confession at the casket or something?"

Terry nodded. "Very possibly. And the Bruces will be outside in the van, getting video of all the mourners." The boys looked at each other, grinning.

"Why do we want video of the mourners?" I asked.

"The killer may return to the scene of the crime."

"But the funeral parlor isn't the scene of the crime," I argued.

"Same principle. Your psychopathic killer likes to observe the results of his work."

Had they sent a vocabulary guide along with the PI equipment? Terry was starting to talk like someone from a TV cop show. I thought it seemed pretty far-fetched that a killer would confess all his sins to an empty burial container—but what did I know?

She was our resident expert on abnormal psychology.

sixteen

Tuesday, and we had two things on our plate: we'd reserved the morning for checking out the dentist, and in the afternoon we planned to canvass the tattoo parlors to see if we could turn anything up on a substitute Darby.

We went online and looked up Adam Gutzeit, DDS. He had his own Web site featuring his bright and shiny staff grinning from their antiseptic yet friendly office. They specialized in "cosmetic dentistry"—no mention was made of fang manufacture. Maybe it was a sideline to brightening the smiles of the rich and famous of Beverly Hills.

"Hard to imagine the Gucci-Pucci set rubbing elbows in the waiting room with vampires," Terry said.

"Should we make an appointment?" I asked.

"Nah, let's just show up. We'll say Shatán sent us."

Twenty-five minutes later we were at the address on Alden Drive. Dr. Gutzeit's office was on the second floor of the Alden

Medical Plaza, where we were greeted at the reception window by a blonde with blinding blue-white teeth. It looked like she was smiling around a glacier. Marla, according to her name tag.

"May I help you?" she said.

"I hope so, Marla," Terry said, leaning casually into the open window. "We were sent here by Shatán. You know, the vampire king? We'd like Dr. Gutzeit to give us some fangs. Real good ones. Permanent and sharp. You know, the kind that don't come out when you're ripping into raw meat."

The corners of Marla's smile hit the desk.

I glanced around and saw a heavyset, exquisitely dressed woman staring at us, appalled. She turned to another woman, who had an overlifted face, and she shrugged back at her.

"You . . . you must have the wrong office," Marla sputtered. "I assure you, we don't do that sort of thing here."

"Course you do!" Terry said. "Word on the vampire circuit is that Adam Gutzeit is the best in the biz. I've heard his fangs can puncture suede, to say nothing of tender neck skin."

The heavyset woman threw down her magazine, grabbed her Louis Vuitton bag, and waddled to the door.

"Oh, Mrs. Rappaport!" Marla called, but the woman was out the door, followed swiftly by the facelift addict.

"Mrs. Krasney!" Marla groaned in despair.

The door closed with a final little click.

Marla turned back to us with a snarl. "You people know you're supposed to come on Fridays!"

Terry looked at me, feigning surprise. "Fridays? No one told us that."

"It's doctor's golf day," said Snarlin' Marla.

"What good would it do us to come when he's out playing golf?" Terry asked her.

Marla sighed in disgust. "He doesn't *really* play golf; it's a cover. You can see what it does to business if you show up when the other patients are here."

"Sorry," I said. "But it looks like he's open now. Can we see him?"

Marla made a big show of looking at her book, as if she were appointment secretary to the president. "I'll check with him. You'll need to have molds made of your teeth. But when you come for the canines, Fridays only!"

She got up and disappeared down the hallway, her rubber soles squeaking on the floor. In thirty seconds she squeaked back.

"Follow me," she said.

The dentist's private office was suitably sterile, with white walls, white cabinets, and a desk of blond wood. The wall behind his desk contained diploma certificates surrounded by *National Geographic* photos of yawning animals baring large, brown, decayed, and misshapen teeth. Obviously the animal kingdom was in dire need of cosmetic dentistry. And there was another oddly whimsical touch, as well—a set of plastic novelty teeth sitting on top of the desk. The wind-up kind with a spring in the back that makes the choppers chop.

Gutzeit smiled and stood up, extending a hand. "I'm Dr. Gutzeit." He was thin and droopy, with bushy eyebrows and a receding gray hairline. One of his eyes veered unnervingly off-center. Gleaming from his unprepossessing face were rows of perfectly aligned, perfectly straight white teeth. Looking at them, I was reminded of a chewing gum ad. I could hear a *ting!* sound and see a starburst of light on his front tooth.

I held out my hand. "Kerry McAfee, and this is Terry."

"Twins?" he said.

"Well, there's no fooling you trained medical professionals," Terry replied.

"Ha ha, very amusing," Gutzeit said, sitting down behind his desk. Terry and I took the client chairs in front. "Now, I understand you ladies would like canine enhancement."

"Tell me, Doc," Terry said, "is it considered ethical to make someone's mouth look like an animal's? Does the Medical Board know what you're doing here?"

His perfect smile was tinged with confusion. "Perhaps I misunderstood. I thought that was why you came."

"We came to get some answers about a murder," she said. "Darby Applewhite's murder."

His eyes opened in alarm, the right orb angling toward the door. "Who are you?" he asked suspiciously.

"We gave you our names," I said. "We're investigators."

"May I see some ID?" He held out his hand for it.

I took out my wallet and opened it to the license. He put on his reading glasses, then picked up a pen and wrote down my name, address, and license number on a pad that advertised Dazzlewhite Tooth Gel.

Then he handed back the wallet. "Thank you." He tapped my license number with his pen. "I've a mind to report you for gaining entrance to this office under false pretenses. There are rules of professional conduct for investigators, are there not?"

"Fuck if we know," Terry said with a shrug.

He reared back in his chair. "I don't appreciate profanity in this office!"

"Fuck if we care," Terry added with a smile.

I realized this wasn't getting us anywhere. "I apologize for my sister," I said. "She suffers from hoof in mouth disease. What we'd really like to know, Dr. Gutzeit, is what you know about Darby's death."

Terry leaned forward. "Alternatively, we could send the police over in our place. Of course, they're golfing on Fridays, too, so they'd probably have to come when you have patients here. And they might want to subpoena your records . . ."

Gutzeit sighed and took off his glasses, slipping them into the pocket of his lab coat. "Ms. Applewhite was a patient," he said. "I don't know what else I can tell you, aside from the fact that I'm very sorry about what happened."

"So her death isn't news to you," I said.

He put on a rueful expression. "She was a public figure. I daresay everyone in Los Angeles County has heard of her unfortunate demise."

"Any idea who might have killed her?"

"Certainly not. Of course, those particular patients lead a rather dangerous lifestyle. But as a health professional, I do not judge. I merely help them to attain a self-image that is appealing to them."

"Well, she's got no self-image at all now," Terry said. "Her body's disappeared from the morgue."

I watched him for a reaction, but his face was as blank as a wall. "Disappeared?"

"Yes. Disappeared," I repeated. "It's very weird, but there you are."

He gave a short laugh. "They more or less specialize in being weird, I take it."

"Yes, they do. Tell me, as a health professional, does it concern you that your patients are drinking blood?"

"What . . . do you mean by that?"

Terry slugged back an imaginary drink. "Human blood. Down the hatch."

Professional consternation creased his brow. "That would put them at risk for any number of diseases."

"I would think so, but it goes with the image," I told him. "They're self-styled vampires. And part of being a vampire is blood-drinking. It's quite the fad."

"I assure you, I had no knowledge of that. My involvement is one of cosmetic dentistry, nothing more or less."

"Yes, but you're promoting this dangerous lifestyle you talked about by giving them fangs, aren't you?" I pressed him. "In a very real way, you *are* supporting it."

He drew in his chin. "Obviously you have misunderstood our mission here."

I leaned back in my chair, crossing my legs. "Why don't you tell us what your mission is?"

"To make individuals feel good about themselves," he said in a righteous tone. "Very few of us are born perfect. It's within the power of the modern physician not only to heal disease, but to lift the spirit by improving the appearance. I consider it a sacred trust."

"Nitrous oxide does a lot to lift the spirit, too, doesn't it?" Terry said.

Leave it to Terry to push the panic button. The dentist's bluster evaporated and there was a flush on his sunken cheeks. He blinked several times. "What are you implying?" he said.

"Do you give your patients laughing gas?"

He took a second before answering. "On occasion, when the treatment merits it."

"Has any gone missing from your office?"

"Missing . . . ?" His head quivered, the right eye wheeling out of sight. "I, uh . . . I would have to check with my office manager on that."

"Go ahead," Terry said, arms crossed over her chest. "Check with her. We'll wait."

He glared at Terry. "My office inventory is none of your concern," he said, shooting up from his chair. "Thank you for stopping by."

"Well, you'll want to do an inventory as soon as possible." Terry stood, staring directly into his good eye. " 'Cause the police are going to be interested in that. Especially if it turns out Darby died from an overdose of nitrous oxide."

He thrust his fists into the pockets of his white coat. "Is there any evidence of that?"

"Yeah. The medical examiner ruled that she died laughing."

It took a second for him to realize he was being jerked. *Very* amusing," he said.

"Just kidding." Terry nodded toward the door and I followed her over. "Thanks for your cooperation, Dr. Gutzeit."

"Oh, you're quite welcome," Gutzeit said, visibly relaxing now that we were on our way out. Then the sales urge kicked in. "And if you girls should ever want to correct those crooked upper laterals—"

"We'll pass," I said, waving goodbye. "But thanks for noticing."

We took La Cienega down to Washington Boulevard, then headed west to Pacific Avenue. It was still warm, but cooler by several degrees here in Venice than it had been in Beverly Hills. Terry found a space on Pacific, squeezing the bike between two SUVs. We cut down a short alley to get to the boardwalk, which was essentially a wide strip of asphalt that separated the beach from the businesses, apartments, and hotels facing the ocean.

It was a weekday, so the seething horde of humanity was a manageable size. There were the usual hawkers and street performers: a man balancing a tourist in a chair on his forehead, another guy juggling live chain saws, a one-man band playing a musical contraption consisting of a harmonica, keyboard, and drums, and the ubiquitous palm readers that were "certified 100% psychic." A gaggle of gulls squawked and dived at the asphalt, ripping into the remains of a corn dog while a heartbroken little boy with a mustard-smeared mouth looked on.

"We'll get you another one," his mother said, rubbing the top of his nappy head.

We wandered into several tattoo parlors, showing around the picture of Darby we'd taken from the Web site. Nobody recognized the woman or the tattoo until we came to a shop south of Muscle Beach.

"Hey, look," Terry said, pointing at a display of sample tattoos in the window. There in the middle was a black widow spider. She held up the printout, comparing the two designs.

"Looks similar," I said.

"Similar? It's the exact same spider."

The place was set up like a beauty shop, with stations partitioned off by four-foot walls. The noise of skin drills filled the air, as if there were a room full of mad dentists at work. The clients lay on examination tables being transformed into living canvases, an occasional groan going up as they suffered for their body art.

Terry showed the printout to the cashier. He pointed us to a station with a girl whose black hair stuck out in a dozen short pigtails all over her head, the body of a multicolored snake spiraling its way up her neck.

The man on her table flinched as the girl jabbed his skin over and over, depositing colored ink into his flesh. A buxom mermaid was taking shape just below his shoulder blade.

The girl stopped drilling and looked up at us. "Help you?" she said.

"Where's the snake's head?" Terry asked, pointing to the girl's neck.

The tattoo artist tilted back her head and showed us the underside of her jaw, where a snake bared his venom-dripping fangs. It had a wicked spark in its eyes, a forked red tongue darting out of its mouth.

"Cool," Terry said, breaking out into a big grin.

"Thanks," the pigtailed artist said, returning Terry's smile. "What can I do for you?" She peered over the wall at the rest of Terry, taking her in with an appreciative look.

I hated to interrupt this little flirtation, but we had business to attend to. "Uh, the guy at the front said you do spiders?" I asked the girl.

"Yeah, they're kind of a specialty of mine. I'm Angie, by the way."

"Nice to meet you." I produced the photo of Ephemera. "Is this yours?" I asked.

Angie glanced at the design. "Yeah, it's mine."

"Do you recognize this woman?"

She nodded. "It's Ephemera, Queen of the Undead, right?"

"Yes," I said, my excitement rising. "Did you give her this tattoo?"

"Um, yeah." She daubed her customer's bloody back with a sterile white cloth. "Take a breather, okay?" she said to him. "Be right back."

The customer let out a big sigh. "Take your time," he said.

Angie stood up and motioned us over to an unoccupied corner. "What's up?" she said. "Are you guys cops or something?"

"Private investigators," I said.

"Is there a problem?"

"We're investigating Ephemera's murder on Saturday," Terry said. "You must have heard about it."

"Oh, I definitely heard about it." Angie looked around to be sure no one was listening, then leaned in to us. "But to tell you the truth, there *was* no murder."

We gave her a curious look.

"I'll tell you what happened," she said in a conspiratorial whisper, "if you promise not to say anything."

We had no idea what she was proposing, but we nodded anyway.

She pointed to the photo. "I did that tattoo for Ephemera, all right. About a year ago. And then a few weeks ago, along comes this other woman who says she wants the exact same tattoo in the same place. She even had that picture with her. I thought she was some wacked-out groupie, so I told her I didn't think I should give her the exact same tattoo, since it was sort of Ephemera's thing—her trademark."

We nodded encouragement and she went on.

"But then she explains that *she's* the new Ephemera," Angie said. "It's been arranged for her to take over the band. She wanted to make sure the tattoo would heal in time for the parade."

"She said she was replacing Ephemera?" I said, poking Terry in the arm.

Angie nodded. "Made me swear not to tell anyone. Said they were doing a whole 'Paul is dead' number. You know, for the publicity."

"Paul who?" Terry asked.

"Paul McCartney. The Beatles apparently pulled some stunt in the sixties, pretending that Paul was dead and that there had been a cover-up. People played Beatles records backwards and heard a voice saying, 'Turn me on, dead man,' and 'Paul is dead, man.' They said the lyrics of 'I Am the Walrus' proved he was gone. But it was all a big joke on the public."

"And she said that's what they were going to do with Ephemera?" I asked.

"Yeah, Ephemera was going to leave the band, this woman would take her place, and everyone would act like nothing had happened. But people would talk, rumors would spread—next thing you know they'd be drawing even bigger crowds because people would be trying to figure out what happened to her."

"So when you heard about Ephemera dying," Terry said, "you didn't really think it was true. You thought it was just a stunt?"

Angie nodded, then frowned as she studied our faces. "Are you saying it wasn't?"

"Yes," I said. "Well, no . . . Actually, it's complicated."

She gave a nervous little laugh. "Sounds like it."

"Did this woman give you her name?" Terry asked.

Angie thought about it, then shook her head. "I don't remember if she did. I do remember that she paid cash."

"What did she look like?"

Her eyes went up in the corners as she tried to recall. "She looked like Ephemera. Not as pretty, but same basic model—goth chick, jet black hair, blue eyes."

"Look, we could really use your help," I said, "but we'd have to have your word that you won't repeat any of this."

Angie crossed her heart solemnly.

"The girl you tattooed a few weeks before Ephemera died, the faker? She may have been killed for real."

The skin beneath Angie's snake flushed pink. "So what happened to the real Ephemera?"

"She may be responsible for the other girl's death, directly or indirectly."

"Whoa," Angie said, leaning on the nearest wall.

"We need to find her," Terry said. "If she's trying to hide, she might have had her own tattoo removed. You must get people who want to do that, right? Who do you refer them to?"

"There's lots of people who do laser removals. I mean, I couldn't tell you definitely who she'd go to."

"What about a list of clinics?" I said. "If we paid you, could you put one together for us?"

Angie shook her stiff little pigtails. "I'll put a list together for you, but I won't take any money. If you guys are gonna nail a murderer, I'd be happy to help. How can I reach you?"

Terry quickly handed over our card. "Call us on the cell," she said.

Angie read the card, then looked up at Terry. "Which one are you?"

"Terry." Angie took the hand Terry offered, holding it for an extra few seconds.

"I could give you a 'T' right here," Angie said, turning Terry's hand over and pointing to her wrist. Then she looked at me. "And you a 'K.' That way, nobody would have any trouble telling you apart." She finally released Terry's hand.

"Sometimes we like it when people can't tell us apart," I said. "We use it to our advantage."

Angie smiled. "Oh, like the girls in *The Parent Trap*?"

Terry and I nodded, grinning back at her.

"Exactly like that," we said.

We thanked Angie for her help, then headed back out onto the boardwalk, Terry giving Angie one last look over her shoulder.

"Cute girl," I said.

Terry shrugged. "Yeah, but I don't know if I could get excited over someone who looks like an ad for *When Cobras Attack!*"

Oh, you little liar, I thought. I'd seen the looks she was giving Angie. But I let it go.

"So I guess I was right," Terry said. "The girl in the coffin wasn't Darby."

"Maybe."

She jumped in the air. "I rock!"

"So who was it, genius?"

Her smile disappeared. "I don't rock that much."

"You think it was Pam? She said the woman looked like Darby, only not as pretty. That could describe the little sister."

She shook her head. "That would mean Darby had something to do with Pam's death. Why would somebody kill her own sister?"

"Only a few thousand reasons spring to mind," I said, giving Terry a punch in the shoulder. "Anyway, why couldn't it have been my accidental death scenario? Pam died, and Darby wanted to disappear from the scene for some reason, so she used her sister's body as a stand-in."

Terry pointed to a woman in a long gauzy dress sitting at a card table, studying the leathery palm of a surfer. What was she reading there? "I see a shark in your future"?

"Let's ask her," Terry said.

"Nah," I said, pulling her past the table. "Let's do it the hard way. It's character-building."

We continued down the boardwalk past paddleball courts,

hamburger stands, and a pickup basketball game. Just as we were about to cut back to Pacific Avenue, we heard a familiar voice calling to us.

"Helloooo, Nancys Drew!"

There was no mistaking it—Cousin Robert. We spun around but couldn't see where his voice was coming from.

"Over here, lovelies!"

I spied his frizzy red hair over the top of the workout pit. This was Muscle Beach, the place where the most dedicated body-builders had come to hoist dumbbells since the days of Jack LaLanne and Charles Atlas in the 1950s, when bodybuilders were still considered freaks. But they'd come a long way since then—from advertising in the back of comic books all the way to the governor's mansion.

The workout pen looked like a prison weight yard dumped onto the sand. There were buffed-out bruisers of every hue, slick with sweat in their tiny briefs, men barely able to circum-navigate their huge thigh muscles as they moved about, massive arms sticking out at angles from their bodies to accommodate the inflated deltoids.

And then there was Robert.

The mounds of his white flesh were covered with sprays of reddish freckles. His coppery chest hair was matted with sweat. He slopped out of the black muscle shirt, arm flab jiggling as he waved us over. A big leather weightlifter's belt cinched his gut, which spilled out over the top like cake mix escaping the top of a bowl.

I shaded my eyes as if to block the sun, but in truth it was because I wasn't ready for the sight of Cousin Robert in work-out briefs.

"Cuz!" Terry said, waving at him. "What brings you here?"

Robert pointed to a blond Adonis hulking next to him. "You remember my personal trainer, Sven?"

Sven gave us a smile and flexed his pecs. "Ja, hello, ladies."

"Sure," we said.

We remembered that Sven had sent Robert to the hospital in his zeal to turn him into one of the few, the proud, the sculpted. I'd hoped the sadistic Scandinavian had found some other fatty to pound into shape after that unfortunate incident, but apparently he was now back in Robert's employ.

"Well, that stint in county jail set my fitness schedule back quite a bit," Robert explained, "so I got back in touch with my trainer as soon as I got out. And now here we are, back on the road to Wellville. Right, Sven?"

"Ja, Mr. Robert!"

"And once we get in shape, who knows? Maybe a run for governor!"

"Ja, Mr. Robert!"

This Sven reminded me of a windup toy with an anatomically correct crotch.

"That's great," I said to Robert. "Glad to see you getting in shape."

"I'll say I am. Here, let me show you what I can do!"

"Oh, no. That's okay—" I started to say, but Robert had already trotted over to one of the weight benches. A black guy with thighs the size of toddlers rolled his eyes at a white guy, then the two of them moved to the other side of the pen and turned their gargantuan backs on the upcoming demonstration.

Robert lay back on the bench, his stomach perched on top of his frame like a sleeping sea turtle. Sven grabbed up a barbell with two huge disks on the ends that looked like they weighed a hundred pounds each.

"I can't watch," Terry said, turning her back.

"Me neither," I said, looking down at my shoes. "Tell me when it's over."

"Okay, girls," Robert yelled, "here goes nothing!"

Morbid curiosity overcame me. I looked up to see Sven lowering the weight bar into Robert's hands. Robert grunted, his elbows quivering under the massive weight. In spite of my most fervent desire to look away again, my eyes were glued to the disaster waiting to happen. Passersby in bathing suits, in-line skaters, gangbangers, and tourists slowed by the side of the pen, drawn to the spectacle. They coalesced into a curious mob, anxious to see if Robert was going to make it.

I sucked in my breath as the weight bar made its agonizing way down toward Robert's chest. Sweat popped out on his forehead, his face was red and contorted into a grimace, his teeth were gritted. His arm muscles shook ferociously as the bar got lower, lower, lower . . . hovering over his vulnerable rib cage. Gulls circled overhead, like buzzards anticipating a lunch of fresh, freckled carrion.

"Go, Mr. Robert!" Sven urged him. "You can do it, you can do it!"

Then, after what seemed like an eternity, the bar miraculously started to move, making its way back up, centimeter by centimeter. The crowd began to shout encouragement.

"Way to go, big dude!"

"Pump it, chubs!"

"Woo-hoo! Look at the fat mother go!"

"URRRRRR*agggggghhh*!"

A supernatural surge of power seemed to course through Robert's arms. The weights soared up and cleared the brackets; the bar clunking down noisily into the prongs. Terry looked at me, her mouth open in a wide smile, and the two of us almost collapsed with relief.

Cheers went up around the pen. The spectators hooted and applauded this victory over the laws of gravity and probability. Robert sat up to accept his acclaim and smacked his forehead right into the weight bar.

Konk!

He plopped back on the bench, unconscious. Apparently it

was a really good smack. A purple spot was starting to materialize above his eyebrows.

A collective groan went up from the spectators.

"Mr. Robert!" Sven dashed to his client, whose head was angled toward us, his tongue hanging out.

"Not again!" I wailed.

We ran through the building at the side of the pen and then back out into the workout area, shoving aside the barbell behemoths to get to where Robert lay lifeless on the bench. Terry whipped out the cell phone and called 911. "Muscle man down!" she shouted at the dispatcher. "Ocean Front Walk, the workout pit at Muscle Beach!"

Sven slapped Robert's wrists. The black bodybuilder swung a half-gallon jug of Gatorade, sloshing the entire contents in Robert's face. After a second, Robert sputtered, blinking.

"Robert!" I said, taking his hand in mine and squeezing it. "Are you okay?"

He moaned as the pudgy fingers of his free hand went to the knot on his head. Then he fixed his bewildered green eyes on me.

"Who's Robert?" he said. "For that matter, who are *you*?"

"Amnesia!" Reba exclaimed through the cell phone. "Well, he'll recognize me. I bore him in my womb!"

I certainly hoped Robert would recognize her, although she in no way resembled the inside of a uterus. "I told the doctor about Robert's fall down the stairs," I went on, "and he told me that amnesia is quite common in people with multiple head injuries."

"Oh, dear, dear, dear. Where are you?"

"We're at Daniel Freeman hospital in Marina del Rey."

We'd followed the ambulance here to the small hospital on

Lincoln Boulevard. It looked more like a veterinary clinic than a hospital—the buildings white and low to the ground, clustered around a parking lot.

"Daniel Freeman!" Reba exclaimed. "I can't leave him to those *amateurs*."

"I'm sure it'll be okay," I said. "The doctor was very nice. He seemed competent."

"Absolutely not. It's Cedars-Sinai or nothing. I'll be right there to have him transferred."

She disconnected.

"She's going to have him transferred to Cedars-Sinai," I said to Terry.

"Maybe he can get his old room back," she said, shaking her head. "You know, there could be a bright side to this."

"Oh, yeah? What's that?"

"Maybe with the amnesia, he'll forget he's a health nut."

I had to agree with her. Being a fitness buff had so far proven to be very bad for Robert's health.

seventeen

*W*ednesday morning passed in a flurry of activity as we got the mobile command center ready for her maiden voyage. I had given Terry the money for a black-and-white monitor (only $99.95!), and the Bruces rigged up a viewing area in the back of the van—a table and swivel chair bolted to the floor, the monitor secured to the table with clamps.

The Bruces, I was learning, had many talents. They proved to be very adept with the electronic equipment, and very capable with design and construction.

But when noon rolled around, there was another desperate call from Reba. She needed our help at the soup kitchen again. We were going to leave the Bruces there to continue working, but they were anxious to lend a hand.

"Well, the more the merrier," Terry said. "We're going to Broadway Court in Oakwood."

We took the bike and the Bruces followed in their van.

Thirty minutes later, we were stopped at a red light on Abbott Kinney. Terry pointed to someone on the sidewalk. I looked over and saw a man of sixty in an Armani suit with a white shirt, a yellow tie knotted beneath his starched collar. Not such an unusual sight, until you looked at his cardboard sign:

NEED FOOD. ANYTHING WILL HELP.

He had his hand out, but no one was stopping. Small wonder. Who would give a quarter to a man dressed better than you?

Maybe he was a former studio executive.

Terry turned all the way around on the motorcycle to show me her baffled face.

I shrugged back at her. "It's L.A."

The light turned green and she buzzed through the intersection. We drove past a stooped old woman pushing a shopping cart loaded with milk jugs, plastic sacks, and assorted other junk. A typical bag lady, until you looked at her dress.

It was a black gabardine, with a waist-length striped jacket and a lizard-skin belt. Her chunky legs were jammed into some Christian Leboutin leather pumps. Terry was staring at the woman so intently, she didn't notice that the car in front of her had stopped at the light. I slapped her on the back and she whipped her head around, slamming on the brakes just in time to avoid rear-ending it.

"What's going on here?" she said when we were stopped. "Did you see that bag lady? She was dressed like a senior fashion model."

"They're becoming very picky at Goodwill Industries," I said. "They won't take shabby clothes anymore."

"Those clothes aren't just unshabby! That outfit would have eaten up our clothing budget for six months."

I shrugged again and pointed to the moving traffic. She turned around and pulled forward, traveling for another block. Soon we came upon two weathered-looking men in front of a liquor store, camped out on an old blanket. The black man was bald and emaciated, the white one was pasty, with long matted dreadlocks. But they were both outfitted in perfect pinstripe suits and wingtips.

The sign at their feet said: WHY LIE? WE NEED BEER.

Terry pulled over to the curb and tossed a quarter into their coffee can. "How's business?" she asked them.

"Sucks," the black man said. "Haven't made a dime all day."

"Nice clothes, though."

The white guy shrugged. "Can't drink 'em."

Terry took off again, the van in tow, then made the left turn onto Broadway. By now I had figured out what had happened. Someone was outfitting the homeless people in designer duds, and I had a pretty good idea who it was.

Terry parked next to the Compassion House, turning to me.

"Reba," we both said at once.

We climbed off the bike, shaking our heads, and walked past the down-and-out patrons lined up for lunch, who were wearing their usual well-seasoned, ill-fitting clothes. Coming out of the house, however, it was a different story. The patrons were dressed to beat the band.

There was a large woman in a flowered yellow frock and a lacquered straw hat who apparently couldn't be fitted for shoes. She was wearing army boots with her yellow fishnet hose. There was a man in a navy jacket with gold epaulets, a white yachting cap, and boaters, who looked like the captain of the USS *Rusty Grocery Cart*. A skinny woman blithered mindlessly as she slapped at the empty air in front of her with a leather riding crop, dressed in brown woolen jodhpurs, knee-high riding boots, and a silk ecru blouse.

"I recognize that outfit," Terry said, pointing to her. "It's Reba's Ascot Opening Day look."

"Yeah, it's already a few months old. No wonder she was ready to off-load it."

The Bruces caught up with us at the door. "Check out the

threads on these homeless people," Bruce One said. "Where'd they get 'em?"

"We're pretty sure it was our great-aunt," I told him.

Two scrunched up his brow. "What'd she do? Hijack a Neiman Marcus truck?"

"She didn't have to," Terry said. "She just had to empty one of her closets."

Inside, the house was full of people who could have held their own on Mr. Blackwell's best-dressed list, leaning over soup bowls, slurping up their lunch. Just then, Reba came flitting up to us from a side room.

"Oh, good!" she said on seeing the Bruces. "You brought help."

I did the introductions as Reba held out her hand to them daintily. "Reba, these are the Bruces. Bruces, this is Aunt Reba."

"Pleased to meet you, Bruces. How delightful that you all have the same name! You should form a musical troupe. Perhaps you could help out in the men's fitting room?" She pointed them in the direction of a bedroom, where there was a group of bedraggled men milling around in their underwear. Some of them wore several pairs, bulging out to their sides like bloomers.

"Where'd you get all the clothes, Reba?" Terry asked.

"I went around Palm Drive and browbeat the neighbors into giving up their old things."

"They look pretty new to me."

"Ha! Some of these clothes were purchased in the last century," Reba said snippily. "I did them a favor, forcing them to let go of the tatty old things."

Then Reba handed the Bruces a box of moist towelettes. "Now, I'm advising everyone to have a little birdbath before donning the new clothes. It'll be so much nicer, don't you think? Do your best to fit them from the things in the corner, boys." She turned to Terry and me. "Think you girls can handle the women while I serve some soup?"

She scampered away again before we could even answer.

We wandered into the women's fitting room, where we found the homeless women poking through the clothes on the floor. I recognized Lola, the Shirley Temple stand-in, who'd managed to outfit herself in a long net skirt like a ballerina's tutu and a sequined top.

"Got any tap shoes?" she asked us, rummaging through the boxes on the floor. "Mine got ruined in the rains."

"What rains?" Terry said. "It's July."

Lola gave her an exasperated look. "The rains of 'forty-nine!"

"Oh, *those* rains."

"Tap shoes, hmmm." I started throwing the lids off boxes. "How about some nice suede ankle boots? These look like they would fit you. Maybe we could have some taps put on them."

"That'd work," Lola said, eagerly grabbing the pair from me.

She shoved one foot into a boot and frowned. "Too small. They'd fit if I cut off my little toes."

"No!" Terry snatched back the other boot. "That won't be necessary. We'll find you a fit . . . Here!"

She pulled out some black patent leather Mary Janes with straps over the instep.

"Tap shoes!" Lola screamed, kicking off the remaining suede boot. "Gimme 'em!"

She grabbed the Mary Janes and stuffed her feet into them. "Crackerjack!" She snapped the straps and practiced a two-step and ball change, then danced on out of the room, warbling at the top of her ancient lungs:

"On the goo-oo-od ship—Lollipop! It's a short trip—to the candy shop!"

Tappity-tappity tap-tap-tap.

"You know what?" Terry said, smiling as she watched Lola go. "She's really pretty good."

An hour later, all of the patrons had been freshened with moist towelettes and dressed in their new finery. They ate their soup while being entertained by Lola's rendition of "The Good Ship Lollipop" some thirty times in a row. (She promised to bone up on some other songs as soon as she got her medication.)

Then the homeless people took to the streets in their swell-looking duds, pushing their shopping carts and begging for change. I hoped the new clothes weren't going to interfere with their livelihoods. I'd never seen panhandlers in designer clothes before. Oh, well. A few days on the street and you wouldn't be able to tell the new clothes from the old, I figured.

We inquired after Cousin Robert's health as we were leaving. "What's the prognosis?" I asked Reba. "Has his memory come back yet?"

"No, he still thinks he's the Brazilian ambassador. But his EEG came back normal, and his neurologist is meeting today with a brain specialist who's flown in from Boston for a consultation. I'm very optimistic about his chances for recovery."

"Oh, good," Terry said. "Well, give him our best, if he remembers who we are."

"Will do!" Reba said, scurrying back to her post in the kitchen. "Ta!"

Later, after we'd put the final touches on the command center, we retired to the house to eat the fabulous homemade pizzas Bruce Two had whipped up from scratch.

"These Bruces are very handy guys," I said to Terry as I bit down into a pepperoni with garlic.

"I know. Let's marry 'em," she said, jamming a slice of sun-dried tomato with goat cheese into her mouth.

We shared a couple of six-packs of beer, and eventually a

poker game got started in the dining room. Terry couldn't lose that night. She won hand after hand after hand. The Bruces were good sports about her taking all their money, but I suspected she was using a marked deck. When she had bilked them of the entire three hundred dollars we had paid them Monday, I took her aside and made her promise to give it back.

"Sure," she said, wounded. "I wasn't gonna keep it."

The Bruces ended up crashing on the floor, piled onto blankets and pillows, the pups snoozing happily amid all that heat-radiating meat. I had to admit, it felt good knowing that if some cloaked evildoer came through the window in the middle of the night, he'd have our three giant houseguests to contend with.

I lay under the coverlet, lulled by the sound of snoring downstairs, and wondered why men made such strange noises in their sleep. Was it an evolutionary thing? Lions wandering by the cave door would hear the nasal rumblings bouncing off stone walls and go on their way, persuaded that there was one bad mamma jamma inside?

Well, I was glad *I* didn't snore. It would be really embarrassing if I got involved with Boatwright, say, and spent the night, and as he was gazing on my sleeping face thinking tender thoughts, all of a sudden I started making noises like a rutting warthog.

I thought about the funeral scheduled for the next day as I yawned and turned over in bed. What would happen? Would we finally learn the truth about Darby and her little sister?

Probably not, despite Terry's fondest hopes. The whole funeral thing would probably be one huge waste of *snnarrrggghhh-*shoooo-*snlugggh*.

$\mathcal{W}$ e pulled up to Valhalla Mortuary a half hour early. The command center was in place when we arrived, sitting in the far corner of the lot. It bore the legend BRUCES' FLOWERS on the side panel. The guys were inside, a digital camera trained on the outside of the building.

We waved in their direction. They responded with a light beep on the horn, the signal that they had successfully delivered the floral arrangement to the funeral parlor, along with the hidden microphone for the casket.

Terry and I entered the building to the downbeat of dreary organ music. The color scheme of the home was soothing roses and beiges, but the vibe was deadly. The main parlor stood in front of us, with a hallway leading off to the right.

"Let's reconnoiter," Terry said to me.

Again with the PI vocabulary. I made a mental note to check under her mattress for a book called *How to Talk Detective*.

We ducked down the hallway and peered into a room full of display caskets in all different styles of wood and finishes—maple, oak, mahogany, aluminum—with everything from ornate brass handles to polished steel hardware. After spending so much time around vampires, I realized I was seeing the caskets differently now, regarding them as furniture instead of mere planters for human beings. There was one coffin with a burled wood veneer that I thought would have made a nice coffee table.

Past the display room was a unisex bathroom. A kitchen was located at the end of the hall. There were two other viewing rooms off the hallway, complete with dead bodies on display, looking like wax statues in fancy shipping crates.

Terry had tucked the FM transmitter into a fanny pack concealed under her jacket. We were also carrying the new lime green cell phones. Terry had had our old number assigned to her new phone, and I got a completely new number. If we got separated for some reason, we could text message each other. I had to admit that all this new paraphernalia was making me feel like quite the well-equipped investigator.

We stepped back into the main parlor, which was mostly empty except for Herb and Sandra in the front row. It was still early.

An elderly woman greeted us inside the door. She was wearing a chrysanthemum that was so huge, it looked like a second head sprouting from her chest. She had a downy mustache on her upper lip, half-glasses on a chain, and her dress was printed with blue cornflowers on a yellow background.

"Bless you for coming," Chrysanthemum Lady said, handing us our programs.

"Thank you," I said, giving her a wistful smile.

She smiled back at me, then made a persimmon face at Terry. "Your headphones are showing, dear." She twitched her mustache in disapproval.

Terry's hand went to her head. "Oh."

"Don't want the bereaved to see us listening to our *gangsta rap* while their loved one is being eulogized, do we? Hmmm?"

"No, ma'am." Terry took off the headphones and stuffed them into her pocket as we went through the door. "Sorry about that."

"Maybe your mother should have taught you manners," Chrysanthemum Lady said to Terry's back.

Terry froze in place, turning around slowly. "Maybe my mother should *kick your ass*—"

I grabbed Terry's arm and yanked her down the aisle before she could smack the crap out of the old lady in cornflowers. She strained to get away from me, finally jerking her arm out of my grip.

"That was one-forty-nine ninety-five well spent," I whispered to her.

She shrugged. "I'll put 'em back on later."

We unconsciously timed our steps to the dirge until we got to the Applewhites. Herb wore a navy blue jacket and gray slacks, his hair combed over the shiny bald spot. He had his arm around Sandra, who was dressed in a black shirtwaist dress and black knee-high leatherette boots. A pillbox hat with netting was perched on top of her bouffant. She took our outstretched hands and gave them a weak squeeze. Herb gave us a nod.

"Thank you for coming, girls," Sandra said. She released our hands to blow her nose into a handkerchief.

"You're welcome," Terry said.

We spouted a few comforting platitudes, then Terry glanced up at the dais. "Ah, look at that beautiful flower arrangement," she said.

I looked over and almost fainted when I saw the Bruces' handiwork. Standing at the edge of the platform was a horseshoe-shaped monstrosity, the kind you see at mobster funerals in the movies—six feet high and covered with pink roses, purple irises, and daisies. On top of the horseshoe was a tiara fashioned out of white edelweiss blooms, and across the front was a pink satin sash with letters in silver glitter: *HOMECOMING IN HEAVEN*.

I stood there a moment with my mouth hanging open, until Terry punched me in the back to snap me out of it. "And there's Darby," she said, nodding toward the casket. "Just as I remember her. I'll be right back."

I turned my attention back to Herb and Sandra, talking to them in somber tones while Terry went up onto the dais. I could see her out of the corner of my eye, pretending to admire the high school portrait of Darby sitting atop the coffin. Blond hair, fresh face, clear blue eyes—Darby had been the prototypical American teen, looking forward to a life full of suburban joys.

Then Terry leaned into the flowers on the casket as if to inhale their fragrance and came up with a satisfied look. She descended the stairs, giving me a subtle eye signal as she passed. I muttered goodbye to the Applewhites, then followed Terry to some folding chairs on the right side of the room.

After we were seated, Terry reached up and slipped the headphones on her head while pretending to fluff her hair. Then she twiddled a button on a small radio and apparently got sound, giving me a covert thumbs-up.

The place began to fill up with representatives of the two sides of Darby's life. The vampires gravitated to the left side of the room, looking like denizens of Jack the Ripper's London. The females wore gowns with plunging necklines and empire waists, hair drawn up like Edwardian virgins', with long white necks ripe for the biting. The men wore velvet waistcoats and long black tails, politely removing their silk top hats indoors.

The "normals" sat with us on the right side of the room. Graduates of Burbank High looking like half-price day at the Gap. The girls had pert haircuts; the men were trending toward male-pattern baldness. I recognized some of the guys as high school football players, who now had the muscle-gone-to-fat look of athletes consigned to desk jobs. Several of the women were also familiar, but not enough to speak to. They were dressed in cookie-cutter mourning-casual, and I noticed they were all angled just a bit in their chairs so they could steal surreptitious glances at the weirdos to their left.

I looked out over the vampire crowd and wondered about Darby's roommates. Lucian had disappeared for some reason, but shouldn't Morgoth be here? I didn't see him anywhere.

Suddenly, I heard noise at the back of the room. I turned and saw the source of the commotion, a huge purple presence just inside the door.

Vishy.

"Am I late, am I late?" he asked Chrysanthemum Lady, all aflutter.

She made a face and thrust the program into his hands. "The ceremony has not yet begun."

"Oh, good!" he said, loud enough for the whole room to hear. "I wouldn't want to miss any of the teeth-gnashing and wailing."

Heads turned as he sashayed down the aisle, fanning himself with the program. He smiled at all of the mourners, enjoying the looks he got in his floor-length purple gown and red silk scarf. His Cleopatra wig was black today, with jingle bells attached to the braids that produced a merry tinkling as he paraded through the rows. I shrank down in my seat, hoping he would pass us by, but he spotted us, waving the program in front of our faces.

"Girlfriends!" he bellowed.

I put a finger to my lips. "It's a funeral!" I whispered.

"*Sorry.*" He lowered his voice to a level that could still tumble the walls of Jericho. "Oh, check out the flowers," he said, pointing to the horseshoe. "Straight out of Tackyville, USA. And, oh—there's our Ephemera, looking quite the wholesome little virgin. So tragic, isn't it?"

I nodded wordlessly, hoping he would get the message and leave.

"Well, I guess I'll go pay my respects," he said. "Later, dolls!"

He strutted up to the dais to look at the photo.

"Big fat faker," Terry whispered to me. "He doesn't even believe she's dead."

"Probably came to start some trouble," I said. "Keep an eye on him."

We watched as Vishy plucked a daisy from the flower arrangement and stuck it behind his ear. Then he leaned over and muttered something at the casket before turning around and swishing to a seat on the right side of the room, ignoring the unofficial protocol and plopping himself down right in the middle of the regular mourners. I heard a folding chair creaking a few rows back.

"Did he say anything?" I whispered to Terry.

"He said, '*Arrivederci*, baby.'"

I rolled my eyes.

A white-bread couple came into the room with a little girl of two or three toddling along next to the mother, who wore a large brimmed black hat. The woman started a little when she saw the group on the left.

The girl pointed. "Mommy, look! Mampires!"

"Shhh, don't stare," the young mother said, urging the little girl down the aisle.

The three of them went up to the dais. They stood for a moment before the flower-laden casket, then the little girl crossed her legs.

"Mommy, I gotta go bafroom!" she cried.

The woman said something to the man, then took the little girl off the dais and out the back exit. The sandy-haired dad stood at the casket for a moment, his shoulders shaking almost imperceptibly. Then he blew his nose into a handkerchief, stepped off the dais, and went back down the aisle, taking a seat somewhere behind us.

I looked at Terry. She leaned over and whispered, "He said he was sorry."

"For what?"

She shrugged.

I turned in my seat and craned my neck to look behind me. Who was this mystery man with the wife and little girl?

Mourners continued to make their way up to the casket, the Gap people and vampires taking turns, each waiting for representatives from the other camp to clear out before they ventured up to gaze on Darby's youthful image.

I saw a look of fierce concentration on Terry's face as she strained to pick conversations out of the organ music. "Hear anything interesting?"

She pointed. "According to those two girls over there, Darby was the blow job queen of Burbank High."

"*Meoww,*" I said, arching my fingers.

The organ music stopped. The crowd settled itself and the whispering ceased as a stern-looking minister in black robes entered the room. He took his place behind the lectern, cleared his throat, and moved his gaze across the room.

"Dearly beloved—" he started.

Weeeeahhhhhh!

An ear-splitting wail rang through the sanctuary like a heavy metal wawa pedal, a sound that could shatter concrete. The preacher jumped back from the mike, startled. The audience grimaced and covered their ears with their hands.

Uh-oh. Looks like our high-tech Soviet toy is defective. Thanks for nothing, Gorbachev.

An assistant rushed onstage and futzed with the switch on the microphone.

Weeeeeeahhhhh!

By this time, I was sure our FM transmitter was the culprit.

I poked Terry's fanny pack. "Get that thing out of here. It's causing interference!"

She nodded, jumping up and hurrying up the aisle to the back of the room.

The assistant turned off the mike and whispered something to the preacher. The preacher nodded and stepped up behind the lectern again, straightening his lapels and taking a moment to compose himself. Then he smiled and began speaking in an ol'-time religion baritone that could raise the rafters even without amplification.

"Dearly beloved, I do apologize for the technical difficulties in this, our time of sorrow."

The crowd seemed to recover from the full-on eardrum assault, soothed by his preacherly manner. They relaxed back in their seats as he began to eulogize Darby the high school beauty, whom he described as enthusiastic and full of life. A cherished daughter, a beloved sister, a good friend to all . . .

He went on in this vein for some time, apparently intending to skip right over the issue of Darby's recent way of life. He made no mention of her consorting with vampires, at least not until the very end. But then all at once his demeanor changed. He drew a deep breath, causing his chest to expand like a bellows, and his face settled into a reproving scowl.

"Little Darby was duly baptized in the church. And insofar as she lost her way, may she be forgiven and taken unto Thy heavenly bosom, Lord."

His voice became louder, more spirit-filled. "For yea, though we walk in the *waaaays* of evil, the Lord hath promised eternal life to all those who accept Him." He leveled the vampires with fiery eyes.

Vampire throats were cleared. There was an uncomfortable shifting of vampire butts in the folding chairs.

"For yea"—the preacher leaned over the podium, pointing directly into the vampire crowd—"though we be surrounded by wickedness in this world—in this *verrry* room—which is filled with the putridity of those who truck with Satan . . ."

Oh, boy, I thought. *Here we go.*

A low hissing started on the vampire side of the room.

The preacher pumped up the volume in order to drown them out. "The Lorrrrrd of darkness . . . who doth *defiiiiile* all that is holy!" The preacher's color rose and spittle gathered in the corners of his mouth, his jowls quivering with revulsion.

"Hissssssssss . . . booooooo," came the commentary from the fanged mourners.

"*Foullllling* the air with the stench of his breath . . . !"

"HISSSSSSSSSS!"

"*Fornnnnnicating* with the very *beeeeasts* of the field—!"

Just as I was wondering how all of this was going to end, someone stood up behind me and yelled, "Hail, Satan!"

I heard gasps and spun around in my seat. Vishy had his arms in the air, his head back. "Hail, Satan, Prince of Darkness!" he screamed at the ceiling.

And that's when the fight broke out.

Someone in the vampire camp threw a folding chair into the Gap crowd. The Gap women screamed. Then the ex-football players and the fanged men in formal wear charged across the aisle at one another, swinging and punching and swearing at the tops of their lungs. The women followed, clawing and screeching and ripping out hair. It was like high school all over again, jocks versus geeks, straights versus outcasts.

"O Lord, strike down the Antichrist in our midst!" the preacher beseeched the Almighty from the dais. "Smite him, *Lorrrrd*! Smite him!"

Speaking of the Antichrist, I thought, *where's Terry?* I'd have expected her to be jumping into the fray with, "Is this a private smiting, or can anyone join in?" I looked around frantically but couldn't find her anywhere.

Too bad. I'm outta here.

I jumped over two women rolling around in the aisle, legs locked around each other like the proverbial two-backed beast. In front of me, a football player tackled a male vampire from behind. The vampire grabbed the coat of the man in front of him, and the three of them thudded down in a heap. I ran right up the football player's back as if it were a skateboard ramp, flying off the end of the pileup and running like hell for the exit.

The horseshoe flower arrangement sailed through the air in front of me and crashed into a stained-glass window depicting the Madonna and child.

If there was ever a moment for a lightning strike . . .

At the back of the room the Chrysanthemum Lady jumped onto Vishy's back, grabbing him around the neck. "Filthy tramp!" she yelled. "Satan's whore!" Vishy spun around in circles, trying to shake the crazed harridan off his back. But she had her legs firmly clamped around his waist, *woo-hoo*ing like a bronco buster, ripping off his wig and waving it in the air like a Stetson.

I saw that his natural hair was a gray buzz cut. Without the wig, he looked like a Marine sergeant in makeup and gown.

The bastard didn't deserve to be saved—he had started the whole thing, after all—but I ran to his rescue anyway. I grabbed Chrysanthemum Lady and struggled to pull her off him. She cursed me, kicking and screeching, but I finally managed to wrench her off Vishy's back, shoving her into the foyer. She stumbled into a table and flipped over it, sprawling on the other side.

"Oops!" I said, horrified. "Hope nothing's broken!"

After a few seconds, she scrambled to her feet and checked her chrysanthemum. She'd lost a few petals but appeared otherwise unharmed.

"That harpy bit my ear!" Vishy wailed. "And they call *us* vampires!"

"You started a riot!" I shouted at him over the din.

He grinned, looking out over the fracas. "Things were getting a little dull, didn't you think?"

"Well, fun's a-poppin' now!"

Chrysanthemum Lady was headed back into the room, beady eyes fixed on me. She pushed up her sleeves and came running. *Uh-oh.*

I turned to run in the opposite direction just as I caught sight of a hymnal flying through the air toward my face. I ducked, and the songbook sailed right past me and clunked Chrysanthemum Lady smack in the middle of the forehead.

She fell over backwards and hit the floor again.

This time she was out for the count.

A half hour later the riot had been quelled, the vampires successfully ejected from the funeral. They'd taken to their hearses and cleared out. The chapel had been put back into some kind of order, although I suspected it would never be quite the same.

Vishy drove past me in his purple hearse, the wig sitting skewed on his head, gray bristles poking out in front.

"Happy interment!" he yelled, then squealed out of the parking lot, laying on his horn. It blared a stanza of the Alice Cooper classic: "*School's out forever!*"

Chrysanthemum Lady's head had been iced. The "normals" were straightening their khakis and smoothing their hairdos, the preacher commending them on their triumph over Satan's minions.

Speaking of which, there was still no sign of Terry.

I watched everybody climb into cars for the burial ceremony, craning my neck in an attempt to spot her. The bike was still there, but she was nowhere in sight.

Sandra came up beside me, grabbing my elbow. "Come on, honey. You ride with us." She dragged me toward a waiting stretch limo.

"Um, have you seen my sister?"

"She's probably going in someone else's car. You can keep us company."

It appeared I had no choice. I got in the back of the limo, facing Herb and Sandra from the jump seat. Sandra produced a flask as the limo began to move, holding it out to me, but I shook my head.

"Good grief!" She toasted me with the flask, then took a slug while Herb stared out the window.

"Still no word from Pam?" I asked her.

"No," Sandra said. "I thought maybe she'd get word somehow, but no such luck. I know I would have heard from her. Oh, well. *C'est la vie.*"

C'est la vie?

"I heard you were threatening to sue the police," I said.

"Who told you that?"

"The detective on the case."

"I just told him that so he'd get off his duff and do something about my baby's body going missing. Can you imagine? Not bad enough I have to bury my little girl—I have to bury her without her body!"

"A crime," Herb said.

"And all those infernal freaks," Sandra said with a shudder, jerking her thumb toward the back windshield. "How dare they show their faces at her funeral. They're the reason she's dead!"

"Bad crowd," Herb muttered.

As we made our way to the cemetery, I found myself thinking about Darby and Pam. They didn't get along, according to Sandra, but "loved each other as sisters." I knew something about sibling attachment, but I also knew that most murder victims are killed by someone close to them. Killings by strangers are more rare than we're led to believe, and murder within families is more common than we'd like to think. Could it be that Pam wasn't in hiding after all, but had died in the place of her more glamorous big sister?

We passed through the gates of the burial park, manicured green lawn unfolding before us. At least the Applewhites didn't skimp. This wasn't an inexpensive place to rest your head for eternity. Assuming your head was actually in your coffin.

To my relief, I spotted the Bruces' van when we entered the lot. Terry was probably inside, I realized, or had otherwise found her way over to the burial site.

The limo driver opened the door for Sandra, offering a hand to help her out. She stuffed the flask into her black patent leather handbag and gave him her hand, then was followed out by Herb. I opened the door on the opposite side and let myself out.

The preacher stood at the head of the coffin, poised over a hole in the ground that was surrounded by Astroturf. His collar was slightly rumpled and his wavy hair mussed, but his color was high and he seemed to have been reinvigorated by the riot. I guess it's not every day you get to go toe to toe with the forces of evil.

I led Herb and Sandra to the reserved graveside seats, then started to join the mourners behind them. Sandra looked up at me with anguished eyes.

"Sit with us, honey."

I hesitated before lowering myself into the seat next to hers.

There was a light wind blowing the leaves and gently bending the grass; a faint rustling was the only sound, except for the occasional sniffle. I looked out across the acres of grave markers and wondered why we devoted so much prime real estate to death. I was thinking I'd prefer to be cremated and have my ashes thrown from the Scream! ride at Magic Mountain when something caught my eye in the distance.

It was a woman, standing behind a granite statue of an angel. The woman's long black hair seemed of a piece with her black dress, strands of it blowing across her pallid face. She looked like a creature from another time, like the ghost of a Civil War widow, or like . . . *a supposedly deceased vampire queen here to check out her own funeral!*

I jumped up out of my chair. Sandra grabbed the hem of my jacket. "Where are you going?" she said in alarm.

I glanced down at her. "I thought I saw—"

I whipped my head back around to focus on the spot where I'd seen the woman. I shaded my eyes with my hand, straining to see her running away or perhaps crouching behind the tombstone. But she had simply vanished.

"Nothing." I sat back down in my chair, shivering.

Great, now I'm seeing ghosts.

At that moment the Bruces climbed out of the van. They'd changed from their deliverymen outfits into black suits and Ray-Bans. They crossed the lawn to the burial site and lined up behind our chairs.

"Psssst." It was a Bruce in my ear. "Have you seen Terry?"

"I thought she was with you," I whispered.

"We were watching the entrance. She never came out."

The preacher cleared his throat and opened his prayer book just as it occurred to me to check my new cell phone. I'd forgotten about it during the hubbub at the funeral parlor. Terry had probably gone running off after some new lead, I realized, and had left me a message on it.

The preacher began the committal service. He uttered a few sentences I didn't catch because I was digging the phone out of my purse. Then I heard him say, "We now commit Darby's body, er, *casket* to the ground."

Concealing the phone by the side of my leg, I clicked on the envelope icon and saw a message on the screen:

Im in coffin

"Ashes to ashes, dust to dust . . ." the preacher said solemnly.

I shook my head and blinked, then looked at the screen again.

Im in coffin

Panic took a seat on my chest. I had trouble getting my breath.

". . . in sure and certain hope of the resurrection."

I looked one more time, hoping I'd hallucinated it. But the text message was still there.

"In the name of the father, the son, and the holy ghost, Amen." The preacher closed his prayer book.

Imagine my dilemma.

Terry had always been a wicked prankster. As a kid, I was continually walking through doors that she'd rigged with buckets of water to fall on my head, usually at the exact moment the carpool had arrived. I'd go to school with my braids frizzed and my perfect homework pages stuck together, my spiffy little outfit all damp and wrinkled. And here she was, adult Terry, allegedly sending me a message from the grave.

Was I supposed to believe it?

But if she was in there, she'd be kicking up a storm, wouldn't she? Banging on the sides of the coffin and kicking the lid with the metal-enforced toe of her boot?

Maybe the padding was too thick for us to hear, I thought. Or maybe she was *tied up*.

Call me crazy, but before I broke up the whole funeral and made them rip open the casket to let her out, I had to be sure. I sent a return message: *Betr be in thr or yr dead meat*.

I gave it enough time for the message to get to her, but there was no response. Well, how could there be? There was no light to see by, probably no air to breathe. She had probably just managed to peck out the message before she passed out.

While I was sitting here dithering, my sister could be suffering severe brain damage from lack of oxygen. And believe me, if I caused her severe brain damage, I'd never hear the end of it.

I retar-dud, an' it all you fault!

The preacher finished up his remarks and nodded to the funeral director, who signaled to the gravesite attendants. They started the machinery of the lowering device, and the casket began its descent into the earth. Someone handed Sandra a spade. She stood up to toss some earth in with the coffin.

I checked the cell phone. No further communication from Terry. I watched with increasing dread as the ebony box inched its way into the hole. I had to do something!

I shot up from my seat. "Excuse me . . . ?"

Everyone turned and looked at me, surprised.

"Has something gone unsaid, sister?" the preacher said, his eyebrows arched.

"Yes—*uh*—I would like to say that perhaps we shouldn't lower the casket just yet."

The lowering device creaked to a stop.

The sallow-faced funeral director cocked his head. "What's the problem here?"

"Oh, no problem, really. I was just wondering, um—would it be possible for me to take a little look-see inside the coffin? Won't take a sec. Then you can close it right back up and bury it."

There was a collective gasp from the crowd. Sandra let out a squawk and collapsed into Herb's arms, flinging her spadeful of dirt in the faces of a nearby Burbank High couple.

The preacher's face was transfused with red. "I thought I'd seen inappropriate behavior today, but you, young lady, take the cake!"

"I wouldn't ask for no reason," I said, my throat tightening and my voice squeezing up an octave. "My sister may be in there!"

Another gasp from the crowd. The funeral director strode up to me, hairy nostrils flaring. "Why do you think your sister is in there?"

"She sent me a message. On this." I held up the cell phone before I remembered the message was gone. The funeral director grabbed the phone and looked at the screen.

"Dead meat? We do not refer to our clients as 'meat.' "

"That was my message to her," I said, pleading with him. "*Her* message said she was in the coffin!"

"I oversaw the loading of this coffin myself," he said, puffing out his chest. "I assure you there was no one in it."

I needed backup. I looked at the Bruces, who were poised for action.

"Say the word," Bruce Two said, cracking his knuckles.

The funeral director snapped his fingers at the gravesite attendants, who resumed lowering the coffin into the ground. Dirty looks were fired at me from everyone in the crowd.

What should I do—use Bruce Power to overcome the preacher and the funeral director? I couldn't let them bury Terry! The coffin was sinking lower, lower, lower.

I looked down at the cell phone. New message: *Helpp*. I thrust it at the funeral director. "Look at this!"

He frowned at the screen. "How do you infer she's in the coffin from this? Step aside, miss, or I'll have you removed by force."

"You're not burying my sister!"

Before I knew what was happening, I had jumped up and flung myself headlong toward the grave. I soared through the air with my arms out like Supergirl for endless seconds, then, as I plummeted down toward the casket, I had a very un-Supergirl-like thought:

Oh, man, this is really gonna hurt my boobs.

I landed with a *whump* on top of the hard wood of the coffin, knocking the wind out of me and flattening my mammaries to pancakes.

"*Ugh!*"

Exclamations of surprise and horror came from the mourners.

I lay splayed on the coffin halfway into the ground, nose jammed in the flowers, wondering what I'd done to deserve Terry as a sister. I must have been Genghis Kahn in a previous life, I decided. Nothing short of a career as a genocidal lunatic could have landed me here. The gears creaked and the coffin began coming back up.

"Terry, what are you doing!" Sandra cried.

"I'm Kerry, and I'm very sorry, but I can't let you bury that coffin with my sister inside!"

"Young lady," the preacher said, "you are deranged."

Two Bruces reached in and grabbed my arms, yanking me up to terra firma. I caught my breath as the coffin cleared the top of the grave.

"We'll just see about that," I said. "Open it or I call the police."

"Outrageous!" The funeral director stomped over to the coffin and flipped the latches. Everyone crowded in to get a better look, no doubt wondering if Terry was going to pop up like a stripper out of a cake covered with whipped cream . . .

She'd better be in there, I thought. *She had just better be in there.*

Sandra stood by with her hands covering her eyes, Herb clutching her waist protectively. The funeral director raised up the lid of the coffin and the mourners leaned over as one to look inside.

The coffin was empty.

"I'll kill her!" I screamed.

The funeral director slammed the lid. "I'm bringing charges, young lady."

"You are going to regret making a mockery of this solemn ceremony," the preacher said.

Beneath my fury and humiliation I was sure Terry was in real trouble somewhere. She might be warped, but even she wouldn't go this far for a joke. She was trapped in a coffin, and she was certainly losing oxygen.

"Sue me!" I said, grabbing two of the Bruces by the hand. "Come on! She's back at the funeral home!"

And we took off running across the manicured lawn, weaving around headstones like they were traffic cones on the Highway to Hell.

nineteen

The van screeched to a stop in the funeral home parking lot.

We piled out and ran in the front door. Deadly organ music filled the air as another ceremony took place in the main parlor.

You had to hand it to them. They really moved 'em through here.

Chrysanthemum Lady was back on duty, a knot poking out on her forehead like a blackened third eye. She reared back when she saw me. "You! Get out or I'll call the police!"

"We're looking for a kidnap victim." I flashed my license at her. "I suggest you not impede our investigation."

"We're in the middle of a solemn ceremony," she hissed.

"Sorry, it's a matter of life or death." I pointed the Bruces to the display room. "Go! Leave no coffin unopened!"

I saw heads turning in the main parlor to check out the commotion. I was sorry to disrupt their tribute to the dead, but I had a duty to the living, and that was more important right now.

If she's still living, I thought, which sent needles of fear zinging into my scalp.

We stampeded into the sales room as a group, and that's when I saw something that had failed to register on my consciousness before. All of the coffins *were* open, their satin interiors gleaming in the overhead lights. There was not one that could be Terry's place of confinement. But the Bruces dutifully ran from coffin to coffin, peering inside each one as if Terry might suddenly materialize from a trick drawer.

"She's not here!" Bruce Three cried, near panic.

I dashed across to the viewing room on the opposite side of the hall. Folding chairs were arranged in front of a black casket with silver handles. I yanked up the lid of the casket and saw an old woman inside. Waxy face. Frozen smile. Raspberry-colored rouge on her wrinkled cheeks.

"Sorry!" I said, slamming the lid. "Rest in peace!"

Chrysanthemum Lady rushed to my side. "What are you people *doing*?"

I grabbed her by the scrawny shoulders. "Are there more coffins somewhere?"

She shrugged off my hands. "Don't you manhandle me!"

"Sorry." I backed off a step. "Where do you keep the coffins? You must have more in a storeroom or something."

She pointed into the display room. "That's everything we carry. The whole line. If we need something that isn't here, we special order it."

I turned to the Bruces. "Search the whole building. Top to bottom."

"See here!" she said indignantly. "You can't do this!"

"Remember my sister, identical twin?" I asked her. "She was the one wearing headphones?"

She glared at me. She remembered, all right.

"Well she's trapped in a coffin somewhere. And unless you want to be charged with"—I searched for an official-sounding term—"*false imprisonment*, you'd better help us find her."

She waved a fistful of programs in my face. "I'm supposed to be handing these out—"

"Leave 'em by the door!" Bruce Three said, bouncing up and down on his feet.

"Here." She thrust the programs at him. "Hand them these and say 'Bless you.' "

"Bless you," Bruce Three said. "Bless you, bless you," he repeated, committing the phrase to memory as he ran to the front door.

The old lady moved into the hallway, pointing. "The kitchen's over there . . . the office is right there. Here's the bathroom." She threw open the bathroom door, pointing inside. "As you can see, no coffins anywhere."

"Where do you store the bodies for embalming?"

She crossed her arms over her chest, shaking her head. "No one's allowed back there."

"This is an emergency! If you don't show me the room, I'll . . . I'll do something desperate! I'll scream—" I drew a big breath.

She waved her hands in the air and spun on her orthopedic heel. "Follow me," she said.

I started after her, still issuing orders. "Bruce One, take the kitchen. Bruce Two, the office. If you don't see her, find us in the back."

The old lady pushed through the double glass doors of the embalming room. I entered, expecting a chamber of horrors— a room full of dead bodies stacked to the ceiling. But there was only one corpse laid out on the table in preparation for the procedure.

He had long black nails. Wispy blond hair. A frail-looking

body with a purple line of abrasion around his neck. Even without his makeup, I recognized him immediately.

"Lucian!" I said, gasping.

"That's not your sister," the lady said.

"I know that," I told her. "But I know *him*!"

"Well, he hasn't been kidnapped. He's deceased."

"God, what happened to him?"

She consulted some paperwork on the table. "Suicide. Death by hanging."

I stood there a moment, paralyzed by confusion. Had Lucian slipped up with the fake noose and done himself in for real?

But I didn't have time now to speculate on the manner of his untimely death. I pointed to a bank of refrigerated drawers. "Open those."

The old lady sighed and began yanking them open. The first one contained a naked old man who was a deep shade of blue. I averted my eyes from the sight of his shriveled little winky. Chrysanthemum Lady slammed the drawer home as I ripped open the other ones.

Nothing. No one.

"You must have a storage room," I said to her, pinching my nostrils. The combined odor of embalming fluid and death was about to make me heave.

"You're free to look yourself," she said. "As far as I'm concerned, this tour is over." I followed her back into the hallway, and she pointed me to a staircase. "Down there."

I threw open the door and ran down the stairs into the musty basement. It was full of boxes, digging implements, discarded furniture. I pulled the chain on a lightbulb hanging in the center of the room. It swung around crazily, illuminating the swirling dust motes I was stirring up, flashing across the dank walls. I ransacked shelves full of spare bulbs, steel drainage pans, assorted tools and electronics. But there was nothing in the room large enough to conceal a human. No closets, no hidden compartments, no alcoves.

I ran through rows of boxes, irrationally banging on them. None was big enough to house Terry.

"Terry! You in here?" I yelled in desperation.

At last I gave it up and pounded back up the stairs, just as all three Bruces met up in the hallway.

"Anything?" I asked them, coughing up dust.

"Uh-uh."

"Come on. Maybe there's something in the back."

I ran through the kitchen, the Bruces right behind me. I shoved through the screen door that opened out onto the parking lot, then stopped cold when I saw what was sitting in the middle of the lot.

A sleek mobile home with a red racing stripe down the side. A top-of-the-line Rialta.

"She's in there!" I shouted.

Bruce One threw himself up the retractable stairs of the RV and yanked on the knob. It was locked.

"Break it!"

One whipped his leg up and smashed it with his foot. The knob cracked off, dangling from the door. He thrust his hand into the hole and flipped the tumbler, then swung the door open.

We rushed inside, heads swiveling as we looked for a body-stashing place.

"Window seat!" I said.

Bruce Two ripped up the cushioned seat atop a storage compartment. It was empty. Three did the same with the window seat on the other side. We ran through the mobile home, throwing open all the cabinets and closet doors.

Terry was nowhere.

"Where *is* she?" All of my panicked energy left me in a rush.

My hands were shaking, my knees collapsing in on themselves. I almost fell, catching myself on the wall of the RV.

I had a view down the short hallway to the sleeping quarters. There was a double bed on a platform, made up with a dark green coverlet. Underneath the platform was a large drawer for storing pillows and blankets.

"That drawer!" I yelled.

Two Bruces took a dive at it, yanking it open.

And there she was.

Terry lay on top of spare pillows, surrounded by them. Gagged, hands and feet tied, clutching the cell phone in her hands. Tears streamed down her face.

"Terry!" I cried in relief.

"*Mmmmmmmphhhggg!*" she answered.

Two of the guys lifted her out of the drawer and sat her on the bed. Her eyes were wild above the gag, and I could hear her thoughts: *Cut these ropes before I lose my shit!*

Bruce Two tossed me a Swiss Army knife. I went for the gag first, sawing on it for a few seconds until it snapped. Terry spat it out and immediately started yelling.

"What the hell took you so long? Didn't you get my message? Where were you guys? I was going crazy, cooped up in there!"

"It took us a while to find you," I explained, cutting at the cords around her hands. And then, furious: "Your message said you were in a coffin!"

She looked around, her eyes adjusting to the surroundings. "I'm in a motor home?" she said, confused.

"Yes!"

"What happened to you?" Bruce One asked her.

"I went into the room where they display the coffins," Terry said just as the rope on her hands gave way. She rubbed her wrists, breathing heavily, and continued: "Someone came up behind me and put a cloth over my nose. That's the last thing I remember until I woke up in the dark."

"Naturally you thought it was a coffin," I said. "That was the last thing you saw before you were attacked. And you were surrounded by padding."

She gave me a weak smile. "Good thing I had the cell phone with the text-messaging feature, huh?"

I laughed and rolled my eyes. "Good thing not even a brush with death can keep you from rationalizing your compulsive buying habits," I said, reaching for the bindings at her feet.

"Whose motor home is this?" she asked. "Herb and Sandra's?"

"Looks like it," I said. "Bruce, go check the registration in the glove compartment."

I didn't hear movement, so I looked up from the cutting.

All three men were staring down at me.

"You didn't specify a Bruce," Bruce Three said.

"*Any* Bruce!"

The three of them ran for the front of the home, getting jammed up next to the kitchen table. They struggled for a second, grunting and pushing, big shoulders shifting, then Bruce Two finally popped out in front.

Terry smiled at me, sniffling. "Thanks for coming to my rescue, Sis."

"Don't mention it."

Bruce Two called out from the front of the home. "Registered to Herb Applewhite of Burbank."

"Son of a bitch," Terry muttered under her breath. "The Applewhites kidnapped me?"

"Don't jump to conclusions," I said. "We don't know how you got here. It could have been an opportunistic move—whoever kidnapped you saw the RV here and decided to stuff you in it."

"Was the door locked?" she wanted to know.

"Yeah."

"Who else would have a key? Who else would know about the drawer under the bed?"

I shrugged, then shushed her because I'd heard voices outside. The Bruces heard them, too, freezing in place to listen.

We heard a woman say, "It's beautiful!"

No doubt about it—Sandra's voice.

"And it's all ours, baby," Herb said.

Footsteps on the metal staircase. "Herb, the door's broken!"

"Huh?"

"We had a break-in at the funeral home?" Sandra whined. "Jeez, is nothing sacred?"

The door swung open and Herb and Sandra stood there speechless, eyes adjusting to the dark interior and the sight of a motor home full of intruders.

"Hi, Herb, Sandra," Terry said.

"You broke the goddamn door?" Sandra glared at me. "You're turning out to be a real pain in the ass, missy."

"I don't think they did it," I said to Terry.

It took ten minutes of quick talking to convince Herb and Sandra that we were innocent victims in this scenario, the Bruces backing us up all the way. I pointed to the cell phone Terry was still holding.

"This is how she sent me the message. Do it, Ter. Show 'em."

She lay back on the bed, hands joined at the wrist as if they were tied.

"I had managed to pull the phone out of my pocket. I laid it on my lap and I pushed the buttons like this. I sent the message, *Im in coffin,* because I thought I was. The last thing I remembered was looking at the coffins in the funeral home."

"Why would someone want to kidnap you?" Sandra asked, perplexed.

"I don't know," Terry said. "A warning?"

Sandra made a face and sighed. "Well, this whole business has gotten me hot and bothered. We got anything cool to drink in here, Herb?"

"We just took delivery on the damn thing!" he said. "You think they stock the bar at the dealership?"

"What do I know about it?" she said. "I never had one a these before. We'd better head home, then. We'll have a bunch of thirsty mourners there waiting for us."

"You girls want a ride in a top-of-the-line Rialta?" Herb asked proudly.

"That's okay," Terry said. "We have our own wheels."

It finally occurred to me to ask. "Why'd you take delivery here, Herb? Why not at your home?"

Herb gave Sandra a worshipful look. "I thought she'd need a little cheering up right after the funeral. I wanted to surprise her."

"You surprised me, all right, you big lug." Sandra bussed him on the cheek and swatted his flat butt. "Mad about the boy," she said, winking at me.

This was *very* peculiar, I thought. Herb and Sandra were acting more like lovebirds headed for their second honeymoon than bereaved parents.

My next thought: *Something's rotten in Rialta*.

We watched as the Applewhites took off in the spanking new mobile home. "Shouldn't we have called the police?" Bruce One said. "I mean, about the kidnapping?"

Terry shook her head. "We have to pace ourselves. Too much calling the police, they'll think we're crying wolf."

"Who's crying wolf?" I said. "You really *were* kidnapped. I really *was* gassed. That was *real blood* on the motorcycle."

"Yeah, but it wasn't really a dead body in the noose when we called them over to Darby's house."

"Uh," I said, remembering the waiflike corpse I'd seen in the embalming room, "it may have been, at that."

Terry gave me a puzzled look. "What?" she said.

"What?" the Bruces echoed.

I nodded toward the back door of the funeral home. "Lucian's in there."

"He showed up?" she said, not getting it. "Where's he been?"

"I don't know where he's been," I said. "But he's not going anywhere."

She gasped. "You mean he's dead?"

"Yeah."

The Bruces gasped.

"Who's dead?" Bruce Three said.

"A guy you don't know."

"Phew," Three said, wiping his brow.

"How?" Terry demanded.

"Would you be terribly surprised to hear it was death by hanging?"

twenty

When we arrived at the Applewhites' house, the reception was in full swing. Sandra was good and looped, and Herb had shucked his navy blue jacket and gray slacks in favor of a golf shirt and checked pants, giving the impression he couldn't wait to hit the links. We'd left the Bruces inside the mobile command center to watch the street.

Sandra approached us with a tray. "Have a cheesh ball, girlsh," she said, her pronunciation sliding downhill.

We each took a toothpick and speared a ball of sharp cheddar rolled in pecans.

"Mmm, good," I said, mushing one around in my mouth.

"Darby loved my cheesh ballsh," Sandra said, dabbing at her teary eyes with a cocktail napkin. "Oh, well. *C'est la vie, c'est la vie,*" she said with a noisy sniffle.

Crocodile snot? I thought cynically.

"Sandra," I said. "There was a man at the funeral who came in with a woman and a little girl, do you remember?"

"Pardon my fingersh." Sandra picked up a cheese ball and bit into it. "A man? What'd he look like?"

"Big man, sandy-haired. His wife wore a floppy hat. They had a little girl."

"Oh yeah." She waved the remainder of the cheese ball at me, flecks of pecan hitting my shirt. She didn't ask me to pardon her pecans, however. "I saw 'em," she confirmed.

"Are they here?"

She cast her gaze around the room. "Haven't seen 'em. Why?"

"I was just wondering who they were."

"Somebody from school, prob—" Sandra gasped. "You don't think they were the ones that kidnapped Terry?"

"We don't know," I said. "The woman left and never came back to the funeral. But really, it could have been anyone in all that mayhem."

It was true. Any one of the mourners could have slipped out during the fight or its aftermath and done the deed.

"Hmmm, don't know them," Sandra said, then she flashed us her hostess smile. "Well, excuse me, girls. Gotta mingle."

We watched her weaving her lopsided way through the crowd, the hors d'oeuvres careening around the tray like nutty little pinballs.

"Does she look like she's in mourning to you?" I whispered to Terry, watching as Sandra "mingled" with the guests.

Terry shook her head. "She looks like Martha Stewart stoned on prison hooch, hosting a party on cellblock C."

"What I mean is, they're not exactly broken up. They couldn't wait to bury an empty coffin. They're hightailing it out of town tomorrow in the Rialta. It all smacks of one thing."

"What?"

"Darby's not dead and they know it."

Terry gloated at me. "Well, you've finally come around."

"And get this," I said. "I could have sworn I saw Darby at the cemetery."

"What?"

I nodded. "It was just a quick glimpse, but there was a woman in a long black dress. I thought I was seeing a ghost, but then it occurred to me—who could resist going to her own funeral?"

"Think Darby was the one who kidnapped me?"

"I don't know," I confessed. "Why would she?"

"Maybe to scare us off the case. I mean, killing me would have been easy. They used ether or something. I was out. They could have stabbed me or strangled me—" She locked eyes with me for a second. "We've got to get Herb and Sandra to admit that she's still alive."

"No way." I shook my head. "They're committed to this charade, for whatever reason."

Terry's face lit up suddenly. "Hey, I've got an idea."

I recognized the wild spark in her eye. "Does this idea involve cold war technology?"

"Yeah, baby." She leaned over and whispered it into my ear.

Terry went out to the mobile command center, and I went to work distracting the Applewhites. I asked Herb to show me his golf swing, then offered to help Sandra pass the cheese. Terry was sneaking back into the kitchen when she caught Sandra's eye.

"Need something, sweetie?" Sandra asked.

"Just a refresher." Terry picked up a highball glass from a nearby table. "Don't trouble yourself. I'll get it."

After a couple of minutes, Terry came back out of the kitchen with an upraised thumb pressed next to her pant leg. She cut her eyes to the front door.

Time to launch Operation Burbank Storm.

I grabbed Sandra in a hug. "We have to go, Sandra. Sorry."

Terry shook Herb's hand. "Good luck in Scottsdale, Herb. Send us a postcard when you get there."

Sandra's eyes misted over. "Thanks for all your help, girls," she said.

"Oh, we're not done yet," Terry told her.

Sandra got a worried look. "Not done?"

"No, we won't be done until we find Darby's killer," Terry said. "*And* her body."

"Well, you gotta keep moving or you'll be consumed by your grief," Sandra said, sounding like the jacket copy of a self-help book.

"So true," I said. "Well, take care."

They followed us out to the front porch and waved goodbye. I looked back over my shoulder to see them standing there with their arms around each other. The bereaved parents, stoic in the face of their loss.

Or a couple of lousy fakers.

We sat in the mobile command unit for the rest of the afternoon, down the block from the Applewhites' house. Bruce One was stationed in the swivel chair in front of the monitor, and I stood watching it over the top of his buffed head. We had a high angle view of the Applewhites' kitchen, thanks to the Pom cam Terry had planted in a ceramic elf on top of the fridge. There was no audio—we'd buried the only microphone we had with the casket—so the video would have to suffice.

If Darby was alive, we were betting she'd show up at her parents' house on this, the day of her own funeral. Failing that, we'd follow Herb and Sandra when they took off in the motor home. Sooner or later, we were sure they'd hook up with the allegedly dead girl.

Terry and the other Bruces were playing poker on the floor, which was covered with pillows and strewn with Burger King wrappers. The interior of the van smelled of onions and fried grease, the gourmet aroma of the burger monarchy.

"Any action?" Terry asked, crunching a french fry.

"Nope," I reported. "Sandra's refilled her drink twice, and Herb came in and put Saran wrap on a couple of cheese ball trays, then stuck them in the fridge."

"Any guests left?"

"No, they're all gone."

"Hit me," Bruce Two said to Terry.

She slapped two cards down in front of him.

"Four," said Bruce Three, placing four cards facedown.

Terry dealt him four new ones.

"Woo-hoo!" said Bruce Three, looking at his hand.

"*Love* the poker face," Terry muttered.

"Oh." Bruce Three clamped his jaw shut and tried to look neutral as he ante'd up another buck. "Coulda been a bluff," he said sulkily.

Bruce Two folded. "I'm out."

Bruce Three peered over his cards at Terry. Terry stared him down, as if trying to read his hand in the pupils of his little brown eyes. Then she tossed another dollar on the pile.

"What ya got?" she said.

Bruce Three fanned out his cards. A king of spades and four twos.

"Nice, but not good enough, buddy." She laid out four eights and an ace of hearts.

"Dang," Bruce Three said, as Terry snapped her cards together and scooped up the kitty.

"Wait a second," Bruce Two said, his eyes narrowing. "*I* had an ace of hearts. How could *you* have one?"

Terry gave him a *Don't be stupid* look. "There can't be two of them, Bruce. You must have had an ace of diamonds."

"Did so," Two insisted. "Ace of hearts."

Bruce Three gave Terry a strange look. "Let me see your cards," he said to Two, grasping for his discarded hand.

Terry snatched up Two's cards, mingling them quickly with the deck. She pulled out a card and held it up for him to see. "Ace of diamonds, dopey. Diamonds."

Bruce Three grabbed for the cards. "Lemme see that deck," he said to Terry.

Terry jerked it out of his reach. "You calling me a *cheater*?"

"Gimme!"

He lunged at her, ripping the deck out of her hands. Terry tried to grab it back from him, and a full-on wrestling match ensued. Before anyone could stop them, the six-footer made of muscle and the redhead made out of pick-up-sticks were locked in mortal combat, rolling around on the floor of the van and screaming at each other.

"Cheaters never prosper!"

"Big stupid lug!"

"Cheatercheatercheater!"

The van was rocking on its axle, threatening to flip over. Bruce Two and I jumped into the fray.

"Hey! You're going to give us away!" I tried to yank Bruce Three's arms off of Terry. His hand flew up and smacked me on the nose.

"Yeow!" Galaxies of stars sprang into my vision.

Terry and Three stopped their tussling, giving me guilty looks.

"Sorry," Terry said sullenly. "*His* fault."

"My fault? You're playing with a loaded deck!"

"Coul' thsomebody please get me some icthe?" I said through a fog of pain.

Bruce Two grabbed a soda cup and poured leftover ice onto a napkin. "Here, this'll keep it from swelling."

"I hope you're pleasthed with yoursthelvesth!" I said to Bruce Three and Terry.

Terry stuck out her bottom lip. "I *said* I was sorry."

"Hey!" Bruce One suddenly yelled from his station. "There's something going on!"

All of us scrambled over the pillows and the playing cards and fast food detritus to see what was happening.

I pressed the ice to my nose, watching the monitor. Sandra was standing next to the kitchen table. Herb opened the side door, the one that led out onto the driveway. She and Herb stepped back in surprise as a hooded figure in a long black cloak swept into the house.

We all held our breath.

Sandra's hands flew up in the air, as if the figure had pulled a gun on her.

"It's Darby!" I said.

Terry held up a finger. "Wait."

Sandra rushed the figure, pulling the hood down and throwing her arms around what turned out to be a young woman.

Terry peered at the screen. "Oh . . . my . . . God." She turned to me, goggle-eyed. "It's Pammy!"

"The little sister?" Bruce One swiveled around to look at her. "Are you sure?"

"I'd swear to it," Terry said, nodding.

The young woman removed the cloak from her shoulders, laying it over one of the kitchen chairs. She did resemble Darby, though she was thinner and plainer. She wore a T-shirt, jeans, and sneakers under the disguise. She turned and grabbed Herb in a hug. Sandra held up a vodka jug, offering her a drink.

Pam shook her head and sat at the table while Herb retrieved a platter of cheese balls out of the fridge. He set them down in front of the girl, who set upon them like a hungry homeless person, which she may well have been.

She pulled something out of her pocket and handed it to Sandra. Sandra stared at the thing in her hand for a second, then stuffed it in her apron pocket.

The conversation was frenzied, both parents asking questions at once. Pam's head swung back and forth, attempting to answer one before the other got the next question out, jamming cheese balls into her mouth the whole time.

Terry turned to me. "What do we do, bust in?"

I thought about it for a second. "She may run."

"We could block all the exits," Bruce One suggested.

"Yeah, but what right do we have?" Suddenly I was feeling much less sure of myself. We wanted to catch Darby coming home undead, but this was something else. The return of the prodigal daughter.

Terry's eyes flashed angrily. "Look at her! She's wearing a cloak in Los Angeles in July! She's the one who poured blood on our motorcycle! She's the one who gassed you and kidnapped me! She's in this thing up to her chinny-chin-chin!"

I stroked the bridge of my nose, trying to focus my thoughts through the ache. "We don't know that," I said. "Just because she's wearing a cloak, it doesn't make her guilty of all that."

"Who else could it be?" Terry insisted. "She's been playing like she's on the run from her abusive husband, so no one's been looking for her. It's a perfect cover. Meanwhile, she's perpetrating crimes and making it look like the vampires did it."

"There's one way we can be sure," I said. "Let's see if there's a black Volkswagen in the neighborhood. Whoever poured blood on the motorcycle took off in one."

"But she could get away!" Terry protested.

I pointed to the monitor. "We'll keep our eye on this. If it looks like she's gonna run, we'll follow. But we can't pin anything on her unless we see the Beetle."

Bruce Three jumped into the driver's seat and cranked the engine. "Where to?" he asked.

"Go down the street a ways, then turn around and come back," I told him.

We combed the street for two blocks without seeing the

black Beetle, then Bruce made a U-turn, retracing his route. We passed the Applewhite residence again, all the while watching the touching scene on the monitor, the reunion of the long-separated parents and daughter.

But *were* they long-separated? Or had the whole underground railroad story been concocted by Sandra and Herb to keep us from discovering the truth: the three of them—parents and younger daughter—were all part of a conspiracy involving the staged death of their firstborn.

At the intersection, Bruce Two pointed down the side street.

"Eureka!" he shouted.

There was the Beetle, parked under the overhanging branches of a willow tree.

I looked back at the monitor. Pam was standing now, pulling the cloak's hood back over her head. "She's leaving. Bruce Two, you stay here with her car. If she gets past us, don't let her get away."

"Roger!" He saluted and jumped out of the van.

On the monitor, Pam was hugging her parents again.

"Burn rubber, Bruce!" I yelled at our driver.

Three spun the van in a squealing circle, then floored it back to the house in the next block, just as Herb was opening the door for Pam on the monitor.

"Quick!" Terry yelled. "She's going out the side door!"

"Don't worry!" Bruce Three pushed the pedal to the metal, jumping the curb at the edge of the Applewhites' yard. We heard the painful scraping of the undercarriage on concrete, then we plowed over the grass toward the motor home in the driveway, blocking Pam's exit.

Pam stood just outside the door on the driveway, frozen in shock at the sight of the van barreling toward her. Then she recovered her senses and turned on her heel, running toward the backyard.

We piled out of the van and took off after her.

"Bruce Three!" I pointed to the front door. "Don't let them leave!"

He turned and dashed toward the front. The rest of us pursued the flapping cloak through the backyard fence and out into the alley.

Pam was quick like a fox and we were slow like pigs gorged on burgers, our legs cramped from sitting in the van all afternoon. Pam darted through someone's yard. We followed, then saw her running across the next street toward another house. We ran up the house's driveway after her, and caught sight of her running down the alley toward the end of the block.

She rounded the corner of a house, and before we could catch up to her, we heard a car door slam, followed by the squealing of tires. We got to the street just in time to see the Volkswagen speeding away from the curb. This time I was able to make out more of the license plate number: DED100.

Dead one hundred?

Bruce Two was lying facedown on the grass under the willow tree. We ran to him, lifting him by the arms to help him to his feet. "She hit me from behind," he said, ashamed. "Ran straight into me and knocked me on my face." He brushed at the newly mown grass stuck to his cheeks. "I tried to get up again, but I slipped in these damn dress shoes on the wet grass." He shook his head. "How humiliating. Knocked over by a girl."

"You're lucky that girl didn't stab you in the back," I told him.

Minutes later we were back at the Applewhites' house. Herb and Sandra answered the door when we rang, but they wouldn't meet our eyes.

"We need to talk to you," Terry told them.

The couple looked at each other, and after a moment's nonverbal communication, stepped back from the door.

"The Bruces are going to be waiting outside, so don't even think about running," Terry warned them.

Herb and Sandra acknowledged this with a nod, then moved into the family room. They sat huddled together on the couch, their eyes trained on the floor. I closed the door, leaving the Bruces standing guard out front.

"We need to know what Pam was doing here," I said as I approached them in the family room. "It *was* her, wasn't it?"

Sandra looked up at me, copping a righteous tone. "I don't see that that's any of your business," she said.

"Not our business?" I said. "You *made* it our business! You and Darby."

"We've been harassed and gassed and tied up," Terry said through clenched teeth. "We might have ended up as dead as that girl in the coffin, whoever she was—"

"Who*ever* she was?" Sandra said.

"Cut the shit, Sandra," Terry said. "We know Darby's not dead. Now you'd better start talking or we're going to go to the police with what we know."

"The police?" Anxiety raised the pitch of Sandra's voice above its usual barroom husk. "Can't you just leave it be?"

"Leave it be?" Terry snorted in disbelief. "There's been a murder, Sandra! And now someone else is dead as well. Darby's roommate, Lucian. Know him?"

Sandra and Herb shook their heads.

"And you never will," I told them. "He was hanged. They think it was suicide, but it's an awfully strange coincidence, don't you think? Now tell us what you know about all this or we're going straight to the cops!"

Sandra lowered her face into her hands. "Haven't we been through enough?" she whimpered. Herb put a skinny arm around her shoulders.

"Been through enough *what*?" Terry said with a harsh laugh. "Enough lying?"

Sandra winced at the sound of Terry's voice. "You can't know what it's like," she said. "You wouldn't say that if you did."

"Know what *what's* like?" Terry demanded. "What are you talking about?"

I tried a more soothing approach. "Tell us what's going on. We're not your enemies." I paused. "That was Pam who was just here, wasn't it?"

Herb and Sandra gave me a tentative nod.

"What was she doing here?"

Sandra pulled a wad of bills from her apron pocket, holding it out to me. "She brought us this."

Terry eyed the money. "That's a nice chunk of change. What's it for?"

"Getaway money," Sandra muttered.

"Getaway from who?"

"Damien, Pam's husband."

"Why do you need to get away from him?" I asked. "Has he been harassing you?"

Sandra snorted and rolled her eyes, as if to say that was the least of it.

Herb sat forward, an elbow on his knee, rubbing his chin stubble, looking exhausted. "He calls us from pay phones and leaves messages: 'You and your bitch daughter are gonna die.' We find dead animals on the front porch, their guts strewn all around. I sit up nights by the front door with my hunting rifle. We never sleep—"

"He was trying to intimidate us, to get us to tell him where to find Pam," Sandra said. "Then he got frustrated and threatened to kill us all. He even threatened to kill Jimmy!"

"He'd kill his own son?" I asked, genuinely shocked.

Herb and Sandra gave each other a look that contained something. What was it? Some sort of shameful secret?

Finally, Sandra fessed up: "Jimmy's *not* Damien's son."

"Not his son?" Terry said. "Whose son is he?"

"Pam had an affair—can you blame her?" she went on. "Damien was beating her! She met a nice boy who wanted to take her away from all the hurt. Damien found out and chased him off, but she was pregnant. That's when the real torture started, when Damien found out the baby wasn't his."

"But he wouldn't let Pam go, neither," Herb said, jabbing at the corners of his eyes with his fingertips. "He made her stay so he could make her suffer, then he started beating on poor Jimmy as soon as he could walk."

I shook my head. "I can't believe he'd take out his anger on an innocent child."

"Man's an animal," Herb said with a growl.

"His first wife disappeared off the face of the earth," Sandra said. "He said she ran off, but . . . no one's heard from her in all this time."

Terry turned and sent me a look: *This is bad.*

"Why didn't Pam go to the police?" I asked gently. "If there was child abuse—"

"She did!" Sandra's hands went out in supplication. "It took all her courage, but she brought an accusation. They arrested him, charged him even. There was gonna be a trial, but he skipped bond. Now he's out there somewhere beyond the arm of the law."

We stood there a moment in silence.

"You have no idea where he is?" Terry asked.

The Applewhites shook their heads.

"Have you seen him in the act, leaving the dead animals?"

"No," Sandra said. "We haven't laid eyes on him in years."

"But you recognized his voice on the phone?"

"He used one of those electronic voice changers," Herb said, jiggling the skin on his neck to demonstrate.

"Then how do you know it *is* Damien who's been threatening you?" I said.

Herb and Sandra looked at each other. "Who else could it be?" Sandra asked.

"We're not saying it isn't," Terry said. "It could be. But I do know this—you can't solve anything by running."

Herb sighed. "We don't know what else to do. We've gone through legal channels, for all the good it did us."

"He's out of control," Sandra said. "First he just wanted Pam and Jimmy. He was frustrated he couldn't get to them, so he came after us. He shot out our windows two weeks ago."

"We'd decided on a whim to go bowling," Herb told us. "Otherwise we'd have been right in the line of fire."

"And the police . . . ?" I said.

"*The police, the police,*" Sandra mocked. "They took a report, okay? They got some shell casings. No one's been arrested. No one's even been questioned!"

"So you bought a mobile home and you're taking off," Terry concluded.

"We're not really going to Scottsdale," Herb told her. "We're gonna stay on the road. Don't know how long, maybe the rest of our lives."

This situation was much more complicated than we had imagined. I decided to take my own advice and follow the money. "Where did Pam get the cash?"

Both Sandra and Herb looked down at their feet. Herb wiggled his toes inside the black socks.

"Does it matter?" Sandra asked quietly.

"It matters if she killed someone for it," Terry said.

"Pammy, kill someone?" Sandra hawked up a laugh. "Our girl would never kill anyone!"

Was that true? We didn't know Pam from a hole in the wall anymore. She was no longer a little girl in the shadow of her older sister; she was a grown woman. A desperate mother allegedly on the run from a violent sociopath. I sighed and turned to Terry. She signaled, *Don't look at me.*

"You didn't even ask her where she got it?" I said.

"I asked," Herb said, with a guilty peek over at Sandra. "But she said she couldn't tell me."

"Didn't it occur to you that it was strange, her coming into a bunch of money just as a girl turns up dead?"

"A girl?" Sandra said with a snort of indignation. "Her *sister*."

"We can't even know for sure it was Darby," Terry argued. "Her body's disappeared."

"But we saw her *before* it was taken! Our baby's gone, don't you understand that?"

Terry put her face in her hands, shaking her head.

"Once and for all," I said to Sandra, "tell us the truth. We have to know—is Darby alive or dead?"

Sandra said vehemently, "She's *gone*, she's buried. Leave it alone!"

Talk about a non-response response.

"Okay. We can confirm all of this about Damien easily," I said, nodding to Terry. "If you're lying, we'll know."

"Why would we lie?" Sandra said.

I almost laughed.

"Listen," Terry said, raising a determined face to the couple, "if we could find Damien and turn him over to the police, would you stop this running?"

"It's no good," Sandra said. "He'll get out again and start the whole thing over. He's obsessed."

"He wouldn't be granted bail again, I promise you."

Sandra stood and snatched a cigarette out of a tray, whipping up her silver and turquoise lighter. "You'll never get him." *Click, click, click.* The flint wouldn't ignite. She snapped the cigarette in half and tossed it against the wall. "They've *tried*."

But Terry wouldn't give up.

"What can you tell us about him? We know he played football—what else?"

Sandra sighed and looked around the room. "Anybody need

a drink?" No one responded. "Oh, yeah, *I* need a drink." She stood up and headed for the kitchen.

Herb watched her go, then turned back to us. "Damien was a first-round draft pick with the Minnesota Vikings, but he crapped out in the second season. Broke a knee in an early game, so he started beating up on his wife."

"He had nothing left but his anger," Sandra called over the clinking of ice cubes. "He needed to blame someone for his failure, so he went after Pam. When the baby came along he got even meaner."

"What did he do after he left football?" Terry asked.

"Don't know," Herb said. "I think he lived on a stipend from the team for a while, but it's probably run out by now."

"How does Pam support herself?" I asked him. "Does she have a job?" I was less convinced than her parents that Pam had a legal right to all that money.

Sandra walked back in, stirring the drink with her finger, a new cigarette dangling from her lips. She must have had a pack in every room. "Pam's smart," she said in a proud mother-hen voice. "She was real good at biology. If she'd been a little more motivated, she could have gotten her MD. But she settled for less."

"What did she do?"

"She worked in a clinic as a phlebotomist," Sandra said.

"A phlebotomist?" Terry said. "What's that?"

Sandra removed the cigarette from her mouth and swigged her drink before answering. "It's someone who draws blood."

twenty-one

*W*e went back to the command center, where the curious faces of the Bruces peered out at us from the windows.

"*That*, ladies and gentlemen," Terry said, climbing into the van, "is what's known as a smoking frigging gun."

"What smoke?" I said, following her inside and closing the door behind me. "And what gun?"

She gave me a look. "What's the matter with you? It's obvious now. Pam killed the girl in the coffin!"

"We don't know that."

"Do so."

"Do not."

"Do so!"

The Bruces swiveled their heads back and forth between us like spectators at a women's tennis match.

"Hello?" Terry said. "Does the word *phlebotomist* mean anything to you?"

"It didn't mean anything to you five minutes ago," I pointed out.

"What's a phlebotomist?" Bruce Three asked.

Bruce One bopped him on the head. "Don't interrupt."

"Ow."

"Come on, Kerry," she said. "It's obvious—Pam had the means *and* the motive."

"What motive?"

"Darby wanted to disappear. She got some girl to replace her, then they killed her. The whole world—the whole world including Damien—thinks Darby's dead and Pammy's underground, then *boom!* The family piles into the Rialta and gets out of Dodge."

"God, could they really be that devious?"

"Devious? Where do you think the money came from, bake sales?"

"What money?" Bruce Three said.

Terry thumped him on the noggin.

"Ow."

"And Herb and Sandra?" I said. "Are they in on this?"

"Have to be. They're covering for their little girls, backing them up."

"But Sandra showed us the money," I said. "She didn't have to. And they seem genuinely afraid of Damien—"

"So they're really afraid. Maybe they're afraid enough to go around killing and stealing to get away from him."

Bruce Three said, "Are you gonna explain this to us later?"

Everyone in the van swung a hand up in the air. Bruce Three ducked under his arms.

"I don't think we can believe anything they tell us," Terry went on. "I think they're all a bunch of liars. And what bugs me most is there's an innocent kid caught up in all of this."

"Little Jimmy? Well, if they're all a bunch of liars, how do we even know there is a Jimmy?"

Terry grimaced. "If they made *him* up, I'm really gonna be pissed. I hate being played with."

"Well, we're not going to solve anything sitting here," I said. "Let's get going."

Bruce Two jumped behind the wheel. "Where to, boss?" he said, looking at me.

At least *he* knew who was boss around here. I ignored the look on Terry's face and said, "We need to pay a visit to the remaining roommate. Let's go find out what Morgoth knows about all of this."

"Sure wish somebody would explain all of this to me," Three complained as the van screeched away from the curb.

"Ow!"

We went directly to Darby's former domicile on Venezia Court and came upon Morgoth, packing all his worldly possessions into the back of the tiger-striped hearse. We pulled up just as he slammed the hatch. He looked over in surprise as Terry and I alighted from the van.

The surprise was mutual. He'd been completely transformed. The fangs were gone and his face was clear of makeup, the skin a healthy rosy color instead of deathly white. Strangest of all, he'd bleached his hair a bright yellow that perfectly matched the lemon stripes in his plaid sport coat. His widow's peak now looked like a canary on his forehead instead of a crow.

"Going somewhere?" Terry said to him. "Costume party? Meeting of the Young Republicans?"

"Oh, hi, uh, glad you could see me off," Morgoth said with a weak smile. "I'm going back to Texas."

"Texas?" I said. "Kind of sudden, isn't it?"

"I'm homesick."

"What happened to your fangs?"

He rubbed a hand over his mouth. "I filed 'em off. It was just a phase I was going through," he said. "I'm ready for something else."

I narrowed my eyes skeptically. "You're ready for mechanical bulls and country music? What happened to the romance of being a vampire?"

He gave me a shrug. "I'm over it."

"Just like that, huh?" Terry said.

Morgoth nodded.

"This wouldn't have anything to do with Lucian's death, would it?" I asked.

He twisted the keys in his hands, looking down. "You heard."

"I more than heard, I saw. He was laid out at a funeral home on the table, cold and lifeless." This statement had the calculated effect. Morgoth's lower lip began to quiver. "What happened?"

Morgoth's eyes began to well up. "He killed himself. I didn't know what else to do, so I had him taken to the mortuary where Darby's funeral was. His parents are coming down from Wyoming to get the body."

"Why would he kill himself?" Terry asked.

"I don't know, but he did. Now I got no one to share the rent with anymore, so . . ." He reached for the hearse's door handle.

Terry put her fingers in her mouth and whistled. The Bruces came thundering out of the van. Bruce Two leaned against the driver's-side door, glancing casually down at his cuticles. Bruce One stretched himself across the hood, reclining on his elbow. Bruce Three propped one foot on the front bumper, an arm resting on his thigh.

"I gotta go!" Morgoth whimpered. "Get those big apes off my car."

The Bruces registered no offense.

"The big apes are going to stay there until we get some answers," Terry said. "We're curious *why* you have no one to share the rent with. Two of your former roommates have died under mysterious circumstances, and you're running off to Texas. Doesn't look good, Morgoth."

"I'm not running . . . and it's Bobby!"

"Bobby?" Terry asked, looking at me.

"Bobby Joe."

"Look, Bobby Joe, we don't want to cause you any trouble," I said, "but two people are dead. First Darby, now Lucian—"

"Michael," he said meekly.

"His name was Michael?" I said, and he nodded. "Okay, look. Tell us why Michael killed himself and we'll let you go."

"I don't know. Maybe it's a curse." He looked over at Bruce Two, who was still blocking the door with his huge body. "Coming with me to Plano?" he asked.

"Too flat," Bruce Two said, not budging.

I put a hand on Morgoth's shoulder. "Did you find Michael dead?"

He nodded, face collapsing. "He was my only friend . . . nobody else would hang out with me."

"What about the police? They don't think it was foul play?"

He shook his head, sniffling. "There was no sign of a struggle. And he had a history of hanging himself. 'Suicidal ideation,' they called it. Plus he left a note."

"A note?" Terry said. "What'd it say?"

" 'Sayonara, suckers.' "

That sounded a little jaunty for a suicide note. Now that I thought of it, it reminded me of "Arrivederci, baby."

"He wouldn't kill himself for no reason," I said. "He had to have a reason."

"Tell us what's going on," Terry urged him. "Does it involve Darby, too? Is she alive somewhere?"

He rubbed his forehead with enough intensity to separate muscle from bone. "She was supposed to be alive. I don't know anymore. If she is, she won't be for long."

I felt my pulse quickening. Morgoth was now admitting that

he, too, knew that Darby might still be alive! "What happened? What caused all this trouble?"

He sighed, his shoulders going limp. "We drank . . . we drank forbidden blood."

I frowned at him. "I thought you had donors. Share and share alike. What's forbidden about that, as long as you're all consenting adul—"

"No!" He choked on a sob. "No, I'm not going to tell you. They'll find me. They'll find me and they'll kill me and—"

Terry grabbed his plaid jacket by the lapels. "I've had enough of this! Tell us who you're talking about or I'm gonna pummel you!"

Morgoth jerked away from her and wiped his nose on his sleeve. "Like that's worse than what they'd do to me," he said.

Terry stepped closer. "Who?"

He looked at her, pleading. "Look, if I don't get out of here *now,* I'm dead, okay? Just . . . get them off my car and let me go. *Please.*"

Terry gave him a look of disgust mixed with pity. He stared back at her, desperate. She relented with a sigh, signaling for the Bruces to move away from the car.

Morgoth yanked open the car door and threw himself on the seat. But Terry grabbed the top of the door before he could slam it shut.

"Just tell us one thing—you didn't kill anyone, did you?"

"I told you," he said, tugging on the armrest, "I'm a lover, not a killer."

Terry released the window. Morgoth or Bobby Joe or who-ever he was slammed the door and peeled away from the curb, the tiger-striped caboose fishtailing down the street.

I waved as we watched him go. "Happy trails, pardner."

" 'Forbidden blood'?" Terry said, shaking her head. "What's that supposed to mean?"

"Maybe it was true vampire blood."

"Oh, so you believe in real vampires now?"

I took a deep breath and let it out again. "I have no idea what to believe anymore."

The Bruces went home for the evening, after we promised to lock all the doors and put salt on the windows. Terry and I spent a few hours searching online for Damien Turnbo. We found notices of his draft pick by the Vikings, articles about his knee injury, and the address of the duplex he had lived in with his wife and son up until a few years ago. After that, he disappeared.

We found a copy of the complaint alleging spousal and child abuse, harassment, and vandalism. There was an arraignment in Van Nuys Superior Court. A notice that Damien had skipped on his bond. A mug shot from his booking.

He had a broken nose, a square face, and brutish little eyes. His light brown hair was cut in an eighties-style mullet—short and furry on top, long and scraggly in back. I wanted to break out into a Billy Ray Cyrus song just looking at him.

Terry read out loud from the complaint. "Cigarette burns on the boy's arms . . . bruises on his throat . . . Jesus, a fractured skull . . ." She turned to me with eyes blazing. "I want to kill this fucker!"

I felt the same way about child abusers. If there was a God, I sincerely hoped he had a very special torture chamber outfitted for them in the hereafter.

"At least the Applewhites told us the truth about that. I wonder why Pam married the guy. She _was_ a smart girl—"

"Oh, come on," Terry scoffed. "She was a mousy nobody, and he was a star football player who was going places. I'm not surprised she went for it. Anyway, they don't start right in with the abuse. They suck you in first, and once you're good and stuck, _then_ they start the torment."

"Yeah, I guess so . . . Well, at any rate, we're out of this, right?"

She looked at me as if I'd spoken Swahili.

I threw up my hands. "Terry, pardon the cliché, but this is a 'job for the police.' I don't care what Herb and Sandra say. We'll tell Bagdasarian what we know—"

"What we *think* we know—"

"And leave the rest of it to the professionals, who actually get *paid* to figure out who killed who, and to put themselves in harm's way in the process."

"Look, we started this, we have to finish it."

"Says who?"

"Says the saying: 'If a job is worth doing, it's worth doing well.' "

"Oh, yeah, like that's your motto."

She gave me an eye roll. "Where's Darby?" she said, challenging me. "Why is she in hiding?"

"I don't know and I don't think I care! My brain hurts from trying to figure it out."

"Okay, who killed Lucian?"

"Lucian, himself. He's cursed, remember?"

She smiled. "But why is he cursed? It's all still a mystery, see? We can't walk out in the middle of a mystery. What would Columbo say?"

"Columbo's not going to say *anything*. He's a fictional character! He doesn't exist!"

She sucked in a breath. "Bite your tongue."

I grabbed my hair in two fists and pulled, throwing myself facedown on the couch. Muffy jumped up on top of me.

"Ugh!" I cried as she landed on the small of my back. "Now I'm a paraplegic."

Terry picked Muffy up and set her on the floor. "Okay, I'll give you a good reason to keep going," she said.

"Why?"

"I'll make your life a living hell if you don't."

"Ha! Too late for that, Hades Girl."

"Come on, please? Pretty please? Pretty please with as many pretties as you please?" She folded her hands and plastered a suck-up smile on her face.

"Ewww," I said, grimacing. "You sucking up is not a pretty sight."

She dropped the pose. "We have to find out for sure whether Darby's alive. If she is, she knows who the dead girl was. She's the key to all of this."

I sighed. "How would we even find her? More surveillance on the Applewhites?"

She paced, biting her lower lip. "That won't work again—they're onto us. What else do we know about Darby?" Terry snapped her fingers and ran to the office alcove. "The Femmes! If we can locate the other girls in the band, one of them may know where to find her. Let's see where they're performing."

She jumped on the computer and pulled up the home page for the Flatlining Femmes. There was a banner across the photo of Ephemera.

REQUIAT IN PACUM. THIS WEB SITE MAINTAINED BY
THE FANS OF EPHEMERA. FOREVER MAY SHE LINGER.

The paragraph below explained that the group had disbanded after the tragic death of their lead singer. Terry clicked on the photos of the band, but the members were listed only by their goth names—Respira, Apnea, and Goreena. We weren't likely to find those in the White Pages.

"Dang." Terry sat back in her chair. "We could probably track them down through the vampire scene, but it'd take a few days."

I went into the dining room and grabbed my shoulder bag off the table, pulling out the steno pad. "If we're doing this"—and as far as I was concerned, I was doing it only to humor her—"we're at least going to be systematic about it. No more stumbling around blind."

"Fine, good," she said. "You're right. We want to be organized. Diagram away."

I knew she was only humoring me as well, but I didn't care. "Okay, let's start with Lucian's death. We saw him hanging from a noose, which was supposedly a gag."

I drew a stick-figure representation of a hangman's noose and body.

"He apparently pulls this stunt to freak out solicitors," I said. "Then, after Ephemera is killed, he ducks out on his job at the morgue, at about the same time her body disappears from there. Then he shows up *actually* dead, strangled. The police refuse to investigate—"

I drew the international NO sign over the hangman.

"*Refuse* is a strong word," Terry said. "Maybe they investigated but didn't find any evidence of foul play, like Morgoth said." She gave me a sly smile. "There's one way we could find out for sure."

"How?"

"Ask!"

Oh, of course. I was getting too wrapped up in our conspiracy theories to think of the obvious. "You want me to call Bagdasarian?"

"Uh-uh. Detective Baggy-Butt wants information from us, but that doesn't go two ways. He's not going to leak anything about an ongoing investigation."

"He told us about the body going missing," I reminded her.

"He knew Sandra would tell us anyway. *I know.* What about Johnny boy? He's always good for a little scoop."

I shook my head adamantly. "I can't call him."

"Why not?"

"Because of . . . because I can't."

"Why not?"

"I can't talk to him until I figure out where our relationship is going."

"There are people who've been together for twenty years who don't know where their relationship is going!"

She stared me down until I caved. "Okay, I'll try him," I said, sighing. "Probably he won't even answer." I knew the best way to reach Boatwright was on his cell phone, so I tried him at his office instead. To my surprise, my whole body got warm when I heard him speak on the voice mail recording.

"Hi," I said. "It's Kerry. How are you? . . . Wonder if you could help us out with a little information . . . It's really no big deal . . . In fact, if you're busy, don't even worry about it . . . On second thought, just forget I called . . . It's nothing. Okay, bye."

I slammed the phone down.

Terry stared at me. "*That's* how you get information?" she said in disbelief.

"I was nervous. I told you I didn't want to talk to him."

The phone started to ring, and I stared at it trilling there on the table. But I couldn't make a move to answer it.

"Pick it up and talk like a human!" Terry said.

"God, you're pushy!" I grabbed up the phone. "Hello?"

"Hi." Damn, it was him. "I was here on the other line, and I, uh . . . got your weird message."

I cringed. "Yeah, about that—"

"You're wondering about the kid who hanged himself, the roommate of the Queen of the Undead, now the Queen of the Actually Dead?"

I had a creepy feeling I was being observed. "How did you know?"

"Lucky guess. He left a suicide note in his handwriting. There's no evidence that anyone else helped him along."

"They didn't think the suicide note was a little cute? I mean, '*Sayonara*, suckers'?"

"Where'd you get that?"

"His roommate, Morgoth. Aka Bobby Joe of Plano, Texas."

"Well, you're right. That's what it said."

"I don't suppose there's any chance he isn't really dead, is there?" I asked, then mentally flogged myself. What was I saying? I saw the guy laid out on the slab with my own eyes. "No, forget I said that."

"Why *did* you say that?"

"I don't know. These people are very strange. They pretend to be dead when they're not, then they actually kill themselves and make it look like a gag."

"Who pretended to be dead when they weren't?"

"Darby Applewhite, the aforementioned Queen of the Undead. We're pretty sure she's still alive."

There was a silence on the line.

"You there?" I said.

"Yeah. LAPD is still treating her death as a homicide, and her disappearance as body theft."

"Well, they're misinformed. Someone else died in her place," I said, realizing as I did how wacky it sounded.

"Who died in her place?"

"That's the mystery," I said.

"Got any proof of this?"

"Well, I—"

"Just curious. Not that there's anything wrong with making up your own version of things just for the fun of it . . ."

My teeth started to grind. "I'm not sure I like your condescending tone."

"I'm not sure I like your tendency to stick your nose into homicides."

"Well, I'm not sure I like you sticking your nose into *my* business!"

"Well, I'm not sure I like your business!"

"I'm not sure I want to keep having this conversation!"

"Then why the hell did you call me?"

"Terry *made* me!"

Oh boy, I thought. *That was real mature.*

We both retreated to our corners, breathing heavily.

"Look," he said, after a long moment, "I didn't mean to be—"

"An arrogant, controlling asshole?"

A beat, and then he said, "I was going to say possessive."

Oh, damn. "Listen, maybe we'd better take up this subject another time." *When I'm thirty.*

"Sure," he said.

"Thanks for the info."

"Anytime."

"Bye now."

"Yeah." He hung up.

I threw the cordless phone on the couch angrily. "I told you that was a bad idea!"

Terry shook her head, laughing. "My fault you can't conduct your affairs like a grown-up?"

My blood started to boil. "*Me* not grown up? Me? I don't spy on you and your dates. I don't go flashing the porch lights when you're kissing."

She peered at her nails. "I've been too busy moving our business forward to *have* dates."

"Oh, I see. I'm somehow neglecting the business. I've got a sort-of boyfriend, so now the roof is caving in."

"You said it, not me."

"And that gives you the right to involve us with vampires and spend all our money on gizmos?"

It was time to confront the reality of the situation. All of this *was* payback, but not for some imagined slight. Terry was jealous of my relationship with Boatwright, and she was acting out because of it. She saw this revelation on my face and suddenly got nervous.

"What?" she said.

"Have you been trying to get my attention with all of this?"

"All of *what*?"

"That's it, isn't it?" I said, nodding. "The vampires, the equipment . . . You're afraid I'm going to abandon you, so you've made sure we're up to our eyeballs in shit so I can't."

Terry moved around the room, picking up cushions, pretending to look under the couch.

"Oprah? Dr. Phil? Come out, come out wherever you are . . . we're about to have a moment!"

"You know it's the truth," I insisted.

She sat down on the couch and glared at me. "That is so . . . insulting!"

I wouldn't let her off the hook. "But true."

"I am not going to sit here and—!"

She stopped midsentence, the fight in her taking flight. Then she nodded, looking down at her boots.

"Yeah," she admitted reluctantly. "It's probably true."

I was too shocked by her turnaround to react. My blood was up, my breathing shallow. And here she was, making a naked admission of guilt. She'd completely hijacked my moment of indignation.

"Well, I wouldn't worry about it," I said, plopping down next to her on the couch. "He's not going to like me after this."

"Don't be silly, of course he will," she said, giving me a painfully sincere look. "Boatwright's a great guy. Probably make you a wonderful husband." She paused. "You know, I only want you to be happy."

I couldn't believe it. I was touched. Could this mean that Terry was finally growing up? "That's really nice of you," I said, swallowing against the lump in my throat. "You mean it?"

"*Fuck, no!*" She jumped off the couch. "What I want is for us to be the best investigators who ever lived, the dynamic duo to the death! I don't want you getting hitched to some cop who's gonna clip your wings!"

I had to laugh. "Well, at least that was honest."

I wasn't sure I was ready for a grown-up Terry, anyway. Might be even scarier than Terry the way she was now.

"Think you could be happy with that?" she asked.

I shrugged. "The way things are going, I think I'll probably have to."

"Great," she said, beaming. "I knew I could count on you."

What choice did I have?

Oprah and Dr. Phil could go jump in the lake. What did they know about coming from the same ovum as someone else, about jostling for space with her in the same womb? (Which is probably where Terry got into the habit of kicking me in the shins.) What did they know about suckling at the same breast with her? (Which is probably where she learned how to poke me in the eye and make me cry.)

She was my sister, yes. But she was more than that—she was literally my other half. And it was my duty to stick by her, whatever the cost.

I parted my fingers in a Vulcan salute. "Dynamic duo to the death!"

"All right!" she yelled, jumping up and down, the pups prancing around with her. "Let's go nail us some vampire killers!"

I got up off the couch and started up the stairs to my loft. "Tomorrow, okay?"

"Well, duh. Hey, don't forget to set your alarm. We have an early appointment with a Dr. O'Brien at the—" She looked down at Muffy and Paquito and whispered, "V-E-T."

twenty-two

The vet appointment the next morning was for Muffy, but we didn't want Paquito to think we were playing favorites, so we arranged to get his toenails cut while we were there. That way he'd feel like he'd had a special afternoon at the doggie spa.

They were so excited about going for a motorcycle ride, we could barely get them into their riding pouches—a blue vinyl Hello Kitty backpack for Paquito, a pink Josie and the Pussycats backpack for Muffy. With their heads poking out of the tops, they looked like tiny canine jack-in-the-boxes.

We sat in the waiting room with a quivering greyhound that was so delicate that it could have been made of balsa wood and wrapping paper; a long-haired white cat who yowled in a carrier case; a man with a tropical bird on his shoulder that kept repeating, "Greetings, Earthlings!"; and a big burly man with an eight-foot boa constrictor coiled up in a moving box.

They called us into the examination room and a young

Indian vet came in to greet us. She had gleaming black hair in a French twist and a diamond stud in her nose.

"You're Dr. O'Brien?" Terry said, surprised.

"My husband's name," the vet said. "My maiden name was Vipujensana. I went from a name no one could pronounce to one nobody believes. That's life in the big city, huh?" She looked at her clipboard. "So what seems to be the problem with little Muffy today?"

"She gained a lot of weight very quickly," I said. "We're sort of new at being dog owners. We thought maybe we're giving her the wrong diet or something. And we wanted to rule out any, you know, pathology."

"Okay, let's have a look."

I took Muffy out of her carrying pouch, and Dr. O'Brien placed her on the scales. "Fifteen pounds, hmmm . . . Pretty porky, aren't you, sweetie?"

Muffy wiggled as Dr. O'Brien felt around her middle, smiling and snorting as if she were being tickled. The vet put a stethoscope to her belly. She listened for a moment, then looked up at us again.

"Congratulations," she said.

"Excuse me?" Terry and I said.

"It's a litter."

"A litter of *what*?" I said, my mind stalled on the word, unable to comprehend the obvious.

"Puppies, of course."

Terry and I looked at each other, agog.

"She's *preggers*?" Terry said.

"Technically, she's in whelp. But 'preggers' will do. You didn't notice the distended teats?" She rolled Muffy over on her side, and Terry and I leaned in to inspect the teats in question.

"Sure," I said, "but I just thought she was, you know, well endowed."

The vet raised her eyebrows. "I take it you didn't breed her deliberately."

"We assumed she'd had her tubes tied!" Terry said.

O'Brien laughed. "Where did you get her?"

"Her previous owner died," I said. "Kind of suddenly. Then we inherited her."

"Oh. Well, if you didn't know she hadn't been spayed, naturally you wouldn't take precautions against her coming in contact with males. And you wouldn't believe what they'll go through to get to a female in heat. They'll trek for miles, jump over ten-foot fences—"

"Oh, no." Suddenly it dawned on me. "He didn't have to trek for miles. He didn't need to jump a fence. He just had to stroll across the living room and *have his way with her*."

We all turned and looked at Paquito. He was panting happily in Terry's arms, his little pink tongue sliding in and out of his mouth. *How about that cigar?* he seemed to be saying.

"You dirty *dog*," I said, shaking a finger at him.

"We thought their relationship was platonic!" Terry said. "What's he doing fooling around? He's not even a year old!"

"Males can reproduce as early as six months," O'Brien told us.

Then a horrible thought occurred to me. "Oh, no. A pug and a Pomeranian-Chihuahua? They're going to be freaks of nature! Tiny little bodies with smashed-in black faces and great big pointed ears? Long fur sticking out all over. They'll look just like—"

"Doggie troll dolls," Terry said, completing my thought.

"Well, that's one possibility," the vet said, laughing. "We'll see soon enough."

Dr. O'Brien thought it might be only a couple of weeks before Muffy delivered the pups, but we opted for an ultrasound just to be sure. And there they were. All snug in Muffy's tummy, just waiting for the right moment to pop out and scare everyone to death with their freakish genetics.

We left the clinic loaded down with prenatal vitamins, a whelping box, a heating pad, thermometer, scissors, towels, baby scales, tweezers, hemostats, a baby suction bulb, milk-replacement formula, baby bottles, sterilizing solution, puppy wormer, and baby nail clippers.

Some of it "just in case." All of it expensive.

"Well, you broke the bank, Mister," Terry said to Paquito as I got him situated in his backpack. "Proud of yourself?"

"Aarf."

I shook my head. "Look at him—'I'm the king of the world! I have spread my seed and it has borne fruit in yon bitch!' Well, there's not going to be anymore seeding after *this* litter!"

Terry placed Muffy in my pack, admonishing her as she did: "Here we are in the middle of a big case, and you have to show up pregnant. This is *not* a good time to be whelping a bunch of troll doll puppies."

I suddenly had an idea. "Maybe it's the best possible time," I said.

"What do you mean?"

"Well, we happen to be tied into the vampire community right now, and they like offbeat, strange things. We could pass them off as a freaky new breed."

"Oh, now you want to place our puppies in vampire homes? What happened to 'They're dangerous weirdos'?"

"Some of them are nice. And anyway, who else is going to want our poor little hybrids?"

She shrugged. "Yeah, you're right. We could make sure they were going to good vampires. No Shatáns or anybody like that."

"Absolutely not."

Now that I was over the initial shock, I was actually kind of excited at the prospect of having puppies. I chucked Paquito under the chin. "It's okay, pal. You were only doing what comes naturally."

"Our fault for not knowing more of your gynecological history," Terry said to Muffy, taking some responsibility for the blessed event. "But after this, you're definitely getting those tubes tied."

Muffy gave a snort of maternal pride.

Then we got on the motorcycle and drove the little horndogs home, their tongues flapping happily in the breeze.

When we arrived at the house, there was a message from Reba. She needed help at the soup kitchen again.

Terry threw her hands up into the air. "What is it this time? Is she doing their hair and makeup? Giving them all mani-pedis? Did she ask us to bring along some cuticle clippers?"

"I don't think so," I said. "It sounded urgent."

"If she keeps this up, we're going to have to ditch the private investigation business and take up social work full-time."

"Come on, we'll go slop some soup and be back in an hour or two. And we'll make it clear that from now on we can't come running every time she calls."

"I wish she and Robert would stay in Beverly Hills, where they can't get into trouble," Terry said.

"Do you have early-onset Alzheimer's, or what? They got into tons of trouble in Beverly Hills! And in Malibu—"

"Yeah, you're right. What was I thinking?"

We grabbed the bike and set out into midday traffic, which is actually midday slogfest. We slipped between the backed-up cars in a maneuver that still makes me nervous, but which is completely legal in California. You treat the spaces between the cars as your own private motorcycle lane, hoping no one tosses a live cigarette or hocks a loogie out the window, or changes lanes without looking when you're whizzing by. It's particularly dangerous in Los Angeles, where motorists are oblivious to anything outside the air-conditioned cabs of their wheeled pleasure palaces. Cars are valuable here. Human life is cheap.

As we got closer to Broadway, I saw a disturbing sight: a large plume of smoke rising into the air. Was there a grease fire in the kitchen?

Terry apparently saw it, too. She gassed it around the corner and down the street to the Compassion House. There, on the front lawn, was the source of the smoke—crackling flames leaping out of an oil drum.

Pollution billowed up from within and joined its parent smog blob in the sky. Even stranger, a bunch of the homeless people were disrobing around the oil drum, throwing their clothes into the flames, shouting and dancing around in some half-naked tribal dance of rebellion.

Terry screeched to a stop next to Reba's Mercedes. We jumped off the bike and ran for the oil can.

"What the hell!" Terry said to a woman who was stuffing a red designer jacket into the blaze. "What are you doing?"

"We can't make any money in these rags!" the woman yelled.

She was joined by the woman who'd been wearing Reba's riding outfit, and who was now gleefully stripping off her jodh-purs. I looked away from the white sagging flesh of her thighs and buttocks, exposed to all and sundry.

"I ain't goin' to no polo match," she screamed at us. "I'm goin' panhandlin'! I need appropriate attire!"

More homeless people streamed out of the house, many of them stark naked and screeching in protest. It was a horror show, a nudie version of *Night of the Living Dead*.

"Not another one!" I said in exasperation. "What is it with L.A. and riots?"

"Reba!" Terry shouted above the jungle din. She pointed toward the entrance of the house.

From the building, a "barely there" mob emerged, hoisting Reba over their heads. She was thrashing and twisting in their hands, but she was no match for muscles built on pushing overladen shopping carts every day. The crowd moved along like an army of ants carrying a tasty morsel to the queen of the hive.

Were they going to throw her in the fire?

Reba spritzed her abductors with the perfume atomizer, using it like a can of mace. "Down! Down!" she screamed. "Put me down!"

"Oh, we'll put you down, all right!" an old man cackled.

"Go pick on somebody in your own economic bracket!" another one yelled.

I spotted Lola in the middle of the throng. "Lola! Let her go!" I pleaded, trotting alongside her. "She was trying to help! She didn't mean any harm!"

"She's going overboard," Lola shrieked. "This here's a mutiny on the Good Ship Lollipop!"

We lunged at them, trying to thrust ourselves inside the naked cluster of street people, but we couldn't even get close to Reba. The mob stopped in the middle of the yard.

It began to sway, heaving back and forth. Someone yelled, "One . . . two . . ."

"They're gonna throw her!" Terry screamed, running to the front of the crowd.

I streaked across the yard, training my eyes on the sky like a wide receiver going out for a Hail Reba pass.

". . . three!"

Reba flew through the air, her skirt up around her waist, pantyhose-encased legs kicking wildly, launching her Jimmy Choo pumps into the air.

I collided with Terry and we fell to the ground just as Reba plummeted down to earth. She landed on top of us, our bodies breaking her fall.

Sirens started to wail in the distance.

"The cavalry is coming!" Reba said.

"Great," Terry said, her voice muffled by Reba's skirt. "Could you get off my head now?"

Reba declined to press charges. It was too soon after that little run-in she'd had with the law in Malibu, and she wasn't anxious to find herself back in the system again. But she resigned her voluntary position at the Compassion House, drawing the line at serving the insurrectionists their soup.

"Let them eat strudel!" she huffed.

Once the police had determined that no one had been hurt, they set about covering up the homeless people with fire department blankets. They and the firefighters had a good chuckle at the situation, sending out an emergency requisition for clothes from the St. Anne's Thrift Store down on Admiralty Way. Meanwhile they herded all the naked people into the lunchroom because they were in violation of public nudity ordinances. There they would await their new, more streetworthy wardrobes.

"So much for my social services career," Reba said as we walked her back to the Mercedes. "So much for noblesse oblige."

Someone had flung a pair of old boxer shorts onto her windshield.

Reba took off a shoe, balancing on one foot. She used the high heel to remove the shorts, flinging them into the gutter.

"Well," I said, "you tried."

"It's too soon for me to become a nun, anyway." She slipped her shoe back on. "There's life in this old booty yet."

Oh, please, let's not start with that, I thought. If Reba was annoying as a philanthropist, it was nothing compared to Reba in senior sex kitten mode.

"Speaking of which, still no word from Eli?" Reba inquired, eyelashes fluttering.

Terry cut her eyes to me. I could tell she was about to lie again, but I knew we couldn't keep the truth from Reba forever. The sooner she was aware of Eli's new love interest, the sooner she could move on with her life.

"Yes, we saw him," I said.

Reba dipped her chin, wiggling her shoulders. "And how was he? Moping around all hangdog and depressed because I rejected him?"

Maybe a blatant lie would be better. "Y-yeah," I said, "that's it, *hangdog.* Just the word I would use. He was hanging just . . . like a dog."

I saw Terry cringing in my peripheral vision.

Reba scrutinized my face suspiciously. "You're lying. You never could lie properly. He's seeing someone, isn't he?" She gripped my upper arms with her viselike little hands. *"Isn't he?"*

Terry wrenched Reba's hands away from me. "Reba, chill!"

"Don't you tell me to chill, young lady! I am not a package of ground beef! Who is she, some little chippie he picked up at the sports bar? Some leather-clad strumpet a third his age with great big bozooms?"

Oh, why had I not left it to Terry?

Don't even expect me to bail you out of this, she beamed to me.

"Actually, she's a classy blonde, about fifty." *The truth is a good thing, a good thing*, I chanted inwardly. "A judge in Superior Court."

Reba's mouth fell open. Obviously she'd never really expected any competition for Eli. She thought she'd play coy for a couple of months and he'd come crawling back to her on his knees, begging to marry her. And the news that her rival wasn't some empty-headed young bimbo apparently hit her hard.

She stood there a few moments, eyes glazing over, her breathing shallow.

Finally she said, "I want her rubbed out."

"What?" we shouted.

"You girls must know the sort of person I need. You must

come across them in your line of work." She moved in on us, a manic look in her eye.

We took a step backwards. "You think we know *contract killers*?" Terry said.

Reba's mouth turned up in a sinister half-smile. "I'll pay handsomely."

"R-Reba," I said, "you can't be serious."

"Oh, can't I?" She arched her eyebrows, homicidal fantasies dancing in her dilated pupils. "Can't I really?"

We stared at her, dumbstruck.

"It shouldn't be too difficult." Reba tapped a plum-colored nail on her upper lip. "She's probably a divorcée, lives alone. A gas explosion, I think. Yes, that would do the trick—"

"Reba!" I shouted.

She looked at me, annoyed. *"What?"*

I didn't know what to say. Our great-aunt had gone from Mother Teresa to Tony Soprano in just under an hour. I knew she was crazy for Eli, but I didn't know she was *crazy*. Talk about your green-eyed monster.

"Think about what you're saying," I said. "Would . . . would Jesus take out a contract on someone?"

She squinted off in the distance, considering it. *"Maybe . . ."*

"Jesus would *not* hire a contract killer," I said with all the spiritual authority of Tammy Faye Bakker.

Reba looked back and forth between Terry and me. She blinked a few times, seeming to come out of her agitated state. Then she smoothed back her hennaed hair, squared her shoulders, and laughed. "Well, of course I was only *kidding*."

Terry and I exhaled in relief.

"I wouldn't kill someone just because she's a dirty, dirty slut."

Terry slapped a hand to her forehead.

"Okay, that's good," I said, not about to argue the slut point. "We're . . . we're very glad to hear that."

Reba reached for the door to her car. "I'll just have to think of some other way of dealing with the situation."

"Checking herself into a rubber room?" Terry whispered to me.

"I'm off to Cedars-Sinai," Reba said, hopping into the front seat. "I've got no business campaigning for sainthood, anyway, with a child in the hospital. My first duty is to my son."

"Please give the ambassador our best," Terry said.

Reba closed the door and lowered the window to blow us a kiss. We could hear Barbra Streisand bleating from the CD player: *"I'm the greatest star, I am by far, but no one knows it . . ."*

That fits Reba's situation to a T, I thought. She'd been the greatest star in Eli's orbit for a brief, shining moment, but he'd lost that loving feeling. I just hoped Reba wouldn't resort to murder in an attempt to get it back.

twenty-three

*S*ince we were already in Venice, we went back to the boardwalk for lunch. We got a table at the Small World Café, an outdoor eatery next to the bookstore of the same name. We drank iced tea and ate turkey burgers, watching as the skaters whizzed by, their sweat glistening in the summer sun.

"What do you think Reba meant when she said she'd find some other way to deal with the situation?" Terry said, munching her burger.

"I don't know, but something tells me it will involve a violation of anti-stalking statutes."

The cell phone rang in Terry's pocket. She answered in spite of my dirty look.

"Hello? Angie, long time no see." She mouthed to me, *The tattoo artist*. "Really? When was this?" Terry snapped her fingers for a pen. I handed her one and she scribbled an address on her paper napkin. "Thanks, that's really helpful . . . Bye!"

"What was that about?" I said.

Terry snatched up the napkin, giving me a exultant grin. "Angie's got a friend at a doctor's office where they remove tattoos with laser treatments. The doctor treated a blond woman a week ago for removal of a black widow on her right cheek. Guess who?"

"Get out!"

Terry signaled frantically for the waiter. "Check, please!"

The waiter dropped off the check and I plunked down enough money to cover us. We ducked through the tables, then ran back out onto the boardwalk and down a side street to Pacific Avenue.

"Apparently it takes a few treatments to fully remove a tattoo," Terry said, jogging toward the bike. "Guess when her next appointment is?"

"When?"

"Right now! Guess where?"

"Come on, spill it."

"Alden Medical Plaza in Beverly Hills! Same as Gutzeit!"

I jumped in the air. "*Ándale, ándale!*"

She pumped her fist. "*Arriba!*"

$We\ zoomed\ over$ to Beverly Hills, keeping to the lane dividers the whole way. We made it blessedly butt- and loogie-free in only forty minutes.

The lobby of the medical building housed a coffee shop and a few small stores. There were lots of well-dressed people coming and going at a brisk pace—the lunchtime business crowd. A number of them were waiting for the elevator, so Terry and I ran up the stairs to the second floor.

We had no way of knowing if our quarry was still in the doctor's office, so I positioned myself next to his door. "I'll cover the office, you take the elevator at the end of the hall," I whispered to Terry.

She nodded and jogged to the end of the hallway.

I opened the door to peek inside. There were a few people in the waiting room, but none of them was Darby. I let it close again, just as the door to the ladies' room swung open a few feet away from me. A woman wearing large black sunglasses, a silk scarf, and a bandage over her cheek stepped out of the bathroom.

We both paused an instant, then she saw me and gave a little gasp of recognition.

"Uh-oh," she said.

"Hi, Darby," I said.

She lunged at me, knocking me sideways into the wall. I bounced off and spun around to see her running to the nearest bank of elevators. Terry was nowhere in sight.

Darby slammed her hand on the call button, then turned and saw me coming for her. She ducked toward the stairwell, yanking the door open. I threw myself against the door, slamming it shut. She whirled around and took off running again. The bell pinged on the elevator at the far end of the corridor, and the doors began to open. Darby ran for it; I was ten feet behind her and gaining. She lurched through the elevator doors at the same instant I dove at her knees. She tumbled forward into the car and headlong into the arms of my waiting sister. I fell onto the floor at their feet, landing on top of my shoulder bag.

"Got her!" Terry said.

I scrambled to a standing position, slinging the bag over my shoulder as I did. Terry ripped the sunglasses from Darby's face. Her blue eyes were like a trapped animal's, darting from Terry to me, to the closed elevator doors. But there was no escape.

"You look great, Darby," I said breathlessly. "Haven't decomposed a day."

She was too shocked to bluff. "Okay, you found me," she said, trying to pull herself together. She smoothed down the hem of her shirt, jerking her shoulders out of Terry's hands. "I guess I ought to explain."

Terry smiled sardonically. "Guess you ought, starting with who was dead in your coffin and how she got that way."

Darby grabbed her sunglasses from Terry, putting them back on. "There's a coffee shop at the base of the building," she said, punching the lobby button. "Why don't we go sit down and talk?"

"Sure," Terry said, "sounds peachy."

The doors opened on the ground floor. Darby stepped out first and I started to follow, but then she spun around with a gun in her hand.

"Get back!"

Terry and I threw our hands in the air. A security guard at the reception desk looked over. He got up from his seat, frowning, and started toward us.

"Look out!" I yelled. "The homecoming queen's got a gun!"

Everyone in the lobby hit the floor, screaming. The security guard whipped out his own gun and crouched in firing position. Darby turned and saw him, then aimed her gun at the lobby ceiling and fired off a round. The shot echoed explosively off the marble floor and walls. The guard spun around and dove behind his desk.

Darby took advantage of the chaos to run for the front door, hopscotching over the prone bystanders as she went.

She threw herself against the push bar and ran outside the building, where a black VW sat next to the curb. She yanked open the car door and jumped in. The engine caught, and the VW screeched out into the street just as we reached the sidewalk, the guard on our heels.

"Let's go for it!" Terry said, running for the motorcycle at the curb.

"Halt!" the guard shouted at our backs, chasing after us.

I yanked a business card out of the side pocket of my bag, thrusting it at him as I jumped on the seat behind Terry. "We'll come back and make a statement, I promise!"

"Why was she shooting up my lobby?" He looked stunned and almost hurt.

"Call the police!" I said, then was almost jerked off the bike as Terry tore away from the curb.

She took full and heedless advantage of the space between cars as we raced through downtown Beverly Hills. The black Beetle was stopped at a traffic light a block ahead of us.

The light turned green. The VW screeched into the intersection going left, cutting in front of the cars in the protected left-turn lane, almost getting itself rear-ended in the process. Brakes squealed and horns blared.

Terry signaled with a straight arm and veered over in the same direction, getting herself honked at and cursed to hell, as she hugged the outside of a silver Camry that was legitimately next in line. A man in the Camry's passenger seat pointed at us, shouting something behind his window.

The driver freaked and jerked his wheel into our space, causing Terry to overcorrect to the right, jumping us over the curb and up onto the sidewalk. A woman on the sidewalk screamed and threw her grocery bag into the air. A milk carton exploded against our front tire and a nectarine bounced off Terry's visor. I looked back and saw the woman do a tuck and roll into the alley next to a clothing store.

Terry kept us from killing anyone through righteous steering and insanely good luck as we sped along the sidewalk, pedestrians taking flight like ducks flushed from the reeds, then we whooshed down a handicapped slope and were back in traffic right behind the VW.

By this time there were a hundred or so honest citizens who wanted us dead, not to mention the woman with the silk scarf and the gun.

Wheee-eee-eeee!

I turned to see a Beverly Hills police car behind us, flashing his lights.

Terry didn't slow down.

"PULL OVER," came the voice on the speaker.

I hit Terry in the back. She shook her head, refusing to stop.

I turned back to the patrol car and mimed *I'm only the passenger*, shoulders shrugged, palms up.

Another patrol car pulled up beside him. Now there were two sets of flashing lights and two sirens going full blast. We turned onto Wilshire Boulevard going west.

"PULL OVER."

Terry stayed on the bumper of the VW, which plowed ahead with nary a flicker of its brake lights. All around us cars were pulling to the side of the road to let us pass. Another police car joined the procession from a side street. Now there was one patrol car on either side of us, one behind.

I looked over at the car to our left. The officer in the shotgun seat had his sidearm pointed at us. *So that's where they got the name "shotgun seat"* I thought stupidly.

"She's a shooter!" Terry yelled at the cops. "Make *her* stop!"

"PULL OVER."

Terry shook her head and kept going down the boulevard, which was now completely cleared of traffic in both directions. I looked back and saw that two more squad cars had jumped into the fray. Five in total, all of us traveling at forty miles an hour toward the freeway. *Oh, shit.* It was a slow-speed chase.

A helicopter materialized out of nowhere, hovering overhead. I looked up and saw a cameraman in a harness leaning out to catch the action. I gave him the *What can I do?* gesture, thinking the footage might save me from a charge of accessory when we were finally arrested. I mentally rehearsed throwing myself on the mercy of the court. *You saw me, Your Honor. I was captive!*

I slugged Terry in the kidney again for the benefit of the camera but she ignored me completely, running a red light as cars screeched to a stop in the intersection. I heard the squealing of tires and the crunching of radiator grills and began reciting the Lord's Prayer.

We came to the freeway and the VW jumped on going west. Terry followed up the ramp, the police cars right behind us.

Word had spread of the pursuit. People were pulling over to the sides of the freeway, leaping on top of their cars to wave at the passing parade, mugging up at the news helicopter. They thrust their fists in the air and egged us on with whoops and hollers. Police chases are considered great entertainment here in the Southland—the poor man's NASCAR. But the real fun would come when we ran over the spikes laid across the freeway lanes, blowing both tires and skidding off the road to crash into an abutment, where we would be stomped by the adrenaline-charged cops into a bloody pulp.

Maybe I could jump off the back of the bike.

I looked down at the asphalt whizzing by beneath my foot.

No good. Even if I managed not to get run over by the police cars I'd end up skinned like a fish, my bones pulverized into dust.

I was along for the whole ride.

Somewhere in a golf club in Florida, O.J. was watching us on cable TV, popping beer nuts and eating his heart out.

They didn't have time to lay the spikes across the freeway, as it turned out, so we followed the VW onto the 10 freeway west with our tires intact, taking the Fourth Street exit. The Beetle had to get off here in Santa Monica or be forced onto Pacific Coast Highway, which would be bumper-to-bumper with beach traffic on a summer afternoon.

It went down to Ocean Avenue and turned toward the Santa Monica Pier, where people hooked for polluted fish, rode on carnival rides, ate hot dogs and played arcade games, completely unaware of the drama about to unfold in their midst.

The Beetle passed under the arched entranceway of the pier,

but instead of plowing down the boards to the end, it pulled up to the edge of the carnival rides. Darby got out of the car holding her gun on the driver, who was a woman of similar age wearing a scarf and dark glasses just like Darby's. Darby was treating her like an unwilling captive, but Terry and I knew better.

This was no hostage situation. The two of them were born confederates—Darby Applewhite and her little sister, Pam.

Terry stopped short of the ride area. I jumped off the bike and turned around, hands behind me with my wrists together for ease of cuffing. I wasn't going to give the cops any excuse to rough me up. Terry did the same, yelling the whole time.

"She shot at us! She's a fugitive! Check with the guard at the Alden Medical Plaza! She endangered a whole lobby!"

Two officers rushed forward to arrest us. The female was Officer Smalley, according to her name tag. She had brown hair in a bun and sharp, merciless features. Her partner was an older male with a substantial gut, named Lindner.

"You're under arrest for reckless driving and evading arrest," Smalley said, snapping the restraints on my wrists.

"I'm so not evading, I'm so not evading!" Terry yelled, waving her hands behind her back. "I'm standing here *inviting* you to arrest me! You can't charge a person with inviting arrest!"

I watched as the rest of the uniforms fanned out over the carnival ride area. They chased the bystanders and tourists to the fringes, then formed a perimeter around the rides, guns drawn.

"I'll shoot her!" Darby screamed at them, jamming the gun barrel into Pam's cheek. "I swear I'll kill her! Get back, or she's a dead woman!"

The cops held their positions while Darby dragged Pam over to the Ferris wheel. Then she turned her weapon on the terrified ride operator, who had one hand in the air, the other on the controls. He stopped the ride to let the Applewhite girls onto a seat. There were several occupied cars above them. The operator stopped the wheel intermittently to let the other passengers off, who then ran screaming toward Ocean Boulevard, pausing only to say a few words to the waiting reporters.

Reporters. Great.

Meanwhile, Officer Smalley rifled through my shoulder bag for my wallet, then reached into Terry's jeans pocket for hers.

"Could you guys *please* confirm my story?" Terry said. "That woman shot up the lobby of a medical building!"

"We got that on the radio," Lindner said. "Was it self-defense? Were you threatening her?"

"No! You can see for yourself we're unarmed!" Terry said. "We're private investigators. We were trying to question her and she took a potshot at us."

Lindner looked up from my investigator's license. "What were you trying to question her about?"

"Her own alleged death," Terry said.

Lindner and Smalley exchanged a world-weary look, but Terry pressed on. "She was supposedly murdered last Saturday at the Dark Arts Gallery in Venice. It was all over the news—a vampire thing. You must have heard about it. Anyway, she turned up alive and we were trying to find out what happened."

Lindner pointed a finger at her. "The law takes a dim view of private citizens speeding through business districts, chasing down other private citizens. Endangering the public. Tying up traffic on the freeway."

"What?" Terry whined. "Whatever happened to the concept of citizen's arrest?"

"Let me explain something to you," Smalley said to her. "*We* are the police. *We* do the arresting. That's how it works. And now we're arresting *you*, little Ms. Citizen, for willful and wanton disregard for the safety of persons and property while fleeing an officer. Tell her what she's won, Johnny!"

"Six months in state prison and a ten-thousand-dollar fine!" Lindner said.

Smalley leaned into Terry's face. "You want to arrest people? Go to the police academy like everyone else, honey."

Terry stomped her foot in frustration. "You wouldn't even know who she was if we hadn't followed her! You wouldn't have caught her if it wasn't for us!"

I glared at Terry, beaming the message, *Quit while you're behind, moron!*

"Well, now we've got a hostage situation developing, thanks to you," Smalley said. "What do we have for people who cause a hostage situation while evading arrest, Johnny?"

"An additional six months to a year in scenic Sybil Brand Institute for Women!"

"She's not a hostage," I said. "The woman with the gun is Darby Applewhite and the woman with her is her little sister, Pam. Darby Applewhite is not dead, and that means the police had the wrong ID on the body in Venice, and that means some-one *else* died in her place."

Lindner looked up at the two women in scarves, now at the very top of the Ferris wheel. He took a second to consider it.

"And you think the woman up there is responsible for that person's death?"

"We don't know for sure," I said. "But shooting off guns in public places and pretending to take a hostage tends to show consciousness of guilt, don't you think?"

"There're a couple of police officers who can vouch for us," Terry said to Lindner. I gave her a *Don't you dare* look, which she ignored. "Detective Bagdasarian of the Pacific Division, and your very own Detective John Boatwright of Beverly Hills Homicide."

I wanted to cover my face with my hands, but due to the cuffs I had to content myself with clenching my eyelids shut while steam came whistling out my ears.

"Oh, you're *those* twins," Lindner said.

I opened my eyes again and saw Lindner grinning like the

Pillsbury Doughboy after being poked in the stomach. He pointed toward the head of the pier. "Speak of the devil. Here he comes now."

And coming he was, though not smiling like the Doughboy. Looking more like the Doughboy with hemorrhoids. Boatwright was striding forward angrily, head cocked at an angle, looking as though he were going to pound me into the planks of the pier as soon as he got within range.

"John!" I said, as he approached. "What brings you here?"

"I heard on the radio there was a freeway chase involving two female subjects on a pink Harley."

My brain took a short holiday. "How'd you know it was us?"

"*Lucky fucking guess!*" His eyes were ablaze, his jaw muscle vibrating at high speed. "What the *hell* were you doing?"

Terry scooted between us, attempting to bail me out. "It was my fault. I was the one driving. She had nothing to say about it."

"We were chasing Darby Applewhite," I said. "We found her alive, just like I told you. And now she's on top of the Ferris wheel with a gun on her sister, pretending to hold her hostage."

The phone in Terry's shirt pocket rang.

All of us stood there a moment, staring at her chest.

"Would you get that?" Terry said to Boatwright. "It could be her. She has my number."

He started to reach toward her breast, then stopped, giving me a sideways glance. "Get that phone, Officer," he said to Smalley.

Smalley grabbed the phone out of Terry's pocket and pulled it open. "Officer Smalley here," she said into the phone. She listened, then turned to Lindner and Boatwright. "It's the shooter. She wants to talk to her." She motioned to Terry.

Terry indicated her cuffs. "Can you take these off?"

Boatwright scowled. "No way. You're not going to talk to her. We'll wait for the hostage negotiator."

Smalley gave a businesslike nod and spoke into the phone.

"Ms. McAfee can't talk right now. She's under arrest. You're going to have to speak to the hostage negotiator."

I heard yelling coming out of the earpiece.

Smalley jerked the phone away from her head. "She says she'll shoot if she can't talk to one of the twins."

Boatwright sighed and took the phone from her. Smalley unlocked Terry's cuffs, then Terry grabbed the phone, punching a speakerphone button so everyone could hear.

"Darby?" Terry said. "Is that you?"

"Thanks a lot!" Darby screeched. "Look at the mess you've got us in!"

"Hey, you shot at us!"

"I didn't shoot at you, I shot at the ceiling. Don't you know what's at stake here?"

"I guess not. Why don't you tell me?"

"Only my sister's life!"

"What about the life of the girl who died in your place?"

A pause. "I had nothing to do with that!" Darby said.

"Nothing except dressing someone up like you, getting her a tattoo like yours, and letting everyone think you were dead!"

Darby's voice became shrill. "You're clueless! You were clueless in high school and you're even more clueless now, Kerry!"

"Terry."

"Whichever! Get out of my life!"

"I'd love to, but we've got two police jurisdictions after us, not to mention a vampire with a gas canister who likes to come in our windows at night and pour blood on our bike and kidnap us at funerals. Look, we know that's Pam up there with you, and we know you're not going to shoot her—"

"I'm not saying anything more. Just . . . *fuck off!*"

Darby disconnected.

I turned halfway and wagged my hands. Boatwright made a face and nodded to Smalley, who stepped up and freed me.

"Now what?" I said, rubbing at the chafed skin on my wrists.

Boatwright looked toward the entrance to the pier. "Now we wait for the hostage negotiator."

"I'm telling you, she's not a hostage!" Terry said. "You think she would plug her own sister?"

Boatwright gave Terry a look that said he thought sister-plugging might be an excellent idea. She stuck out her tongue at him.

"No," I said edgily, "she's not going to . . . *even if the sister richly deserves it.*"

"We only have your word that it *is* her sister," Lindner said.

"Yeah," Smalley added. "And there are people still in jeopardy. She could shoot the Ferris wheel operator. She could shoot a police officer."

I turned to Lindner. "Have you done a search on that license tag, yet?" I don't know where I was getting the attitude. Lindner made a signal to Smalley, who got on the radio in the car. After a second, she came back.

"Registered to Pamela Applewhite."

"That's what we've been *telling* you," Terry yelled. "It's Darby and Pamela Applewhite."

Then the phone rang again. Everyone looked at Boatwright for direction. He considered it for a split second, then nodded.

Terry hit the speakerphone. Darby's voice came through, sounding much more calm and in control.

"We're willing to give up."

Terry pumped a fist in the air.

"On two conditions," Darby added.

Boatwright grabbed the phone. "This is Detective John Boatwright of the Beverly Hills PD," he said into the speaker. "What are your conditions?"

"We want a lawyer. Now."

"Fine," Boatwright said. "You're entitled to a lawyer."

"And we need to go to the bathroom."

"We'll let you go to the bathroom and we'll get you representation. But first you must lay your firearm down at your feet and put your hands in the air. We need to see empty hands."

"And we don't want a lousy public defender," Darby said. "We want someone good, or no deal."

Terry stepped up to the phone. "We'll get you a great criminal lawyer, name of Eli Weintraub. He's the best. He got our aunt and cousin off a murder charge recently."

The patrol officers looked at her with raised eyebrows.

"Bum rap," she whispered to them. "They were stone innocent."

"Okay," Darby said through the speaker. "Go get him. And hurry. My sister has to go to the little girls' room."

And then she disconnected for the last time.

twenty-four

$\mathcal{H}$ours later, we were watching the news coverage on TV from the relative comfort of our couch.

"The kidnapper agreed to let the terrified passengers off the Ferris wheel," the reporter said, pointing over her shoulder. "You can see them behind me, running the gauntlet of police officers lining the perimeter. Things are anything but *amusing* here at the pier's amusement park on this summer afternoon, and it may be some time until it opens up again to the tourists, who are the very lifeblood of this city by the sea." She nodded sharply. "Back to you in the studio."

The anchorman looked out into our living room with a grave expression. "We'll bring you more on this afternoon's bizarre hostage situation at America's fun spot, the Santa Monica Pier, right after this short break."

Terry grinned, muting the commercial. "You know, we're getting even more publicity for this than we did for the terrorist thing," she said, sounding very pleased with herself. "Pretty cool, huh?"

I didn't respond. I lay on the couch, silently planning to kill her.

I know, I promised to be the Dynamic Duo to the death—but I don't think you heard me specify whose death it would be, or when it might take place.

On second thought, even with a charge of voluntary manslaughter, I'd be facing ten to fifteen years in the pen.

Better to kill myself.

I put a pillow over my mouth and nose, wondering how long I'd have to hold it there and how much force I'd have to apply until my lungs exploded and I was delivered from this nightmare that was now my life.

I must have sought solace in the minideath of sleep, because I awoke when Terry shook my arm.

"Hey, look! They've got a psychologist on, talking about us."

"What?"

I jerked the pillow off my face and saw an image of Terry frozen on the screen. She was in the back of Lindner's radio car, hand thrust up to the window with her fingers digitized out of the picture, presumably because she was flipping someone the bird. Her eyes burned like Aileen Wuornos's with intimations of serial killings to come.

My sister the psycho.

Cut to the psychologist in the studio, a slope-shouldered man with a furrowed brow and the last surviving pair of aviator glasses in the free world, who subjected us to instant on-air analysis.

"The girls are orphans, Dan. That explains their pathological need for attention. The terrorist episode gave them their first taste of fame, but as you know, the public is very fickle. As soon as they were no longer getting what they considered their fair share of notoriety, they involved themselves in another publicity-garnering event to get that rush—that *high*—they get from being in the limelight," he said, smug as only a PhD on TV can be.

"So fame is like an addiction for these girls?"

"Most definitely, Dan."

"They were national heroines after Flight 212. Now you're saying that they'll do anything to stay in the public view? Even if it involves becoming outlaws?"

"Yes. It's comparable to what we saw with Paula Jones, who went on *Celebrity Boxing* and posed nude in *Penthouse* to keep the public interested in her when her moment in the sun had expired. You haven't seen the last of the McAfee twins, Dan. They'll be staging another stunt before too long, mark my words—"

"*Eat* your words, Dr. Know-It-All!" I jumped up and grabbed the remote. "Eat 'em and choke!"

Click!

The TV went dark.

"Excuse me," Terry said, reaching for the remote in my hand. "I was learning something about myself there."

I stared at her for a long moment, my jaw hanging limp, and my whole body began to tremble with fury. "Oh, it's self-knowledge you're after, is it?" I winged the remote to the couch like an out-of-plumb boomerang. It bounced off and hit the floor, breaking into its component parts. "That's what this is all about? You need insight into your warped little psyche?"

She gave me a worried frown, eyes darting around as if searching for the nearest exit.

I moved toward her with short, jerky steps, my voice strangled. "Well, next time you're wondering what *motivates* you to jam up the whole west side while leading the police on a slow-speed chase and endangering the lives of innocent citizens and getting us arrested in the process, then why don't you ask me?

'Cause I'm the one that knows you, Ter . . . I'm the one who can read you like a cheap novel . . . You want to know what you are? *I'll tell you!* You're . . . *glarrggggrhhhrgggluhlaaa*!"

I slammed my mouth shut, amazed and horrified at what had just come out of it. I'd never before been rendered inarticulate by rage. This was a new low.

Even Terry looked alarmed. "Does your head hurt? Tongue feel kinda thick? Any lip numbness?"

"I am not having a stroke!"

She snapped back as if she'd been zapped with the phaser pain blaster. I took a small measure of satisfaction from that as I spun on my flip-flops and started up the stairs. But the satisfaction didn't last.

"Don't you want to see if we made Keith Olbermann's show?" she called after me. "Starts in five minutes."

I stopped on the staircase, my back to her. "Do we have any razor blades in the house?"

She took a moment to answer. "Just those pink Lady Gillettes, the plastic ones . . . Why?"

"No reason," I said as I made my way to the loft with the heavy tread of the damned.

"Okay, you can see it on tape tomorrow," she said cheerfully. "I'll let you know if Jay Leno says anything about us."

"Oh . . . *goody*."

I crawled under my bedcovers and prayed for oblivion.

Instead, the events of the day played out over and over again in my head, as if on some diabolical video loop.

After the pier, we'd been taken to the Santa Monica police station on Main Street—the Applewhites in one car, Terry and me in another. Eli followed in his gold LTD with the white vinyl roof, with Boatwright bringing up the rear.

Between Eli and Boatwright, our booking charges were knocked down to a misdemeanor violation of the vehicle code.

Could have been a lot worse—*felony evasion*. Terry's second strike under the three strikes law, two-thirds of the way to life imprisonment.

We were fingerprinted and released on our own recognizance, a "promise to appear" at a future court date.

I wasn't too worried about the charge. Eli would finagle something for us in court. He wasn't above using our national heroine status to get us leniency from the judge.

What was keeping me awake was the prospect of spending the rest of my natural life keeping Terry out of prison. Would she always need twenty-four-hour supervision? I wondered. Would I never have a life apart from her?

And if I wasn't my twin's keeper, who was?

twenty-five

*M*onday morning we were seated in Eli's office drinking coffee from mismatched chipped mugs. He had called us there to bring us up to date on our case.

Terry threw her black Pat Benatar boots up on his desk. "So what are we looking at? Jail time, a fine . . . what?"

"O ye of little faith." Eli shook his head mournfully. "I'll get the charges dropped."

"Really?" I said. "What makes you so sure?"

"We drew a great judge. A very fine and fair jurist, in my opinion. Name of Helen Lampert."

"Omigod," Terry said, cracking a smile. "Your new squeeze is our judge?"

He grinned back at her. "I think I can *squeeze* her into dropping the charges."

"How'd you do it?" Terry asked, slapping her thigh.

"Helen's clerk had a little talk with the clerk of the assignment judge—the two of them are dating, as it turns out. Anyway, we got the case assigned to Helen's courtroom."

"You are completely without ethics," I said, never so glad to know someone I could say that about.

"So disbar me." He chuckled, jowls jiggling with mirth.

"How do you know she'll go all the way and drop the charges?" Terry said.

"Well, if her disposition of the Applewhites' case is any indication . . ."

"*They* got her, too?" I shook my head. "What were they charged with?"

"Negligent discharge of a firearm, felony evasion of arrest. I pled them out on the first charge and the judge dropped the other one on the grounds that they were really evading *you,* not the police. She gave them a fine and probation."

I was aghast. "That's the worst they get for leading the police on the longest chase since O.J.?"

"O.J. didn't have the sympathy factor. These are two young women on the run from an abuser."

"But one of those poor young women is supposed to be dead, and the other one has some very shady source of ready cash," I said.

Eli waggled his eyebrows. "The better to pay her attorney with."

"Has everyone forgotten about the dead body?" Terry asked. "The one at the Dark Arts opening?"

"And what about Darby's parents?" I said. "They buried an empty coffin!"

"In good faith." Eli shrugged. "Far as I know, there's no law against it. They paid for the plot."

"This is unbelievable," Terry said, rolling her eyes. "Do we even have a crime here anymore as far as the police are concerned?"

Eli jabbed a thick finger in the air. "Number one, it is not a crime *not* to have been murdered."

Terry and I frowned at each other, trying to follow his logic.

He popped up another finger. "Two—Darby didn't take anyone hostage. She was with her sister at the pier and the sister denied any coercion, so no crime there. They said they thought they were in danger from you two because you wouldn't stop for the police."

"Oh, please," I said, groaning.

Finger number three. "They pulled the stunt on the Ferris wheel because they figured it was the only way to get their story heard, and to get safe passage from *you*. Incidentally, they wanted to get a restraining order against you, but I advised against it."

Terry gawped at him. "A restraining order! *We're* the victims here!"

"Let's not play the blame game, okay?" Eli said, sounding a lot like Johnnie Cochran rehearsing in the mirror.

"There was a dead body," Terry said. "We saw it. We touched it. And someone's sure as shit to blame for that!"

"Well, if someone produces this alleged body—"

"Oh, now it's an 'alleged body.' " I gave Terry a cynical smile. "I get it. As long as it's an 'alleged body,' your clients can't be arrested for murder."

"Bingo." He grinned at me. "No habeas corpus, no habeas crime."

Terry began shaking her head.

"Our main problem now is the abuser." Eli scratched his crotch, a sure sign that his mind was engaged. "Now that the girls are out in the open, he can get to them."

"Where are they?" Terry asked.

"At their parents' house. I want you to go talk to them."

"About what?" I practically shouted. "You just said they wanted a restraining order against us!"

"Yeah, but I persuaded them that I needed you on the case."

"Why?"

"Because they say they didn't kill the girl in the coffin, and I believe them. But sooner or later her body's gonna turn up, putting my girls in jeopardy of being murder suspects." I felt a twinge of jealousy when he called the Applewhites "his girls."

"I want you to locate this Damien scumbag." Eli leaned forward and punched the coffee-stained blotter for emphasis. "I think he killed the girl, believing she was Darby. If we can find him and nail him for the murder, then he goes to prison and my clients go their way in peace."

I looked over at Terry and saw she was thinking the same thing I was—*How did this figure? No one ever said Damien had threatened Darby before.*

"Well," Terry said, "we offered to find him so he could be locked up for child abuse, but Sandra and Herb turned us down. Of course, they were still pretending to believe Darby was dead at the time, so we didn't know which end was up."

"Well, thanks to you, she's not dead anymore. Which means she's in danger, as well as the little boy and the rest of the family. So I want you on the case on my tab. It's the least you can do since you outed them."

"The least we can do, huh?" I looked at Terry, who did a palms-up with her hands.

"You know what our fees are," she said, getting to her feet.

"By the way," Eli said, shuffling some papers on his desk, "how's your aunt doing?"

We stopped in the doorway, taken aback. What about the blond judgey-poo he had in his pants pocket?

"She's okay," Terry said. "She tried to turn her life over to a good cause, feeding the homeless. But it didn't work out so well."

"Why not?"

"The homeless people rioted and threw her out on her ass."

Eli's eyes bugged. "What for?"

"Spritzing them with perfume and dressing them in designer togs. They couldn't make any money on the streets."

Eli's guffaws made the windows rattle. "Ha! What a piece of work!"

"I think it's all been a reaction to your breakup," I told him. "She doesn't know what else to do with herself."

He stopped laughing and toyed with the curled edge of the blotter. "Oh."

"So . . . how serious are you with this judge?" Terry said.

His eyes went to the ceiling. "Serious? I don't know about *serious* . . ."

"Then she's just a good time?"

"Hey. Don't bad-mouth good times. There's few enough of them in this life."

I had to ask. "I thought you were having a good time with Reba?"

"Sure, I was—until she went to work on me."

"What do you mean?"

"Always trying to change me. My clothes, my hygiene, my speech. Hey, if I want a makeover, I'll call the fruits from cable TV."

"I know she was madly in love with you," I said, "just the way you are."

He rolled back on his chair casters and threw a foot up on the corner of the desk. The DNA that I shared with Reba forced me to notice that the heels of his wingtips were worn to nubs.

"Let me tell you something. I've had three marriages, so I'm sort of an expert. It happens the same way every time. In the beginning, they think you hung the moon. Prince fucking Charming.

"Then little by little they discover all the things that are wrong with you, and they peck away until you don't even dare pick out your own shorts in the morning. It's 'Wouldn't you like to try this nice dandruff shampoo, dear?' and 'Wouldn't you rather eat with your mouth closed?' What am I, six years old? I don't want someone to love me for my 'potential.' I'm potentially *dead* in a few years. I'd like to enjoy the time I have left."

I sighed, shaking my head. "It's not just you. She tells *everybody* what's wrong with them. I guess she should take a look at herself once in a while."

"Well," he said, pulling his foot down and bellying up to the desk again. "It is what it is, right? In the meantime, we got work to do. You girls get on up to Burbank."

"Don't go changin'," Terry sang to Eli as we headed for the door.

He laughed, picking up the phone to make a call. "Tell Priss to get the paperwork started, and get back to me as soon as you have something, okay?"

Priscilla was Eli's office manager. We caught up with her in the reception area.

"Hey, Priss," I said, "we're back on the payroll."

"I figured." She handed us the contract, ready to go, along with a pen.

"You're so on top of it," Terry said.

"We wouldn't get very far around here if I couldn't read the fat man's mind. Initials here, here, and here, please . . . Sign here and date."

We did as she asked, and promised to take her out for a vegan lunch as soon as all this craziness was over.

"Bye, girls," she said, waving as we went through the door. "Keep your garlic dry."

At the Applewhites house, Sandra threw open the door excitedly and enveloped us in her skinny arms, crushing us to her ample bosom. She had on a floral scent today, a big improvement over her usual eau de fermented juniper berry, and no highball glass in hand.

"I've got my babies back, and I owe it all to you two!" she cried.

Then she dragged us into the kitchen, where her offspring sat with Herb, eating pound cake and drinking coffee at the table. Darby was well scrubbed and blond once again. But without the vampire makeup, I noticed she was drawn and older-looking.

She jumped up and seemed about to hug us, too, but she stopped when she saw the look in Terry's eye. "I'm sorry about the shooting," she said. "I panicked. You know I would never have hurt you."

Terry decided to cut her a break. "You were aiming at the ceiling," she said, shrugging. "We weren't *on* the ceiling."

"Would you girls like some pound cake?" Sandra asked.

We declined.

"Thank you for the wonderful lawyer you found for the girls," Sandra said with the hint of a crush. "What a gentleman. He had that judge wrapped around his little finger."

And other parts of him, as well.

"He just hired us to work on your case," Terry told them.

"Oh, yeah?" Darby said, exchanging a look with Pam as she sat down again at the table. "I thought our case was all sewn up."

Herb stood to go, putting his dish in the sink. "Excuse me. I've gotta go gas up the Rialta. Thanks a jillion, girls."

I looked at Darby. "Gassing up the Rialta? Does your probation allow you to leave the state?"

"Isn't that great?" Pam said. "Eli fixed it so we can."

"What if Damien follows you?"

The girls looked at each other. Sandra went to the sink and began to run water over Herb's cake dish.

"We're pretty sure he won't," Pam said.

"How can you be so sure?"

"Trust us," Darby said, which caused Terry to bark out a

laugh. Darby lowered her head. "I guess I deserved that," she said softly.

"That and more," I said. "Sandra, will you excuse us for a minute? We need to talk to the girls."

"Oh, surely. Help yourselves to a cocktail, if you like." She waggled her sparkly gold acrylic nails at us and left the room.

After she'd gone, Terry skewered the sisters with a look. "If we're going to work this case, we need some answers."

"Answers to what?" Darby asked, as if everything up to this point had been crystal clear.

"Questions Eli can't ask you because he's an officer of the court," I said. "He can't suborn perjury if he has to put you on the witness stand one day, so there are things he can't know, such as whether you've committed a crime." I knew Eli would have no such compunction, but it sounded good. "You follow?"

They nodded cautiously.

"Who was the dead girl in the coffin?" Terry asked Darby.

Darby looked at her sister for her cue, getting a faint eye signal in return. "One of my band members," Darby said. "Her name was Nina."

"How did she get there?"

"I was going on the road with our folks and Pam," Darby said, twirling a strand of hair around her finger. "We were going to put as many miles between us and Damien as possible."

"Yeah, and . . . ?"

"The band was starting to draw big crowds, making good money. The other girls didn't want to break up, so we worked it out that Nina would take my place. She looked enough like me to get by in makeup."

"So she got your tattoo and was going to pass herself off as Ephemera?" Terry said. "And someone killed her, thinking she was you?"

"Right," Darby said, not looking terribly upset about it.

"She was your friend, and you're not more concerned than this?" I said, doing little to hide my disgust.

"Of course I'm concerned! Nina was a good girl. Not too quick on the uptake, but she had a beautiful voice. She was kind of a lost soul, needed the vampire scene to give her life meaning. I feel *awful* about what happened to her, but I can't take it back."

Well, there was a little remorse, at least. About enough to fill a thimble.

"Who killed her?" I asked. "You must have some idea."

"*None.*"

"You don't think it was Damien?"

She shook her head. "I only met him once. I'm sure he would never have put it together that I was Ephemera, Queen of the Undead."

Terry asked, "Well then, could it have something to do with the rival vampires you mentioned when you hired us?"

She frowned. "Rival vampires? I don't recall saying that."

"All right," I said, keeping my exasperation in check. "But this thing doesn't stop with you. What about your friends Morgoth and Lucian? Why did one of them hang himself? Why'd the other one skip town?"

Darby's eyes went up to the corner of the ceiling. "I . . . I just don't know," she said in a lame attempt at befuddlement.

Terry sandbagged her. "What's 'forbidden blood'?"

This question stopped Darby cold. She'd had ready-made responses to the other ones, but Terry had taken her by surprise, to judge by the redness creeping up her neck, the sudden rigidity of her body.

She gave us her biggest blue eyes. "What do you mean?"

Terry started tapping the bright pink nails of her right hand on the table. *Clickety clickety click.* Darby and Pam correctly interpreted this as the precursor to violence. They looked at me for help.

"You guys had better stop pissing her off, or there's gonna be blood on your mother's kitchen floor in about five seconds."

Darby forced out a little grunt of protest, but Pam held up a hand to silence her big sister. She looked me square in the eyes and I held my breath, sensing I was going to hear the truth for the first time.

"It's blood that came from someone who didn't know he was giving it."

Terry squinted at her. "Like who?"

Pam hesitated, tongue pressed against the inside of her cheek. "Like . . . someone who'd had blood taken at a doctor's office for analysis."

It took me a second, then comprehension exploded behind my eyes like flash fire.

Pam could have been a doctor . . . She was real good at biology . . . but she settled for less . . .

"Oh my God, *you* supplied it," I said, staring at her as if I were seeing her for the first time. The shy little sister who had grown into a woman engaged in an abominable enterprise. "You worked as a phlebotomist and you traded in blood!"

Pam's gaze moved past me and fixed on a wall plaque that said WORLD'S GREATEST MOM.

"That's *horrible*," Terry said. "That's worse than identity theft! Blood is really . . . *personal*."

"I was desperate," Pam said evenly. "I had to make money to get away. I figured they'd never miss a couple of milliliters here and there."

"Who, they?" I said. "Whose blood was this?"

She hesitated before answering. Terry started tapping out jungle rhythms of death on the tabletop with her nails again.

"Celebrities," Pam said softly. "They bring the highest prices."

Terry jumped out of her chair, sending it crashing over to the kitchen floor. "Are you fucking kidding me?"

Pam pulled a *Don't kill the messenger* face. "Look at the world we live in," she said. "The cult of celebrity is insane, but what can you do? People crave their photographs, their cast-off clothing, anything they've touched. Vampires are no different, except they take it further. They think that by drinking the blood of famous people they can 'absorb their essence.' "

I slumped back in my chair. "I am not believing this," I said. My voice sounded hollow to my own ears.

"It goes on all the time," Pam said. "Medical techs save blood from overdoses, or siphon some off when it's drawn for tests, things like that. A tube of William Shatner's blood brought twenty-five thousand dollars recently from a die-hard Trekkie, although I doubt he drank it. He probably built a shrine to it."

Terry's head was gyrating on her neck like a bobblehead's. "This is some freaky shit," she said. "And I've seen some *freaky* shit in my day."

"I was her broker," Darby related in an oddly blasé tone. "I was tied into the vampire scene, right? So I did the dealing. We were doing really well, then everything went to hell."

"The wads of cash," I said to Terry, who nodded back at me. "What went wrong?"

Pam spoke in a near whisper. "I got ahold of something unique. Some really special blood—"

"Whose?" I said, embarrassed that I was no less susceptible to fame than anyone else. Did she have Brad Pitt's leukocytes in a test tube?

Pam rose to close the swinging kitchen door. "You'd never believe it."

"Try us," Terry said.

Pam sat down again, placing her palms flat on the table in front of her. "Ever hear of someone named Marilyn Monroe?"

Time stood still as the name reverberated off the kitchen walls. Terry and I looked at each other in shock.

"You mean *the* Marilyn Monroe?" I said.

Pam nodded.

"Where on earth would you get her blood, from her grave?"

"God, no. You don't have blood in your grave after being embalmed. You don't have anything but some shreds of clothing and bones, maybe a little hair."

"Sounds like you know a lot about it."

"I'm *not* a grave robber," she said, her tone implying that purveyors of celebrity blood occupied a higher social rung than people who stole dead bodies.

Who knew?

"I worked for a man, old Doc Poole. He was an emergency room intern at Santa Monica Hospital in 1962. Get it?"

"Not yet," I said.

"Marilyn died in '62."

"Oh," Terry said. "Didn't she overdose? I thought they found her dead in her bedroom."

"Yeah, but she didn't die at her house. She was picked up by an ambulance early in the evening and was taken to the hospital. She died there, then they moved her *back* home and called the police after they'd had time to stage the scene."

"Why would they do that?" I was getting caught up in spite of myself. This discussion was beyond belief. We'd be talking crop circles next.

"Ever hear of the Kennedys?"

We nodded.

"Marilyn had affairs with both Bobby and Jack."

"So it's been rumored," I said. "And?"

"She kept a record of all their conversations in a diary. Apparently they couldn't keep their mouths zipped any more than their pants. They blabbed about everything—the Cuban missile crisis, JFK's mob buddies, Sam Giancana, people like that. They wanted that diary back, and they needed to make sure there was nothing else in the house that connected them to her."

"Why?"

"She was doing drugs, coming unglued. They thought she was going to go public about the affairs *and* about the mob."

"So they offed her?" Terry said.

"You tell me," Pam said, locking eyes with her. "The overdose, if there was one, came after Bobby Kennedy was seen by the neighbors going into Marilyn's house that afternoon."

Okay, this was definitely a bombshell, no pun intended. But I wasn't buying it yet.

"So she was taken to the hospital, and while she was there the doctor drew her blood," I said. "Can you keep blood for forty-plus years?"

"Sure," Pam said. "You add a glycerol cryoprotectant to it—a kind of antifreeze—and store it in a special freezer. When the doc opened his own lab he transferred the sample there."

Terry frowned. "Antifreeze—that's toxic, isn't it?"

"Yeah, but it wouldn't kill anybody at these concentrations. Probably no worse than sniffing a few fumes at the gas pump."

"Where is the blood now?" I said.

"It's safe."

"Okay then, *why* did the doctor keep it?"

"He was convinced the Kennedys had some involvement in Marilyn's death. Peter Lawford, too. The official story of her death was that she swallowed barbiturates, but witnesses said she'd been given an enema."

"Suicide by enema?" Terry scrunched up her nose. "Kind of an unglamorous way to go. Can you really die from one of those?"

"It's just another delivery system for drugs, same as swallowing them. But it's an even quicker way into the bloodstream. The point is, she couldn't have swallowed a bunch of pills, contrary to the official story. There was no pill residue found in her stomach. No drinking glass found in her room. The bathroom was being renovated and the sink was out of commission, so she couldn't even have scooped water into her mouth. And she was locked inside her bedroom when the police found her."

Normally I'm a big fan of conspiracy theories, but normally I'm not asked to take them on faith from a former homecoming queen and her twisted little sister.

"Okay," I said skeptically. "Then what?"

"Doc Poole hid the blood away along with a testimonial that it had been taken at the hospital on the night of her death. He hung on to it, waiting for the right time to bring it to light—when the political climate was different, or when the major players were dead."

"What players?" Terry asked.

"You know, J. Edgar Hoover, the Kennedy boys, Peter Lawford."

"Well, aren't they all dead?" I said.

"Apparently not."

"Why do you say that?"

"Because someone is trying to kill us for it. The same someone who killed Nina."

I looked at Terry, who was leaning against the refrigerator, arms crossed over her chest. She looked as gobsmacked as I felt. After thinking in terms of rival vampires and violent ex-husbands for so long, now we were being asked to do a radical about-face and accept that a forty-year-old conspiracy was at the heart of the matter?

It was too bizarre to be believed.

"Why should we believe this wacked-out story?" I asked her.

Pam gave me a helpless look. "Who could make this up?"

Who, indeed? I thought my head would split like an overripe cantaloupe from trying to assimilate this information—if it *was* information.

"What happened to the doctor?" Terry asked. "Did they kill him, too?"

"No. He died a natural death six months ago. When I heard about it, I used my old key to get into his office and took the blood. He'd shown it to me years ago, hidden away in the freezer. I guess he never felt safe enough to come out with it while he was alive. I also got the letter he wrote, attesting to the fact that it was Marilyn's."

"And what were you going to do with the blood?" I said.

Pam shrugged. "Sell it to the vampire freaks to drink in their graveyard rituals."

I stared at her. "How about setting the record straight on Marilyn's death?"

She did a scornful shake of the head. "Nothing would come of it. No one wants to know the truth. We thought we might as well use it to finance our escape." Her voice went low and frightened. "Now it looks like it could *cost* us our lives."

"These people who are trying to kill you, these shadowy conspirators," I said, "how'd they find out you had it?"

"I put the word out on the vampire market," Darby said. "We figured it'd bring a big price. Can you imagine a bigger thrill than drinking the blood of the greatest screen goddess of all times?"

"Offhand, *yeah*," I said.

"A lot of people thought it was a joke," Darby continued, ignoring my sarcasm, "but apparently some people believed it. The offers started coming in. We accepted a blind bid of a hundred and fifty thousand. It seemed like an insane amount of money, but there are some real nuts out there. We got a good faith advance of twenty-five thousand dollars in exchange for the doctor's testimonial. We get the rest when we deliver the blood."

"How are they going to know it's hers?" Terry said. "How can they confirm it?"

"I don't know," Darby said.

"You don't know?" I blurted out. "Who was the bidder?"

She started to balk, but Terry wasn't having it. "Come on, who was it?"

"I really don't know," Darby insisted. "I went through an intermediary—a dentist. The one who does all the fangs in the community. He's got a very rich clientele."

Terry and I turned to each other, rolling our eyes. "Gutzeit," we said together.

Darby's eyebrows went up in surprise. "How'd you know?"

"Trust me, we've met him," I told her. "So he found you a bidder and gave you a down payment."

"Yeah, then the next thing you know, I'm dead in my coffin."

We all took a second to absorb this. What a crazy scenario. Movie stars and politicians and vampires—dealing in blood, doling out death.

"Why did Herb and Sandra identify the body in the morgue as yours?" I asked. "They had to know it wasn't you. What was up with that?"

Pam jumped in. "They believed Darby was dead at first. Then I told them she was alive but said they had to act like they still thought she was gone. They had to identify the body as Darby's, bury it, and then we'd get out of town."

"You were willing to bury that poor girl without any investigation into her death? Without letting her family know?"

"She *had* no family," Darby said, defensive. "But I *did*. My family was under threat. We did what we had to do."

"Who took her body from the morgue?" I asked them.

Darby and Pam looked at each other, shrugging.

"Why did you call to cancel us on the day of the opening?" Terry wanted to know.

Darby looked down at her hands. Her nails were unpolished now, with no trace of the black, undead look. "I went by the house on the morning of the parade to pick up some clothes and found Nina dead. That's when I knew things had gotten out of control, that I was in real danger. I thought you might—you *did*—investigate before we had time to get rid of Marilyn's blood and disappear."

"Did you answer your cell phone later in the day?" I asked Darby.

"Yeah." She gave an embarrassed laugh. "It was totally Pavlovian. I answered it before I remembered I was supposed to be dead."

Terry ratcheted up the pressure. "Who did we see driving away from the Firehouse restaurant in a black VW?"

"That was me," Pam said. "I put the blood on your bike. When Darby said she hadn't been able to reach you, we thought the only way to keep you out was to scare you away."

Well, this much of their story was making sense. Within obvious limits, of course. But there was a whole new set of problems staring at us now, leering like red-eyed, hunched-over little devils in the dark.

I tilted my head back and exhaled. "Okay. The question now, I guess, is what to do with the blood."

Darby looked at me as though it were obvious. "We make the sale, of course." When she saw my expression, she protested, "I came *that* close to getting killed for it! It's probably the reason Lucian is dead—"

I leaned across the table. "Come on. You really want us to believe that dark forces from the past are going around bumping people off left and right?"

"Who else could drain Nina's body? Who else could steal her body from the morgue? These people are connected. They can do anything they want; they can get to anyone. We're carrying around a live grenade, don't you see? The safest thing for us to do now is to get rid of it."

It suddenly occurred to me—*Do these shadowy conspirators climb through skylights dressed like vampires? Do they kidnap people at funerals?*

I supposed it was possible, if they wanted to make the whole thing look like internecine vampire wars. But that would mean that whoever was after the blood must have believed that *we* were involved in this business, as well. I didn't much like that thought, although I wasn't entirely sold on the existence of Pam's dark forces.

"Did it ever occur to you that you're obstructing justice?" I got blank looks from both of the sisters, as well as from my own. "I mean, if the blood can prove that there was a conspiracy to keep the time and manner of Marilyn's death a secret, then there's a good chance she was murdered."

"Duh!" Darby said.

"And no one's been convicted of the crime. You're helping the murderer or murderers to get away with it."

"They *have* gotten away with it!" Pam said, frustrated at my naïveté. "Don't you know your history? Anyone who has any information on one of these big conspiracies gets dead one way or another, and the evidence goes up in smoke!"

"You could take it to the FBI," I said. "We know someone there."

"Oh, yeah," Pam said, with a cynical laugh. "Like the FBI's gonna admit they kept the whole thing quiet so J. Edgar could blackmail the Kennedys with it. The Los Angeles police chief took the file on Marilyn to Washington, D.C., and—*poof!*—it's gone forever, just like JFK's brain. The public doesn't want to know what happened, and no one who's looked into it has lived very long."

That was a sobering thought, I had to admit.

"Look, if someone's rich and crazy enough to buy the blood for a hundred and fifty thousand, let them have it," Darby argued. "Then we can use the money to find a safe place to live. What's more important, the solution to a forty-year-old murder, or our lives?"

This was way too sticky a wicket for me. I was determined not to get involved any further. "Looks like you're somewhere between a rock and a hard place," I said.

"Yeah," Darby said. "We've got the blood and we can't get

the money for it without getting ourselves killed." She sat silently for a moment, chewing on her lip, then her eyes opened with fresh inspiration. "Unless *you'd* help us."

"No!" I shouted.

Terry looked at me. "Why not?"

"Ever heard the term 'blood money'?" I surveyed the faces around the table, all of which were unmoved by the concept. I was surrounded by people with the moral sense of bacteria. "I'll help you turn it over to the authorities . . . but that's it."

"Hey, if you had a pair of Marilyn's shoes, you'd sell 'em to a collector, right?" Terry said in I-can-rationalize-anything mode. She looked at me expectantly, as if she'd just solved the world's problems and was waiting for her Nobel Prize.

"Please tell me you recognize the difference between selling someone's old shoes and selling blood that's evidence of their murder."

She gave me a quizzical look.

"I'll explain it to you later," I said, standing. "Come on, we're out of here."

"You won't help us?" Darby said.

"You're on your own," I said. "And you're on pretty shaky ethical ground, if you ask me. I'm glad you're alive and everything, but we're done here."

I threw open the kitchen door, almost creaming a towheaded little boy on the other side. He looked up at me with startled blue eyes. After a second's hesitation, he cornered around me and ran into the kitchen.

"Mommy?"

It was the sweet sound of a puppy's whimper for its mother.

"What happened to your nap?" Pam said, opening her arms to him.

"I can't sleep." He buried his face in her chest, hugging her.

"It's all right, sweetie," Pam said, as she stroked the boy's silken white hair.

"Jimmy?" Terry asked softly.

Pam nodded over the top of his head. "He has nightmares every time he closes his eyes. He dreams of the beatings. He's afraid Damien's going to find us and kill us all."

She took a piece of pound cake off her plate and offered it to him, but Jimmy shook his head. There's nothing so heartbreaking as a kid too upset for a treat. I noticed how thin he was, how fragile-looking. He had the haunted look of a child who's been through the wars, witnessing horrors far beyond his ability to comprehend.

"I need to go sit with him for a while." Pam took his hand, leading him out of the kitchen. "Come on, sweetie. We'll go sing the bad dream song, okay?"

"Okay," he said, but he sounded dubious to me.

I watched him pad across the living room on his bare little feet and thought, *Oh, no, not guilt. Anything but guilt.*

Darby turned to me, tears in her eyes. "Someone's willing to kill for that blood, they've made it obvious. Unless we can find some way to dispose of it, we're dead. *He's* dead. Maybe not today, maybe not tomorrow, but soon—and if they don't get us, Damien will. We're sitting ducks any way you look at it."

I turned and saw Terry looking at me like I was a convicted child molester buying a day pass to Disneyland.

I threw up my hands in surrender. "Jesus Christ, all right!"

Terry grinned at me, beaming with a sense of adventure. "Okay, where do we start?" she asked Darby. "Gutzeit?"

Darby let out a long breath, dabbing at her eyes with a paper napkin. "That's your best bet. He's got the buyer."

"Come on, Sis," Terry said, grabbing my sleeve. "Let's go see Dr. Goodtime."

We started out through the kitchen door.

"Be careful," Darby said to our backs, and I almost burst out laughing.

Why start now? I thought.

$\mathcal{U}$nfortunately, the guard in the lobby of Alden Medical Plaza recognized us from the shoot-out. We were standing next to the elevators when he came running up behind us, panting and flushed in the face.

"You, there! Redheads!"

We turned and pointed to our chests, feigning innocence. "Who, us?"

He jerked a thumb toward the front doors. "Out."

"It wasn't our fault!" Terry said. "We were the victims!"

"I barely got to hold on to my job," he said, pointing to a scaffolding next to the elevators. A workman in coveralls was plastering the ceiling. "I don't need any more crap outta you today."

I pulled a twenty out of my wallet and slipped it into his palm. "For your pains." I batted my eyelashes.

He looked down at the bill in his hand, hesitating. "I got

more pain than that," he said. "I got angina. Angina's wicked painful."

I pulled out another bill and tucked it into his breast pocket. "We'll be out of here in fifteen minutes."

"Who're you going to see?" he asked, reasserting his authority.

"Dr. Gutzeit, on the second floor."

"If you're not back down here in fifteen, I'm sending Joe up there to get you." He pointed to another uniformed guard on a stool, leaning against the wall and sawing logs, his cap pulled down over his eyes.

"We'll be back down before he wakes up," I said. "Guaranteed."

The guard did a little flick of his head toward the elevators, and Terry stepped over to punch the call button.

"Okay," she said on the way up to the second floor, "what's the plan?"

"We brace him. Put our cards on the table. If he denies knowing about the blood, we walk. If it looks like he's going to deal, we just go along with whatever he says."

"Whatever he says?"

"Yeah. Make out like we're on the take."

"We aren't?"

"No!"

"What if he pulls a gun or something?"

"Duck."

She snorted. "No wonder you're number one at the agency."

"The dentist is not going to pull a gun," I told her. "You've seen too many movies. Remember—we have to get him to name the buyer."

"Why?"

"We have to be sure he's not in league with the shadowy conspirator-types that have allegedly been killing everyone."

"Gotcha."

Snarlin' Marla saw us in the reception window and snatched

up the phone before we'd even spoken, never taking her eyes from our faces.

"Doctor? The redheaded young ladies are here." She listened for a second, then hung up. "He'll be right with you."

"No hurry," Terry said. She smiled at a well-coiffed matron in the waiting area and picked up a copy of *Redbook*. "We'll be here looking up interesting household uses for human blood."

The matron buried her nose in a romance novel. The rest of the patients did their best to ignore us, as well.

After a moment, Marla poked her head out the connecting door.

"This way, please."

We followed her as she minced down the hallway to Gutzeit's office. He stood, gesturing us to the guest seats. There was a vase of fresh flowers sitting on the credenza behind his desk.

"Thank you, Marla," he said as we sat down. "Close the door, please."

She paused, curiosity writ large on her face. Gutzeit gave her a firm wave of his hand.

"Yes, Doctor," she said obediently, ducking outside.

When the door was closed, Gutzeit's professional demeanor left him in a rush. "*Now* what do you want?"

Terry took her time answering, looking directly into his good eye. "It's what *you* want. We have it."

"Oh? And what would that be?" He reached out for the novelty choppers on his desk, sticking his finger between the rows of teeth. He tapped the top denture, giving himself a light nip.

We waited for him to stop playing, drawing out the moment. "Something that someone is willing to pay big money for," I said finally.

He picked up the teeth, using them as a puppet to mime his next question.

"Gold crowns?" said the choppers. Gutzeit giggled at his little puppet show—a deranged girly sound. I wondered if he wasn't a few molars short of a full set, himself. In fact, he was starting to scare me.

"No. Something more perishable," I said. "Blood."

"I don't have much need for transfusions here," he said coyly. "I rarely puncture an artery when I'm doing caps."

"This blood is special."

"Oh, really? And what makes it so special?"

Terry started to stand. "It looks like we made a mistake, Ker—"

Gutzeit sprang from his chair and stopped her with a hand to the shoulder.

"It's *her* blood," he said.

"Whose?"

He waited a long moment before answering. "M.M.'s," he whispered.

"Right."

The two of them sat back down in their chairs.

"We're told you have a buyer for it," I said.

"Correct. But I don't intend to be cut out of the deal."

"Nobody's trying to cut you out," Terry said. "We're here, aren't we?"

He put the choppers down and popped the spring on the back. They skittered around in a circle, biting at the air like a dog chasing its tail.

"Ho-*ho*," he said. "What about that cute business, switching the girls in the coffin? It was obviously an attempt to duck out on me."

"What about your part in that cute business?" I said. "We know you gave her some kind of drug to take to make her look dead."

Her drew himself up, indignant. "I had no idea she would use it to murder that poor girl. It was supposed to be a publicity stunt, but you never know what's going to happen with those *vampire kids* . . ." He *tsked* like an old fuddy-duddy at a group of rambunctious youngsters.

Terry frowned at him. "Are you saying you think Darby murdered the girl in the coffin?"

"Who else?"

"Darby seems to think that there's someone *else* after the blood," Terry said.

He frowned at her, pulling off his glasses.

"Who?"

My gaze started to follow his right eye on its wanderings. I snapped my attention back to the center of his face, staring at the tip of his nose to keep myself oriented.

"She thinks it's someone involved with Marilyn's death," I said.

"Nonsense." But there was a new uncertainty in his tone. "She's soft-soaping you. Probably trying to go directly to the buyer—"

"How can she do that?" Terry said. "She doesn't know who it is."

"Then perhaps she has another buyer altogether?" he speculated.

We shook our heads.

"Well, I suppose I have to take your word." He thought about it a second. "May I assume, then, that everything is going according to the original plan?"

"Yes, you may," I said. "Speaking of which, what's your end?"

"Thirty percent."

"Fifty thousand dollars?"

He gave a short laugh. "Times six."

" 'S'cuse me?" Terry said.

He spoke like an exasperated math teacher to a remedial student. "Thir-ty per-cent of one mil-lion is three hun-dred thou-sand."

"Holy cannoli," Terry said, as the number sank in.

Gutzeit's thin lips curled up into a smile. "Obviously you were misinformed about the scope of the exchange."

"Or our clients were misinformed," I said.

"Or they're lying little bitches." He popped the teeth with the end of a pencil and they started chattering again, biting my nerves with each snap.

"Who has that kind of money to spend?" I asked him.

"That's none of your concern."

"What's his motive? Surely he doesn't plan to drink it?"

"Or she," Terry said.

"I assure you it's a he," Gutzeit said, pulling open a desk drawer and reaching inside. He whipped out a .38 snub-nosed revolver, pointing it at us.

"Hand it over," he growled.

Terry slapped the arms of her chair. "Dammit, I told you he'd have a gun!" she yelled at me.

Gutzeit jerked back at her outburst, then he remembered he was the one holding the weapon.

"Quiet," he said, pointing the barrel of the gun directly at my face. "Or I blow her away. Now hand it over."

Terry leaned back in her chair, eyes turned to the ceiling. "Hand what over?" Doing her tough-bitch thing.

I knew she was formulating a plan of action, but I was too panicked to read her mind. I hoped it was something good enough to get us out of here alive.

"The blood," Gutzeit said. "The hemoglobin. *El sangre*. Give it to me!"

"We don't have it," Terry said evenly, lowering her eyes to his face. "And you wouldn't shoot her, anyway. Not with all those people in the waiting room."

Easy for her to bluff. I was the one looking at the business end of the gun, trapped between Terry's chair and the wall.

Gutzeit picked up the phone. "Marla, dear. Cancel my appointments and take the rest of the afternoon off . . . Yes, make some excuse. Thank you." He hung up and gave Terry a superior look.

She shook her head. "That's pathetic. You don't think other people on your floor will come running when they hear the shots? You don't think they'd call the cops right away?"

"I'll take my chances," Gutzeit said.

"There's no two ways about it," Terry insisted. "If you'd ever actually *fired* a gun before, you'd know how loud it is. It sounds like a bomb going off."

"Well, then," he said, rising from his desk. "Suppose I muffle the shot by placing the barrel directly on your heart—"

He started around the desk, eyes locked on hers.

That's why he didn't see her stick her foot out to trip him.

Gutzeit's ankle hit her boot and he stumbled sideways. His hands went out in an effort to catch himself and the butt of the gun slammed the wooden desk. It went off, blasting a hole in a framed diploma on the wall. I ducked the flying glass.

"Eeeee!" Gutzeit shrieked.

Terry jumped up and wrested the gun from his hand. Apparently he was too shocked to resist. He hadn't expected her to trip him, let alone spring like a lynx.

Footsteps pounded down the hallway and the door flew open. Marla stood on the threshold and saw Terry holding the gun on a pale and shaking Gutzeit.

"It's not what you think," Terry told her.

"It—it's all right, Marla," Gutzeit assured the anxious woman.

Marla's voice was squeaky with fear. "It's not all right! She's shooting at you!"

"No, she's not. She'll give me the gun right now, won't you?" he said to Terry, holding out a trembling hand. "Come, come." He snapped his fingers. "There's a good girl."

Terry flipped open the cylinder and dropped the bullets to the floor, kicking them to the side of the room. Then she handed the gun barrel-first to Gutzeit, who recoiled at the touch of the hot metal, dropping the gun on the plastic teeth and cracking the upper denture wide open. The bottom layer poked up through the remains like an underbite with dire consequences.

Well, at least there'd be no more chatting with fake teeth.

"Should I call security?" Marla said.

"They're on their way up," Terry said. "We told them if we weren't down in fifteen minutes to come get us. We thought there might be trouble."

The bell at the reception desk buzzed. All heads swiveled in that direction.

"Go get 'em, Marla," I said. "I'm sure they'd like to watch Dr. Gutzeit taking target practice in a professional office with live ammunition."

"We'll be done here in a moment, dear." Gutzeit smoothed the few silver strands on the top of his head. "If they ask about the noise, kindly explain that the bit came loose from the new drill and hit the wall, or something. I'll finish up with the young ladies and come speak to them."

"A-all right," Marla said. "If you're sure . . . ?"

Gutzeit nodded and she closed the door.

Terry crossed her arms and gave him a jaundiced look. "Now that we've established that you're a homicidal thief, where do we go from here?"

"I wouldn't have hurt you." Gutzeit lowered himself into the desk chair. "But they've tried to undermine me before. If you'd had the blood, I assure you, I would have made the transaction and paid everyone what they were due."

"They didn't try to undermine you," Terry said. "We explained that already. Someone else tried to kill *them* for it."

"Look," I said, turning to Terry, "this is getting too complicated. I say we go to the cops with the blood, let them sort everything out."

"No!" Gutzeit came out of his chair again. "What are you, fools? Do you know how many fangs I have to manufacture to make three hundred thousand large? How many caps I have to install?"

I held up a hand. "Calm down, okay? We'll make the deal. But we have to know who the buyer is."

"That's impossible," he said.

"Why?"

"He's very shy."

"Look," Terry said, "our clients don't trust you, and you don't trust them, and the two of us don't trust any of you. We have to know who the buyer is. How do we know he's good for it?"

"Oh, money's not the problem," he assured us with his sick little giggle.

I crossed my arms over my chest. "We're not coming to the party unless you tell us who the host is. It's too dangerous."

Gutzeit looked at us for a long moment. "He's a collector," he said finally.

"Of?"

"Marilyn."

"Explain that," Terry said.

"He's got a million-dollar collection of Marilyn paraphernalia. Her shoes, handbags, costumes, hairbrushes, family photos . . . anything that's on the market, he bids for. He's a patient of long standing. I did his dentures."

"He's old?" I don't know why this should have surprised me.

"Quite. Ancient, you might say."

"And he wants one last Marilyn acquisition to go out on?"

"He wants one more to go out *with*. He plans to be cryogenically preserved along with the blood. It's his particular fantasy to be resurrected at a later date when cloning will be an everyday occurrence. He'll be revived, and Marilyn will be reborn from her own DNA. Then he'll raise her up to be his bride."

twenty-seven

O h, man!" Terry said, looking at Gutzeit like he was sprouting snakes from his head. "That's too sick for words!"

The dentist shrugged. "We all have our dreams. People with his kind of money can afford to dream a little bigger."

"He's going to be frozen," Terry said wonderingly. "He'll be a corpsicle!"

"He wants to use Marilyn's DNA to bring her back, and she's got nothing to say about it?" I asked indignantly.

"It won't *be* Marilyn," Gutzeit said. "It will be a perfect facsimile. He plans to raise her in a foreign country with, shall we say, more lenient notions of when it's suitable to take a bride. A place where no one will recognize her."

"There's nowhere she wouldn't be recognized . . . and what do you mean, 'lenient notions'?" I felt a shiver of revulsion as the implication sank in. "Are we talking child bride? Where is *that* okay?"

He shook his head, indicating ignorance or a refusal to say. Unfortunately I could think of some countries where such practices existed. West Virginia, for example.

"I don't care where it is," I said. "She'd be a human being. She'd have the right to say what she wanted to do with her own life!"

"But would she be a 'human being' as such? Who knows what laws will be enacted between now and then to deal with the issue? Will a cloned being have rights, or will it belong to the person whose cell structure was used to produce it? Will they be used for organ donation, or as some sort of servant class? The ethics of it all are beyond me, frankly. I really don't give a damn. I intend to live one lifetime, and I'd rather spend what remains of it on some exotic beach than slapping caps on Beverly Hills matrons and would-be vampires."

Terry's face was turning green with revulsion. "This is so unbelievable."

Gutzeit dismissed her horror with a wave of his hand. "Don't be so dramatic. The technology isn't there yet, Dolly the ewe notwithstanding. We don't even know if a cloned human would have cognitive function. Would they be able to think as we do, or would they sit there thinking nothing, eating and excreting like some oversize baby doll . . . ?"

The door swung open and the downstairs guard stood there, hand on his holster, ready to rumble. "Everything okay in here, Doc?" he said, glaring at us.

"Everything's just fine, isn't it, ladies?"

"Yeah, except I need a vomit bag," Terry said.

"Thank you for checking," Gutzeit said to the guard. "We're fine."

The guard frowned at the hole in the plaster. "What happened there?"

"Never got it fixed after the Northridge quake," Gutzeit said. "Bad of me. Now if you'll excuse us . . ."

The guard gave Terry and me a warning look, patting the gun in his hip holster. He pulled back, closing the door behind him.

"Okay, what's this wacko's name?" Terry said. Gutzeit was still hesitating. "No name, no deal."

Gutzeit gazed past us, pondering his next move. Then he sighed and brought his eyes back to us. "His name is St. Ives."

"St. Ives, like the lotion?"

"Not *like* the lotion. He *is* the lotion."

I laughed, incredulous. "We're talking about the lotion king?"

"I guess keeping his skin soft and smooth isn't enough anymore," Terry said. "He wants it fresh frozen."

"We'll see how you feel when you're pushing one hundred," Gutzeit said. "You might be a little more concerned with your mortality then."

"I think I'll make my peace before that time," I told him.

He gave a little shrug. *So you say.*

"How's he gonna know if it's really Marilyn's blood?" Terry asked.

"He has a partial PCR from a follicle found on her hairbrush, bought in the sixties, when cloning was the stuff of science fiction, not science fact. The man's a visionary, I'll give him that. He's been buying up any and all personal items in the pursuit of suitable cellular material, with no luck. This blood is his last hope. The root of the hair provided him with enough DNA for comparison purposes. If the blood matches closely enough, he'll take it on faith, along with the documentation already delivered, that it's hers. If the blood contains cells that are clonable, there'll be a million-dollar bonus."

Terry's jaw dropped. "Two million total?"

"Two million would be cheap, if he were able to accomplish it," Gutzeit said. "Think about it—it's a sort of immortality. An eternity with the most beautiful woman God ever created. The two of them continuing through history, cloned over and over again in an endless cycle of death and rebirth—it's the stuff of Pharaohs."

"Well, this is a much larger transaction than we thought," Terry said. "I guess we'll have to renegotiate our fee, eh, Ker?"

I gave her a mercenary smile. "Whatever you say, Number Two."

Gutzeit got a smug look: *You see? Everyone has a price.*

"When do we do the trade with St. Ives?" Terry asked him.

"We never speak on the phone. I leave a note for him, then he gets a message back to me confirming a meeting."

"And where do you leave the note?"

"In the flower vase hanging on Marilyn's crypt in Westwood Cemetery. Perhaps I could persuade you to do the honors?"

"Write us a note and we'll take it to her grave."

Dr. Gutzeit scribbled what looked like code on a prescription slip. He pulled a rose from the flower arrangement on the credenza, wrapped the note around the stem, securing it with the thorns, and handed the rose to me.

"Give the lady my best," he said.

The thorns were pricking my chest underneath the jacket. I hadn't wanted to put the rose in my shoulder bag for fear of destroying it, but now I wondered why I'd bothered. It was destined for destruction from the second they cut its stem—from seedhood, actually. Its entire destiny was to flower into beauty, then fade.

Only beauty doesn't do anything so gentle as fade, does it? It dries out, crumbles, rots into mulch, and ultimately turns to dust.

If Marilyn had lived to be eighty, I wondered—if she had outlasted her looks and died old and wrinkled—would the world still be as obsessed with her?

Pointless question, really. Like wondering what would have happened if Jesus had lived to be sixty and died of diverticulitis.

I watched the slick Beverly Hills storefronts whizzing by as we made our way down Wilshire Boulevard, tracing the path of the slow-speed chase. This was without a doubt the strangest case we'd ever had, and we'd had some. But trading in a screen goddess's blood topped them all.

Soon we were on the stretch leading to Westwood. Terry signaled and turned left onto the driveway next to the AVCO Cinema, passing the theater to arrive at the iron gates of the cemetery.

We knew the location because we'd happened on to it once by mistake. We had gone to see *The Sixth Sense* at the AVCO, and Terry got turned around afterward while looking for the exit, accidentally driving us straight into the cemetery. We hadn't known it was there, and to find ourselves surrounded by marble crypts after seeing the movie about dead people had really wigged us out at the time.

But we'd decided to do some exploring instead of turning back around immediately, and that's when we'd come across Marilyn's crypt.

Terry parked on the service road inside the gate. To our right was a small green stretch of lawn with a few grave markers flush to the ground. The brick structure at the edge of the property was probably a chapel.

She turned off the engine. It was preternaturally quiet back here. You couldn't even hear the traffic on Wilshire.

Terry pointed. "Over there, isn't she?"

I nodded and we walked past a large sepulcher housing the Armand Hammers—a family of dead philanthropists. Next came the first of several gated alcoves containing marble crypts, stacked on top of each other in rectangular sections that reminded me of filing cabinets for the deceased. The alcoves bore brass plaques with the names SANCTUARY OF DEVOTION, SANCTUARY OF TENDERNESS, SANCTUARY OF TRANQUILITY.

And beyond them—but not in a gated alcove, not protected by anything other than a video camera trained on it from a neighboring roof—was Marilyn's final resting place. Or the storage vault for her biological residue, for the unsentimental.

Two rows from the left. Five rows up from the ground.

MARILYN MONROE
1927–1962

That's all it said. I saw lip marks on the plaque, left by some fan with shiny pink lipstick. A small conical vase was affixed to the marble, containing a bunch of drooping posies.

I replaced the wilted flowers from the vase with the fresh rose. Terry reached out with a finger and traced the lettering of Marilyn's name. As she did, the marble bowed inward, loose from the thousands of idol-worshippers who'd pressed on it in the same way over the years. Terry jerked her hand back, sneaking a guilty look up at the video camera.

I stared, transfixed, at the tomb. Marilyn's name used to be in lights, and now here it was on a cold piece of stone. Had she made her peace before dying, I wondered—or had she not had time, being unprepared for her end at the hands of a murderer?

Someone tapped on my shoulder. I jumped, uttering a terrified squeak, then turned to find a man in a chauffeur's uniform standing behind me. He was tall with a regal bearing, somewhere between forty and fifty years old, wearing reflector sunglasses and sporting a natty little chin beard.

"Is that for my employer?" he said with an upper-crust English accent, indicating the rose.

I cut my eyes to Terry. "Um, who's your employer?"

"Beg pardon, ladies. My mistake." He tipped his chauffeur's cap and turned on his heel.

"Excuse me?" I said, and he turned back around. "I think it's probably for your employer." I plucked the rose from the vase, unrolled the piece of paper and handed it to him. "Mr. St. Ives?"

He didn't answer but read the piece of paper, holding it by its curled edges, then tore it into little pieces and stuffed them into his pocket.

"We'll be here at midnight with the money," he said. "The gate will be unlocked."

And without another word, he was on his way.

As soon as he had gone, I called Darby. "We've made contact," I said, deliberately being obscure.

I heard a small gasp. "With the buyer? Who is it?"

"Can't tell you that."

Her voice was petulant. "It's *our* buyer."

"Not on a cell phone."

"Oh. Well, what about the dentist?"

"We saw him, but he doesn't know we've made the connection."

"Where are you now?"

I decided not to give her our exact coordinates. "Westwood, outside the Bruin Theater."

"Meet us at Acapulco," she said eagerly. "We'll be there in half an hour."

I agreed, then closed the phone.

"She wants to meet at Acapulco," I said to Terry. "Could you go for some life-affirming supernachos?"

"Yeah, baby." She flipped her braid and gave a little shudder. "Let's go shake off these death cooties."

We took a booth in the main room of the restaurant and ordered our nachos. The brightly colored tile work, huge paper flowers, and cheery Mexican music made me feel like I was on vacation south of the border. The natural light in the sunlit room was a nice change from the vampire gloom of the last couple of weeks.

Darby and Pam entered the front door, outfitted in their headscarf-and-shades disguises, and spotted us in the corner. They slipped into the booth across from us, then Darby took off her sunglasses and got right down to business.

"You saw Gutzeit?"

"Yeah," I said, "he held a gun on us."

The two of them appeared shocked.

"Are you okay?" Darby asked.

I shrugged. "As you see us."

"Well, what did he say?" Pam wanted to know.

Terry leaned over the table, lowering her voice. "He said that the . . . *item* . . . was worth a million dollars to the buyer."

Darby took a second to let this sink in. Her eyes grew furious, turning a darker blue. "He told us a hundred and fifty, the lying little twerp!"

Terry put a finger to her lips. "Obviously he was going to try to rip you off. He said the buyer was willing to pay twice that amount if it checked out."

Darby and Pam exchanged excited looks. One hundred and fifty thousand was chump change next to two million. Two million would pay for years of peace of mind.

"Checked out?" Pam said. "You mean, as far as its origin?"

"Yes. He has access to a substance for comparison."

"What substance?"

"A hair follicle."

"Wow," Darby said, sitting back in the booth. She helped herself to a chip heaped with guacamole. "Why do you think he came clean with you about the amount?"

"He's afraid of losing out altogether. You scared him when you showed up dead. He wants to incentivize you. Guess he didn't kill you, after all."

"How did you make contact with the buyer?"

"Gutzeit sent us with a note to a rendezvous place. But what he didn't know was that the guy's chauffeur would be right there, waiting. He made a date with us there for tonight."

Darby grabbed another chip, shoving it into her mouth. "Tonight! And he's bringing a million?"

"That's what he said. Less the twenty-five thousand you already have, I assume."

"He must want it bad. What's he going to do with it?"

"If you knew," I said, "you probably wouldn't go through with it."

A worried look crossed their faces.

"Tell us," Pam said.

"The buyer's an old man. A gazillionaire who's going to have himself cryogenically frozen along with Marilyn's blood. When the technology's advanced enough, he plans to have them both thawed out and Marilyn's body cloned. She'll be reincarnated—without her soul, obviously—and raised up to be his bride."

After a few seconds of silence, Darby began to snicker. She put a hand over her mouth and turned to Pam, whose own eyes were wide with horror.

"That's wacked!" Darby said, then she hitched up her shoulders. "But it's no worse than drinking it, I guess."

Somehow this was not the reaction I was expecting. "So you're still willing to sell it?"

"Sure. Why not?"

"Call me crazy, but I thought you might be a little freaked out that the guy wants to make a sex puppet out of Marilyn's clone."

"Look, if it wasn't him, it'd be someone else," Darby said. "There's always gonna be crazies out there. He's just a stalker with a ton of money."

This girl is cold, I thought. Well, what could you expect from a homecoming queen? Just like Miss America—all sweet smiles and glossy hair on the outside, the heart of a predator within.

She must have read my face, because she immediately started

to backpedal. "Anyway, you can't really clone people, can you?" she said, looking to Pam the talented biologist for her answer.

"Well, it's illegal to try in most parts of the world. It looked like South Korea was making progress, but it turns out they falsified their data." She sat back in the booth. "The real question is whether cryogenics will ever work. The only thing that's ever been successfully unfrozen is a human kidney. Doing the same with the whole human organism is tricky at best. So this guy, whoever he is, will probably stay frozen for eternity."

"There you go," Darby said, smiling at us. "The stalker's on ice forever. Feel better now?"

Hardly.

"Anyway," Pam said, "there's no guaranteeing they'll get usable DNA from the blood."

"I thought you said it was preserved," Terry said.

"Yeah, but Doc Poole wasn't using state-of-the-art methods for preservation. It was 1962, remember. Later he moved it to a more sophisticated apparatus, but any variation in temperature could result in a low yield of DNA. Just taking it out of the deep freeze to give it to this guy could corrupt it."

Darby sat up triumphantly. "There you go—no Marilyn clone. We're getting paid at least one million for some cruddy old blood, and nobody's going to enslave anybody, okay? Are we on?"

She could tell I was still hesitating. "Look," she coaxed me, "Pam's little boy deserves a decent life. With a million dollars we could set ourselves up in the Bahamas or someplace. Dumb-ass Damien would never be able to get together the airfare. We'd be clear of him forever."

"Aren't you forgetting something?" I asked her.

"What?"

"Gutzeit's commission. He's supposed to get thirty percent."

Darby waved a chip in the air. "Forget him. We don't need him anymore. And he lied to us, the prick. Tried to cheat us."

"If you think Damien's a problem," I told her, "try having Gutzeit on your tail for the rest of your life. He *does* have the means to come after you, and the man is mental, if you ask me. He'd kill for three hundred thousand."

"We'll give you his share," Darby said airily. "If you promise to keep him off our backs."

Terry frowned at her. "And how are we supposed to do that?"

Darby lowered her chin, her voice creeping into damsel-in-distress territory. "I don't know. Couldn't you think of something? I mean, for three hundred thousand dollars . . . can't you get a little creative?"

She was talking about killing him. Why did everyone seem to think we knew contract killers or were killers ourselves? Had we acquired a bottom-feeder look in the last few months? I realized it was getting harder and harder to know the good guys from the bad guys in this scenario.

" 'Creative'?" I said, kicking Terry's foot under the table. "No, I don't think we're creative enough for that. I guess you'll just have to take your chances."

Darby gave me a feminine little pout.

Pam didn't seem quite as concerned with the prospect of having a deranged dentist after them. "So when's the meet?" She snagged a jalapeño for her nacho and bit into the pepper without flinching, as if it were a pat of butter.

"Midnight."

"Where?"

Terry shook her head. "If we tell you, why do you need us? Why should you pay us?"

I had no intention of taking money for this job, but we were obliged to help them, as Eli's clients, and I wouldn't let him down. We were also obliged by the image of an innocent young boy who deserved to live without fear, and I didn't think I could live with myself if something happened to Jimmy. But it had been canny of Terry to make us appear financially motivated. That was something that Darby, at least, clearly understood.

"Right." Darby gave her sister a quick sideways look. "So, how's ten percent? Is that enough?"

Terry and I nodded.

"You'll pick us up at eleven-thirty with the blood," I said. "We'll take you to the rendezvous."

"Give me your address."

I wrote it down for her.

"I'll be there." Darby jumped out of the booth and Pam scooted out after her.

"Just you?" I asked Darby. "Pam's not coming?"

"I told you, I'm the go-between," Darby said. "Be sure to come armed. We can't trust anybody."

You can say that again.

"By the way," Terry said to Pam as they turned to leave. "That's an adorable kid you have. Very special."

What she was saying was *We're only doing this for him.*

But Pam took the compliment at face value. "I know," she said, her eyes softening. "He's the best."

I felt marginally better after seeing her transformed at the mention of her son. Maybe you couldn't fault these women for doing whatever it took to preserve their *own* DNA from ruthless predators. Or maybe I was still rationalizing the whole sordid business.

We watched as the disguised Misses Applewhite skipped out the restaurant door, whispering to each other. They looked somewhat giddy to me. Probably stoked about all the fun they were going to have on the road with a million bucks.

Finally, Terry looked back at me. "Where to, Numero Uno?"

"We've got a lot of time to kill. Let's go home."

What we couldn't know at the moment was that there was already someone else at our house, killing time.

twenty-eight

The second we walked in the front door, I knew something was wrong. Fear frosted my stomach lining and my palms went tingly. I sensed a foreign presence.

I grabbed Terry's jacket. "Ter, someone broke in."

"Huh?" She looked around the room. "You're right," she whispered. "Our things have been moved."

A horrible thought occurred to me. "Where're the dogs?" I raced into the living room, yelling, "Muffy! Paquito!"

Hearing their names, the pups came trotting in from the kitchen, apparently unharmed. I bent down to inspect them, running my hands over their little bodies to check them for injuries.

"Are they all right?" Terry said. "Are you all right, babies?"

"They're fine. But look—the couch is in a different place. See? It's closer to the fireplace."

"And where'd that come from?" She pointed to a small table

behind the couch holding a vase of fresh flowers—irises and carnations and tiger lilies. One pink rose.

Terry and I frowned at each other, mystified.

She looked at the stone hearth. "Am I going crazy? We didn't have brass fireplace tools, did we?"

"Uh-uh."

We moved cautiously into the dining nook. There was a blue glass bowl full of oranges that definitely wasn't on the table when we'd left. Terry lifted a small silver saucer to her nose. "Potpourri? Hey!" She pointed to the table. "This isn't ours!"

Sure enough, our garage-sale special had been replaced with a lovely table of rough-hewn oak.

"What kind of burglars are these?" I said in amazement. "They break in and redecorate?"

"SURPRISE!"

Three giant men jumped out at us from the kitchen.

"Yahhhhh!" Terry and I screamed, jumping into each other's arms. We recovered from the shock as soon as the Bruces came into focus.

Terry pushed me away from her. "What are you guys *doing*?" she shouted at them.

"You like?" Bruce Two gestured around the house, beaming. "It's feng shui!"

"You scared the feng shit out of us!" Terry fumed. "We thought a killer had broken in!"

"Please watch your language," Bruce One said, pointing a digital camera at her. "This is a family show."

I fought to get my breath under control. "You're recording this?"

He nodded behind the camera. "We're making an audition video."

"Yeah," Bruce Two said. "No offense, but private detection really isn't our thing. Too rough-and-tumble. We're going back to what we know."

"Oh," Terry said, putting a hand to her still-heaving chest. "You're going back to acting?"

"Well, yeah, but there's no production going on these days except for reality programming. And since makeover shows are all the rage, we decided to make *ourselves* over and go for it!"

"A home improvement show?" I said.

"Not just that," Three said, his eyes shining with excitement. "It's something completely original. A combination of home improvement and home defense. We're gonna refurbish houses while teaching the owners martial arts. Guess what it's called?"

Terry and I shrugged.

The three of them shouted in unison: *"Kung Fu Feng Shui Bruces!"*

Our mouths fell open.

"Hope you don't mind that we experimented on your house, but to tell you the truth, the place was looking a little *Tobacco Road*," Bruce One said.

"Not to mention the bad vibes caused by your furniture placement," Bruce Two put in. "The angles were all off. They were definitely blocking the flow of chi."

"Plus, your window treatments were not at all auspicious," Bruce Three added.

I looked at them in astonishment. "But who . . . who paid for all this?"

"Product placement," Two said, bursting with pride. "We've already got a design store on board as a sponsor."

"What'd you do with our old table?" Terry asked.

The boys turned to each other, grinning.

"Why don't you see for yourselves?" Bruce Two said, clicking on the TV and reversing his way through a recorded program in the deck. Bruce One stood to one side with his camera, ready to memorialize our reaction.

Bruce Three appeared on the TV screen. He was standing in our backyard behind the table, dressed in a black satin dragon robe. He bowed to the camera, palms together, then reeled back, whipping his right hand up in the air.

"Ai-*eeeeeeee!*"

The hand came down and chopped our old table in two. The halves fell to the grass.

Then the other two Bruces came forward, bowed to the camera, and the three of them commenced a free-for-all, chopping and kicking and howling like banshees. Two minutes later, the table was a pile of briquettes.

"Recycling!" Bruce Two said. "Very auspicious for the environment."

Terry blinked a few times. "That was a perfectly good table. We could have given it to Goodwill."

"They never would have taken it anyway," I told her. "It wasn't up to their standards." I turned and smiled gamely at the Bruces. "Well, gosh. The place looks—and smells—just great. What can we say, except *thanks*."

"Say you'll let us use it for the pilot episode!" Bruce Three squealed.

"Well, it certainly looks like a winner," I said truthfully. It was just the thing for today's television market.

"Yessss!" Bruces Two and Three threw their arms around our shoulders in a group hug and spun us around, jumping up and down, causing the house to bounce on its foundation. One of the newly installed pictures jumped off its nail and fell to the floor—*crrrasshhh!*

"Cut!" Bruce One said, like a natural-born director. "Okay, let's get that glass cleaned up, then we'll do another take of the homeowners' dance of joy."

$\mathcal{T}he$ $\mathcal{B}ruces$ $left$ us to go edit the pilot episode. Terry and I heated up some of their leftover gourmet pizza for dinner. But neither of us had much of an appetite thanks to the supernachos we'd had earlier, combined with anxiety. Three nail-biting hours to go till the rendezvous.

The phone rang. Terry answered and handed it to me. "Boatwright," she whispered.

Oh, God, I wasn't ready for this. I hadn't even spoken to him since the snafu at the pier. But I took the phone from her, trying to psych myself up as I did.

"Hi, John! How are you?"

"Fine," he said. "How's it going?"

"Fine."

"So . . . you staying out of trouble?"

"Yep, staying way out of it." If you didn't count riots and murders and forty-year-old conspiracies. "Thanks for helping us out with the cops at the pier," I said. "With Terry's record, it could've been bad. A second strike. You saved her from the slammer."

"I didn't do it for Terry," he said pointedly.

"Well . . . thanks, anyway. From both of us."

"You're welcome. You know, I miss you. A day without you is like a day without sunshine." He paused, then: "Three days without you is like nuclear winter."

I had no idea how to respond. Finally, I forced myself to speak. "That's . . . really sweet."

I could hear the smile in his voice. "Thanks, I worked real hard on that one. Listen, what are you doing tonight? Want to go out for a drink?"

"Sorry, that won't be possible. I'm going to meet a billionaire cosmetics king in Westwood Cemetery to sell him Marilyn Monroe's blood so he can be unfrozen with it in the future and live happily ever after with her clone."

That's not what I said. What I said was, "Sorry, I can't. Our dog's about to have puppies. I have to wait around for the blessed event."

"Puppies? Great. Need another midwife? We could open a bottle of wine at your place and celebrate."

"Oh, uh . . ." I said, fumbling for an excuse. Reba was right—I sucked at lying. Terry got all the good liar genes. Wait a minute—we had all the same genes. So how come she could bullshit her way through any situation, whereas I got all tongue-tied and awk—

"That's not the real reason, is it?" he said finally.

I sighed. "No, the real reason is that I'm going to meet a billionaire cosmetics king in Westwood Cemetery to sell him Marilyn Monroe's blood so he can be unfrozen with it in the future and live happily ever after with her clone."

I really said it this time. Truth is supposed to be stranger than fiction, and in this case it might just be too strange to believe.

"Oh, I get it," he said. "You've already thrown back a few."

"Yeah, that's it." I faked a hiccup.

"Well, how about tomorrow?"

"Tomorrow?" I looked into the kitchen and saw Terry getting pizza plates down from the cabinet. Her movements were artificially slow, as though she was straining to hear my side of the conversation.

"Um, John. I think I'd better pass."

"For tomorrow?"

I bit my lip. "For . . . the time being."

Another silence. "Ouch." I heard him breathing in the silence that followed. "Listen, I didn't mean to be so hard on you about the chase—"

"That's not it."

"Is it Terry?"

"Sort of."

"You know, she's old enough to take care of herself."

"That's debatable." No, it was demonstrably false, but I wasn't going to argue with him about it. "And I don't know if I'm ready for what you said . . . you know—*permanent*."

"I'm sorry," he said, sighing. "I really liked you."

"You don't have to put it in the past tense," I protested weakly.

"I thought you just did that. Bye, Kerry."

He hung up and I listened to the dial tone for a second.

Then I set the phone in its cradle, and sat down at the nice new table.

I put my head down on my arms and thought about crying.

"You could have gone out with him," Terry called from the kitchen. "I can do the exchange on my own."

I sat up and pinched the bridge of my nose to squelch the tears. "And let you have all the fun?" I called back. "Dream on, bitch."

Later, we went out in the backyard to practice with the phaser pain blasters.

"How do you do it?" I asked Terry.

She shrugged. "Point and shoot."

"You *did* read the instructions, right?"

She gave me a look. "Just do it."

I held my arm out straight, the blaster thing aimed at a Diet Coke can on our new picnic table. I pushed the button and the aluminum can shot back and hit a rock on the ridge behind the house with a clang.

"Yikes! Go make sure I didn't hit any wildlife."

Terry ran up the ledge and scoped out the area. She picked up the smashed aluminum can, waving it around for me to see.

"Killshot," she said.

"I didn't hit any bunnies?"

"No, but this Coke can is worm food."

In a couple more hours, I thought, we might get the opportunity to use the blasters for real.

twenty-nine

The VW pulled up outside our house at eleven-thirty. Terry was watching the street through the snazzy new window treatment in the alcove: beige curtains with a mod red trim.

"Showtime," she said, letting the curtain fall back into place.

We petted the pups, telling Muffy not to go into labor while we were gone, then packed up our phaser blasters and went outside to meet Darby.

She was at the wheel in her scarf and black glasses, wearing the old makeup—white pancake, dark lipstick. Terry started to get in on the passenger side, but I pulled on the sleeve of her jacket, yanking her back.

"Maybe we should take the bike," I whispered in her ear.

"You afraid to get in the car with her?"

"I don't know if we can trust her."

She looked into my eyes, and I prepared myself to be wimp-slapped. To my relief, she nodded. "You're right."

Terry walked around to Darby's window. "We're gonna take the bike," she said. "You follow us in the car."

Darby shrugged. "As long as you're there to look out for me. You've got weapons, right?"

"We have stun guns, sort of."

She pulled down her sunglasses, showing us her heavily lined eyes. "You don't have a real gun?"

"Sorry," Terry said. "Best we could do. You got the blood?"

Darby picked up a plastic cooler, waving it around. "Happy birthday, Mr. Pres-i-dent," she sang in a breathy voice.

Ick. I didn't need that little reminder of what a ghoulish errand we were on.

"Okay, good," Terry said. "We'll take Beverly Glen down to Wilshire, then cut up to Westwood."

"What's in Westwood?" Darby asked.

"You'll see."

"Okay, let's go." Darby popped the glasses back on her nose.

She stayed close all the way down the canyon road. We hung a right on Wilshire and took it toward Westwood, then swung onto the service road beside the AVCO cinema.

Terry slowed to a crawl, the VW on our bumper. As promised, the iron gates were open. I looked around for a guard but saw no sign of one. I guess if you have a few billion dollars to throw around, you can corrupt a few rent-a-cops.

It was dark, but there were some lights shining from the back of the movie theater, and one gas lamp at the entrance to the cemetery. It was enough to discourage people from vandalizing the place but not enough to keep us from our mission.

I decided the place wasn't bad, as burial sites go. No wasteful grassy spaces with headstones poking up from the ground like stone extensions of the skeletons below. And the crypts looked more like shrines, with all that pink marble glowing softly in the night light.

Terry cut the engine and we got off the bike. She pointed to some cables hanging from the base of the video camera aimed at Marilyn's crypt.

"They've disabled the camera."

"Good thing. Wouldn't want to get caught on tape doing the grave robbers' dance of joy."

Darby got out of the VW with the cooler, looking around. "Is this where Marilyn . . . ?" she asked, her voice trailing off.

Terry nodded.

"Creepy," Darby said, hugging herself.

The Queen of the Undead was creeped out by a cemetery? Or was it the knowledge that she was selling Marilyn into white slavery that was giving her the willies? If I were to be honest, it was doing the same to me. Not that I really believed it could be done—it was more the idea that anyone would think to do it in the first place.

Darby blew out a sigh and looked at her watch. "Where is he?"

"We're a couple minutes early," I said.

"You think he'll really have the money?"

"Why not?" Terry said. "He seems like a motivated buyer."

"Can't you tell me who it is now?" Darby asked. "I mean, what's his name?"

"His name is St. Ives," I said. "And yes—it's the hand lotion guy."

Darby's eyes bugged, then she let out a whoop of laughter. "Whatever," she said, shaking her head. "Wish Mr. Hand Lotion would get here already."

No sooner had she spoken than a black limousine turned into the service road with its fog lights illuminated. Darby drew a sharp breath. Terry put a hand on her arm.

"Steady," she whispered.

The limo pulled up beside us, slowing to a stop.

After a moment, the back door opened.

"Get in." The voice was thin and hoarse, with barely enough energy to carry it to our ears.

We looked at Terry, who stepped up first and climbed in. I followed, Darby behind me with the cooler.

The three of us sat facing the rear of the car. There was a lone figure in the middle of the backseat, wrapped in blankets. His bony pate was backlit—wide, round, and hairless. His face was completely in shadow.

"Good evening, ladies," he said, the breath whistling sharply through his dentures. Gutzeit must not have given him a very snug fit, I thought.

"Hello," Darby said to the old man.

He looked at Terry and me for a moment. "You're twins," he rasped at us. "You share the same features, the same DNA."

"Yes," Terry said, "but never the same underwear."

The old man leaned over, hacking. I thought for a second it was laughter, but then he produced a handkerchief and wiped sputum from his lips. "I have little use for wit at my age," he said, folding the hanky with gnarled fingers. "I have no use for anything that won't prolong my existence. Your *wit* won't get you a minute more of life, young lady. Remember that."

"We'll remember," I said, preempting another smart-ass comeback from my sister. I didn't want the old man to balk. I just wanted to get this exchange over with.

"But I'm being terribly rude," he said.

He reached over to the control panel on the armrest and flicked a switch. In the overhead light, his wizened face looked like a rotting raisin, the hawkish nose casting a black shadow down the middle of his chin. His eyes were rheumy pools of blue, their expression fathomless.

"Here you see the ravages of age," he said almost proudly. "I was quite handsome in my youth. Now I'm extremely rich. But I was never handsome and rich at the same time. There's the rub, eh? When we have the means, we no longer have the way."

The way to do what, bang beautiful women spawned in a petri dish? I needed to get out of there. The idea of this horrific old cadaver making love to Marilyn Monroe was making me want to throw up.

Terry was impatient, too. "Do you have the money?" she said.

He inclined his buzzard head to the side, squinting at her. "Oh. Am I boring you?"

"Yep."

"Good," he said, phlegm rattling in his throat as he laughed. He hawked and spat into his handkerchief again. "You're learning. Don't spend your precious time on earth with things that bore you." He pushed a lever on the armrest and spoke into a microphone. "Williams, the suitcase, please."

I saw the shadow of the chauffeur's hat as he exited the car. He opened one of the back doors, placing a black alligator suitcase on the floor. Then he withdrew, standing a respectful distance from the open door.

"Have you the blood?" the old man said.

Darby pulled on a pair of latex gloves, then opened the cooler and took out a steel cylinder. She twisted open the lid of the cylinder with the *whoosh* of a broken vacuum seal. Then she reached inside and fished out a small glass vial with a rubber stopper.

She held out the vial to the old man, her hand trembling slightly.

"Closer, dear."

I actually heard Darby swallow. After a second she got up from the hurricane seat and leaned over to pass the vial to the old man. His palsied, spotted claw of a hand reached out and closed around the vial, then he emitted a full-throated groan of pleasure.

"*Uhhhhhhhhhhhh . . .*"

It was obscene.

Darby fell to her knees in front of the suitcase and flipped the latches. The case was full of crisp bills surrounded by white paper bands. She took it in excitedly, as if she were gazing on a chest full of treasure from a Spanish galleon. Then she started counting.

The old man had much the same greedy reaction to the vial of dark slush in his hand. He held it up to the map light, the better to admire it. His breath was coming quicker, his chest rising and falling under the blanket.

"Hello, my darling," he said, as if it had ears to hear him. "I've waited such a long time for this pleasure."

It was all I could do not to bolt. This was a preview of the nightmares I'd have that night, probably every night from here on.

Darby thumbed through the money, then frowned all of a sudden.

"Wait a minute," she said, looking up at the old geezer. "There's supposed to be close to a million here. There's only a hundred thousand."

The old man's eyes settled on her face. "Who said anything about one million?"

"Gutzeit did. He said the first installment was for a million. And another million if you get usable DNA."

"Did he indeed?" St. Ives shook his withered head. "What a pity he's not here to back up your claim. I take it you've decided to cut him out, bringing in our redheaded friends here." He gave us a snide look.

"Gutzeit cut himself out," Darby said, her voice on the knife's edge. "He tried to cheat us."

"Honor among thieves," St. Ives said wistfully. "Another quaint notion bites the dust."

Darby grabbed for the blood. "Give it back. If you don't want to pay, there are people who will."

He jerked it out of her reach. "Sorry, my dear. It's spoken for."

Williams whipped a gun out of his pocket and aimed it directly at Darby's head. She hesitated a second, watching him, then stretched out her hand toward the suitcase.

"Um, all right. I guess we'll just take this and go . . ."

Williams brought the gun down hard on her forearm. She recoiled with a gasp.

"What are you doing?" Darby cried, cradling her wrist. "We held up our end of the bargain!"

"Such charming trust," the old man said. "You hold up your end, I hold up mine. But as I said, it's an outmoded idea." His hand went to his neck, pinching the loose skin at the base of his throat. "And no one ever said there was honor among *vampires . . .*"

Huh?

The old man cackled and pulled the wizened face right off his head—*it was a latex mask.* The light caught the swirls of dark green on his cheeks underneath, giving him a surreal, almost psychedelic appearance. He stuck out his black split tongue and waggled the points at us.

"Boo!" Shatán said.

Holy shit. The big vamp on campus!

Williams kept the gun trained on us as he reached into the limo. He snapped the latches on the suitcase with his free hand, then grabbed it and chucked it into the front seat.

"You lying bastard!" Darby yelled at Shatán.

"You dumb slut," Shatán said, grinning. "You've been had."

"Give me that money!"

"No. The money's mine, payment for the blood."

Darby let out a grunt, venting her frustration at us. "You totally screwed up," she said. "I hope you're happy."

Terry ignored her, focusing instead on Shatán. "Good work, man. Never would have recognized you without your yellow contacts. And I guess you use clip-on fangs?"

He nodded, smiling. "I have a whole collection of them. I keep them in a jewel case with my cuff links. I'm quite the fang horse."

She paid him another grudging compliment: "Great mask, too."

"It's Nosferatu, my spiritual father," Shatán said. "Creepy

little fucker, isn't he? He was designed by the special effects guy from *Buffy the Vampire Slayer*. I wear it every year to the Halloween ball." He chuckled and flipped open a gold lighter, lighting the flame under the vial. The blood began to melt.

Darby sucked in a breath. "You're going to ruin the DNA!"

"DNA's not the issue, babe."

"But what about St. Ives?"

"You silly bitch, don't you get it? There *is* no St. Ives! Gutzeit and I had a good laugh when he told me about improvising that story for the Doublemint girls here." He nodded at us. "They were insisting on knowing who the buyer was, when his gaze happened to rest on a bottle of the lotion on his shelf. He spun out the story on the spot. Very clever of him, I thought. He was afraid he'd blown it, but I assured him you were too stupid to catch on."

"Looks that way," I said. "Although it's a good thing for him it wasn't Lubriderm on the shelf. That *might* have clued us in."

Darby shook her head as if to clear it. "I don't understand," she said. "If not for the DNA, why do you want the blood?"

"I've sold it to a very exclusive group of connoisseurs who are even now waiting at my club, anxious to imbibe Marilyn's essence. That's their money in the suitcase. You wouldn't believe who some of them are—studio executives, celebrities, politicians. I'd tell you, but then I'd have to kill you."

Terry glanced at Williams, who smiled back at her over the barrel of the gun. "You're going to kill us, anyway, aren't you?" she said.

"Well, technically, yes. But I'm discreet to the end."

Darby fulminated with rage as she finally began to see the whole picture. "*You* killed Nina, thinking she was me . . . You were trying to get the blood for free!"

"Actually, that was Gutzeit," Shatán said. "He realized he'd killed the wrong girl, and he couldn't find the blood on the premises. When you girls came to the club and accused me of Ephemera's murder, I thought perhaps you had it. I sent someone over to your house to get it, but you know what happened then." He winked at me. "I hear you're pretty handy with a frying pan."

I nodded at Terry, giving her the credit.

"Whichever."

"What happened to Lucian—did you kill him, too?" Darby wanted to know.

Shatán's eyes flickered with momentary regret. "I used him to remove the body from the morgue. We couldn't take a chance on them discovering the nitrous oxide in her system, somehow tying her death to Gutzeit. Lucian obliged me by wheeling her right out the back door and into my waiting hearse. Naturally, I couldn't let him walk around with the knowledge afterward."

"You slime," Darby said. "He worshipped you!"

Shatán gave a little shrug. "Then he can sit at my right hand in hell."

I don't know why, I had to ask: "Why didn't Gutzeit take the body from the house that night? Why leave her in her coffin to be discovered at the opening?"

"Too cumbersome to move, and too risky—he couldn't be sure how the roommates would react. Besides, watching everyone freak out when she plopped out of the coffin was such fun." He laughed at the memory. "We're *all* about fun."

I looked over at Terry. She turned away, unable to meet my eyes. But I hadn't meant the look as a reproach. I'd merely wanted to say goodbye.

"Now," Shatán said, holding up the vial, "I'm going to have a little taste of immortality, right here where Marilyn's spirit lingers. And you'll get to watch."

Williams had us covered. There was no getting out. Shatán

filled a shot glass with mineral water from a bottle. Then he pulled the stopper from the vial with his teeth, pouring a few drops of blood into the glass.

"You're diluting it?" Darby said in horror, as if it were a fine, aged wine.

"Can't be greedy," Shatán said, capping the vial again and setting it on the armrest. "I have to leave some for my customers."

He bent over the shot glass and muttered something in Latin, then tipped his head back and tossed the blood into his mouth as if he were taking communion. He sucked air through his teeth, swishing the blood around on his split tongue. After a few moments, he swallowed.

He jerked back against the seat, rigid, whipping his head from side to side. Moaning, his arms and legs spasming with erotic tension. I could barely stand to watch his horrible, sexualized thrashing, but I couldn't look away. While he moaned and writhed on the seat, Williams looked on, getting a vicarious charge, his own lips wet with saliva.

Then after what seemed an eternity, Shatán finally experienced release. He let out his breath, his body stilled. Slowly, he opened his eyes. Eyes that were shining with the thrill of his abomination.

"*Yeaaahhhhh!*" he said. "I have drunk the blood of Miss Marilyn Monroe!"

That did it. I made a dive for the door handle. Williams reacted quickly, jamming the barrel of his gun into Darby's head. She whimpered, eyes wide with terror.

I released the door handle and sat back down.

Shatán replaced the vial in the canister, sighing with contentment. "That, you pathetic mortals, was a pleasure you will never know."

A pause, then Darby said, "I'm glad you enjoyed it, Damien."

Shatán's head jerked around on his neck. He stared at her, his blood buzz seeming to evaporate before our eyes.

"Sorry?" he said. "What did you call me?" He wore a nervous, caught-in-a-compromising-position smile, as if trying to charm his way out of a social faux pas.

Darby grinned, ripping the dark glasses off her face. If eyes could sing, hers would have been belting out the Hallelujah Chorus.

"I called you Damien, scumbag. It's your name." She carelessly pushed Williams's gun out of her face. Confused, Williams took a step back. "You thought you were safe behind all your tattoos and your snake tongue, didn't you? Well, guess what? You still smell. I tracked you by your foul odor."

Shatán's lower lip began to quiver. "How long have you known?" he whispered.

"Oh, I've had your number for months. Years, actually. We only met the one time, remember? But that was enough. When I asked you what had happened to your first wife, you called me a nosy cunt. Sorry, but I didn't much feel like supporting the marriage after that. That's why I didn't come to your wedding."

Shatán's eyes darted around as he tried to pull a coherent thought out of his brain. "I had discovered who *you* were," he told Darby. "After the funeral, I mean. But I didn't imagine you knew who I—"

She didn't let him finish. "Guess I'm better at disguising myself than you are, Lizard Boy. Tell me, just between the two of us—you murdered your first wife, didn't you?"

He didn't answer her. But the fear on his face told the story.

"Are you wearing a wire?" he asked, raking his eyes over Darby's chest.

She shook her head. "Only the two in my bra."

"Did you . . . tell anyone about this? Who I am?"

"No, I wanted to confront you on my own."

Shatán sighed and threw Williams a relieved look. Both of them seemed to relax. Williams stepped up again, aiming his weapon.

"But I know you murdered her," Darby said, leaning in to Shatán. "That's where you got your taste for all this, isn't it? You discovered you liked killing. You liked spilling blood so much, you decided to make a career out of it. And it was even more 'fun' to torture an innocent young child."

Shatán hesitated a moment, then burst into hearty laughter, as if suddenly remembering who had the advantage. After all, *his* man was holding the gun.

"Well, good for you," Shatán said. "You're smarter than I gave you credit for." He motioned to Williams with his head. "But it's not as if you can do anything with the knowledge, is it? Unless you can somehow communicate from beyond the grave."

He and Williams both snickered at this.

"No, I wouldn't know how to communicate from beyond the grave," Darby said. "Maybe you can figure that out." She consulted her watch. "Shouldn't be long, now. There was enough cyanide in that blood to kill a horse."

It took a few seconds for this to sink in. Shatán's striped forehead wrinkled and his eyes bugged as he began to understand the enormity of his mistake. The prongs of his tongue went to his lips with tentative little flicks. Then his eyes slowly traveled down to the canister in his hands. He let out a wail and dropped the canister to the floor of the limo. It rolled over next to my feet.

"Buyer beware," Darby said with a sly chuckle.

A bubbling gurgle came from Shatán's mouth. His hands gripped his throat. He made a noise that was somewhere between a whimper and a wordless curse as he dove out of the car.

"Williams!" he croaked.

He ran out into a pool of lamplight, his body whipsawing and jack-knifing—his screams filling the air. Williams watched open-mouthed, the gun forgotten in his hand, as Shatán did a dance of death on the asphalt. Flailing and shrieking like a wounded jungle bird, digging his fingernails into his throat as if he were trying to rip it right out of his neck. Twisting and writhing again—but this time in agony, rather than ecstasy.

Then he collapsed to the ground.

The chauffeur stared at his boss—and probably his idol—jerking spasmodically on the asphalt in his death throes. Then the rage boiled up in Williams and he sprang into action. He grabbed Darby by the arm, dragging her out of the car, stabbing her in the ribs with the gun. She twisted around, screaming, knocking the gun out of his hand with her elbow.

It skidded across the asphalt.

Terry and I scrambled out of the car. Williams had his hands around Darby's neck, choking her. Terry did a running jump and delivered a powerful kick to Williams's leg above the knee. He howled in pain, stumbling away, releasing Darby as he did. She tore away from him.

Williams then recovered from the kick and threw himself forward on his good leg, lunging for Terry just as she whipped the phaser blaster out of her pocket and hit the oncoming chauffeur in the chest with a powerful blast.

He arched up and flew backwards through the air, smacking the marble wall and falling into a heap at its base. I ran to Shatán, kneeling at his side. He was hovering near death, his eyes desperate above the gaping mouth. The last thing I wanted to do was make contact with his horrible snake's tongue, but I couldn't just stand by and watch him die.

I tipped back his head to give him mouth-to-mouth, and got a whiff of burnt almonds.

"I wouldn't do that," Darby said, grabbing me around the waist, yanking me to my feet. "Even a tiny amount can be fatal."

I spun around to face her. "Call 911!"

She shook her head. "It's no use. The poison works in seconds. He'll be dead before they get here."

And in an instantaneous fulfillment of prophecy, Shatán gave one last gasp, his eyes rolling up in his head. Then his whole body went limp.

Darby looked down and kicked him in the ribs.

"That's for Jimmy, asshole."

She gave a satisfied sigh, full of slaked bloodlust.

"Thanks for the help," she said to Terry, retrieving the chauffeur's gun and stuffing it into her waistband. She reached into the limousine and grabbed the suitcase from the front seat, then opened it and took out a few packets of bills.

She offered them to us.

I stared at them dumbly. Before I could get my mind to wrestle with the idea of taking a gratuity from a murderess, Terry grabbed the money and stuck it inside her shirt.

"I wish I could spare more," Darby said, "but we're going to need it to go underground."

I was slowly recovering from the shock. "You're not going anywhere, Darby. You just killed a man."

"Sometimes you have to take the law into your own hands," she said, casting a hateful glance over at Shatán's body. "He would've killed all of us, given the chance. He tried to, many times."

"You knew who he was! If you'd told the police—"

"He'd never *stop*, don't you understand? He'd still be the king of the vampires in prison. He'd send someone after us!"

She pointed to the chauffeur, who was beginning to stir. "He's got twenty more goons where that one came from. A hundred! And they all think he's some kind of god. He'd send them to kill us, as many as it took!"

I couldn't argue with that. Shatán had been a charismatic psychopath, surrounded by acolytes willing to do his bidding.

But I couldn't shake the idea that there had to have been some legal means of dealing with him.

"How did you find out he was Damien?" Terry asked her.

"I'd heard a rumor that he'd gone vampire, so I got into the scene. I was good at it, I have to admit. He thought no one knew of his past, but I was able to find out who he really was."

"You infiltrated the vampire scene just so you could kill him?"

"Yeah, but he was always surrounded by his groupies. I thought I'd never get the chance. Then Pam came up with the idea of selling him Marilyn's blood—pure genius. We knew he couldn't resist. And we figured we could take him for some money at the same time, to buy our freedom. That little shit Gutzeit is a blood drinker, too, by the way. It really gets his rocks off."

That was *way* too much information. The image of Gutzeit dressed up in a black cloak and fangs, sipping human blood in some sort of erotic ritual, caused the stomach acid to flare up my esophagus.

"What if Damien hadn't drunk the blood in the limo?" I said, as the implications of this started to dawn on me.

Darby shrugged. "I knew he would."

"But what if he hadn't? What if he'd taken the blood to his club and given it to all those people?"

"Oh, that'd be a real tragedy," she said. "A room full of dead bloodsuckers."

I shook my head in disbelief. She'd been willing to commit mass murder?

She read the look on my face. "I'm telling you, I *knew* what he'd do."

Darby had taken a chance on our lives, as well, but that hadn't yet occurred to Terry. She was still caught up in the moment.

"Who would believe it?" she said, shaking her head in wonder. "Marilyn Monroe's blood used as bait to kill Marilyn Manson."

Darby spewed out a laugh that bordered on the hysterical. "It's not really Marilyn's blood," she said.

Terry and I turned and stared at her.

"What did you say?" Terry said. "Not her blood?"

"What does that mean?" I asked Darby. "Whose was it?"

"Whose?" Darby shrugged. "I never did catch his name. I guess we could call him Rocky. He was killed trying to cross Van Nuys Boulevard with a nut in his mouth . . ."

Terry's eyes bugged. "What are you *saying*?"

Darby giggled. "It's squirrel's blood."

Terry smacked her forehead. "All of this . . . over squirrel's blood?"

"Yep." She gave us a shrug. "People are pretty gullible, huh?"

Terry and I looked at each other, acutely embarrassed. I guess you'd have to count us among the gullible hordes.

"I never really understood the whole celebrity thing, anyway," Darby said. "Who gives a shit if you're famous? I mean, under the skin we're all the same, right?"

I had one fervent hope at that moment, and it was that under the skin, I was not the least bit like the woman standing in front of me. Not to mention the vampire lying at my feet.

"Was there ever any celebrity blood?" I asked her.

"Nope."

"And the whole story about the emergency room doctor who treated Marilyn?"

"Urban legend."

"How about the testimonial from the doctor that you exchanged for twenty-five thousand bucks?"

"Forged."

"This is unbelievable," Terry said. "So who kidnapped me at the funeral, you?"

"Me and Pam." Darby made an apologetic face. "Once we knew this exchange was going down, we did everything we could to uninvolve you—but you're so damn *persistent*."

I looked at Terry, who gave me a blameless face.

"Terry was the one who wouldn't let go," I told Darby. "I appreciate your trying to keep us out of it, but here we are."

I got out my phone to call the police. Shatán's death may have been justifiable homicide, but that was for a jury to decide.

"Don't worry. Eli will get you off with voluntary manslaughter," I said. "The guy tortured your family. He endangered your nephew, harassed you out of your mind—"

She pulled the gun from her waistband, raising it to the level of my chest, fixing me in her sights. My finger stopped after punching in the numbers 9 and 1.

I slowly raised my hands into the air.

"It's good you brought your own transportation," Darby said. "You can tell the cops I held the gun on you and threatened your lives."

"Threatened . . . ?" Terry said. "Would . . . you would shoot us for real?"

Darby took a second to answer. "Please don't test me."

"Okay," I said, raising my hands even higher. "We won't, we won't."

Darby backed up to the VW, the gun trained on us the whole way over. She opened the door and threw the alligator bag into the car. "I'd appreciate a ten-minute lead."

Terry reached over and took the phone from my hand, dropping it to the ground and crushing it with the heel of her boot. "She held the gun on us and busted our phones," she said, rehearsing her story for the cops. Then Terry reached in her jacket for her own phone, destroying it, too.

"Thanks," Darby said, smiling gratefully at her. "I always thought you were cool." She looked at me. "And I knew you'd come around eventually."

Then she got in the VW and spun the car in a tight circle, peeling out onto the service road as we watched her taillights disappearing in the distance. The homecoming queen turned goth goddess turned vigilante executioner. Talk about reinventing yourself.

I looked back at the chauffeur, who had raised himself to his knees at the base of the crypts. I walked over and helped him to his feet. "Your boss is dead," I told him.

He looked at me, then over at Shatán's body on the ground. Without a word he stumbled past us, jumped in the limo and started it up, jamming it in reverse. With the driver's door still hanging open, he screeched out of the cemetery, slamming the door as he sped down the street.

"Should we have tried to stop him?" I said to Terry.

"Why?"

"He's a material witness."

Terry shrugged. "Well, what were we supposed to do? Lay our bodies down in front of the tires?"

We stood there for a long moment.

"Hey, Terry?"

"Yeah?"

"I think I'd better book our jobs for a while. You okay with that?"

"As long as you reinstate my salary."

"Done."

"And make me vice president."

"You never know when to quit, do you?"

thirty

$\mathcal{W}$e flagged down a car on Wilshire, asking the driver to call the police. When he heard the words "dead man," the poor driver went into shock and fumbled with his cell phone. Terry grabbed it from him and called 911.

The cops took us to the West Los Angeles station on Butler Avenue to make our statements.

We told them everything just as it happened. With a couple of harmless omissions.

We didn't mention the money that Darby had given us, which was locked in our saddlebags at the time.

Neither did we tell them about the phaser pain blasters. Terry had neglected to get a license for them, see, so we'd buried them in the grass next to a burial plot.

We told the police we'd overcome the chauffeur with brute force. They looked askance at this, skinny redheads that we were, but Terry assured them that we were schooled in the martial arts. (We planned to have some lessons from the Bruces soon, so it was only a little white perjury.)

Happily, the cops had enough on their plate without charging us with breaking and entering the cemetery. Neither did they regard us as accessories to murder. We convinced them we had no prior knowledge of the plot to assassinate the king of the vampires, and we were supported in our claims by our friend Bagdasarian.

An arrest warrant was issued for Adam Gutzeit for the murder of Nina Herman, Darby's bandmate. The murderer of Lucian had arrived at the morgue DOA—Shatán, the yellow-eyed monster who spoke with forkèd tongue—felled by his taste for forbidden blood.

An arrest warrant was also issued for Darby, but she was headed for parts unknown, along with the rest of the Applewhites. But they probably weren't the Applewhites anymore. They'd have new identities by now.

Little Jimmy would be starting the second grade somewhere in the breadbasket of America, probably. I hoped he could sleep soundly at night wherever he was, but I guessed that the bad dream song would have to be sung for a long time to come. When he got older, he could trade in the song for some heavy therapy.

I like to imagine that Darby has started a finishing school for beauty contestants, honing and polishing pretty little girls into glass-hard competitors. Either that or training them for Special Forces. If ever you date a beauty queen, boys, better treat her like a lady. They don't mess around.

I also like to imagine that Pam's putting her skills to work in a veterinary clinic, doing penance for her abuse of Rocky the Squirrel. And that Herb and Sandra are drifting from campsite to campsite in the luxury Rialta, enjoying their cocktails under the stars, stopping in every now and then to visit their girls and their sweet little grandson.

But I'll never really know. The police have looked, but they haven't found them. The case is officially still open—but the truth is, bringing the killers of scumbags like Shatán to justice is never a top priority.

Bagdasarian and Kenneally were able to tie Shatán to three unsolved homicides in the vampire community, as well as to Lucian's death. Shatán's first wife is still missing, but her case has gone stone cold. Maybe someday her body will surface.

Anyway, nobody sheds too many tears for dead child-beaters, whether they're paid to care or not. Almost magically the investigation into Shatán's murder sank to the bottom of a big pile of unsolved homicides.

Happens more than you know.

epilogue

$\mathcal{H}$i, we're here for the test screening," I said to the woman with the clipboard.

"Your names?"

"Kerry and Terry McAfee."

"Oh, the big stars," she said, smiling. "Go on in."

"The *big stars*," Terry whispered to me. "Kiss my sweet ass, Lindsay Lohan."

We entered the screening room and took one of the reserved seats in the front.

"I'm so excited," Terry said, slouching down in her seat.

The lights dimmed and we were treated to the chronicling of our house makeover, along with the demise of our old furniture, edited to music by Justin Timberlake, and followed by a segment in which the Bruces taught us some handy martial arts moves. The crowd erupted into cheers when Terry threw Bruce

Three right over her shoulder, flipping him onto his back on the grass.

She stood in her seat, facing the crowd, raising her fists to even more applause.

By the time we got to the "homeowners' dance of joy," the audience was on its feet. I foresaw a whole new career for our pals the Bruces. They were headed to the top of the ratings. Afterward we attended the reception, shaking hands and gabbing with the audience, drinking white wine.

Now that it was all over, I had time to think. As I watched Terry beaming at her fans, sharing war stories about the production, demonstrating a few karate chops, I saw how happy she was.

She was happy. The Bruces were happy. And I was—

Not.

I realized with a pang how much I missed Boatwright. *Dammit, why does life have to be so complicated?* I wondered. Why should having a great man in your life and taking care of your sister be mutually exclusive?

Someone tapped me on the shoulder. I held my breath as I turned, instinctively knowing who I'd see behind me. It was just as if my thoughts had conjured him out of thin air. Boatwright flashed me a megawatt smile, holding out a bunch of red roses.

"For you," he said.

I stared at him, speechless. I hadn't expected to see him ever again, let alone with a bouquet of flowers.

"Unless, of course, you don't want 'em." He started to pull them back.

I ripped the roses out of his hands and stuck my nose in them. "How'd you know about the screening and everything?" I asked him.

He nodded to Terry, who walked up to us wearing a big grin. "She invited me," he said.

I turned to her, shocked. "You did?"

"I know what you tried to do," she said. "You passed on a great thing so I wouldn't feel abandoned. That was incredibly selfless of you." I felt myself turning red. "But I'm not spending the rest of my life with a goddamned martyr, so get over yourself and go out with the guy."

I turned and smiled shyly at Boatwright. "You still want to go out with me?"

He nodded. "I'll try not to crowd you, and I'll *try* not to rush you." He reached into his pocket and pulled out some tickets, waving them in front of my face. "Dodger game Sunday?"

I pointed at his hand. "You've got three tickets there."

"I know better than to try to come between you two." He looked over at Terry. "You free?"

She assumed a prissy posture, crossing her arms. "I'll have to check my social calendar."

"Oh, you're free." I smacked her with the roses, a shower of petals falling at her feet.

Just then, Bruce Three came running over to us. "Hey girls, we need you for a press photo."

"Oh, no," I said. "Not me!"

"Come on, just one!"

Terry and Bruce dragged me over to the media corner, where the Bruces locked arms, bending down. They hoisted Terry and me up in a pyramid, balanced on their strongman arms à la Cirque du Redheads, while the entertainment press snapped away.

"You know, we're never gonna live this down," I said to Terry as we gripped each other for balance.

"Who wants to live it down?" She laughed. "I'm going for a spot on *Leno*!"

The puppies entered the world on national TV in an episode of *Kung Fu Feng Shui Bruces,* midwifery being a surprise addition to the Bruces' list of astounding talents. Each of the guys adopted a dog and named it Bruce Jr. (even though two of the pups were female). Angie the tattoo artist took the fourth puppy. She named him Trollie, and with his batlike ears and black wrinkled face, his image is now one of the most requested tattoos on the boardwalk. Look for him next time you're in Venice on shoulders, arms, and backs. Also on T-shirts, for those who don't care for needles.

Terry and Angie have been hanging out a lot. They haven't actually gone on a date yet, but there are pheromones in the air.

A few weeks ago, Judge Helen Lampert was offered an appointment to a federal court on the island of Maui in Hawaii. Being an avid surfer (who knew?), she found it too tempting to pass up, and she and Eli decided to forgo a long-distance relationship. We never did learn who interceded on Helen's behalf, but I have a sneaking suspicion the intercession wasn't divine—but rather by someone with very deep designer pockets.

Cousin Robert recovered fully from his barbell accident, regaining his memory and then some. After his two cerebral mishaps he claimed to have acquired psychic powers, and when he started talking about setting up shop on the boardwalk as a palm reader, Reba decided it was time to move back to Beverly Hills. She bought the other three condos in her building on Vernon Avenue and turned it into the Reba Price-Slatherton Home for the Financially Disadvantaged. (Fortunately, the neighborhood was already zoned for low-cost housing and public tap-dancing.) Lola and some of the rest of the gang maintain an official residence at the home, but they prefer to spend most of their time on the streets.

As for my original dilemma, Franzen is still MIA, but that's probably for the good. Good for the country and good for my conscience. I fully intend to experience hot monkey love with Boatwright one day, but lately all of our dates have been—*ahem*—chaperoned.

~~THE END~~

That's just an excuse. He's too much man for the little wimp.

THE END

For toe-tag key chains, chalk-outline towels, and other fun death-related tchotchkes, go to Skeletons in the Closet online: www.lacoroner.com

about the author

JENNIFER COLT is a screenwriter in Santa Monica, California. She has written for Dimension Films and Playboy Enterprises and worked in the Home Entertainment Group of MGM/United Artists in LA.

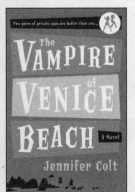